LEVIATHAN

Paul Falshaw

ISBN: 9781981075973

Image Credits
Front cover image: ID 64323122 © Chrisp543 | Dreamstime.com
Rear cover image (print edition): ID 23164332 © Oleg Doroshin | Dreamstime.com

Web: www.shuckstale.com
Face: Shuckstale

- One -

>Keegan Chase

The day I became a detective again was almost my last.

I woke late, confused and aching, half-twisted in the chair where I'd dozed off in the small hours. In the background I could hear the TV and over it the relentless, rising chime of my phone. Scrambling up I grabbed the old handset, forced a deep breath to calm myself, then answered, probably a little sharper than I intended.

"Yeah?"

"Morning Chase."

"Raissa!" It was unmistakably her, the voice warm and eloquent, gently amused.

"Got some work for you: there's been a fatal incident at the Maxim Mall. Someone, ID unknown, took a dive right through the main atrium. Unclear whether it's a murder yet, but it's suspicious enough to engage us, anyway. I've earmarked it for you, if you fancy it?"

"Ok, sure, that'll be fine". It would have to be. I'd not expected to hear from the office today particularly, but I knew it was going to happen soon or later.

"Great, it's yours then." She left the most artful of pauses, and then: "How was your trip?"

"OK. It was good to visit New York again, and I enjoyed Rome."

"Cool! Ok, have to go. Keep in touch, Chase."

Neither of us had mentioned Paris, but memories flashed through all the same. I stood there for a few moments, not particularly thinking anything, just conscious that she was gone and aware of the sudden anxiety she'd left behind. Shrugging, I shook my head and then moved to get ready, raising the volume on the TV as I went through to the bathroom. The news was mostly bad, with more refugees on the move, fleeing from drought or conflict in one zone and floods in another, extremes of season and scarcity combining.

Once I'd showered, I headed into the bedroom to change. The company liked a suit, and all mine were bagged and hanging neatly in the wardrobe at one side, nicely spaced as though it might hide the fact that the other half was empty now. I couldn't remember which was which so I chose one at random, a dark blue, and then picked a cream shirt to go with it. On the way past I checked myself over in the mirror, turning my head this way and that in the half-light, checking for the last traces of injury still etched there. The face that looked back at me was younger than I felt, but still a little grizzled at the edges.

I wasn't exactly on the clock, but I needed to get moving. The rest of my stuff was in the secure cabinet in the lounge, where I'd left it. It felt strange to strap on the stun gun again and feel the weight of it against my ribs and across the shoulders, its outward design and construction sharing that of a regular automatic and possessing about the same physical heft. The next things were the earpieces and 'lenses in their fitted case and the smartpad they both linked to. All of it was company issue, so I'd not touched it in a while, which meant I'd have to recharge everything on the way.

The news had moved on to the business section, a piece about the impending lawsuit between two of the major robotics firms, OraCotek and Hallistiks, so I shifted channels only to be met with a report on the mall case, quickly switching off before I could hear any of the details.

One last look round the flat, checking I hadn't forgotten anything. I ran a hand gently across the strings of my guitar where it rested in the corner, saw again the walking stick still propped up behind it, and then lingered for a few moments over the pictures on the walls. They were mostly family photos, Dad with Ellie and the kids, and his old academy graduation portrait next to my own, crisp navy whites on black skin, his a darker, deeper tone, the only thing that really set us apart. There was nothing else to delay for and I left as the final tones of the guitar faded from its strings as they slowed to stillness.

Time to get back on the horse.

> Reznik

Despite a strong effort Reznik was still not drunk enough. To help him along the way he could have scored any number of substances, some not so much illegal as re-purposed, but that would have made it all too easy. It was rare for him to indulge, so it really should have been more fun, but there was no getting around the fact that he could still walk in a straight line and chew khat at the same time.

Somewhere along the flow of the previous evening he'd ended up in one of the area's less hospitable bars, and had inevitably navigated towards its darkest corner, though that was relative now that the sun was out and punching through the mycoboard roof in several places. It was almost pretty, the way that the dust motes were highlighted in their Brownian dance.

He'd been the centre of his own cloud of motion for a while last night, having collected a small retinue once he started buying the drinks, but he'd lost most of them again along the way, except for the final two who were now draped over the table, sleeping. The bar had been quiet for the last couple of hours, with just the occasional thud of glass on wood over a background murmur of TV and bad dreams.

Reznik had old eyes peering sharply from a weathered face, mostly tanned except for a few small light coloured patches. They were old lesions, badges of survival that spoke of luck he didn't feel. After draining the final dregs of his beer he contemplated ordering another, the expressive fingers of one hand gently tapping in rhythm on the table, while the other smoothed back his dark hair before resting lightly on his stubbled chin. Instead, he stood and gathered his leathered jacket from the back of the rough chair, stepping lightly round and over his sleeping entourage. Now that he was upright and mobile, his tall, slim frame was more obvious, lending his movements a relaxed grace despite the cheap-looking clothes he wore, a light hoodie and old cargo pants. Reznik headed out, weaving a path around the other customers, solitary drinkers sipping beers in private isolation. He never passed closer than a couple of yards to any of them as he moved toward the exit.

Before pushing the bead curtain that functioned as a door aside Reznik pulled up his hood and donned a pair of sunnies and a cheap disposable facemask, similar to the ones he'd seen locals wearing. The area was still semi-quarantined, but the last outbreak had been a half-mile away and several weeks ago, long enough that even the conspiracy theories had grown old. Though it was only mid-morning the sun was already fiercely hot. He hoped to be out of it before it got much later because the sea breeze was light today, barely stirring the humid air. This area of the city was a little out of the way, but was more anonymous and non-descript than rough. The noise was as constant as the heat, and left him no doubt he could lose himself in the bustle. It wouldn't take long to get back to where he was staying if he took the minimal level of evasion, and he saw nothing to indicate any real need for greater caution.

Realising his movements and thinking were close to optimal he moved off, knowing his system would clear the last of the alcohol soon enough. Reznik gave a wry smile behind the mask, which reached only so far as the wrinkles around his eyes before stopping dead.

> Cara Dalca

"You expect me to believe that? Of all the crap you've come out with lately that has to be the worst!" She continued, her voice growing in agitation, "No, I don't understand. Why can't you just keep your head down? Why do you always land yourself in more trouble? You're due before the parole board next month, for fuck's sake!"

Cara Dalca, if anyone had been observing her, would have seemed like some modern mystic, gesticulating and talking angrily to empty air. There were no visual clues to inform an observer, no handset to suggest that she had in fact been talking to her brother Petre, though she would have loved to have that physical prop right then so she could slam it firmly onto the desk. Instead, all she had was a tiny, bean-like device stuck behind her ear, her short punky hair and pale complexion doing little to hide it. She could unpeel the thing and throw it across the office, but the impact would be so miniscule as to be pointless.

"Ok, ok, I know you didn't mean for this to happen." A pause, a sigh, drawn and deep. "Look, I'm sorry. I just hope you'll be out soon. I haven't been able to get up to visit you in ages, and Dad would love to see you." This was all so bloody frustrating, though she knew the person who would suffer most from this was Petre himself.

Phone-time was soon over though and they wrapped things up, Cara a little tearful, struck by the sadness of it all and reacting to the catch in her big brother's voice as he said goodbye.

It was Dad she was most worried about. The virus had touched him lightly during the war and returned with a vengeance now, its progress, if that was the word, aggressive and tenacious. It was killing him an inch at a time, ravaging his lungs and nervous system, always running ahead of any treatment they could offer. Cara had started to research his condition herself but stopped when she became overwhelmed with bitterness. There were newer, more effective procedures that would have kept her father alive and in greater comfort, perhaps even heal some of the damage, but they were outside the hospital's expertise and budget. They were certainly outside hers. At least he was in Auldwiche Central, the best she could get for free.

Petre had taken the news stoically, said his goodbyes over that last dinner they'd had together before he was arrested again. He had seen their father only a couple of times since, while the old man had still been fit enough for visiting, but that was it. For Cara it was much harder to let go. Everything was happening before her eyes, and any distance she might find for herself felt like betrayal.

Nothing she could do about any of that now though. She still had at least another couple of hours of work to do before she could even think about knocking it off for the day. Someone had to keep their shit together.

Frost headed cautiously down the steep valley sides in a half crouch, the dry earth sliding away in small tides of scree as she dug her boots sideways into the loose surface. The angle of the slope made progress more difficult, forcing her to stretch out her left hand in places to keep her balance as she moved downward in a rough lateral, her right arm steadying the rifle harnessed against her chest.

It was dark and cold this early, breath fogging the air ahead while her enhanced vision cast everything in a green-tinged light. She could hear the careful movements of the others trailing behind her against the cries and scuffles of animals and birds; Jakobsen's footfalls always heavier than Tsukino's, who moved like a ghost. As Frost descended, the soothing trickle of the stream running along the old riverbed at the apex of the valley became louder. When she reached the bottom she waited a few moments to take a breather, allowing the other two time to catch up.

Somewhere up ahead was The Wolf.

- Two -

> Chase

The mall complex rose like some great sea-beast in the centre of the block, its structure all long, serpentine lines and organic curves, carbon-traps like great fins along its blue-grey back. Situated amongst a mix of old and new buildings, stone against sheet glass, it blended with neither, save for a common scattering of solar panels and external foliage, the lichen and moss clinging to its outer skin like parasites.

I'd arrived there a little past one and parked up nearby, aiming to just sit and watch for a little while to get a feel for the place. The 'lenses and earpieces had charged up so I put them on and opened their wireless link to the smartpad, playing with the zoom and enhanced modes as I studied the crowd to make sure the systems were functioning.

The foot traffic was varied, a rare office worker rushing around on a lunch break while other pedestrians meandered along more casually, some of them senior citizens in robo-frames. Cliques of school kids cut through noisily on their own paths. If any of them knew at all that a man had just fallen to his death inside, they showed no obvious sign of it.

I'd skimmed the basic details of what had happened from the files Raissa sent, so I knew the quickest way in was through the southern entrance. As soon as I reached the main hall I was struck by how busy it was. A crowd had gathered around where I guessed the body would be and as I drew closer the yellow barrier posts jutting over their heads became ever more obvious, the black lenses of embedded cameras focussed outward to watch the harder edge of onlookers. The press were also there, mainly small crews from the majors.

Despite the mass of people and the media presence I had to walk through with my head high, looking into faces and making eye contact against all natural instinct, allowing the smartlenses to capture as much data as possible. After brief flashes of my security ID, and the occasional tight smile or nudge, I was able to reach the outer barrier, where I could see the faint shimmer of a privacy field and hear the static of the white noise it was generating. I waited there a few moments before one of the uniformed officers let me through, and then I was inside the perimeter.

This first area was quite large, as it had to accommodate not only the officers but also the forensic technicians and their equipment. At its centre was a second, more substantial barrier arranged around the crime scene itself. It looked as though the preliminary examination was almost over as the techs were packing their small aerial drones back into carry cases, whilst a larger quad robot, with its scrubbed white shell and plastic-sleeved manipulator arms, sat idling just inside the second cordon. As I'd first approached I'd not really been aware of it, but here there was a sharp smell of disinfectant in the air and that, along with the technician's pale green hooded overalls, almost gave the impression that we were in the middle of a hospital rather than one of the city's largest malls.

Both techs were familiar from previous cases, but only Anish came over to exchange pleasantries while he issued me with protective clothing. Karla merely glanced up from what she was doing to nod a quick greeting. Once I'd suited up I was allowed through to the inner area. It felt calmer and cooler inside, away from the press of the crowd. Over the body itself they'd positioned a tent to hide the worst from the onlookers and perhaps restore a little dignity to the scene. Outside of this and to one side stood an android, holding its position as though in vigil.

As soon as it had opened the mall had drawn a lot of attention for its embrace of modernity and commitment to ecology, though opinion was divided on how well it met those ambitions. The interior was as bold as the exterior, with a high vaulted ceiling hosting large stained-glass panels in abstract designs, casting colour across the pale walls as the sun made its transit. Walls and walkways flowed in smooth elegant lines around the main atrium, formed around a large, central space in the shape of a curved teardrop. Over and through this hall hung a vast array of banners in various colours, illuminated by the natural light from the stained windows and theatrical spots.

Through this brilliant canopy, level with the upper storey and just a few feet from the edge in places, a colony of sleek male and female 'droids in various chromed or metallic shades would glide and tumble amidst the neo-silk pennants in a display of exquisite acrobatics, scattering light which flickered across the wall and floor surfaces below. I knew from the brief summary I'd read that the victim had fallen straight through this display from somewhere in the heights of the building, taking one of these Acrobots with him whilst another fell in their wake.

I walked over to the second android where it stood immobile beside the tent. Up close and at rest the robot was far more machine-like than it would ever seem in motion, its outer shell of moulded ceramics and composites etched with the monogram of one of the great fashion houses whilst the matte black tubular chassis beneath was badged more subtly with OraCotek logos. There was no sign of damage on it, and it made no movement in reaction to my presence, yet the thing pronounced its place in the future like a shout just by standing there.

Realising that I might be stalling I moved toward the tent, paused just for a moment to steady myself, and then went inside. The victim lay undisturbed in the centre, misshapen and broken from the fall, his head smashed open. Trapped beneath him was another android, equally damaged, the two forming a rough 'X' shape crossing at the abdomen, like an unintended riff on da Vinci. Everything was starkly lit with a pure white light, and the chemical smell was stronger here. It was a relief to see that the worst of the blood spatter had already been collected, and I guessed it would only be a short time until the rest of the remains were taken away, but it was clear enough that the cause of death was most likely the severe head injury he'd suffered. Despite the almost clinical setting it was an unpleasant sight.

It was impossible to make much of an assessment of who the victim had been from the state of the corpse. His clothes were good quality - black, loose fitting cargo pants and a sandy coloured top - but they were creased and grimy, as though they'd been worn repeatedly for a few days. Both sleeves had been crudely ripped from the top, and at least one had been used to bind his feet, which were shoeless and bloody from several cuts, as well as being quite dirty. Whatever electronic devices or personal items he had carried would have been collected, but I already knew that there hadn't been anything that gave us an ID.

Every now and then a victim turned out to be a life-logger or uplinked in some way, but it didn't look likely this time. If he had been, the final moments before his fall might have been recorded, the sights and sounds he experienced digitised and downloadable, but that would be unusually fortunate. I myself was following standard practice and recording everything I witnessed straight onto the smartpad through the wireless link, slowly viewing the body from all angles to pick up as much detail as possible with the 'lenses.

I wondered how things had appeared when the body had first fallen here, before the forensics team had move in to sanitise the environment, and decided I'd take a look. Using the smartlenses, I called up a visual overlay from the database. I had to tilt my head and squat a little to reduce my height, but small arrows in my field of vision guided me into place. Once I was in position, I saw what the forensics team had recorded when they first arrived.

The scene was even bloodier than I'd imagined, and rendered perversely worse by the shattered circuitry and lubricants from the Acrobot, its vital fluids mixing with the victim's in a spatter that reached out across the floor. It had been some time since I had seen something like this and the rawness of it shocked me, snatching my breath away and pulling the bile from my stomach. I switched the overlay off and closed my eyes, telling myself that the image quality had improved a lot while I was away.

> Reznik

He'd waited as long as he thought wise under the canopy beside the food shack, appreciating the shade as much as the cover. The falsa wrap he'd bought wasn't bad and he was hungry enough to enjoy it, but the thick, spicy tang of the sauce couldn't completely hide the slightly rubbery texture of the vat-grown meat.

There was a checkpoint at the top of the market square about 50 yards away. A small team of medics were using portable scanners to examine anyone passing through the barrier for signs of infection, while two bored-looking police officers looked on. This crossing point was one of many at the far edge of the outer quarantine zone, more of a nuisance than anything else now that the contagion had abated.

While he licked the last of the sauce from his fingers, Reznik watched a police quadrotor loitering over the market. As with many localities, city ordinances banned drone use for most purposes, but the Police and other state agencies tended to be exempt. He wasn't the only one to spot it, and one or two people pointed up toward it directly, their hand gestures quickly turning more explicit.

Reznik let the size of the crowd build a little more before pulling his facemask back into place and crossing over to an electronics stall, all the while walking steadily and looking more or less straight ahead. Ducking to avoid a loose flap of brown tarpaulin, hanging at the outer edge of the tent, he went inside.

Under the canopy the heat was stifling, but the stall was large enough that there was plenty of room to wander and browse. Tech was roughly piled and sorted by function, if not era, on a rectangular ring of tables set up around the sides. Old spot lamps gave dim illumination from the scaffold-pole frame at the corners while the centre ground was filled with an island of junked robots and flat screen TVs. Some of the monitors were switched on but muted, giving off further light as they cycled between soap operas and violent sports, while the blank screens of the others reflected the blink of LEDs and digital displays. Two teenage girls ran the stall, circling round like patient sharks, scattering small shoals of household helper-bots with each step. Mostly the customers were left alone as they rummaged, their excavations and the scurrying bots giving off the only sounds.

Apart from the main entrance on the square, there was another of sorts at the back. Reznik circled casually toward it, picking up the occasional item as he went as though to inspect it, before leaving two banknotes on the table nearest the exit. He then slipped outside past a couple of old power-assisted frames entangled messily together in the corner. It was hard to judge the right amount to drop, but he'd been this way once before and there'd been no complaint.

Reznik moved past a stack of boxes and then carefully along a short route behind the backs of the jostled market stalls, their limits defined in a range of mixed materials: wood, tarpaulin, fibreboard, metals and plastics. He could only guess at what most of the stands sold, though a few gave off aromatic wafts of foodstuffs and the clean heat of cooking that just about cut through the stink of livestock and humanity. Everywhere was noisy and busy and he was glad when he finally came out in another empty space, this time a gap between more permanent structures of grey concrete and sandy brick. At the end of this short, dusty alley was an eight-foot wall.

Glancing quickly to the right and upwards to check for anyone watching, Reznik moved briskly toward the high barrier. He jogged for a couple of strides as he neared it and then jumped, catching the concrete edge and hauling his body upwards while pushing off the building wall to the left with his legs. Pausing for a moment to look down he then dropped on the other side, landing almost silently.

Reznik remained in position after clearing the wall, squatting down low and alert for any signs of alarm. He was in a deep concrete box, edged by buildings on both sides and high walls at either end, the floor uneven and filthy from accumulated rubbish, crap thrown inside and forgotten. It was surprisingly dark here for midday, the shade embracing and cool. Nothing flew overhead but an occasional bird while in the near distance he could hear the sound of traffic and life.

Walking gingerly across the floor of the alley to the other side, as much to avoid the more unsavoury looking rubbish as to maintain silence, he then climbed up the wall in the corner until he could peek over. Apparently satisfied by what he saw he hauled his body up the rest of the way in smooth, sure movements before clearing the top and dropping back down on the other side.

Pausing only briefly he moved onwards, turned sharp left and then walked casually forwards into brighter sunlight, removing and pocketing the facemask and pulling back his hood as though to better hear and feel the increasing noise and bustle of the road ahead. Turning right, Reznik now moved onto a much busier street, finally merging into the flow of people.

He was sweating, wishing he'd not taken his jacket last night, the smart fabrics unequal to the heat. A couple of blocks further on was a bus stop and he headed toward it, matching the pace of the crowd, hoping to grab a bottle of water on the way.

> Cara

She did her best to throw herself into her work, pushing back the mild depression that worried at her as soon as she awoke and didn't let go until the afternoon. Fortunately, the Reingard job was absorbing enough that when she did find some focus the time passed enjoyably enough. It was almost a treat to be working manually on some coding for a change. Most of the software glitches in the program suite were from common enough problems, but a couple of things needed her to delve through layers of antique code like an archaeologist.

No one had yet completely replaced all the older software protocols from the first decades of computing, as the cost and effort involved had always seemed too daunting. Now that AIs were writing routine software much of the time it seemed inevitable that demand for a nice, clean restart would grow, but it hadn't happened yet. Fortunately, most of these expert systems were so singular of purpose that they lacked the capacity to realise that the excess effort and inefficiencies they were dealing with might properly be called frustrating.

Cara could only guess what a truly intelligent machine, an AGI or Artificial General Intelligence, would think of it, assuming you could find a quorum of academics to agree you actually had one. They were all hellishly expensive, so far the playthings of only the very richest organisations and confined to research labs and secret bunkers – the very stuff of spy thrillers and conspiracy theories.

She thought about Petre again, stuck inside, and then did her best not to as there was nothing she could. There was always Dad: she could at least do something for him. He wouldn't really be expecting another visit this soon though, and she could do with an early night. Unless Ethan was back of course, and did a good enough job of apologising.

Before they'd argued Ethan had said there was a solid piece of work coming through, but it would mean he'd have to go away for two or three weeks, and be out of contact most of the time - something to do with site security for the project and part of the confidentiality agreement he'd have to sign. That had been a few days ago now, and if pushed she'd expected him to be in touch to patch things up before he left.

Cara thought about calling him instead, but was damned if she'd make the first move. He still had Emma's palmtop, despite promising to bring it along on their last date, and that might give her an excuse. She was supposed to get it back to her soon, so she might not have a choice.

The Wolf had signalled for them to proceed, but Frost still exercised all caution: there was no room for error with either him or the hostiles, and she wanted to keep on his good side almost as much as she wanted to avoid a contact. Her HUD showed a clear path marked on the ground that The Wolf had vouched for, and movement was much easier on the valley floor, but she was on point and responsible for the others. Mines and such were one concern, but Air was the big worry. They had limited overwatch from their own assets until they had the security hacked, and whilst it looked like the way was clear for now things would only get tenser as they moved up to the perimeter.

Ahead of them was a crude dam reducing the meagre flow of the stream still further, a shallow pool built up behind it. She led Jakobsen and Tsu back up the side of the valley on the right and along past the pond. The Wolf had left another waypoint here, and she crouched down in the cover of an old stone wall to await the next signal, her heart loud in her ears.

- Three -

> Chase

Up on the second floor, up close, I couldn't help but pay more attention to the Acrobots. They were running a slow, graceful display, some of the 'droids spinning high over the audience amongst the silk banners whilst others swung around the edge of the central void, level with the public balcony. They were smoothly impressive in motion, catching the light and scattering colour, and I could see at this distance that they had all been individually customised with outer shells from different designers, most of them emphasising their futuristic curves and elegance of motion.

Every now and then one of the robots would make eye contact with a spectator as it moved by more slowly or paused in flight. My own turn for this simple gesture came, and as I gazed briefly into the softly luminous jade eyes of the sleek femme form just a few feet away I broke into a bright grin. All the robots had visual sensors of their own, and their multiple viewpoints might give us new perspective on the scene. If these inputs were stored, they might have recorded something useful.

I'd come up here for another reason though. From the balcony I could look down on the impact site, though I had to imagine the tent wasn't there to appreciate the perspective. None of the witnesses interviewed so far were able to pinpoint where the victim had fallen from, but they all agreed that he fell through the Acrobot display from above, not from this floor. I activated the more advanced AR settings on the smartlenses for a while, overlaying the reconstruction of the scene as it had first been recorded, but it was an early rendering and less useful than I'd hoped.

Leaning back against the rail I looked toward the ceiling, saw there was another balcony level higher up and closer to the outer wall, which I guessed might be a maintenance area of some kind. Despite the brilliant lighting in the atrium the top floor was in deep shadow, so it was hard to make out any detail even with the 'lenses. It was most likely the body had fallen from there, and when I checked the file Raissa had sent it indicated that the area had been sealed as a second crime scene. I would love to have a look round, or at least pilot one of the small forensic drones for a flyover, but I'd have to wait for Anish and Karla to document the scene first.

When I first entered the basement it was striking just how functional and utilitarian it was compared to the public areas, but it wasn't long before I'd moved into what was clearly an office space of some kind, with brighter, less severe lighting and decor that had seen much more attention. I was met there by the mall's security manager, who seemed a creature of both worlds, his clothes and appearance cared for but plain.

"Detective Chase?" he enquired, hand half outstretched.

"That's me," I replied as I extended my arm to complete the handshake, grip firm but not overly so, matching his.

"John Harris. I understand you have some questions? We've already spoken to the police and given them everything they asked for."

I showed him my ID and replied, "I know, but I just wanted to make sure of a few things." I smiled, all friendly. "It's mainly about the security you use. According to the uniformed officers you don't have any particularly sophisticated systems in place, and there's no surveillance up on the maintenance balcony - that about right?"

"Yes, that's right. We use standard commercial level stuff, nothing fancy. Mostly we rely on static cameras for the public spaces and secure access for the more private areas. We do have some mobile security drones, but we tend to keep them out of the way while the customers are around. There's definitely nothing permanently in place up there."

"Ok, what about access? I assume there's a service lift – any stairwells?"

"No, to that floor. There is an emergency access ladder, but the easiest way is the lift, one of the main ones in the maintenance areas runs right through the building from the sub-basements up to the top gallery."

"I don't suppose it's monitored?"

"There might be a record of the lift traffic. The building's systems collect a lot of background data – there could be something in there. I could take a look anyway."

"Thanks, that would be helpful. What about members of staff or customers: there's no one unaccounted for, or missing?"

"No, definitely not."

He seemed honest and on the level, and I hardly needed the advantages the smartlenses gave me, with their subtle assistance in reading the micro-expressions of his face. A few more questions though. "I was wondering if anything out of the ordinary had occurred over the last few weeks, anything at all, even if it seemed trivial at the time?"

"Nothing I can think of - not this last couple of weeks anyway. We get an occasional shop-lifter, now and then a drunk or whatever, but nothing lately."

"OK, nearly done. Is there any chance that the Acrobots themselves might have seen something and if there would be a recording or back up?" I kept my voice level, not wanting to place too much emphasis on the question.

Harris paused for a moment in response, apparently reflective. "I'd not thought of checking the Acrobots. They're just shells really, slaved to a networked AI that monitors their performance through its own sensors, so they don't have much on board. I suppose it's possible they might hold some images from their own optics on internal memory – I'll have to check."

"Thanks. So if you'd send me any security data you have, anything the robots might have recorded, and a list and contact details for any staff who were on duty, and where they were stationed, that would be excellent."

"Yes, ok. I'll ask the system to run a full check, including all the 'bots on site. It might take some time to pull everything together." He was still showing no signs of evasiveness, and it probably would take a while to collate all the info I'd requested, so there wasn't much more I could do for now.

Before leaving the mall I stopped by the main crime scene again briefly, but there was nothing new. On the way out, I picked up a double espresso, knowing that it would disagree with me but enjoying the slight buzz it gave me all the same.

I'd been in the mall a couple of hours and all I'd bought was a tiny coffee. It was probably for the best; I'd had enough therapy lately, retail or otherwise.

> Reznik

By habit and choice he'd crossed town on a random route, improvised as he'd travelled, switching direction and mode of transport but always in the thick of things, one amongst many.

There was a limit to how effective such measures could be. Whilst he'd no reason to believe the authorities would have any specific interest in him he knew they had access to many of the latest technologies and routinely monitored public spaces. Alongside a multitude of static cameras they also used a variety of aerial drones, most of them quiet and difficult to spot, sometimes the size of an insect though often larger. Smartdust and stickydust were probably the hardest things to deal with, thousands of tiny mikes, cameras and other sensors scattered like sand. All of these various sources of intel would be collated and interrogated by analytical AIs, tirelessly and unceasingly alert. No matter the size of the crowd you moved through there was no real safety in those numbers.

Despite all of this Reznik had come to regard his apartment building as a place of relative safety, clean and comfortable and with quiet, disinterested neighbours. It was a converted townhouse, moderately sized, with plenty of light throughout. The owner had taken the trouble to install a few pot-plants, some of them trailing long strands of foliage down through the central stairway. His contact, Araya, had suggested the place and it had been near perfect.

He'd already checked his own modest surveillance net as he approached the building, but now he was in his own apartment Reznik opened up a small laptop he retrieved from a backpack under the bed. A couple of minutes spent running a more thorough check confirmed there were no alerts. Placing his 'pad down next to the laptop on the lounge table he then rose and made his way to the bathroom, shedding his clothes and dumping them on the floor as he went.

Once inside the shower he poured a thick, gritty blue gel from a sachet into his hands before spreading it thoroughly all over his body and hair. The gel fizzed gently on his skin almost as soon as Reznik had applied it, and he stood and waited for a couple of minutes while the reaction continued.

When it was done, he stood at the inner edge of the cubicle and turned on the water. It quickly ran hot and he stepped into the flow and rinsed the foam off, revealing patches of clean skin and hair beneath as he did so. His body was leanly muscled and athletic, but covered in lighter patches of skin, traces of old wounds, and the ghosts of deleted artwork on his arms. Tiny dates were etched beside some of the larger, more topographic scars and a faded colour portrait of a gnarled, majestic old wolf covered most of his back.

After he'd dried off and dressed he went into the kitchen. There was a large grocery box on the counter, which he briefly rummaged through before pulling out an olive green plastic packet. His optics instantly translated the labelling: 'Field Ration, Meal 9 - Spicy Chicken' and a use by date still months in the future. From within this outer wrapper he took a smaller foil package and activated its chemtab to heat the contents before gingerly peeling off the lid. Grabbing a plastic fork, he returned to the lounge to eat his daily dose of nutrients and supplements, following it with a small pale green pill he swallowed down dry.

The previous day had turned out fine. He'd begun with a late lunch and drinks before meeting with his contact Espina in the one of the bars. The rest of the evening had been for show, really, though as there wasn't much else left to do it would have been rude not to make a proper night of it, especially as the news was good.

Lagorio was still out in the country, hunting and whoring, but he'd apparently made plans to return to the city in a couple of days. Polzin was there with him, very much part of the gang, so she should be back soon as well. Knowing her it was hard to imagine she would fully appreciate all of the entertainments, but it would be worth her while to get close to such a client, doubly so when she gained the protection his company afforded.

It had taken a long time to track her down, but they were close now. Reznik paused for a moment, savouring the anticipation of what should come next.

Almost time to set things right.

> Cara

She'd been standing in the corner of the hospital café for some time now, a thin plastic half-cup of coffee grown cold in her hand, staring through her own reflection like a stranger. Cara gave a thin, sad smile and came back to herself, nearly spilling the forgotten drink as she adjusted her stance. It was dark outside and she really should get home soon.

It had been a rough hour with Dad. She'd decided to visit him after all, and was relieved she had, as the old man looked bad today, tired and very poorly. Tubes and wires carried fluids, gasses and data back and forth - a new nervous system writ large - while he lay there old and aching. Monitors and medical arcana showed no change, but from his wracked, rattled breathing, he sounded worse to her. They'd barely spoken: neither of them could really stand the effort.

The roads were quiet as she crossed town so she drove back herself, calculating that she was still within her monthly self-drive limit. It was her Dad's car but her own policy, and she could do without the premiums rising. Patching into the traffic management system wouldn't really be much of a benefit at this time of night and the old car's autodrive tended to be more cautious than she was.

Her flat was in a reasonable area and a nice property, but a little lonely now and then as it was a too far from any of her friends to be convenient. As Cara drove up to the estate she could see there was a group of youths hanging around. Even though she was only 24 herself they seemed like another species, their clothes loose and baggy with oversized cowl-like hoods pulled up and over, trapping the cold illumination of the smart displays they obsessed over. It wasn't the first time they'd been there, but they always made her a little uneasy as she waited there at the entrance, the sensor slow to recognise her car as though it expected better of a resident.

As soon as the gates opened she drove through, and it was a comfort to see them already swinging shut behind her. The gang had mostly ignored her, barely glancing in her direction as far as she could tell, and she was grateful for that even while she admonished herself for being paranoid and out of touch.

The car was running on auto again now, and as it parked itself up Cara looked up at the flat. There was just the low lighting in the lounge, with the curtains half-open. For a moment she'd hoped Ethan would be there, a surprise, despite the row and his business trip. She was weary, and needed a hug and someone to talk to. He had a key, as she had a key to his, but they'd not quite had that conversation about moving in together. They would often go three or four days apart when they were both busy with work, and they were chilled enough about it not to be messaging all the time. Things were fairly casual and relaxed between them really, but now and then when things with Dad or Petre got on top of her she needed him that bit more.

Sighing, she locked the car and walked up the single flight of concrete steps to the landing outside her apartment. Once inside Cara was still disappointed to find that the only one that greeted her was the house *aigent*, welcoming her back. The warm tones of its voice and the soft lighting made her feel the emptiness for a moment but before she had time to get a full grump on it had the shower flowing, a meal warming and her current playlist running through the flat.

>Conrad Schuler

He leant lightly against the old balustrade at the head of the stone staircase, his outstretched hand savouring its texture, weathered from centuries of service and warm from the afternoon sun. At his feet was a sunken garden, immaculate and mature, bordered on three sides by the villa, its fourth edge reaching to infinity down a long straight avenue of scented pines. The garden gave voice with the soft rustle of the breeze and the calming chorus of birds and crickets.

Schuler had been there some time, still and quiet as the stone he leant on. He was tall and well dressed, classically smart in a neat suit, his hair dark and luxurious to his shoulders. By complexion he was tanned European, almost Mediterranean, perfectly placed in the garden despite the modern dress and more northern ancestry. He greatly valued the classic gentility of the villa, a haven from the ugliness he so often found elsewhere.

Then that other world intruded, its messenger pulsing in rhythm against his breast like a second heart while his own beat a little faster, interrupting the stillness of his thoughts. He exhaled luxuriously then reached into his jacket pocket and pulled out the phone, glancing at the screen briefly before bringing the device level with his ear. His voice was gentle, measured; every word polished and definitively pan-European.

“Ms. Harper, lovely to hear from you. How can I help?” He stood straighter now, his long frame gaining height and authority as he listened.

"I see. Yes, your associates are right to be concerned. The unit's behaviour may well draw attention, and the police's decision to involve an outside agency will further complicate matters." He paused again.

"Certainly. I would be happy to resolve the situation for you. I'll send you my new terms. I'm afraid my compensation will have to increase, given the greater difficulties and need for direct intervention." He caressed his chin with a free hand as the caller continued.

"Oh yes, I'm sure I can be of help. I rather specialise in this sort of thing, neutralising risk factors. Cleaning up other people's messes, as it were." He smiled reflexively, though there was no warmth in it.

"Excellent. I look forward to receiving the files from you. Please be as thorough as possible, I would hate there to be any misunderstandings at this stage." The call over, his phone went back into his jacket.

He felt little doubt. He would be able to offer assistance and at least mitigate the problem even if it was too late perhaps to remove it entirely. The increased fee was on a point of principle. They really should have taken his advice, that it was the wrong time and place for their experiment.

It would be unwise to allow himself to become complacent of course, but the corporate security outfit the police had engaged were unlikely to be a real concern. They were a quality professional outfit and therefore predictable, following established protocols and progressing their investigation methodically. In all likelihood they had only just begun to gather their information and forensics. Perhaps generosity would be the best solution: find a way to give them even more to work with.

Smiling with satisfaction, he resumed his quiet appreciation of the old garden. It looked its best, he thought, in the late autumn, when the sun was more bearable and the rain came again.

She lay flat, almost pushing herself deeper into the dirt from sheer will, hoping the tiny drone wouldn't spot them. Tsukino had seen it first as it came in from the east, her eyes a little sharper than Frost's. This was exactly the kind of thing they'd feared.

There was no way of telling if they were safe. The stealthed fatigues they all wore should help, but it could have tagged them before they even hit the ground. There'd been no obvious alarms, and nothing else had arrived at their position, but the tension was threatening to overwhelm her. The damn thing loitered there just a few yards away, drawing a slow circle in the sky.

A beep in her ear, soft as snow and loud as thunder. The Wolf had sent a burst transmission down the comm. They were good to go, apparently.

- Four -

> Chase

From the outside the office was an ordinary enough building covering several floors, modern but not particularly innovative. The outer construction featured smoked glass and curves flowing around an exposed metal frame, while on the inside natural light gave the atrium and reception areas an open, airy atmosphere. Lush beds of tailored foliage were featured in planters throughout the interior and in terraces on the exterior, blending with the tasteful park area running through the rest of this modest commercial zone at the river's edge.

There were a number of these individual units of various sizes on the site, many of them similar but others quite different, more blocky and utilitarian. Nearly all were occupied. Without a working knowledge of the tenants or AR tagging it was hard to guess what they were all used for. Most had some form of corporate plaque outside, actual and virtual, and in their varied designs it was clear where the creative vision of the different tenants was allowed greater expression. Cadejo Security Services S.A. had one of the more sober displays, a modest, vaguely Latino font giving the company name while smaller italics spoke of Cadejo's place in the Aschbank Concord. In the background was a depiction of the head of a large white wolf-like creature, shown in profile, beautifully rendered in 3D.

That morning was the first time I'd been back there in a long while. Somehow, the sight of it made my return to work more real than the crime scene had done. I knew there would have been changes inside, new faces and maybe a remodelling here or there, but I knew much would be the same. Cadejo was many things in many places, and whilst the domestic branch offered only legitimate security and investigative services the heat from some its more ethically challenging foreign operations could still be felt back here on occasion.

I'd arranged to meet up with Franklin, a forensic technician, at one of the holographic suites. We'd worked together before so knew each other well, and she was one of the few people at Cadejo I'd actually call a friend. I knew I could trust her to keep my visit quiet, and I'd timed things so I was there at lunchtime, when there was regular movement of staff in and out of the building and people were a touch more relaxed.

Franklin rushed over and grabbed me for a hug as soon as I entered the room, and it was impossible not to feel my mood lighten. We parted quickly, both a little embarrassed, and after exchanging a few pleasantries got down to work. There was a model of the crime scene reconstruction already up and running, a near perfect ultra-high resolution 3D hologram of the mall atrium, frozen in time.

"It's good to see you back Chase. Ok, we've received plenty of raw data from the forensics and the mall manager. We've still no ID for the body though: there was nothing in his personal effects, and the coroner's not released a formal identification yet. In the meantime, they've started building a detailed profile from his DNA and they're trying to work up a facial reconstruction."

"I'll not hold my breath on that – it looked as though he fell face down, and his head was probably the first point of impact. Good to see you too."

She smiled before replying, "Yeah, well, it's worth a try. We have the detailed scans from the crime scene, and in theory the skull would have shattered in a way that left uneven breaks in the bone that you could match up, given enough time. We might end up with only an approximation of his appearance, but it's better than nothing."

I had an intimate knowledge of how impressive the reconstruction software could be, but this would be like doing a jigsaw puzzle with only a vague idea of what the final picture was – even with the appearance profile they could build from the DNA work. Hopefully the coroner would come through with an ident, but if they didn't we'd be able to use everything we could discover to make our own enquiries, once we had the formal permissions.

I walked over and stood at the edge of the holographic image, forming the rough shape of a butterfly with my hands, palms outstretched. As I took control of the haptic field around the hologram the display changed in sync with my hand movements, showing new angles and viewpoints, zooming in as I brought the model up through to life-size and beyond before pulling right back to give a more distant view.

The reconstruction was designed to capture the timeline of events surrounding the victim's death, as well as the moment itself, giving us a strikingly real image of the fallen body and the Acrobot trapped beneath it. All the available information and evidence was included, and the model was honest enough to reflect the many points of uncertainty regarding the precise movements of some of the eyewitnesses, showing them as fainter, ghost-like images.

The forensic AI had estimated the height and trajectory of the body's path, confirming that the victim had most likely fallen from the balcony area high up on the maintenance floor. I watched in slow motion as he plummeted downward, head first and apparently silent as far as we could tell from the audio we'd obtained so far. The real focus of most of the video captured had been the Acrobots, and I had to admit to being impressed again as I watched a replay of their routine and the elegance and grace they displayed as they wove between the hanging banners, leaping and gliding, giving motion and texture to the silk which swayed and rippled in their wake. It was truly gorgeous watching this in slow motion and I was almost as lost in it as the spectators had been – until the body dropped into frame.

The victim fell in a path that took him almost precisely through the centre of the display, missing the banners and all the Acrobots save for one. You could see the shocked reactions of the crowd at the balcony edge as he struck the android bodily, his weight carrying it before him, past the point where it could grasp a banner or the outstretched arms of another 'droid, a second robot falling in their wake, undone by the chaos of the moment as the rest of the Acrobots scattered like startled birds.

When he neared the ground I slowed the frame rate to a crawl, allowing the forensic record of the injuries sustained by the body as it impacted to play out at a rate I could comprehend. In the clinical detail of the presentation it was nasty and brutal, the catalogue of organic damage more like a lengthy beating at this speed. The robot didn't fare much better as its head casing shattered against the hard floor, its legs kicking spasmodically at the empty air.

I signalled with my hands to replay the sequence, and was then confused for a moment as my gestures received no response and the sense of immersion was broken. Looking over to Franklin I could see her expression was one of surprise and concern, and as I turned fully around it was clear why.

Iyer was standing there, with her arms crossed and her perfect face scowling in obvious anger and distaste.

> Reznik

He stood in his apartment, casually watching the street outside from the large windows of the lounge area. Reznik found the constant flow of people moving by restful, as though their to and fro absolved him from any personal need for activity. Tradecraft suggested that he should stand further back, be less openly on view, but he allowed himself a few minutes respite from the constant edginess and cultivated paranoia every once in a while. A small balcony ran in an 'L' shape around the corner of the apartment, and he would have enjoyed going outside. There was work to do though.

Moving over to the couch, he sat down in front of his computer where it rested on the low table, soft light flickering from the screen in the shade away from the windows. Touching a few keys and the mouse pad opened up a series of 3D maps and photos, abstracted topography and virtual light focussing on a tall, graceful sliver of glass and exotic materials, a skyscraper of twists and curves in the centre of Maravilhosa. Now the objective was in front of him again his thoughts solidified and sharpened.

There were any number of ways he could target Polzin, but he'd very much like to be free and clear afterwards. Minimising any collateral damage wasn't so much a matter of conscience as professionalism, and it was in any case generally best to keep things simple. As a member of Lagorio's entourage Polzin would be protected as a matter of course by his security, and given the affluence of her host that was good security indeed.

Lagorio owned a penthouse near the apex of the skyscraper, at its rear an open balcony with a spacious patio area surrounding a large infinity pool. There was another more modest balcony at the front. Reznik guessed the vantage from either would be spectacular, covering the whole of the bay from the seawalls to the favelas, with the mountains and beaches curving round on either side and the algae farms further up the coast. In the distance the ocean glimmered, once a source of simple beauty but now a threat, the high tides pushing against the barriers.

He knew from previous research that Lagorio made much use of his patio, holding regular parties for the rich and well connected. From his reputation, Lagorio was just dirty enough to be useful to the more respectable types whilst also attracting the most ambitious rising stars, who perhaps imagined they saw in him a kindred spirit. He was a fixer in the main, a go-between with friends in all manner of places and smart enough to be discrete and free from true scandal. As Polzin was a guest she would surely be obliged to attend any upcoming events, and the intelligence he was buying from Espina gave him a solid idea of when those would be held.

The apartment's open balcony would in theory make her vulnerable to a sniper, but the skyscraper was one of the tallest in the city. There was only one other building nearby with a good enough vantage point, but it would be a tough shot from there as the winds were strong across the bay at that altitude, almost a private microclimate for the loftiest citizens. Those same winds also served as a natural barrier to drone flight when they blew hard, as most of the smaller, stealthier designs were too underpowered to deal with the gusts. Reznik was grateful that Jakobsen was on board for this op. His presence running the cyber side of things gave them a lot more options, many of which were significantly less messy than he would have easily managed on his own.

Jakobsen was undoubtedly an asset, reliable and effective, but for this mission he was more than that, personally invested and emotionally driven. Of the two of them, Jakobsen had by far the brighter, hotter anger whilst Reznik's smouldered, a dull orange glow, steady and slow to cool. His was a more complex combustion, an alloy of personal loss and professional chagrin. Jakobsen thought more about mates and might-have-beens.

This may well be their last gig together, and if so, it was a fitting way to end things. Jakobsen had met someone, he said, and wanted to try to make something of it, a normal life. Reznik sighed, and wished him luck with that. There were things he needed to be on with, preparations to make before the hunting party returned to the city and Polzin became prey.

> Cara

She'd been going to sleep in, but the bed felt a little empty today. Right then, Cara was missing Ethan for other reasons, but her *aigent* distracted her with a few new messages as soon as she was more awake. It wasn't strictly speaking intelligent, but it was damn good at seeming like it, assessing her moods and needs, providing support and smoothing out the little lumps of life. Most people had one of some sort, at least to help run their home or diary, and many relied on it entirely. Hers had already filtered the latest messages for her, whittling them down aggressively to the things she really should bother herself with.

Cara was a freelancer, and had plenty of work in for the next few weeks. Beyond that, it was typical for things to look a little thin and then fill up later. The majority of her commissions came through individual recommendations, repeat bookings and the small, discrete tags she placed on her finished pieces. She excelled at satisfying her client's desire to have a more personalised digital presence, offering a combination of website design, profile management and *aigent* customisation. Many people and businesses felt the need for an occasional upgrade, so she was kept busy enough, and every now and then there'd be some proper coding work to do, which she loved.

Over the last year or so she had made a move into profile pruning, a sort of digital embalming, at first because of Dad and more lately because she could at least help other people. Realistically, it was probably too late for her own father: he'd been unusually resistant to the attractions of a digital life and had left only a tiny presence online, but for others, whether life-loggers or just those with a rich virtual existence there was a strong trend toward maintaining a permanent digital presence, ready for the promised technological leap that might bring virtual immortality.

Already there were a number of commercial organisations, uplink centres and independents like herself, who offered to take the reams of personal data available, edit it and run it through neurological emulators and AI software to create a digital ghost, almost a personal ancestor spirit, always available in the electronic afterlife. Like many in the industry, she usually referred to them as an ArPer - after Artificial Personality - though rarely in front of a client, as that could often lead to upset and confusion, given their similarity to simple AIs. It was all highly controversial, with plenty of religious groups loudly declaring their spiritual objections just as others argued that the human mind was too complex to encode in lines of software. Enthusiasts in turn labelled their opponents as luddites or fools, pointing to the human capacity for adaptation and acceptance, citing the popularity of *aigents* with their entirely simulated personalities and the unending flow of chattering technology. Cara could well imagine the fuses that would blow the first time anyone succeeded in transferring their persona from an old, broken body to a brand new clone or permanent digital life, as the techno-progressives insisted was inevitable and perhaps imminent.

Dad thought the whole thing preposterous, an affront to Nature – definitely with a capital 'N'. All the same, she'd considered encoding him anyway, and doing the work herself, ever since they'd first had the diagnosis. In the end, though, the whole thing would be too icky, like running her fingers through the wet humanity of his inner self. There were people she knew who would do a good job, some she had recommended to others, but the truth was that any attempt to capture her father's essence would be more conjecture and stock code than she could stomach. There just wasn't enough of him on record: when he went, he would be gone for good.

This felt unfair to her, ironic but with no sense of amusement that he should die when eternal, tangible salvation was a leap or two of R&D into the future. It was a cruelty almost as great as the manner of his illness. He would pass at the wrong time, at the threshold between candlelight and plasma. Nothing like her mother's death, which was so long ago now that only in old pictures was her face remotely clear.

She swore and shook her head. This wasn't what she wanted to be thinking about. A text from Emma reminded her of their date that night. Cara wasn't really in the mood, but she knew that Em would only allow her to talk about the negatives for a while before distracting her. Emma was always so busy it was rare for them to get together so she was loath to cancel without the strongest of reasons.

Cara returned to her work, selecting new personality traits for an upgraded *aigent* for the 13-year-old daughter of one of her clients, enhancing its cultural database with a customised extension and adding a more complex suite of emulated behaviours, long on emotional nuance and empathy. If her next few years were as confusing as her own had been she would need it.

The drone moved off, so silently she almost missed it. Over the next few moments the tension peaked still higher as they held their position, nervous that at any moment the sky, or at least explosive ordnance, would fall. The seconds ran up to a minute: it seemed they were safe. Frost breathed deeply and then got back gingerly on her feet, sending a quick response to The Wolf as she led the others off.

They followed the valley again until they reached a turn in the riverbed, which ran along to the left where it would eventually reach the main gated entrance to the base site. Their path took them right, up the valley side and over an outcrop of rock. Here there was less cover so they made the quickest time they dare in climbing up and over the ridge and down the other side, where a steep, broken slope lead onwards to a gap in the rusted security fence, partly hidden by gnarled trees. Up ahead in the near distance she could see the next target.

- Five -

> Chase

Iyer, more than anyone, was exactly the person I'd wanted to avoid. As always, she looked immaculate and professional, thoroughly business-like. In another life, and if I were honest in this one, she would be immensely attractive, her fine Indian features classically beautiful, but her obvious disapproval was never far from the surface. The limited contact we'd had while I'd been on leave only seemed to have made things worse, but she was my boss, at least technically, and I was stuck with her. I kept my expression as neutral as I could, whilst Iyer stared back frostily, arms still crossed, before she arched an eyebrow, lending a further acidity to her expression.

"So, the prodigal returns. Glad you could finally join us. I trust you're feeling better, Keegan." The coolness of her tone contradicted almost every word she said, and the limited confidence I'd begun to feel once I'd started the investigation was beginning to ebb away. I was determined to maintain a positive front though.

"Yes thanks. Raissa assigned me the mall case, so I thought I'd take a look at the current crime scene model."

"I'm aware of that. I hope you're up to this."

"I think so. We'll see, I guess."

"I'm sure we will. Do me a favour though: try to keep the guessing to a minimum if you could." She shook her head slightly, and then turned crisply on her heels to walk away, casting a brief glance toward Franklin as she left, who looked both chagrined and embarrassed.

I stared at the closing door for a moment while Frankie continued to make herself look busy at the controls of the console where she'd spent the whole of Iyer's visit. After a few seconds the hologram image began to move again in the corner of my eye, and I turned back to the centre of the room, grateful for the distraction.

The first images Franklin brought up were a confused pattern of partial footprints, smeared in blood across the plain grey floor of the maintenance balcony. A long soiled piece of cloth lay twisted on the ground, one of the missing sleeves from the victim's top. These were the results from the second crime scene, and it looked as though he'd arrived there in the lift, stepped across to the centre of the floor, where he then seemed to have moved more or less in place before stepping back toward the edge of the balcony. At the edge was a railing, too high to easily leap over, but as there was no trace of any blood there, he'd probably not climbed over it either. One thing that was conspicuously absent was any form of suicide note or direct communication from the victim, though by now I wasn't really expecting anything.

Other signs indicated there had been someone else up there, either at the time of his fall or shortly afterward. Whoever it was, they'd been careful to leave as little evidence as possible, just a few fragmentary boot impressions in the blood trail. It was a remarkably clean area, with only a few forensic traces.

As a matter of course the lift had also been examined for evidence, and the techs had run brief scans of all the floors it had stopped at, but apart from confirming that the victim had used it they'd found little else. Everywhere below the top level was scrupulously clean, which Harris had confirmed was due to the building's automated cleaning schedule, which was both regular and thorough. No one had thought to interrupt it, and there didn't seem to be any security monitoring of the private areas either.

I had more questions than answers, and it was looking increasingly likely this had been a murder. The state of the body, especially the feet, indicated that the victim had been in some distress, and if anyone up on the maintenance balcony had seen a suicide they were being suspiciously close-lipped about it.

I spent some more time with the reconstructions, letting Frankie demonstrate her expertise to illustrate particular points. The next thing to do would be to review the autopsy file in detail when it came in, especially anything that might give an indication of the victim's identity. Satisfied I'd seen as much as I could for now I shut down the haptic field, gently closing the butterfly's wings.

> Reznik

Late morning found him sat in the back of a quiet café at the edge of the same downtown zone he'd passed through the previous day, alone save for the bored waiter and an elderly couple. It was a decent enough place, but the recent outbreak nearby had cut the through-traffic in the area dramatically, even though a few streets over things were as busy as they'd ever been. This was very much an official district of the city still, fully part of its municipal fabric, but marginalised and forgotten.

After finishing lunch, he left enough money on the table to cover everything and went to use the restroom. Reznik was confident he'd be undisturbed and went straight into one of the cubicles, closing the door behind him. He put the seat down, and then stood atop it to reach up to the cistern. Placing his hand into the water for a couple of moments he pulled out a small plastic bag containing a black, cylindrical object, smooth and roughly three inches long of either metal or hard plastic.

At the top of the cylinder were a trio of tiny LEDs, all lit a soft, pale green. His expression gave little away, but the device had obviously served its purpose as he used both hands to grab each end of the cylinder before robustly twisting them in opposite directions. There was a soft crack, and then the cylinder gave off a faint wisp of grey smoke from its centre. A moment later the LEDs flickered and died. Opening the neck of the sealable bag, releasing a sharp chemical tang, Reznik reached back up to the cistern and gently tipped the object into the water. He could hear a gentle fizzing begin.

Climbing down he tore off some toilet roll to wipe the trace of his boots from the seat before lifting the lid and dropping the used paper into the pan. He left the cubicle, threw the plastic bag into the trash, and then washed his hands thoroughly at the sink. Leaving the restroom he went through the back of the café to a service door that he knew would take him out onto a narrow road that ran behind the property.

It was then that things lost a little smooth.

Up ahead, in the direction he intended to take, he could see a police cruiser parked across the end of the street, solidly blocking the exit, its lights flashing. There was the sound of some commotion around the corner there, violent resistance, and he turned and walked briskly away, taking the nearest path, an alley narrower even than the back street he'd just been on, too tight for patrol cars.

He kept going, determined to stay away from trouble but not completely sure where he was heading now. Whatever was going on back near the cafe seemed to be escalating, the noise growing even as he moved away, more sirens arriving and some sort of crowd gathering. As he continued, the paths became ever more jumbled and confusing, every now and then another one branching off or joining on, each just as rough and anonymous as this. He began to meet other people here, hurrying along as he did, some toward the fracas, some away.

At first he'd not been too concerned when a group of youths entered the alley a few yards behind and begun to follow, their pace casually matching his own. Reznik took a quick look back and then ignored them, but in that single glance he'd seen enough. They dressed like teenagers, but were perhaps a year or two older. There were three of them, and at least one was armed, judging by what looked like a handgun sticking from the waistband of his shorts, a long baggy yellow t-shirt dropping down around the pistol grip. He'd not thought himself close to gang territory here, but things were fluid these days, unpredictable, the traffickers more desperate now their regular incomes and routes were disrupted by the quarantines. The fact that many of the social bonds that held the favelas together where also strained in the wake of the plague didn't help.

Reznik carried on, glancing back only briefly to take stock: they were still trailing behind, keeping the same distance, their expressions hard and focussed. He kept his pace steady, his bearing confident. There were less people using the alleyways now, and it was becoming clear to both himself and those following that they were on the same path. The air was hot and thick in his lungs as he breathed deeply, keeping his heart rate low, controlling his body's reactions as best he could while he looked for another route to take, another option. There were fewer exits from this stretch of the alley though, and each one seemed rougher than this.

In the distance, somewhere up in the hills, there were gunshots, the rip of rapid fire and the deeper crack of heavier calibres in response. A pause, another outburst, and then the barking of startled dogs, ever alert to sudden noise. There was a growing unease, a spike in the tension, and suddenly he'd had enough. With a speed that almost surprised himself Reznik ran off, feet skittering occasionally on the dusty and uneven surface as he raced down the alley. From behind he heard shouting, threats and curses, and the sounds of fast feet as they sprinted in pursuit. He fancied his chances of outrunning them, but couldn't be sure there wouldn't be a straight enough length of alley ahead where their guns would close the distance, letting them reach out across the yards to stop him dead.

He ran on, too fast to keep anything but a direct course, weaving a little when his paranoia began to build up on the straights. They were still running after, further back now, and had given up shouting after him, needing their breath for tiring muscles and racing hearts.

As he rounded the next corner Reznik slowed to walking pace, suddenly wary. Behind him, he heard the footsteps of the youths slow to a stop, even as they started to laugh in between great gulps of air. Ahead, up the alley from Reznik, two men had turned square toward him, far more openly menacing than his pursuers.

> Cara

Her phone pulsed behind her ear and Cara, momentarily distracted as she juggled too many thoughts at once, answered it without checking the caller ident.

"Mornin' Cara. Been a while. I was wondering if you could pass on a message to that boyfriend of yours, if it's not too much trouble." She wasn't quite sure at first, but it was a voice she knew with old intimacy; one she had never expected, or wanted, to hear again.

"Who is this? How did you get this number?"

"I asked someone for it. Not your boyfriend, don't worry. Don't suppose you told 'im about the old days did you? Not clean Cara, no, wouldn't suit you for 'im to find out about all that. Needn't worry though. Just want you to tell 'im your old pal Nada was asking after 'im, like."

"He's out of town, not that it's anything to do with you." The realisation that she was talking to Nathan Daniel Thorne had grown slowly. She'd not seen him since he'd run from the police faster and further than she had way back when. Cara had been caught and sentenced, a heavy fine, community service and curfew followed along with the heavy hand of her father and the mother of all groundings.

"Ah, well you see, this is just a friendly word, like. Been doing a little bit of business with your feller see, and 'e's a little late on paying up. Nothing too serious – I'm sure it's just slipped 'is mind, as it were – but I'd appreciate it if you could let 'im know I've been in touch."

"Fine, whatever. When he next bothers to ring me I'll be sure to let him know."

"Ta, very decent of you. Out of town, you reckon? Don't suppose 'e mentioned where at all?"

"No, he didn't."

"Ah well, fair enough. Been lovely chatting and all that. Take care of yourself." He rang off.

She saved the number to her *aigent* so it would alert her if he rang again. His voice, even slimier than she remembered, was all the more intrusive for being piped straight into her head through bone conduction, as though hearing it in the ordinary way would have been less dirty somehow.

Dan bloody Thorne. Whilst on probation for that first incident she had still been in touch with him on the quiet and he had somehow managed to implicate her in his next failed caper even though she was supposed to be his friend - at the very least - and staying the hell away from any more of Nada's schemes. After a short stay inside a juvenile detention centre Cara had vowed fervently never to go back there or have anything more to do with him, or hacking in general.

It had just been a bit of teenage vandalism and amateur pranking really, turning all the traffic lights to red and exploding paint bombs over the stationary cars, but the police had a particular shortage of humour when it came to anything they could classify as cybercrime. Nada had been sloppy rather than malicious, using code Cara had written weeks before to prise open the system, but he'd left her virtual fingerprints all over it and none of his own. The worst thing was how her Mum had reacted after the police came. Dad had raged, threatened, and shouted his disappointment as he ran red with anger. Mum had just stared at her, and then shaken her head in wordless condemnation and shame.

Cara had been released a few weeks before her Mum died, but things were never quite patched up between them. There were the silences at meal times, the long prayers of grace and always the icy formality. Things would probably have been ok in the end, been fixed, but then there was the car crash, at that same intersection Cara had been accused of griefing, and suddenly there was no more time. She'd had to grow up fast then. Petre was away – Christ knew where - and Dad was lost for a while.

There had been other friends, at the edge of that same circle of miscreants, which she'd resumed contact with after a time through obscure chat links and darksites, partly for professional reasons, but she'd never once been in touch with Thorne or anyone too close to him. But now he was back, and Ethan was mixed up with him somehow. She had no idea what Nada was into these days, but she didn't think it would be legit.

She tried Ethan's phone, but got nothing but his *aigent.*

They'd been in position for a few minutes now, quietly observing the old concrete pillbox across the broken ground. Polzin had assured them the abandoned sentry post was still linked into the base network. That and the access codes she'd sold them were Jakobsen's way in.

Frost led the way, running fast and low up to the front side of the box. Stopping hard against the wall, she threw a fist-sized object straight into the nearest gun slit, ducking straight back down again. She waited a few moments, checked her display, and then signalled for Jakobsen and Tsukino to follow her as she moved around the pillbox in a crouch, snug against the wall until she reached the entrance at the rear.

The Wolf grinned at her from where he crouched in the corner furthest from the door, lowering his rifle as she moved inside. Frost retrieved the small IyZon bot from where it hovered in the centre of the damp concrete room and moved over to confer with him. Jakobsen went straight to the electrical box on the wall, much newer than the rest of the structure, and pulled a laptop from his pack. Tsukino shook her head and moved to cover the doorway.

- Six -

> Chase

I'd gone back to the flat after I left the office, tried to play the guitar to find some calm but ended up even more frustrated as my head refused to settle and my hands forgot how to move. Even the simplest of things felt unfamiliar, and I had to put it back in the corner, knocking over the walking stick Jo had bought for me. As I picked it up and set it back I ran my hand slowly along it, relishing the texture of the carving, turning it this way and that to watch the serpent endlessly eating its own tail. I missed her, but was almost grateful I didn't have time to think about her now, the details of the case fresh and pressing on my mind.

Despite not having the exact things I needed from the mall's security manager we did have everything he'd given the police, including a copy of all the footage captured by the static cameras in the few hours running up to the victim's fall. The video had already been analysed by an AI to see if anything suspicious had occurred, but no one had done anything to draw attention to themselves. Once we had a face and more details for the victim we could run the software again and perhaps pick him and his assailants out as they moved through the building, but until then it was giving us nothing.

It was possible that they might have arrived on the previous day or even earlier, but unless they'd been holed up somewhere completely out of sight they should have been fairly conspicuous to the mobile security drones, which openly patrolled after hours when there were no customers around to be offended. These would have been very alert to any people still in the mall without permission.

It was more likely that they had entered sometime on the day he was killed and stayed away from the public spaces entirely. They clearly had access to the service areas, which might easily have afforded them a covert and unrecorded way into the building. The information Harris had sent over didn't cover all of the possibilities, but if we were lucky it might just be because he hadn't thought to include everything.

I kept coming back to the same key issues: the lack of any ID for the victim and an absence of witnesses or security footage from the mall. Without knowing who the victim was, or anything about him, we couldn't begin to reason out a motive or possible killer, or even positively rule out that he'd committed suicide.

The autopsy report, when it arrived, would tell us more. Cadejo had donated much of the equipment used by the state pathologist, including the latest deep scanners and auto-surgeons, so I knew the work would be of a similar quality to what we would have produced in-house. If there were still no positive identification for the victim we would hopefully be granted permission to expand our own enquiries at last.

With the high saturation of surveillance technologies, pervasive social media and sophisticated forensic and data analysis techniques a significant number of crimes were resolved quickly and without much fuss, especially when many serious incidents involved people who were known to each other. In some respects this case was similar given the huge amount of amateur footage available, but for us the critical part was how the body had fallen and from where, and no one seemed to have any shots of that. The videos that did exist had circulated wildly online, going viral before the body had even cooled. Other media channels had picked up on the story and covered it as a trending topic - news about news in effect - which increased its profile still further.

The case was typical of the ones Cadejo were contracted for, small in scale and yet relatively intensive in terms of its technical and forensic requirements. The Police still handled the majority of criminal investigations, but their more specialised detective departments had been stripped back to priority activities such as terrorism and organised crime. That left quite a lot of serious incidents, murder included, which they couldn't always resolve quickly, if at all, leaving the way open for private contractors like CSS.

I glanced at the clock and realised if I got on with it I'd be able to give Ellie a call. It had only been a week or so since we'd last spoken, but she would want to know I was back at work, and it would be a good to catch the kids. In no time we were reminiscing about my last visit home and planning the next one.

> Reznik

One of the men up ahead was an intimidating figure, tall and bulky with a shaven head, but the other was much less physically imposing. There was something about him though, something in his stance or bearing that spoke of cruelty. From the look of things it seemed they were in the middle of a deal, most likely for drugs or data. They were most definitely in his way though, and had turned to block most of the alley. Back behind him, the youths had stopped at an easy distance, braced against the wall to catch a breath. Beyond the two men, perhaps twenty or thirty yards away, the alley ended at a broader street. An occasional car rolled by as he watched, not fast but steady, so it was more of a side road than a main route. There were no other exits from the alley that he could see, the buildings crowding in on either side, plain walls with only an occasional high window.

He began to walk forward slowly, posture relaxed and easy. Reznik hoped he looked like a tourist, and no particular threat, which was realistic enough given that he carried no weapon beyond a short-bladed knife. The situation was balanced on the edge of nasty, so he let some of his nerves show, walked with a little less confidence, took a perfectly natural look backward toward his pursuers, who'd begun to edge a little closer now. It didn't seem that the two groups were working together as such, but they were more likely to find common cause with each other than him. Reznik called out, his voice calm to match his body language, palms out and open: "Hey fellas. Sorry to interrupt your biz but I'm just passin' through. Not lookin' for any trouble."

"Yeah? Well you found some motherfucker – or maybe you brought some with you?" It was the meaner one who spat out the words, indicating with a glance behind Reznik. His associate, who kept close to the left-hand side of the alley, stayed silent, his angry glare and steady rock back and forth on planted feet the only clear sign of tension. The smaller, mouthier one looked wired, scruffy to the point of dereliction and a little frenetic in his movements. He took a step to the right, more definitively blocking the way, trying to weave a lazy eight in the air with a dull grey blade he'd produced from somewhere but failing, his hand stuttering through the pattern as though it were new or only half-remembered.

Reznik kept his breathing and heart rate as steady as he could but slowed the tempo of his movements a touch as though less sure, edging forward still, openly switching the direction of his gaze between the men, risking a quick look back to see that the three youths were moving up slowly, their guns still stowed but more openly on show. They were a bit younger than he'd first thought and appeared both nervous and edgy, moving with a brittle bravery that promised violence. He was grateful the older men ahead were apparently either without firearms, or at least more cautious in using them.

He called out again, softer now, attention ahead. "Honestly, I'm just lookin' to get by. If you'd let me pass I'd appreciate it. Then I'll be on my way." All the while Reznik moved steadily nearer, posture and palms open, non-threatening. There was no relaxation in the stance of either of the two men: the knife continued to dance awkwardly in the air while the other looked on, sullenly hostile and suspicious.

"Don't come any closer. We can see you well enough from here."

It wasn't going to be. Reznik knew this might be seven kinds of stupid, but he was stubborn and short of time. Moving with graceful assurance, focus just beyond and to the side of them, he closed suddenly and then moved to the right of the smaller man for a step as though trying to go around him. As his feint drew the other man forward a touch Reznik cut back explosively, stepping in, striking at his assailant's outstretched knife arm with his left hand whilst simultaneously thrusting at the smaller man's neck with his right, jabbing him neatly in the throat with his knuckles, not too hard, feeling the impact against soft flesh and cartilage.

The smaller man dropped the knife as he recoiled from Reznik's attack, gagging and reaching for his throat as Reznik jabbed at his exposed abdomen, forcing him back and into the path of the bigger man, who was reacting now, trying to move around to get to Reznik. The two thugs collided, and in the momentary confusion Reznik aimed a hard snap-kick at the larger man's leg, connecting soundly with his knee. Off balance and in pain the shaven-headed man rocked backward, exposing his face to Reznik, who jammed the heel of his hand sharply into his nose, feeling it collapse messily against his palm. Reznik moved around, punched hard at the big man's side, and again, felt the ribs give, and then circled away, breaking the contact.

He ran for it straight toward the end of the alley, staying close to the wall. Behind he could hear the pained curses of his assailants as they gathered themselves up and shouts from the youths who'd pursued him first. He would just as soon have left bodies, but that would have made noise of another kind.

As he left the back street and turned along the main road he slowed to seem more ordinary, but was ready to sprint forward again. His palm and wrist were wet from the big man's blood, while his knuckles throbbed dully with the echoes of contact.

Across the street a car was parked up, two men inside chatting to a couple of young girls through the open windows. Guessing they might be lookouts he hoped they would stay distracted long enough for him to make the next corner and get out of sight.

> Cara

She looked herself over in the mirror one last time, pursing her lips to apply a final sparse touch of makeup. Cara was attractive in a cool kind of way; slim, a touch androgynous, certainly pretty but not striking. She had dark, edgy hair, and wore tees and skinny jeans like she'd invented them. For her style had substance and fashion had none, and anyone – any guy – that didn't like her look was probably not for her anyway.

Emma was the only friend she spent any regular time with that shook that conviction, even a little. Nothing was ever said, but Em managed a comfortable fusion of both fashion and style so effortlessly and effectively that Cara would occasionally feel she might have gotten it a little bit wrong. Accordingly, it was almost a rule when meeting her to be as glamorous as the setting would allow, even if that occasionally meant resorting to a dress and really uncomfortable shoes. At first it had been mildly annoying, but now it was just a fact of their friendship. Tonight, though, with the evening they had planned she could get away with a little less, something closer to herself.

They had first met when Emma had wanted an ArPer of her recently departed father creating, and resumed their acquaintance later that month, bumping into one another at an exhibition of ancient South & East Asian art. The reverence for renewal and rebirth struck them both as apt under the circumstances. Discovering they both loved many of the same things their friendship survived and thrived. Mostly they would meet up to visit some gallery or other, and it became a semi-regular thing.

Cara wasn't entirely clear about what Emma did exactly. The ArPer she'd done on her father had been unusually sketchy as well, there being so little data to work with, so she'd no real sense of who Emma was from her dad's history. At first Cara had thought there was something odd there, perhaps the faint whiff of criminality, but it was nothing she could put her fingers on. Emma herself always claimed to have a dull, boring job, though it admittedly paid quite well. Whatever it was she never complained about the cost of anything, so it must be working out ok. While there were times when Em was too busy for a catch up, and she very occasionally cancelled on her, in general Emma had been there, sometimes at her worst times. If she were honest, Cara didn't mind that there were a few unknowns between them. She certainly hadn't told Emma everything about herself.

The taxi pod arrived on time, as though it would ever do anything else, and she headed downstairs to meet it after checking herself in the mirror again. It was a two-seater, fully automated, plastic and bright, shaped like an old computer mouse or cycle helmet, fat-end first. Nothing like her father's car, older and unfashionable. As she settled herself inside the window tint darkened, increasing her privacy.

When she arrived, Emma was on great form and the food was excellent, as usual. They were near to the gallery here, so this was a favourite spot, with a nice level of recognition and remembrance from the staff. Cara had briefly filled Em in on her news before Emma took the conversation in another direction. She didn't mind so much as they had talked at length about everything when they'd first got Dad's diagnosis, and Petre's history was nothing new. Emma had been hugely supportive but there just wasn't much to say about it all now, at least not without dragging the mood down.

Boys were a more contentious subject. Cara talked about her last row with Ethan, and that he'd not been back in touch yet. Apart from anything else she'd been trying to help him by getting him to see a doctor and perhaps a therapist, as it wasn't normal to sleep as little as Ethan did, or to have such vivid and distressing dreams that he would wake up from them, sweating and scared. He'd said it was due to a car accident he'd been in as a child, in which his sister had died, but as painful as dealing with it would be it was surely better than ignoring it? Besides, she found it hard to get a good night's sleep alongside him.

As always, Emma's general advice was to adopt a policy of zero tolerance, or at least a three strike rule, which as far as she was concerned Ethan had exceeded a while ago. Emma had never been that keen on Ethan truth to tell, though they'd never actually met in the flesh. Cara had a few pictures, and as soon as Em had seen one she seemed to take against him a little, which was odd as he was fairly hot by any normal standard, and not too far from Emma's usual type.

Em could have a point though: it was past time he stopped sulking and got in touch, especially after Cara had passed on the message, more or less, from Thorne. There was the palmtop as well, which he'd forgotten to bring along when she'd last seen him. Cara did have a key to his flat: maybe Emma would go with her to pick it up? It would feel a little weird going there when he wasn't home. At first, Emma had been reluctant, but then had finally agreed over the course of dessert and a couple more glasses of red.

Within moments Jakobsen had the junction box open and leads attached between his Hallistiks laptop and the exposed terminals, but the minutes that followed while he worked stretched out like hours for Frost. It was chill and damp inside the pillbox, her breath clouding in the pre-dawn cold.

Bright illumination suddenly flooded the interior as the laptop's display flashed into life for a moment before The Wolf growled at Jakobsen to dim the screen. Frost directed a wry glance toward Tsu, who responded with a warmer smile. She returned it, shaking her head.

Jakobsen's software had wormed its way into the control net: they could now exert influence over the patrolling drones and stop any alerts from reaching the human operators inside the main complex. The Wolf spoke softly by her ear, his voice still rough-edged even as a whisper. It reminded her of home, a different South a long time from here. He would set off now and scout ahead. Jakobsen would stay in the pillbox to monitor the security network.

In 20 minutes she and Tsu were to head out directly for the main buildings.

- Seven -

> Chase

I poured my third straight black coffee, wished I had something stronger, and watched as the hot steam tickled the nearest edges of the hologram display. The call had come in around eight that the pathologist's report was finished and I'd gone straight over to the office to view it.

In front of me was a life-size image of a naked corpse laid flat on its back on a metal autopsy table, a couple of clean white coverings over the head and hips, everything pin-sharp and bright under the medical lighting. The victim had been a fit, well-muscled white male with an exemplary level of general physical health. Mid-30s, almost exactly six-feet tall, with a medium-build and a weight of 175lbs. He wore his light brown hair cropped short and had a four or five day growth of facial hair, but his head was such a mess from the fall that I still couldn't stand to look at it uncovered for long. Evidently it had given the coroner some problems, as they were still unable to confirm his identity.

Formalities first: the likely cause of death was massive trauma to the head and upper torso caused by the impact with the ground, after which there had been extensive and rapid haemorrhaging. The time of death estimate matched to known events, but from there things got more complicated. Because the body had landed from such a height, it was hard to determine whether there had been any pre-mortem head or shoulder injuries, or even to confirm with absolute certainty that he had been alive before the impact.

The rest of the body was relatively intact, and there were indications of bruising in several places, mostly quite faint, evidence perhaps of minor injuries suffered in the last few moments of his life. There were also clear signs of ligature marks on the wrists and ankles, indicating the victim had been restrained at some point, but they looked like they were a few days old and had been starting to heal. Other recent injuries showing on the body were minor lacerations to the abdomen caused by the chassis of the Acrobot pinned beneath the victim as they made contact with the ground, as well as a number of bruises and cuts to his feet, some of which still had small pieces of glass embedded. Something we could perhaps match to another location later.

I thought about the fainter traces of bruising found on the shins, forearms and chest area, imagining myself in a boxer's stance for a moment, visualising where they were all located. It seemed as though these might be a mixture of impacts from a fight, and that the victim had been primarily on the defensive, as there were hardly any signs of contact on the usual points like the knuckles or feet. It was impossible to tell who had initiated the violence but it seemed clear that our victim had come off worse. From the general state of his health and physical condition and the extensive signs of old calluses it seemed he'd been a trained fighter, which made the fact he'd apparently been so outmatched even more interesting.

More thorough scans revealed signs of older wounds. His skull had been repaired at some point in the last few years, and there was a suggestive pattern of past fractures and injuries across the skeleton and in the deep layers of flesh. I nearly stumbled when I unconsciously reached out to support myself on the edge of the table, forgetting it was nothing but an image. Stripped of recognisable features the body was almost a twin of my own, shattered then sutured back together again.

The story his corpse told us was one of a probable military or security background, and there was perhaps another hint of such a past. On his left bicep there was a large tattoo, Celtic in style, but the deeper scan had revealed hints of a much older piece beneath that. The details were hard to define though, perhaps the mast of some kind of sailing ship set within a border. It could be a unit badge of some kind - then again it could be almost anything. He had a number of other tattoos, mostly decorative, a mixture of knot-work, tribal and more symbolic designs. These were of various ages, and showed a typical pattern of gradual collection over some years. The freshest one was on the left forearm, a stylised yellow rose and white chrysanthemum, their stems intertwined. None of these meant much to me, though they might help in identifying the victim.

As well as the autopsy itself various other tests had also been run, giving some interesting results. The general condition of his skin and hair showed that he'd not bathed as such for a few days, though he had been using cleansing wipes quite liberally. The contents of his stomach indicated he had recently had a very bland diet of bottled water and pre-packed food, and the state of his clothes increased the sense that he had suffered some recent deprivation, as he'd probably been wearing the same ones for a few days straight going on their appearance and the biologicals present. At some point during that time he had also soiled himself, and despite the mess caused by his fall some older bloodstains were evident on his shirt. There were also traces of light oil stains on the cuffs and inside the rear waistband of the cargo pants, with a corresponding one on his underwear.

This was starting to look more and more like some sort of botched kidnapping, but despite the range of physical evidence recovered so far there was absolutely nothing that gave us any real insight about his attackers. They were likely to be physically capable and technically sophisticated, but on the other hand they'd killed him in a very public and ostentatious manner that was bound to draw police attention. It looked as though their aim might have been to send some form of message, but who exactly that was intended for I couldn't say.

Perhaps things would seem clearer in the morning, but it seemed like the only thing that could bring to light any possible suspects was a look through the criminal intelligence records for known kidnapping gangs. More knowledge of the victim's life and recent activities would help immensely, but that was something we could barely start to investigate until we had his name.

> Reznik

The lock-up was in a quiet backstreet, and there was no one around, though he could hear a couple arguing nearby through their second floor window, wide open in the afternoon heat. He'd waited for a while nearby, but was now approaching the warehouse almost casually, quickly bending down to check a grip-tie he'd left sealing the base of a large roller-shutter. After cutting through it with a knife, he used a key to unlock the heavy padlock beside it. Standing, he used another key to open a smaller side door, before pulling a fresh filter mask over his face and slipping quietly inside.

He stood for a moment to survey the scene. It was a high-roofed industrial building, the interior spacious but gloomy as the bright sun strained to penetrate the narrow strip of grimy windows set high up in the front wall, their thick covering of dust undisturbed by the faint flow of air through the narrow vents nearby. A little more sunlight sliced under the roller-shutter, its metal not quite meeting the floor. After a time his eyes settled on a pair of small aerial drones, tracking them as they sketched a lazy, random dance in the heavy air.

In the centre of the warehouse was a battered old van, white in its prime but now as much primer as paint around the wheel arches and sills. Its windows were as dirty as the garage's, except for a cleaner arc of windshield carved out by the wipers. To the side of him was a smaller room, about the size of an office, a cheap and temporary construction separated off from the open interior by thin ply walls.

Reznik went inside the small room, returned a few minutes later to the main warehouse space, carrying a large torch that he switched on at the threshold. In his other gloved hand was a holdall, bulky and probably heavy. Along with the facemask he now wore a faded blue one-piece overall on top of his clothes and industrial work boots fitted with disposable covers.

After placing the holdall in the driver's compartment of the van he began walking through the garage, shining the torch about methodically, its powerful beam illuminating the open framework of the roof supports and rough, unfinished walls. About a third of the way up, at regular intervals, were a number of black, non-reflective half domes about a hand-span across. He paid particular attention to these, picking out each one with the light and following along the line of plastic-insulated wire that ran between them, a continuous loop around the walls of the garage and back to the side room. Other wires ran from this main loop up to more of the half domes located up in the rafters, and he inspected these as best he could from the floor below.

Once he was finished, he then turned to the van to give the exterior a similar close examination before checking the insides. Apparently satisfied, he took a phone-sized smartpad from a pocket and entered a few commands. Moments later the two small aerial drones flew down and settled at his feet. Picking them up, he put them in the rear of the van and retrieved a large unmarked aerosol, its surface unfinished metal.

Next, he crossed to the front wall of the garage to operate the roller-shutters, watching as they clattered open. After getting into the van he drove outside, stopping as soon as he was clear of the doors. Reznik then returned to the garage interior to close the shutters, spraying the controls liberally from the aerosol, then repeated the process once he was outside and the side door was locked. He tossed the aerosol into the cab as he climbed back into the van, and then drove away at a steady pace.

Up in one of the narrow air vents, high in the wall, a Spydar drone stirred minutely, one of its many legs scratching in the dust. With black-lensed eyes it stared into the garage space, untroubled and unwavering as a tiny red LED on its belly flashed briefly into life, pulsing rapidly, then going abruptly dark.

Five minutes later, or thereabouts, the roller-shutters rattled for a moment, as though caught in a gust of wind. A fine mist of dust puffed out from underneath, unnoticed in the empty street.

> Cara

The gallery was in an old industrial building by the riverside, long since emptied of machinery, the crowds inside echoing around its vast spaces. A TV crew, running a live link for one of the arts channels, stood amongst a small island of calm, forcing everyone to go around them as they moved past. The Norling exhibit was up on the second level, so Cara and Em walked briskly through, almost bushing the wall, before heading straight up the stairs.

Norling had come to the fore some ten years ago and had retained much of his notoriety, though more from his creative methods than the actual message of his art, which was simple enough in its directness. His work was highly sought after, whether the visually arresting canvases or his 'trans-organic sculptures', both featuring a brutal insertion of the machine with the pastoral. Many of the visitors were heading directly toward the sculptures and installations, Emma included. Cara went instead to the hung pieces arranged around the walls.

The first was a large oil-on-canvas, some three feet across, which showed a colourful, slightly cartoonish rural landscape with a jagged mass of machinery, all spike and cog, dropped right into the centre, painted with some skill in a super-real style. It was one of Norling's early pieces, and opinion was still divided as to its quality. Another painting was of a stylised Manhattan island, the tall skyscrapers casting a nether-world reflection of cutting spikes and barbed metal through the scarred mouth of the Hudson. There were similar pieces modelled on other metropoles, cities old, new or not yet built, light and clean curves darkly reflected as endless slum and sacrifice.

In the next collection the gallery featured a more diverse mix of work in different media, much of it more recent, including slim sculptures designed to hang on walls, but she still found herself growing slightly bored. The trans-organic work beckoned, the outreached arms of the core installation drawing her toward it.

Norling attracted controversy and high valuations in equal measure, a synergistic growth in shock and draw. The central piece had no title, just a catalogue number like much of his work. In essence, the installation featured a naked human male cadaver, frozen in mid-motion, running toward or from something across barren, parched earth with yet another mass of jagged metal erupting from its torso. Everything was rendered in faded, washed out colour, but it had to be admitted that the plasticised body had been posed with great skill, the outer flesh peeled away in places to enhance the interplay of muscle and bone, with even the faintest trace of blood and fluid removed. The face in particular was done exquisitely, its expression pained and pleading.

When it was first released Norling declined to comment on how this or any other works were created, but a police investigation revealed that he had purchased a live medical clone, perfectly mindless and designed for surgical practice and organ-farming, and shot a mass of rusted scrap metal through it before flash-preserving the body. Technically no harm but still somewhat foul, it made no sense to her that the sculptures eyes seemed to show so much emotion. It was one of those things you had to see for yourself to judge properly, and now that Cara had she didn't like it. Her feet may have been a little unsteady from the wine, but she was sure she was seeing straight enough. Whatever point Norling was really trying to make there were probably better ways of doing it.

Emma had also had enough it appeared, as she was off to one side chatting animatedly with a man Cara didn't recognise, tall and tanned, long dark hair brushing the shoulders of an excellent suit. She caught Em's eye, who seemed non-plussed for a moment but then smiled when Cara grinned and winked at her. Em mouthed 'call you later', as her new acquaintance turned briefly toward Cara and then back again. Handsome, and probably loaded.

Cara left soon after, calling another pod for the trip back. She switched the media player off and rode home in comfortable silence, the interior a bright bubble of light in the dark.

Frost was beginning to get a little tired of this pattern. She lay on her belly on the ground again, Tsukino about 30 feet behind her and equally still. She'd risked using the IyZon, which was hovering above the next ridge giving them visuals.

In theory Jakobsen had tagged them as friendlies on the network, but they would cause less of a disturbance if they moved cautiously and avoided attention. The security grid here would be monitored at some level by smarter minds, so the less he intervened the better. Besides, he'd have his hands full keeping an eye on their own support drones, which would be moving into place now.

They were holding position again as a security robot passed by, a medium sized hexapod unit, surplus materiel from the last war. Even over the uneven ground it held its main weapon on an almost flat trajectory as its turret tracked back and forth, and she knew it could match this performance even if it moved at greater speed. Its legs and segmented body rose and fell in irregular, alien rhythm as it crossed the rough terrain like a stalking spider.

- Eight -

> Chase

The email came in while I had the car drive me to work, a simple message from Harris with a couple of video clips attached. He said he didn't know how useful they'd be, but it was all he'd been able to get. I set the multipurpose display in the car's dash to its maximum size and pressed play.

The clips were poor quality corner-of-the eye images, fuzzy and indistinct. These were recordings stored by the Acrobots in the mall, just brief moments captured in their peripheral vision. I watched both files in quick succession, at first a little underwhelmed until I convinced the car's playback to run them at a slower speed. The sequence of useful images was broken and uneven as the 'droids themselves were in motion, but once the intervening sections were ignored they showed the victim out in the air space up above the Acrobots display, already in free fall. In the background some fleeting shots of the maintenance balcony showed something else: there was a figure there, glancing briefly over the edge, dressed in an oversized hooded top of some kind, leaving their outline blurred and their face entirely in shadow.

I sat back in the seat, surprised and elated, then leant forward again to watch the clip a second and third time. The other file Harris had sent was similar, though from slightly different angles. There was nothing in either that could give us a clear description of the second figure, but we still might be able to learn something once the clips were properly analysed.

I'd intended to call Harris at some point anyway so I dialled from the car, thanking him for the email once we'd exchanged brief pleasantries. He'd looked at most of the robots that were in the display that morning, and only found two with anything new. The others did have footage of the victim falling, however, and they would improve the accuracy of the digital reconstruction of the crime scene when he sent them over later.

Whilst I didn't want to seem ungrateful, we were still waiting for details of the on-duty staff and lift traffic for that day. It occurred to me that it would be best if he just gave us everything they had on file for the previous 48 hours, however tenuously it might link to the case.

"Are you sure that's necessary? I would have thought with everything we've already provided or agreed to you'd have enough." He was clearly reluctant, obviously anticipating the level of effort it would require and the reaction of his superiors.

"I need information, Mr. Harris, the more the better. I don't know what details might be hiding amongst the files you have there, or how important they might be, but I need it all."

After a brief moment of hesitation he replied, "I'm sorry, I didn't include the extra files because I just assumed that you'd have what you needed."

"I get it. But it would be really help if you'd just send me a copy of all your records from the mall for that day, and the day before just to be on the safe side. They may well have used private areas to move through the building so those locations are at least as important as the public ones."

“Ok, I can do that, but it will take me a while. The mall’s a big building and a lot of routine information is collected and logged. Most of it’s to do with micromanagement of the power and environmental systems to run everything at the optimum levels.” He paused a moment. “I suppose then as there was someone up there with him it looks less like a suicide?”

“We’re treating the death as suspicious at this time. I really can’t tell you any more than that.”

“I see, fair enough. Well, I’ll try to get you all the information as soon as I can then. I’ll have to check with my manager, but I’m sure there’ll be no problem under the circumstances.”

“I hope not. The sooner we have everything the sooner we can move forwards.”

It was my first proper return to the office, and it went better than it might have. I didn’t get away with it completely of course. After arriving at about nine, casually, as though everything were routine, I found my usual desk seemed to have been left unused in my absence. That was the story the rest of the criminal investigations team were keen to emphasise anyway, with piles of paper folders left stacked all over, a few plastic spiders and a whole can of fake cobwebs sprayed on it to complete the scene.

The fact was it was good to see some of them again, and the ‘welcome backs’ seemed genuine enough. There were a couple of new faces as well, obviously curious about the whole thing. I was a bit disappointed to see that Mallory wasn’t around, though she had left a note stuck to my monitor, ‘About Time!’, and one of her roodles. Took me a while to find it under all the fakery, but it gave me a smile when I finally did. She was the closest thing to a direct peer I guess, and an occasional partner, so it would be good to see her again.

While I waited for further info on the victim there was a short list of items to follow up on, but the first priority was checking the databases for any intelligence on previous kidnapping cases or missing persons. The basic checks had already been done but there was every reason to have a look myself. I didn’t find any likely candidates though, and the files on recent kidnappings weren’t too helpful either. After peaking about ten years ago, the numbers of recent cases had dropped sharply when the police Serious Crimes Division made their investigation a higher priority.

Looking into the public records for the mall was another necessary step. Much of the raw research was complete so I was fortunate to be able to read from the case notes. The building was owned by a number of private investors, the majority share belonging to an offshore holding company based in South America, which in itself had a number of private and corporate backers. It was hard to dig much further given the confidentiality and legal agreements that were in place, and probably not worth it given that everything looked innocuous enough so far.

The mall also had an excellent safety record with no significant accidents or code violations in its brief history. Police reports listed a few minor public order incidents over the last couple of years, but that was nothing unusual for this kind of place. The most recent occasions were a fracas caused by a mentally disturbed homeless man who did not like being moved off the premises at closing time, and a burglary from an electronics store that had a few high-end computers stolen. Nothing that really gave me any concerns or informed my investigation.

I actually enjoyed being back in the office, surprisingly. The team had obviously made a priority of the case and it felt good to have their support. Shame it didn't feel as though I had the same from Iyer. We'd never really gelled, and despite giving it plenty of thought I couldn't really pin down why. Maybe it was just a personality clash, one of those fundamental differences that you get every now and then. It seemed as though my long absence had only increased her antipathy, but I didn't think there was anything she could do about it as long as things went smoothly with the case. Give her a reason, though, and she could certainly make things more difficult.

> Reznik

He was lounged against an interior wall of the high-rise, not far from the outer edge, taking in the superb view to his left and the strong wind that gusted by. Lagorio's penthouse suite was in the centre of his vision, some 120 yards away and five storeys up.

This level, along with its neighbours, was undergoing a major refurbishment. Everything had been stripped back to its bare frame, with thick plastic sheeting stretched across the exterior edge to substitute for absent glass while the permanent structures of hard interior walls and support struts were the only interruptions to the otherwise empty space. Builder bots trundled and flew to and fro, their hazard-marked shells dusty and battered.

Apart from a cursory inspection every few days and some supply drops there were no humans on site. Mostly things were automated, with some of the more complex work being handled by teleoperation from another location. Jakobsen had supplied a number of modified construction drones, which had integrated seamlessly with those that belonged here, piggybacking with the local control network to add their efforts to the building work. Even though he had delivered them himself Reznik was barely able to distinguish them from the rest of the robots.

It was all by careful design. Reznik had installed cameras and a net monitor some weeks ago, and Jakobsen had then used the intel this provided to source and customise their own drones to blend in with the rest. This was the first time Reznik had returned here since that visit, bringing their own builder bots up in the service elevator, still boxed from the warehouse. After unpacking and initialising them he'd sat back to watch while they activated in sequence and joined their brethren, everything controlled by the black box Jakobsen supplied. Their first task had been to install a few pieces of additional gear in preparation for the main job, removing and recycling the equipment he'd brought on his first visit.

Satisfied, Reznik rose smoothly to his feet and gathered up any remaining pieces of unused equipment to take with him. The packaging from the drones he'd brought would go straight into the building's recycling centre on his way out.

Traffic was heavy so the drive away from the building took longer than he'd have liked, though the sheer volume made his journey all the more unremarkable. Sheer volume was a good description: there were plenty of older cars still running on cheap biofuels, their rumble drowning the whisper of any electric drives, with horns, shouts and bass beats adding their own random syncopation to the low pedal tone. It was hot in the van, and grimy, and the overalls and heavy boots he still wore added to his discomfort. Up above, he could see traffic cams on gantries and a couple of mini-drones in the distance, so he left the side windows closed.

Finally, he made it to the next exit and headed off the freeway toward the airport, picking up a little speed. There was a large multi-story car park there, where he could leave the van unattended for a few days. As he drove along his phone handset chirped, a simple two-note pattern. Only the edges of his mouth and eyes gave the briefest of betrayals to his reaction, two taps of his index finger on the steering wheel echoing the rhythm of the phone signal. Reznik continued on his route, a little faster now, lane changes sharper.

High above one of the mini-drones followed, unseen.

> Cara

She hesitated, keys in hand, her foot already on the doorstep, Emma a couple of feet behind. The memory of an evening just over a month ago flashed into focus, and Cara paused for a moment as it washed over her. Ethan had stood by her side while she tried the key he'd just given her in that same door, and she had looked toward him and seen a perfect reflection of her own warm smile. Though she'd visited a few times since it had never been while he was out, and standing here now, at the threshold, if felt a little wrong. Emma, though, had insisted they come after Cara had first mentioned it, saying she needed her palmtop, that Ethan should have returned it by now.

Shaking her head Cara pressed on, working the lock and pushing the door open as quickly as she could, stepping in and over a small pile of mail, then closing it firmly as Emma moved past her into the lounge. The flat's *aigent* greeted her by name, just a disembodied voice rather than a hologram or visual display, exactly as she preferred at her own address. Whatever it looked like, or didn't, she knew that if Ethan checked later that the AI would keep a record of their visit. She could probably alter its log but didn't really fancy going through the hassle. May as well use it.

"House, when was Ethan last here?"

"Friday morning of last week, Miss Dalca." It was Friday again, so that was a full week ago. She had last seen him the evening before, on the Thursday, when they'd had dinner. The flat certainly had that particular emptiness of being uninhabited for a few days, a certain cool stillness, that was more than just the *aigent* keeping the ambient settings low. She turned around and picked up the post from the mat, just as Emma called through from the other room: she'd found her palmtop. Cara quickly tidied the mail, flicking through the envelopes. There was nothing obviously useful, so she set it down on the worktop.

Cara moved into the lounge where a modest desk sat in the corner. She had rarely seen Ethan using it, though he most likely did given the size of the desktop PC that was crammed underneath it. There were some open letters piled neatly on the edge of the desk and she scanned through them, quickly, with some level of guilt, as though he might walk into the room right then and catch her. Emma was stood by the window, absently looking outside.

As she was there, Cara thought she may as well have a quick look round. The lounge didn't reveal much. It wasn't that Ethan was especially tidy, more that he resented clutter. The room was mostly about the oversized, comfy settee and television sectioning off the back corner of the room: there was little space for anything else, and he certainly had no taste for ornaments or knick-knacks. Dust traps, he said.

Cara next moved onto the more private rooms. In the bathroom she could see no obvious gaps amongst the various things he had arranged in the shower cubicle or by the sink. From the look of the bedroom it didn't seem like he'd packed much either. As far as she could tell the few cases he kept on top of the wardrobe were all there but she couldn't be sure. It wasn't as though she had paid any special attention to that kind of thing on previous visits.

Emma popped her head around the door then, glanced around for a moment and suggested they get moving, maybe grab a bottle somewhere? That sounded fine to Cara: the flat felt unpleasant in its emptiness, and they'd found the thing they'd come for.

On their way back through the kitchen Cara paused and asked the house AI if there'd been any contact from Ethan since he was here last? No, there had not.

"Did Ethan say when he would return?"

"He did not, Miss Dalca, though he had no luggage with him and had not made any travel arrangements to my knowledge." Many people would use their *aigent* to make those kind of plans, though not everyone did.

"What about the police, did you notify them?" The question was out before she'd thought it through.

"I did not, Miss Dalca. Mr. Grant changed a number of standard response parameters when I was installed, so he has not been absent for a sufficient length of time. Nor have I have received any suspicious or unusual messages." There was a pause, before it continued, "Are you concerned Miss Dalca? Do you believe I should contact the police?"

For a moment her mind was empty, blank and unresponsive, but Emma was shaking her head, impatient, and so she replied in the negative. He was probably just away on that contract, and had forgotten to let anyone know. Ethan often installed security grids and robotic systems for wealthy clients, so confidentiality tended to be at a premium. This wasn't the first time he'd been out of touch when he was working away. It was a little odd that he didn't seem to have taken much luggage, but she imagined he would tend to travel light.

Cara told the house *aigent* to get in touch if it heard from Ethan, to let him know she'd been around, and then left, closing and locking the door firmly. She trusted Ethan as much as she trusted anyone, but there was something to this she didn't like. For a moment she wondered if there might be someone else, but she didn't think so. Cara liked to believe she was smart enough to spot some sign of infidelity, even though she knew everyone probably believed that. Surely, though, he'd have made every effort to give her a good cover story and keep in touch enough to allay any suspicions if he was cheating on her?

Perhaps she was overreacting – this was not the first time Ethan had been out of touch for a few days – and realised finally that Nada's call had unsettled her more than she'd first realised.

The Wolf had signalled for a stop, so Frost held station in a low depression in the ground, Tsu not far away. The terrain here was rough, though not nearly as much as the country they had moved through on their way up to the boundary. There were no trees or bushes, just coarse grass, straw-like but damp from the previous day's rain.

The main complex was straight ahead of them, and they were close enough to see the human complement of guards stationed around it through their optics, along with numerous robotic and surveillance systems covering the inner perimeter. So far everything looked ok, though they'd not expected this much security.

Another signal pinged in on the comms. The Wolf had attached a relay box onto a different part of the network so that Jakobsen could exploit and compromise more systems. The Wolf had tagged a clear path ahead for them in the HUD and she followed it, moving up to the next piece of relative shelter, ready to provide fire support.

- Nine -

> Chase

Cadejo had been busy while I'd slept. Raissa called to brief me, this time using a full video link, her disembodied voice running over a silent montage of recent news reports. "Morning, Chase, that's twice in one week now. It's good to have you back." Her voice was as exquisite and curious as ever, excellent English with an accent you could never quite place, but always warm and cheery.

"Thanks, it's good to be back. What have you got for me?"

"Plenty. First though, you should know that media interest in the case has increased. It's a key story in the regular bulletins on most of the prime channels, and it's getting even more attention elsewhere. There's been some new footage uploaded to YuTu, but it's nothing that helps us much."

Raissa continued, "The best news is we have an ID for the victim! I think you're going to like this, Chase."

As she talked the promise of new information was inspiring, but her last comments also made me a little suspicious. From experience I knew that when Raissa's interest was piqued in that way it tended to mean things were about to get complicated. Still, I had to ask, "Sounds intriguing. And a little bit like trouble."

"Maybe, maybe not. The victim has been identified as Karl Jakobsen, but he's only showing up in some of our, shall we say 'non-standard', databases. There's nothing much under that name in the official records. I'll send you all the new data. Let me know if you need anything."

"Thanks, Raissa, I'll look at the new info and let you know."

"Awesome! Thanks Chase, catch you later."

You could criticise her for being a little flippant and disrespectful for discussing a murder investigation with such a light tone, but that would miss the truth of my own reaction. I was fully alive and aware, keen to dive in again. She'd read me perfectly.

Once they'd completed the facial reconstruction as best they could, and received the relevant permissions, the support techs at Cadejo had sent the images, along with the fingerprints and DNA profile, through a range of governmental, law enforcement and military channels, official and otherwise. They did get an ID for the victim, and within a relatively short time. The trouble was the results were confusing.

One of the more esoteric lines of enquiry we'd followed listed our victim as Karl Jakobsen, a naturalised Norwegian who'd served in his country's regular and Special Forces for a spell before switching to the corporate sector. His expertise was in small unit operations, robotic systems and electronic warfare. The surprise was that Jakobsen shouldn't have been here at all: he'd been listed as 'Killed In Action' two years ago.

His last known employer, a small PMC I'd never heard of named Onkalegann, had reported his death, though a body or other remains had apparently never been recovered. I could see why. After that, the only records of Jakobsen we could discover were official enquiries made by the Norwegians and various legal judgements regarding his estate, which was pretty modest. His family had obviously believed the worst as they'd held a funeral service some time ago, a small affair apparently for a handful of relatives and old friends. We were still confident about our identification though, as the various physical characteristics all matched the profile we'd received.

Tracing the victim's history further through his Jakobsen identity would be challenging, but necessary. I would ask Raissa about assigning some local resources to look into the Norwegian end of things, but I had a definite feeling that this wouldn't be one of those nice easy cases where Cain killed Abel in an argument over who got custody of the family tractor. More than likely this would all tie back to his professional life, which was looking particularly murky at this point. I'd conducted investigations in the past where false identities had been involved, usually for criminal purposes, but this appeared to be something else.

In addition to discovering the victim's ID the techs at Cadejo had also analysed the footage Harris had downloaded from the Acrobots in the mall. Despite the poor quality of the images, they'd been able to provide a very basic description of the hooded figure up on the maintenance balcony: 5' 8", with a slight frame. Going from that we couldn't be sure of their gender and we still had no idea if they were just a witness or directly involved. The additional data had also helped refine the crime scene model, and we knew now that from the trajectory and angle of his fall that Jakobsen had more than likely been thrown bodily from the balcony.

Hopefully there was more evidence still to come. We'd not heard back from any of the government databases and there was still a good chance those enquiries would give us something. It was likely that Jakobsen had been operating under an assumed name, and if we could discover which it might tell us why someone had wanted to kill a man who everyone thought was already dead.

> Reznik

The phone handset was in pieces by the wall where it had fallen, the empty-line tone still sounding in mockery. There was a slight mark on the paintwork from the impact, a dark smudge and shallow dent. He walked over and stamped on the case a couple of times until the signal finally died.

As soon as he heard its chime on the way to the airport he knew it was bad news. The message itself was a simple notification of a new email, sent to a number that was only on this particular handset and entirely separate from the rest of his comms, so he had waited until safely back in the apartment before accessing it. Jakobsen was in trouble, was the long and short of it. The email was a pre-written alert notice, time-delayed to be sent from a secure web address only if he had not activated a regular stalling message: a Dead Man's Switch, in other words.

He couldn't be sure Jakobsen actually was dead of course. He may have been in an accident and be too messed up to keep on top of things, or he might be unable to use his email safely. Protocol demanded he plan for the worst, however, as there was a possibility Jakobsen had been compromised. There was little chance this was a simple error or lapse in memory.

Reznik got up suddenly and headed to the kitchen, pulling another ration pack at random from the cardboard box and tearing aggressively into the outer packaging, spilling the contents out over the worktop. With one hand he stirred the individual sachets around like a shell artist, before scooping up a couple at random, popping the chemtabs on his way back to the lounge.

As he ate his mystery meal he stared without focus toward the window, his thoughts slowly expanding in all directions, twisting and knotting as they crossed. Jakobsen was key to the operation as originally conceived, so his absence gave Reznik major problems. In truth, he himself would have been more of an observer at the final stage if things went to plan, a contingency in case of a last minute hitch. The culmination of the mission would have been in Jakobsen's hands, and his excellent drone piloting skills. Finding someone to replace him would be difficult at this late stage and reaching Polzin by a different method would present too many fresh challenges.

Unfortunately, Reznik's concerns went deeper than that. Jakobsen was familiar with almost every detail of the operation as it was currently planned, and if one of the more sinister possible explanations for his absence were the real cause, such as his abduction or arrest, then they were screwed. The entire mission as it stood could be compromised.

There was his own skin to think about as well: he could be under imminent threat, and that danger may just possibly extend to his sponsor. He had maintained strict information discipline throughout and told Jakobsen nothing about where the money and occasional assistance came from, suggesting that this was an entirely private affair, but in reality he was simply on an unusually long leash. If Jakobsen had been intentionally targeted then their extensive precautions may have failed.

Only at the end did he consider what he could possibly do for his comrade, in the event that he was alive and in need of help or assistance. Professionally speaking his best option was to make discrete enquiries, in part to try to ascertain the scale of any security breach. Personally, he was more focussed on the mission than the man. He knew that was cold, and a betrayal of the revenge motif he had traded on to draw Jakobsen into this, but he also knew himself and that this was his true reaction. Back when he'd been obliged to play along with mandatory counselling and evaluation he'd come to understand himself rather well, and was realistic regarding the labels that would be attached to his behaviours. None of that concerned him. He'd lost the better part of himself, his morality and finer feelings, back in the Zone long ago.

> Cara

The café was busy but Emma had been quiet, at first, though she was distracted by her palmtop, which she wanted to check was working. Ethan had obviously managed to fix it, and by the time of their first refill things were lightening up again. Cara tried to draw Em on the man she'd been talking to at the Norling exhibition, but Em was having none of it.

They only had the one bottle, and Cara ran a couple of errands on the way home, a quick bit of grocery shopping, which she promptly regretted, wishing she'd just let her *aigent* automate the order as usual. After that she'd dropped into see Dad again, just a quick visit to say hello, which had hardly lifted her mood though it had at least given her a bit of perspective.

On reflection, she didn't feel quite so bad for dropping by Ethan's flat. Really, she ought to be annoyed with him for his lack of consideration, rather than worried he would be upset with her. Cara posted a message to his social media accounts to see if that would help, just a 'Hi, give me a call', but she knew he used them sparingly at the best of times, and didn't really expect much to come of it.

Before settling down for bed Cara reached out to her friends from the old days to see if anyone knew what Nada was into now. Like Cara, he wasn't known to have done much hacking of late, but he was still a member of that community, providing a range of interesting items on the quiet, depending on the buyer and their available cash. Never anything dangerous or truly naughty though, nor in large quantities.

Cara started the next morning with a determination to put all the distractions to one side and concentrate on business. Mostly she enjoyed her work, and certainly appreciated the relative variety of freelancing. When the doorbell rang it was a nuisance, an unwelcome distraction. Another ring and then her *aigent* spoke to inform her of a courier delivery. She would have to sign for it, whatever it was.

As she opened the door the daylight made her blink a little, the sun having brightened since she last took note. Cara traced a scrawled signature on the greasy screen of the courier's handset to sign for the package and accepted it as it was passed over. He wasn't from one of the bigger firms, his badge and company logo indicating a local service she'd barely heard of.

The parcel was a brown cardboard box, unmarked, about the right size for a large book. Cara was surprised at what was inside: a hardback copy of Hollis's biography of Boyle, a book she already had - one of only a small number of print books in fact - which resided on a low shelf by her favourite chair. A smile broke through before turning quickly wistful. Ethan was also a fan and she remembered they talked animatedly about it on their first date.

A strange thing to receive in the post, especially as there was no sign of who'd sent it. Only a handful of people knew of her interest and they would guess she might have the book already. A mystery for another day, as someone would surely mention it, perhaps to ask if she'd received it. Leaving the book on top of its packaging on the table Cara went straight back to work.

Someone had really screwed them over with the intel, because the defences here were much tighter than expected. They'd marked a number of targets that would be taken out quickly by the support drones they'd brought, but the odds would still be a long way from even if things did go hot.

Frost and Tsu held position, a few yards apart. The main complex was close enough now that even human eyes could see them if they were careless, so every movement had to be slow and considered. Dawn was far enough off that they still had the dark, and the expected storm would not break for some time yet.

Their sense of brittle calm ran right up to the last moments, until a small drone thudded down next to Frost, its shell splintering with the impact. A hole bored all the way through its body gave off trails of smoke and sparks. For a heartbeat she stared at it until her surprise found voice. Rolling away and back, she bellowed into the comm. "We are compromised! We have a drone down! Repeat, drone down!"

Seconds later the flashes and explosions of gunfire shattered the night like lightning.

- Ten -

> Chase

Harris called just as I was thinking about finishing for the day. After receiving the victim's ID in the morning, things had settled down to a steady grind as lines of enquiry for the last two years of Jakobsen's life were followed. Nothing had come of it so far.

His apparent fate as a KIA had been final enough until he died for real four days ago.

"Detective Chase? It's John Harris from the mall. I've been working on that data you asked for. I think I've found something, I'm not sure. Could you come over? It would be easier to talk face to face." He sounded both confused and a little alarmed.

"Ok, sure, I can finish up here. Have you found something in the security footage?"

"Err, no, it's not that. There's too much data!"

"Sorry...What do you mean?"

"I'm not sure but the system seems to have too much activity. Look, it'd be easier to show you. I've just found it and I don't know what it means yet."

"I'll be over as soon as I can. There's a game on this afternoon and I'm the other side of town so it might take me a while to get to you."

"Ok, fine. I'll stay and carry on working until you get here." That sounded promising. Quite what the significance of the additional system traffic was I couldn't say, and Harris didn't seem too sure yet either.

It turned out he'd have plenty of time to work on it. Congestion was murder south of the river and there was a problem with the traffic management system, which was trying to route things through the Civil Safety Zone. The roads there had been closed for years, so it was either a serious glitch or some protest group or other had hacked into the system. In the end I just got sick of it, parked the car up in an Armabay, and took the underground. Unfortunately, that wasn't running to schedule either.

When I finally arrived at the mall it was quite late and much less busy than on my previous visit. Everything appeared normal again in the atrium and there were no signs left of the disturbance from earlier in the week. Harris had left a pass for me at reception, but I had another delay there. A young couple were ahead of me, complaining loudly about something, and the whole thing was getting quite heated before I cut across them, waving my ID to get the receptionist's attention. Once I had the pass, I retraced my steps from the other day, taking a service elevator to the basement levels.

Things were just as quiet down there as before, a world away from the bustle of people just a few yards above. It wasn't until I reached the intersection where I'd first met Harris that I encountered any problems. I'd assumed he would be there waiting for me, so I was surprised to see one of the mall's small security drones hovering in place at the junction, rotors quietly buzzing and tiny air navigation lights flashing. The robot was equipped with speakers and it relayed a short message from Harris as soon as I approached, asking me to follow it to where he was working. I replied that I would and trailed after the drone as if flew off. Harris had evidently not remained in direct control as it would rush off along each corridor and then return and loiter while I caught up.

I played along with the whole 'follow my leader' thing until we reached what was presumably our destination, deep in the basement of the building on a lower level than I'd previously visited. The atmosphere here was entirely utilitarian, everything plain and sparsely lit.

On the left-hand side of the corridor we had arrived at was a doorway. The warning signs outside were the first splash of colour other than the drone's lights I'd noticed for a few minutes now, and I took a moment to study them. This was some kind of server room from the legend, and access was forbidden to unauthorised personnel. I took the fact that the door was propped open by a large fire extinguisher as an invitation.

I called out to Harris as I crossed the threshold, assuming he would be inside. No reply. Racks of servers and other equipment partitioned the room into corridors and corners. The overheads were off, so it was dark, save for the flickering status lights on the server panels and another more constant glow in the far corner. Fans set in the walls whirred away, joining the servers in a muted chorus of hums. The faint tap of a keyboard provided rhythm in counterpoint, momentary breaks like a breath mark. I pressed on, treading lightly.

Rounding the next corner, I called out to Harris again. There was someone else there, a man wearing a dark suit. He was sitting at a narrow workstation, typing quickly on a keyboard. Some of the monitors in front of him showed system analytics and progress bars while others were full of static. It wasn't Harris, but I could see a body laid on the floor nearby, which might have been him.

I moved forward, drawing the stun gun, and called for the stranger to stop and turn around. He paused for a moment, his fingers now still on the keyboard, and I began to step sideways, trying to improve my line of sight, glancing across toward the prone man for a moment as I moved around.

Suddenly everything changed, my body stiffening in unbelievable tension as a fist-sized patch of muscle in my back went into spasm. I was frozen there, almost suspended in time, wracked with pain. And then just as abruptly the agony ended and I stumbled, losing my balance and falling uncontrollably toward one of the server racks, cracking my head hard as I went to the ground, black emptiness rising.

> Reznik

He'd spent the last couple of hours checking and extending his surveillance net. There was an increased risk that someone could discover one of the various devices now that he'd installed more of them, but he'd expanded the range of his intelligence gathering capability enough that the trade-off was worth it. Instead of just monitoring his own building he now had a much wider reach, covering the approach to the property and the surrounding streets.

All of this had come after he'd called Murdoch. Once he'd calmed down and got his head around the Jakobsen situation there'd been no real sense in delaying any longer than it took to rehearse the conversation he was about to have. Reznik went into the bathroom, covered the tiny window with towels, and activated a small white noise generator before dialling a number straight from memory.

The phone rang three times before an unfamiliar male answered. "This is an unexpected pleasure. We'll need to call you back in a short while, he's just in the middle of something." The phone then cut off.

Well, that might be for the best. Gave the man chance to control whatever negativity his call might provoke. Reznik knew that he particularly disliked these kind of surprises but it couldn't be helped. The whole mission may have been compromised and it would be poor protocol not to inform his sponsor.

A few minutes later the phone rang: "I can see why you called. Bad news from over the water." Murdoch's voice now, gruff and cultured.

"Yeah. I received a message from an old friend. Wasn't sure how to progress from here."

"Just a moment..... Ok, the line checks out. Here's what we know. Your friend has been very unlucky. Died in an accident it looks like."

"How?"

"We don't have all the details yet. The case has been handed over to some corporate security outfit, but they're just making routine enquiries. There were no suspicious circumstances, and they only have his current cover details at present. They'll probably stop digging before too long."

"Let's hope so."

"Agreed. Even if they do put out a trace through other channels and come back with something, they'll only get tied in knots for a while. Listen, I might have another job lined up for you, so best get this business finished. If you need to find some replacement talent locally you should be able to trust the previous contact. He's been useful to us in the past."

"Ok, understood. So, to be clear, there's nothing to be too concerned about? He caught one, but there's no sign of a problem otherwise?"

"No, no problem, just bad luck. An accident, no sign of foul play. The police there have zero awareness of our friend so there won't be any issues."

"Ok, thanks. Sorry to trouble you."

"Not at all. I understand your concerns, no need to apologise."

Murdoch hung up and Reznik switched off the white noise. It was a useful toy, but it tended to fratz out his internal audio a little, making the other caller sound compressed and unnatural. Made it harder to pick up some of the inflections as well. Without it running there would be no chance of a direct conversation though, so it was just something he had to accept. Protocol.

Reznik was relieved, and a little sorry to hear of Jakobsen's death. That it was some random dumb luck rather than a killing made him feel far more secure. There were still problems to sort out, and it sounded as though he should move quickly, but it seemed like a few extra security precautions were all that were necessary, just to be on the safe side.

Once the grid was extended, he busied himself with preparing an emergency exit from the apartment, before quickly going through his personal belongings to identify anything he didn't need and could safely leave behind. The rest of his stuff he stashed in a smaller backpack that he could quickly grab in a hurry, along with some energy bars and hydration pouches. Other critical stuff would be kept on his person. He'd generally left his handgun in the apartment on most of his previous excursions, hidden in a shielded air-and-watertight pouch keyed to his own biometrics. The gun itself was an older model and much less high tech than its case. The only other incriminating thing he usually carried was a short knife and a few small strips of pills, designed to look like over-the-counter meds. You would have to suspect these were something more to give them any attention.

It was a shame about Jakobsen. Losing him so late in the game was unfortunate, but at least there was nothing to worry about.

> Cara

She knew better but she really couldn't help herself. It was obvious to her that Dad wasn't responding well to the most recent change of treatment advocated by his doctors, but they weren't there to speak to. The nurses were, and she gave them a piece of her angst and worry, sharp manner and short words. Almost as soon as she'd spoken Cara regretted it, but apologies would take a strength she lacked at this hour. It was almost the end of visiting, when the hospital would return to its private practices, a rhythm and routine for the care of its more permanent guests.

Cara understood perfectly their wish to discharge her father and have him cared for at home, or at least in a hospice, where he would be someone else's problem and expense. It made fiscal sense no doubt, but it was a line she didn't want to cross, a final admission that Dad was near to his end and could not be helped. Scaling back the active intervention, as they'd put it, would only hasten that moment.

To be fair, they'd tried every treatment available to them, as had she, and there were no other medical programmes she could get her father on. She had even, with great self-consciousness, tried prayer, but the only tangible results Cara could detect from that was an influx of old memories, especially of Mum, though she supposed that was how it usually worked. There had certainly been no miracle cure.

Exchanging goodbyes for the day Cara kissed her father's cold cheek and then headed for the café area. There was no food service as such this late, but the vending machines were always on. She hardly saw anyone else once she left the ward, and the café's only other occupant was a robot cleaner. They often met in the quieter hours, their routines almost as ingrained.

Her brief, soulless meal over she headed for the exit and the car park. The quickest route took her past the A&E department. It wasn't so busy yet but she knew there would be an influx of injuries and human errors – it was a Saturday night after all.

There was a sudden crescendo of light and sound as a crash team rushed in some casualty. She couldn't see much of him; a head restraint obscured his face, though she was sure there had also been a fair amount of medifoam involved. The rest of him looked ok, even if a suit was overdressing for the situation. Whoever he was, a couple of police officers followed in their wake, so he was probably either a criminal or another cop. She couldn't tell which.

> Schuler

He had to admit to being pleased so far. The detective had been dealt with for now and the mall's security manager was no trouble. They'd both looked perfectly peaceful laid on the floor, though he'd had to shift Harris when he recognised the opportunity that the situation afforded him. It was simply too good to resist, just a simple rearrangement of the bodies and the trail was nicely muddied. There was every chance, looking at the cut on his head, that the detective would suffer at least a touch of concussion, which could only help matters.

There were a couple of outstanding jobs to do to finish things off here but he was confident that it would be hours before the police got around to searching the basement properly, which should allow him plenty of time. The main task was already complete, so the rest was just a little insurance.

He almost felt sorry for them both. Harris was simply unlucky, in the wrong place at the wrong time. It was interesting that he had identified an issue with the computer records, but now that the system had been crashed it was not an insight anyone else was likely to repeat in a hurry. Most of his sympathy he reserved for the detective, something of a kindred spirit perhaps, though he supposed that might be a little perverse considering. At least he'd left him alive.

Jakobsen had felt some of his tension gradually fade away as the weapons platforms moved into place, stealthily completing the final stages of their pre-programmed routes. The news from Frost was solid as well, everything green, everyone in position. He had even begun to relax a little, his own work mostly done.

A sudden starburst of colour flashed through the inside of the bunker, startling him and shattering his complacency as his screen lit up with alarms and action reports. Jakobsen scrambled to answer the warnings, frantically trying to override the defence grid and shut everything down, but a firewall had dropped into place with all the finality of a guillotine, severing his access to the complex's intranet.

In the near distance angry guns grumbled and spat.

- Eleven -

> Chase

I was confused, sleep dragging me down as I awoke in saw-tooth steps, smells and sounds drifting into sharper focus as I became more fully aware. I realised I was in a hospital or clinic, somewhere strange and yet familiar, and for a few brief, distressing moments the last few months were nothing and I was back in a wrecked and ruined body again.

There was no one there when I opened my eyes fully. I half expected to see Jo waiting beside the bed as she'd done so many times before. Things were still fuzzy, but once I'd realised the throbbing I felt in my head was a real thing, not part of a dream, I knew I was most of the way there. I checked my limbs, moved my head and face, everything feeling remote, unconnected. My mouth was parched, teeth feeling sharp and strange as I ran my tongue around. I couldn't yet remember what had happened or what had brought me here, but apart from a monster headache and feeling generally rough everything seemed physically intact, a lot better than the last time I woke up in hospital unexpectedly.

The visuals and acoustics in the room were set to simulate a warm summer's day, but the illusion of tranquillity they were projecting wasn't really working. A nurse came in after a while, a young woman, who smiled and asked me how I was feeling. I tried to reply, but my mouth wouldn't work. She smiled again and crossed around to pour some water into a plastic cup and hand it over. I took a couple of good gulps then a shallower sip, working some of the liquid round. It felt wonderful, splashing back the dryness, cold and clear as it plunged down my throat. The nurse left, saying a doctor would be by to visit. After another half hour a doctor did indeed arrive, a uniformed policeman following her into the room. I nodded at both and tried a smile, which only the doctor returned.

I had suffered a head injury last night. The scans they'd taken showed that whilst there wasn't any major trauma I'd had a hefty concussion, for which they'd given immediate treatment. I should be ok to go home soon, depending on some more tests, though as she said this there was a look toward the police officer, who was otherwise almost invisible for all the disturbance he'd made.

What could I remember? Not very much, I said, explaining that I had no recollection of how I'd been injured, or anything before that. She gave me another professional smile and said that was entirely normal, and that everything should come back to me in time. They left then and I was returned to the solitude of the room, confused by a brief look the doctor shared with the officer. The room's atmospherics still gave off the warmth of summer, but I felt a colder air breeze by.

I must have slept a little, or at least dozed off, until I was pulled back from wherever my thoughts had drifted off to by the sound of visitors. As I turned to look at them, I glanced at the clock: it was almost seven.

There were four people in the room with me now, which seemed a much smaller space with their intrusion. I was not entirely surprised to see Iyer there, but she had another two detectives with her. The older man was Robbins I thought, while his companion was a much younger woman I didn't recognise. My fourth visitor was a male nurse, who didn't seem entirely comfortable with being there, hovering around the side of the bed and keeping from out of their line of sight. All of them had severe expressions on their faces, but there was also a trace of some concern there for a moment or two.

"Detective Chase. I'm DI Roberts - we have met – and this is DS Williams. We've a few questions for you if you don't mind." They both produced their IDs as he spoke. This wouldn't be an entirely informal chat then.

"I'd be happy to help, though if it's about yesterday I'm afraid I don't remember much."

"Yes, we spoke to your doctor on the way in. You took quite a nasty knock on the head. Whatever you could recall would be most helpful." It was Roberts who spoke, Williams and Iyer obviously content with his lead for now.

"Ok. I think I was working in the office yesterday, and then went across town. It was busy: there were lots of people around, lots of traffic, and I was running late for something. The next thing I remember was following someone through some dimly lit corridors, like a basement. Then I woke up here. That's about it."

"I see." Roberts again. "You say you don't know where you were. Do you remember being at the Maxim Mall at all?"

"A little. There was a murder there wasn't there? I suppose that would be the case I was on, so I could have been there yesterday. What happened?"

Roberts looked thoughtful for a moment, and opted not to reply. I looked between them all for some suggestion or help, locking eyes with Iyer for a moment. She returned my gaze unflinchingly, blanking me and giving nothing away.

I spoke up: "Look, I'm sorry I can't tell you much, I just don't remember anything."

Roberts: "I suppose that will have to do for now. We'll definitely need to speak with you again, and there'll be a uniform on duty outside for the time being. If you do remember more, just tell the officer." He looked pensive, disappointed, but his voice and manner as he spoke seemed reasonable enough.

They had a brief exchange there, in the corner of the room, then Roberts nodded a goodbye and left, Williams following, and I could see them both speaking to their uniformed colleague just outside. Iyer remained, arms crossed. There was only the slightest relaxation in her posture, which remained stiffly formal. I asked her what was wrong, and she refused to answer at first until I asked again.

"We don't have all the details yet, but you were found unconscious on the floor in the lower basement of the mall. The security manager Harris was also there, shot dead. No sign of anyone else present. Does that jog your memory?"

It didn't and I said so, as strongly as I could.

She shrugged. "Well, don't worry about it for now. You're on sick leave again until the doctors give the all clear. Maybe when you recover some memory we can make some sense of this mess."

> Reznik

There was no real way around it: Araya didn't look himself today. He wore every one of his years openly on his face and then some, the mantle of mature authority he normally projected suddenly gone from his body, leaving just grey weariness in its place. The light coloured suit he wore, usually dapper, today only emphasised how drawn and pale he appeared. Reznik had watched him amble slowly over to the al fresco area of the café, choosing a table in the shade of an awning whilst his bodyguards positioned themselves nearby. The morning sun was hotter than even the last few days and there was almost no breeze.

Reznik was sitting across from the café, on one of the many wooden benches positioned around a large ornamental fountain in the centre of the plaza. It was undeniably pleasant to be sat there, the excited droplets of water cooling the air just as the sound of it gently cascading calmed the spirit. It was less busy here today than he had seen it before, and then he remembered it was a Sunday, when many of the locals would be preoccupied with family and faith, and was glad he'd dressed more smartly than usual.

Deciding there was nothing apparently amiss Reznik stood, folding his newspaper and setting it down on the bench. He covered the few yards to Araya's table across the plaza at a relaxed pace, smiling and inclining his head in greeting as soon as he caught the other man's gaze.

"Mornin'. Hope I didn't keep you waitin'."

"No, not at all. How are you my friend?"

"I'm ok. Been busy, lots to do. You don't look so good."

"I am a little the worse for wear to be honest. Picked up some virus or something. Still, have to keep busy. The world won't stop because I'm feeling a little sorry for myself!" They ordered fresh coffee and a light pastry. The small talk continued as they acted the part of friends and companions. Business would come a little later.

It had been some time since they had seen each other in person. They were both keen on meeting when Reznik first arrived in town, but since then everything had been arranged through secure messaging. Araya had provided a few things, small and large, which had strayed on a meandering course between different points on the legal compass, and Reznik was grateful that so far the sailing had been smooth. Up close it was clear Araya was more than just under the weather, but Reznik's enquiry was met with a dismissive wave of the hand. It was probably time to move the discussion toward his reason for calling.

Reznik needed help again, and was short of time. The essential details of the plan he had formulated with Jakobsen were sound, and the sharp end of the operation could still be done with the drones, but without the skills of a good operator to guide the swarm in it would be much less likely to succeed. The only way forward he could see was to find some local talent to handle the insertion and distraction stages of the plan, leaving him to seal the deal and kill Polzin himself. Reznik relayed as much of this to Araya as he thought prudent as they finished their meal. The coffee was excellent, the pastry less so. Araya listened with an expression of frankness and close consideration as he explained things.

Out of respect for Araya, and a sense that they may have need of each other in the future, he didn't omit that the job would ultimately draw police attention. It was all discussed obliquely of course, in the smoothly abstracted lingo of corporate speak, as though they really were two old business colleagues meeting for morning coffee. He presumed Araya understood his meaning plainly enough, though his expression remained admirably neutral throughout.

When he had finished Araya paused for a few seconds before asking, "The expertise you need, one person could do this, yes? It does not sound as though you will need more. The bigger problem might be in acquiring the necessary equipment and a secure place to work from. It is a shame you are on such a tight schedule."

"Yeah, I'll be leaving soon, so I need to have this over with before then."

"Leave it with me. There are one or two people I can think of but I'll ask around - discretely of course - to find you the best one. I'll call you later."

They drained their coffees and parted, business done.

> Cara

She had done her best to waste the morning properly with a late lie-in, but Sunday or not she was restless, and more than a little hungry. After showering, Cara made a quick breakfast, carrying it through to the lounge where she settled down in front of some old spy film, smiling wryly as the handsome agent infiltrated some kind of secret base that was disguised as an industrial plant. She'd watched a similar movie with Ethan once, and enjoyed his amused critique of the film's naivety and 60's kitsch. It was good to think of him laughing; he hadn't done that as much lately. She cursed at reminding herself about him, and then thought about the Hollis biography she'd received. Maybe Ethan had sent it, not realising she had a copy already? It was still where she'd left it the day before, nestled atop the cardboard packaging. Wouldn't hurt to take a closer look at it. From the cover it was a newer edition than the one she already had.

As she returned to her place on the sofa, settling into the warm imprint her body had left, she thumbed the movie forward a little. It had gone a bit slow and considering she wasn't really watching it properly there didn't seem any harm in skipping on. The next scene was of some villain's secret base, and she watched as a troupe of sombrely dressed men stood agape as the room transformed itself from a relaxed lounge area into a command centre. Her amusement grew as a wall panel retracted to show a large black and white reconnaissance photograph, rather than the display screen she automatically expected. Furniture flipped and swivelled to reveal clunky analogue tech, drawing a laugh from Cara as a handful of blinking lights and buzzers announced the equipment's status. There was every chance she would see a tape drive computer the size of a small house if she carried on watching.

Cara opened up the book and checked the first few pages for an inscription, but there was nothing. Marking the thirds were two bands of glossy white paper, and she turned to the first of these expecting photographs. As she looked through the pictures most were familiar, though there were one or two she didn't recognise.

She flicked through to the next set of glossies, but these proved more troublesome. At first, she was able to open the book up as expected, finding another photo that she didn't remember from the earlier edition. As she tried to continue she discovered that there was something wrong with the binding. The pages wouldn't open fully and she wondered if some glue had strayed where it shouldn't and partially sealed them, but that didn't seem to be it. Confused, she opened the covers back on themselves and looked through the tube formed by the stitched binding and the spine of the cover. There was something there.

With the covers still bent back Cara tipped the book up and shook it to try and dislodge the object, with no success. She tapped the book against her knee, first gently and then with more vigour, but the blockage was stuck fast. Agitated, she almost leapt to her feet before going to the kitchen, returning with a knife that Cara poked into the space behind the binding, carefully using it to prise the object away from its mounting. Cara felt it give and come away, so she turned the book over and let it fall into her lap.

It was a flash drive, an unusual design about the length of her thumb but much flatter and thinner. Cara wondered what was going on. She gave the spy on the TV a hard stare as though he were responsible, and stabbed at the remote to cut him off mid-quip. She was rewarded with a screen as dark as her own thoughts.

Picking up the flash drive, she activated a switch on the side, sliding out a mini-port that would fit any number of devices she had lying around. There was her old ‘pad, which would be able to open the drive and view the contents list if she plugged it into the mains to get some charge. Cara decided it was best to proceed with a little caution, as she had no idea what this was all about.

What the hell was on this thing, and why had it been sent to her?

Frost hadn't entirely lost it but she was close. She'd run with all the speed she could back the way they'd come, Tsukino just behind her, any attempt at stealth long abandoned. It was hard going over the uneven ground, rough on the legs, but they had to get the hell out of there before they were targeted. Once or twice there'd been a near miss when shattered chunks of some drone or other rained down nearby, but luckily that was as close as they'd come.

She'd no idea of The Wolf's status, or Jakobsen's. Their comms were offline and the boss could be anywhere, but they had agreed in advance to scatter if things went this far FUBAR, so they'd done exactly that.

Frost slipped and fell at the top of the next hill, landing just over the ridge. Tsukino kept her feet and ran smoothly half way down, slowing a little to turn and look backward. Their eyes met for a moment before Tsu's flashed wide, two baseball-sized holes suddenly punched right through her chest in a spray of red mist.

- Twelve -

> Chase

The next afternoon at four we got the band back together. For the benefit of the tape, there was DI Roberts, DS Williams, Iyer and myself. I could see the subtle glint of smartlenses over their eyes, and wished I had my own. None of us had said much on the way into the room, just the minimum of polite greetings.

It began easily enough. They asked plenty of questions, some subtle and conciliatory and others less so, and I answered them calmly and with full frankness from the knowledge I had, which at that moment wasn't much. I confirmed my previous statement, with apologies that I still couldn't remember any details from the night I was injured, though now I could at least recall more about the days leading up to it. They were clearly hoping for more, but I knew they would have spoken to the hospital already. I'd had to spend another night there, and they'd not let me go until the results of a fresh scan were in, so it had been past lunchtime when I was discharged. It was a relief when I could finally walk out of there, reasonably intact if not unscathed.

I had questions of my own, and as I wasn't under arrest or a formal caution I felt free enough to ask: "I presume you have my smartpad? Whatever I was doing at the mall there's a good chance I recorded everything on it. Should fill in some holes."

"We don't have it yet. That was one of our first thoughts as well," Roberts replied.

Williams continued, "It seems pretty convenient that it's gone missing."

"Really? It doesn't feel so convenient to me. I'd like nothing better than to see from my own eyes what happened, because I'm damn sure that I wouldn't have shot anyone without good cause. And how was he fatally injured with a stun gun anyway?"

Roberts reply surprised me. "He wasn't killed with a stun gun. Ms. Iyer here" - he nodded toward her - "assures me that the weapon you were issued with was indeed non-lethal in design, but that's not what you were found with. Instead you seem to have used a different gun, a fully lethal one." He let that one sink in a moment before continuing. "Can you tell us why that's so, Detective Chase?"

"No, I really can't. The only firearm I use is my service weapon. Have you found it? I would have had it with me, same as the smartpad. It's standard issue, and I wouldn't leave it behind." I tried to keep calm as I spoke, not let the pressure of the situation get to me. This was an uncomfortable place to be.

Roberts again: "Well, the absence of those key objects puts you in a bit of a difficult position, gives us cause for some suspicion." He paused a moment, and looked as though he would say more, but I interrupted before he could continue.

"Or it could be argued that whoever shot Harris removed the objects from the scene, to cast doubt on my testimony or implicate me. Maybe you should look again to make sure they're not there! Anyway, what about GSR?"

"That doesn't help you I'm afraid. We didn't find anything on the swabs we took from you in hospital but the weapon found at the scene is an advanced model, using liquid propellant. It burns much more efficiently than gunpowder and doesn't really leave as much residue, so I'd call that an open question. What we did find were your prints on the gun grip and trigger."

"Doesn't mean much. According to you, the hospital and my own headache I was unconscious on the floor. Anyone could have pressed a gun into my hands."

Roberts didn't seem to have a ready reply to that, so Williams picked up the baton. "Tell us about your first couple of days back at work then. I understand you've only just returned after a long period of recuperation due to some injuries you sustained?"

"That's correct. What are you getting at? I was medically cleared to come back a few weeks ago. I just took some personal time first, that's all."

"I'd have thought you'd had enough time off. Maybe you weren't quite ready. Perhaps the pressure of the investigation got to you? We've all been there. I understand that you weren't making too much progress?"

"I was doing fine thanks. We're heavily reliant on forensics on this case from what I understand, and we'd only just got an ID. If it were an easy or straightforward enquiry you'd have handled it yourselves." They didn't give a lot away, but from their expressions they didn't like that so much.

Williams again: "Still, I know you guys in the commercial sector are under a lot of pressure to succeed, targets and service agreements and all that. Maybe it got on top of you a bit, your first case back. Maybe you just snapped, made a mistake. We'd all understand, it could happen to any of us." Roberts agreed with her, cracking a small smile, conciliatory and understanding as if we were all good friends.

"Look, unless you're cancelling the contract with CSS then I think the investigation is still ours. Harris is linked somehow to the death of Karl Jakobsen, even if only as a technical witness, and the mall is where both crimes happened. Whatever I was doing there it was obviously tied into the case. I'll be happy to let you know what I remember when it comes back to me, but until then maybe you'd better let us get on with things?"

That was enough to set the fat cat amongst the pigeons. They suspended the interview and went next door to talk it over. I was grateful for the pause: it felt hot in there, close, and my head was starting to pound again. A few minutes later they all returned. No one said much, or gave an explanation, but I was free to go for now. From her expression Williams was clearly pissed off, though Roberts was more guarded. Iyer was her usual stony self.

I followed her as far as her car, but it was clear I was on my own from here when she spoke: "Until you're fully recovered from your concussion you're off the case and on medical leave. I don't want to see or hear from you, or about you, for the next few days. Now fuck off home."

She got into her car and reversed in a quick turn, scattering gravel as she then accelerated quickly away, leaving me stranded and very much alone.

> Reznik

The heat was almost unbearable, the air thick and humid outside in the street. Brown dust coated everything in a fine film that rendered the whole scene in sepia-toned antiquity. A sickly breeze would occasionally wheeze through, stirring the dust into brief motion before setting it back down again mere inches from where it began. There'd been no rain for a few weeks now, though the sea was high and a big storm was due.

He'd been watching the hotel entrance for the last few minutes from the deep shadows across the way. It was an old colonial style place, the exterior run-down and heavily graffitied with a near continuous scrawl of tags, politics and profanity covering the brickwork and boarded-up windows in an unbroken flow. Here at the top of the hill a few outbuildings edged close, last remnants of an older age, but everything downslope was lean-to and temporary.

Araya had been at his best, calling back within a few hours of their breakfast yesterday. He'd named a contact, Santos, who could help, and set up a call. The two of them had talked and arranged a face to face for this next day, but the drone pilot would only meet on familiar turf. A place where he was welcome, and Reznik was not. He'd used one of the local taxi firms to travel in, paid a little up front to try and smooth his exit later. On the way, he'd tried to keep an eye on the driver's satnav to get at least a rough sense of the geography. The display was as detailed as you would expect for the main road, but as soon as you looked a few yards from it there was only the vaguest sense of a surrounding street plan, as though the region were plastic, not yet fully formed. They were literally off the grid, far from the clean areas of the centre and the permanent zones.

The rest of his journey had been on foot, up steep hills and rough steps, heading out from the old favela into something newer, more desperate and precarious. Three times he was stopped by armed youths, challenged as to his business, and he'd had to negotiate his way through with careful words. Whoever this Santos was, he was obviously well known here, his name opening the way.

There was no point in watching any longer. Reznik waited until the doorman was looking in the other direction and then stepped out from the shadows, crossing the street with feigned nonchalance while inwardly zenned against the possibility of sudden violence. He had taken a few steps already before the man turned and noticed him, though from his lack of reaction he was clearly expected. Apart from a tightening of his posture and a theatrical roll of his heavy head across the enormity of his thick neck there was no change, no sign of trouble.

Reznik drew closer. The guard called back into the dark recess of the doorway, summoning help. He was joined by a woman, someone who could have been his cross-gender clone with all the similarities they shared.

"What do you want?" Her voice spoke oddly accented English in a slightly nasal tone. The doorman didn't say anything, simply stood there and radiated suppressed menace. Reznik waited until he was a touch closer, allowing him to speak softly rather than bellowing as she had done. "I'm here to see Santos. He's expecting me." She merely grunted in response, so pressed on. "I'm a friend of Araya's. Everything's already arranged." She glared at Reznik belligerently, but turned to re-enter the building, glancing back over her shoulder with the same fixed expression of generic hostility she had borne since he first caught sight of her. The doorman simply stood, slightly to the side and just far enough away to not be imminently dangerous. Reznik took little comfort from the fact that no violence had occurred yet – there was plenty of time and opportunity for things to devolve.

Perhaps not today though: she returned and gestured with her head, adding verbally that Reznik should follow. He'd been eavesdropping as she talked on a phone and so fully expected the invitation, but was still relieved that she relayed the instructions without further delay. Her male counterpart remained behind as Reznik followed her inside.

Whatever the hotel's past there was little sign of former grandeur, as the reception area was empty save for some random pieces of battered furniture. There was a stench from deeper inside, an overpowering stink of unwashed bodies and human filth. Reznik was not exactly surprised by it, but the strength of it caught him a little off-guard. It was worse than anything he could remember in similar places, and he wondered if it were deliberate, a way to keep out the curious. If his guide either noticed or cared about his discomfort she gave no sign.

The interior looked abandoned and derelict in the half-light, but from the noises and momentary signs of reluctant movement he glimpsed through open doorways the building was very much occupied. They went deeper, following a twisted and complex route through a maze of temporary and broken walls, until they reached a stairwell in what was probably about the centre of the building. There was an elevator there, but from the condition of it – doors half-open, barely containing a pile of mixed garbage – it was some time since it was last used. His guide set off up the stairs, choosing her path with evident caution. As he followed her it was clear why: he suspected a lab could be kept busy for months analysing the decaying organic mush and general filth smeared everywhere.

He followed her upwards, treading carefully with every step.

> Cara

She was relieved to see Ethan again, even on a screen, but it left her surprised, worried, and more than a little numb. Somehow, the fact she cared for him so much had escaped her, passed her by. What she'd mistaken for mere fondness was something more. If the melodramatic tone of the video message he'd left for her on the flash drive was at all real, and not just some sick joke, it was perhaps too late.

"If you're watching this then something's happened to me. I'm really sorry."

Bastard. His hair was a little longer than usual, but she remembered he had worn it like that for a short while a couple of weeks ago, until his preferred barber was back from a long snowboarding trip. The period she would have guessed at lined up pretty well with the video's date stamp. He needed a shave as well. Had needed.

"The fact is I'm not entirely who I said I was. Most of it is true, but not all. My name's not really Ethan. All the stuff about being a software engineer, and drone and RPV operator, that's all true, more or less, and I did spend some time in the military. It was just different regiments, different places. I do love you though. That's absolutely true, for real." That wasn't a word he'd used much to her face, nor one she thought applied to them so strongly.

"The thing is, I had some old business to take care of, a final mission if you like, helping out an old friend. Just this last job then I'm done, no more of that life, just a life with you. Thing is, for all that you have to keep things straight and pretty normal, I know there's more to you than that. You're more for real, if you know what I mean. Real enough to maybe make sense of me, maybe. I've done some crazy shit."

When she first heard that, she knew somehow that he wasn't talking about some boyish adventure, though he was completely vague about what he did mean. He looked adorable and gorgeous in that thin oatmeal sweater, the buttons on the right shoulder half-undone, scruffy but sexy. He smiled then and she melted a little, again, before remembering she was annoyed. And worried.

"Still have some crazy shit left to do I guess. Don't want to talk about that; don't want to put you in any danger. The less you know the better. I don't know how far this goes, but I do know I want this to be nice and smooth, and be done and finished with."

He looked imploringly, intensely at the camera then, reaching over to zoom into a headshot as he spoke. The close up brought his eyes into sharper focus, and she could see the subtle change in colouring and reaction that betrayed his smartlenses. She wasn't keen on them, but he always half-smiled and said they were part of the job, without really saying what the job was.

"If you're watching this though it means things didn't work out quite so well, unless I'm showing you this for old time's sake, when we're both old and grey and this was just some youthful indiscretion."

She hated that he planted and stole away such a warm, cosy image in the same sentence, and that she enjoyed the image quite so much.

"I'm sorry things haven't worked out. I'm sorry that I didn't get to spend more time with you, and tell you how I feel to your face. Maybe this is the best I can do until this is all over, but maybe I'm being a selfish bastard for leaving this till now."

"I love you."

There it was again. And yes, Ethan Grant, you are so being a selfish bastard!

"If things have gone wrong they've probably gone really wrong. I sent you this message this way because you might be watched. I don't know, the police or someone else might get involved, and they might track me to you. I'm not sure, but I haven't told you much so you don't know enough to be in real danger. God, I hope not. I really love you. Forever. Past this life and into the next."

She loved him too. Maybe not so eternally, but for here and now, for sure.

Frost would swear that someone had altered the terrain, adding contours and generally making the surface more irregular and uneven since she had last been this way. At least the ground's roughness made her weave, varying her path and making herself a more difficult target, but it also prevented her from running flat out.

Her mind was elsewhere. She had stayed with Tsu as she passed, catching her and easing her to the ground, brushing back her hair to watch the final light fade from her eyes. Everything had slowed as she laid Tsu down gently and then turned and run in clumsy, sliding steps up the side of the bank, away from her friend and the incendiary she had dropped to cremate her.

There had only been a couple more brief exchanges of gunfire since then, which worried Frost, allowing her milspec pessimism to run as fast as her feet, twisting and turning but always racing on in the near dark. She was already out of hope but grit and bloody-mindedness made her keep going.

The same old patterns of survival saved her as she slipped, her legs finally giving way on the rough ground. Frost scrambled back up and brought her rifle around sharply to cover her rear, immediately dropping low again and firing at one of the hexapod drones as it crested the ridge.

- Thirteen -

> Chase

I was on the underground when it first came to me, though typically on the wrong line and heading in the wrong direction. Although I'd been judged fit enough to go home and been discharged by the hospital I felt rougher and less together than I had in some time, and I couldn't help but think of the long dark days of recovery and recuperation after Paris. Some of it must have shown on my face, as I caught more than a couple of appraising looks cast in my direction from the other passengers as they glanced up from their 'pads and paperbacks. For anyone to take note on the underground I must have been looking fairly grim, especially as there were several ARtifacts in this carriage, where various holodisplays were interacting messily with each other and giving off vivid colour-sprites. I had my own personal flash of light when I suddenly knew exactly where I should go.

The mall was where the murder I'd been investigating had occurred, and it was where I'd apparently been found on the Saturday night. It was obviously at the centre of something, though if I'd known what that was before the concussion I didn't now. Although I was on sick leave much of it was an inherently public space, so there was little anyone could do to stop me paying a visit, so long as I didn't draw attention to myself.

Once I'd made it back there I opted to walk around the perimeter first. Somehow it looked a lot bigger in context, viewed alongside the older, more mainstream architecture it nested with. I remembered then that some significant portions of the building were given over to commercial office space and still others were unused, effectively mothballed, so I had more than likely seen only a fraction of the place on previous visits.

I'd covered a good two thirds of the exterior when I decided to head inside, passing quickly through the main retail spaces until I reached a second atrium. At its core was a tailored biosphere, hefty lumps of weathered rock down which a modest waterfall flowed. The designers had selected the flora carefully to appeal to particular species of butterfly and ladybird, as well as some form of sting-less honeybee the geneticists had dreamed up. There were what looked like small rodents and birds as well, but these were actually robots on a tightly programmed leash.

It had seemed like a good place to stop and think, but it wasn't long before I grew restless and returned to the main commercial areas, this time moving through more slowly. The mall was more about the experience of shopping than the shopping itself. A steady swarm of Lifestyle Consultants buzzed around, keen to draw attention to their particular brand of stereo-lithographed blobjects and fast fashion. Everything here could be printed, formed or stitched to specification in the time it took to enjoy a skinny-something in the coffee shop next door. The few stores that catered for more lavish goods were almost cul-de-sacs, selling high-priced handmades and ancient kitsch. After a while I got tired of it, the endless banners and flashtags for 'Sales' and 'Savings', projections of hard light and harder economics.

I went back outside, to take a look at the rest of the building. As the mall was placed in amongst the existing structures on the block much of the outer shell was inaccessible, but it wasn't long before I found a vehicle entrance that threaded through the frontage of one property down a short tunnel into the mall's private, more functional spaces. Only a rough sense of geography and the faintest of blue-grey tints to the walls gave me any indication that I was looking at the exterior of the mall again. The space was entirely utilitarian, with none of the design flair or character that was visible elsewhere. There was a shutter door and an ordinary one to the side, while the vehicle access continued around through the tunnel to the right where it reached daylight again further on.

I followed the road around and came to a much broader access way cut through the block leading to an impressive goods bay, clearly designed for heavier and more frequent traffic. The whole area was well lit and busy, with a couple of human personnel and plenty more warehouse robots shifting packages, much of it foodstuffs and bulkier items too large or complex to be made on site.

Returning the way I'd come, I looked again at the smaller loading area. I'd seen most of the mall's exterior now, at least at ground level, and this seemed like it might be the easiest way to slip inside. Moving up closer to the keypad and card reader beside the small door, I could see that the outer cover was loose in the bottom corner, and that the little LED light on the unit was showing a steady green. I reached for the door handle and turned it gently. The door clicked, and I pulled it open a few inches, and then a few more when there was no sign of an alarm.

Inside was a perfectly ordinary loading bay, large enough to cater for a big van. There was a conveyor system running deeper into the building through hatches, while a couple of autoloaders were hanging idly from tracks running across the ceiling. I couldn't see any people around, but there was a door toward the rear of the room that probably lead further inside. As far as I knew no one had investigated this area. If they ever did they might now find traces of my presence here, along with whoever else had been this way, so I pulled out a personal smartpad I'd brought with me and took reference photos and video, just in case.

I'd come here hoping to bring back some memories, but instead I had the feeling I might have found something entirely new.

> Reznik

By the time they'd reached the top, five flights up, he was a little tired and out of breath, though it was satisfying to see that his guide was faring worse. It wasn't the physical exertion: what made it so hard was trying to breathe in as little of the stained air as possible in the stifling heat while keeping a near constant watch on his footing. Things had improved as they climbed higher, but the experience was distinctly unpleasant.

There was a small lobby at the head of the stairs, and here the smell finally cleared, tamed by subtle chemicals and the sharper tang of skunk. Once they'd passed by another two bodyguards the top floor was completely open, almost a loft apartment save for the rough furniture and boarded windows. A number of people were sat or laid in various small clusters, many of them smoking, some with faces shining in a bright wash of screen-light, others zoned out or enraptured by whatever they saw in the more intimate displays of their smartlenses.

He ignored them all and was ignored in turn, making straight for the far corner of the room where it was lightest. As he approached, he felt the strong shift of air from a line of fans mounted on tall stands blowing constantly against the smoky atmosphere, pushing it back toward the lounge. There were fewer people here in the corner, and they watched his approach openly, without guile. A couple of mid-sized racks of computers stood in the centre of the space, lights flashing energetically.

Santos turned out to be a 16 year old with almost as much attitude as acne. He'd been assured by Araya that the specialist would be up to the task. That was all that stopped Reznik from turning around and going straight back where he'd come from.

The kid had done his best to project cocky competence and professional edge, but he mostly just came across as young and arrogant. As he arrived the boy was berating one of his entourage, cursing and criticising the man with an unending stream of invective, barely pausing for breath or response. Santos's accent was so thick and furious Reznik had a little trouble following the entirety of it. Deciding that patience was both a virtue and an operational requirement, Reznik merely stood and waited for the flow to stop. He was mildly surprised at how long it took.

When he was done, Santos finally turned to face Reznik. "Sr. Araya said you had some work for me, and that you'd pay me well. What do you want?"

"Did Araya also tell you I like to keep my business private?" Reznik didn't bother to indicate toward the watching entourage.

"These are my...associates. You can say anything you need to in front of them." Reznik wasn't convinced. The people surrounding Santos regarded him with a certain low-key hostility, dislike without passion or purpose.

He pressed his point: "I need you and your expertise, I don't need an audience. Now, either our business is private or we have no business."

"I'm not sure I like you, Mr. Reznik. I'm not sure I want to work with you." Santos crossed his arms defiantly, raised his shoulders. Reznik stared back, kept his posture relaxed, barely moving.

There was a long pause, until abruptly Santos started talking again. After a little more back and forth the boy finally agreed, and they left to go to the next floor down, where there was almost no one to overhear. Once Reznik had a chance to explain what he needed without the distractions, Santos surprised him with a series of probing and considered questions. He stayed on topic and didn't question Reznik's grander designs or motives, but stuck largely to the parameters of the job. It looked as though Araya had been right about him, though a little more info up front would have been nice. On the other hand, he probably wouldn't have gone for it, so Araya had played it perfectly.

Their business concluded, and at a price he found only mildly extortionate, Reznik was free to leave. The doorwoman accompanied him again, leading the way. The trip down was exactly as unpleasant as he'd imagined.

> Cara

"Sorry love can't help you. Don't know what Ethan was mixed up in. Didn't want to know, to be honest. Not my business."

She studied Thorne intently, not caring if he was aware of it, looking for any sign he was lying or hiding something. He looked back at her with equal frankness, meeting her eyes calmly. She could see nothing that contradicted his words, no tick or tell.

Cara had called him, with great reluctance, to arrange a meet. Nada had accepted her request a little too readily, and had chosen a bar more appropriate for a date than business, but he was here as agreed, looking leaner and somehow even less respectable than when she'd last seen him, his hair colorfixed black. Her strong misgivings at renewing any acquaintance with him, however briefly, were something she'd just have to swallow. She needed to know where Ethan was, and what was going on, and hoped that Nada could tell her. Unfortunately, he didn't seem to know.

"Ok, tell me what he owes you for, and what business you were doing together."

"You offerin' to settle the debt? If that were the case, we would 'ave business and my business with 'im might be shared, if you see what I mean. I'm sure 'e wouldn't mind given your close association, as it were. Otherwise, as a gentleman, I'm not sure I could help you any further. Though I would be happy to buy you dinner. For old time's sake and all that."

Cara was barely surprised by his last offer. He had never paid much regard to social norms and seemed to care little who he might upset. Every moment with him was a reminder of their past, but the mood for her was closer to nausea than nostalgia. She wanted to keep strictly to business and her reason for calling. If she let him get to her, she might give him a mouthful and lose any chance of his cooperation.

"Don't think I can make it, sorry. What amount are we talking about here? What does he owe you?"

"Well, I can't recall exactly but I believe it was about four-fifty, give or take. Not such a stretch for you I'd guess, you being an independent contractor and all."

It was a stretch, as it happened. It was money she had, technically, but there were other things it had been destined for, like rent. "That's a bit vague. Any chance you could be more specific? I don't know, maybe give me an invoice or something?"

He sucked his front teeth a moment, furrowing his brow. "I'm sure I could dig up some paperwork or whatever, if I was sufficiently motivated. Maybe I should do you a bit of a discount, as a sweetener, to mark the renewal of our friendship."

She really didn't think so. "Look, we both know I want what you have on Ethan. If I have to clear his debt to get that, fine, but this is the one and only time I'll pay you for it, and I want no tricks. No bullshit and nothing held back. Am I clear?"

"Ceed, I'm hurt, we're old friends! Honestly, it's only my professionalism that causes me any conflict, I'd love to just tell you all I know. I thought you'd understand."

"Oh I do understand Nathan Daniel Thorne, and it's precisely because we were friends all those years ago that I don't trust you. You dropped me in it you little shit, and you never even had the decency to apologise." Ah, that was it then. There it was.

He paused, leant further back in the chair, and looked at her more coldly. There was little trace of his smooth bonhomie, or cultivated mockney left. "Fair enough Cara Dalca, I believe I do understand you. Four-fifty and the debt's closed, then I'll tell you everything I know, though I warn you it's not much. I'll even tell you if I hear anything new, any whispers. And that *is* for old time's sake."

Cara had no choice really. She needed to know what Thorne knew, and he wouldn't tell her for free, never mind old times. Reluctantly she stretched her hand out to shake on it, grabbing for her purse as she did so. Thorne left her hanging for an instant before leaning forward, returning her firm but straight handshake, his expression neutral and appraising. She touched smartpads with Nada and keyed the fund transfer, sitting back to watch the progress bar as Thorne checked his own display and nodded to confirm acceptance.

"So, you want to hear about my dealings with Ethan?" There wasn't much, he'd been straight about that. Nada had supplied a few drones a few weeks ago that had come his way. They were quality industrial grade models, with limited flight capability, something you might see on any construction site. She guessed that they were probably stolen, but she didn't bother to enquire. Ethan had asked quite a lot of questions about the condition and specifications, and was obviously particular about what he wanted. Thorne had other, similar items at the time that he showed absolutely no interest in. And that was it. He'd only been paid for part of the deal but as he knew Ethan from some other business, 'a while back' as he put it, he accepted his word that the rest would follow. Wanted to move the items on to make room for more stock, Nada said, or as she guessed because they were too hot. He'd delivered the goods to Ethan's lock up the next day.

She had the feeling that he was holding something back, though he said he'd told her everything. It could be something to do with the business he'd done with Ethan in the past, but he said that wasn't part of the deal and refused to talk about it. Cara knew he couldn't be pushed into revealing anything else if he didn't want to.

As the conversation wound up she kept her face straight, thanked him and finished her drink, though she couldn't help smiling to herself as she left. Cara hadn't known that Ethan kept a lockup, and now she had the address. It wasn't as much as she'd hoped for, but it was something.

Jakobsen had never felt this stressed or frustrated. The laptop screen was flashing with so many amber and red warning lights he could barely track them, and none of the codes Polzin had given them were working anymore. Worse, even their own assets had ceased responding, blithely ignoring the commands he sent them.

In the first few seconds of contact they'd scored some clear successes, machine logic immune to the shock of the moment, but every shot betrayed a position for immediate retaliation from the complex's defenses, and there'd been no way to bring up enough fire support of their own. In reality they were fucked as soon as the shooting started.

With the comms blocked, he'd no way to contact anyone. The Wolf should have been finished before the shit storm began, but if he were honest it was Tsu and Frost he was more concerned about. They'd worked together before and were close, but right now there was nothing he could do for either of them.

- Fourteen -

> Chase

When Mallory dropped by it was a total surprise, and it took me a couple of seconds to recover and buzz her in. She came straight over and gave me a hug, holding on firmly for a few beats before pulling back. I let go and she smiled, gently pushing me away.

"What have you done, you idiot! Iyer will have your arse for this if you give her chance!" She shook her head ruefully.

I was pleased to see her, and told her so, but we had moved to opposite ends of the lounge by then, a more professional distance dropping back into place automatically. Mallory was beautiful, caramel skinned with a slim and athletic build. Her fine features were partially hidden by mid-length kinked hair, which she pushed back casually, smiling again. Everyone I knew at Cadejo had at least a soft spot for her. She was thoroughly educated and by upbringing thoroughly posh, and swore exquisitely.

I offered her coffee and she accepted, following me through to the kitchen area as I went to make it. "So, what happened? I hear you were found unconscious at a crime scene, near the body of a witness."

"That's about as much as I know myself. I wish I could remember more, but for now I'm waiting to see what the forensics come back with to try and make some sense of things, same as everyone else. Hopefully, I might recover some memories on my own before then, but there's nothing much I can do to make that happen."

"I know that's what you told Iyer and the police, but is there anything else? Maybe something you're not sure about, just a feeling or impression?"

"No, there really isn't. I went back to the mall where the crime scene was – just the public areas – and had a walk around, but it didn't bring anything back. It's only the events of the Saturday I'm not sure about, I think I'm fairly solid on everything from earlier in the week." I almost told her about the service entrance I'd found, but thought I maybe shouldn't yet.

"Perhaps if you looked at some pictures of the basement it might help, the route from where they think you took the lift on Saturday through to where you were found? Just a thought anyway."

"That's a good idea. I'll see if I can get access to some photos, see if anything comes back to me."

We chatted for a little longer as we finished our drinks, until she had to leave. I showed her to the door and we said our goodbyes at the threshold. I thought she was done, but she had more to say: "By the way, I really don't believe for one moment you're guilty, but if you are I'll help them fucking bury you. Nothing would disappoint me more than to find out you're dirty. Not that I think you are of course." She smiled warmly and then turned and walked off, leaving me standing there in the doorway.

I came back to myself and went back inside, making a point of shutting the door gently in case she was still in earshot. I'd seen her test a suspect with a similar strong statement and then wait just around the corner before heading back quietly to eavesdrop on their reaction. I was sure she was on my side, but right now I couldn't be too careful.

When I found the memory stick that she'd left on the kitchen worktop a few minutes later I could have kissed her.

There was plenty of content on the flash drive, and I went straight to the files that dealt with the first murder to update myself on the original investigation. We'd had a response from government records, which had finally caught up with the intelligence databases and provided some results from our ID search. It wasn't quite what we expected.

Rather than returning information to us under the name of Karl Jakobsen, we received a wealth of data for a different ID: Ethan Grant. At first glance all the indicators were that the identity was perfectly real. There were his birth records, details of residency throughout Europe, most recently here in Auldwiche, as well as banking, credit and tax reports. He even had a presence on social media, though he wasn't a prolific user. In short, there was nothing about him that stood out or raised any obvious concerns.

Only when CSS techs looked beneath the surface were there any indications that the Ethan Grant ID was fabricated. There were small patterns and inconsistencies in his back-story that to a trained eye suggested some level of forgery, and it looked as though the Ethan Grant identity had been freshly created about six months after Jakobsen's reported death. From that point forward it had been in daily use, and the various strands of data wove together much more convincingly. This whole thing was redolent of tradecraft: a deep-cover mission of some sort, or at the very least a serious attempt to go into hiding.

Our investigator in Norway had been able to confirm some of the details of his military service from public records, and there was a lot of early biographical information, but in her opinion there was nothing particularly suggestive in any of that so far. His only listed next of kin was an older sister, his father having died about nine months ago in hospital after a long period of illness. His mother had also passed, when he was still in his early teens. The period of Jakobsen's life that he spent working for PMCs was much harder to investigate. Cadejo would continue to pursue the enquiry, but there was no telling how much they would uncover, particularly in respect of his last recorded mission. The mercenary outfit he'd been working for was a shell company that had been wound up a few months after his disappearance.

There were plenty of leads to follow regarding Ethan Grant though, not least of which was the flat he'd been living in. It would be relatively easy for CSS to secure a search warrant for the address, but as yet they'd either not visited the place or not written it up as there was nothing in the files. What I did find curious about all this was that the level of detail available for the last eighteen months was much more extensive than might be expected for a mere cover identity. There was a private company registered under the Grant name offering consultancy services on robotics and security, and he'd filed proper business accounts and paid taxes. Everything about his current activities seemed genuine enough. Perhaps Jakobsen had intended to remain as Grant for good.

> Reznik

Reznik was already in position, belly down on the roof of the skyscraper. His sights were aligned with the swimming pool area on Lagorio's balcony, and the rifle was nestled comfortably into his shoulder, most of its weight resting on the small bipod at the end of the fore grip. Everything was hidden beneath a smartfabric camouflage net whilst Reznik himself was likewise covered, his ghillie suit a new design using similar materials. Within the suit were a number of self-inflating pads that cushioned him from the hard surface and made the wait a bit more comfortable.

He'd heard from Espina again. There would definitely be a party tonight at Lagorio's penthouse, some sort of schmooze for an overseas robotics corporation, Hallistiks, who were keen to win support in their legal dispute with another firm from closer to home, OraCotek. It would be a full production number, the biggest one since he'd come back from his hunting lodge in the country, and Polzin was certain to be there. Lagorio's security would be kept busy and forced into a less aggressive stance, though the task of identifying Polzin amongst so many guests would be made more challenging.

To prepare Santos he'd run through the op in simulation as thoroughly as he could that morning, but the more emphasis he placed on success the more the boy would start to question the cover story that they were issuing a warning to a business rival. He'd been given only the barest level of background detail, but there was a good chance he might have worked a few things out for himself. To be useful the simulation had to be accurate, and Lagorio was a well-known figure, famous for exactly the kind of party he would be throwing that night. The actual kill was Reznik's responsibility, both to keep the boy's hands reasonably clean but also because he didn't know him near well enough.

Given his own more limited piloting skills, Reznik had been forced to revert to a more direct method and use a sniper rifle. The conditions at that altitude were difficult, the winds unusually brisk and unpredictable as the first wave of the expected storm moved in. Fortunately, Jakobsen had outfitted some small drones to act as spotters as a contingency, and this would provide Reznik with accurate climate data. Santos would create a distraction with the rest of the RPVs and then herd everyone out into the open on the balcony, including Polzin. He hoped that she would become separated enough from the others, or that Santos could nudge her along, but as plans went it would rely, if he were honest, on a little too much luck. It would be easier to use an offensively armed drone in the first place, which had been the original plan, but he couldn't trust the boy that far.

From his earlier research Reznik had determined that the best vantage point was atop this building, along the main road from the construction site where he'd left Jakobsen's modified 'bots earlier in the week. It was a slightly older design based on a large oval, split into mixed use for small to medium offices, retail, services, and apartments. The central core had been left as an open space, intended as a light well, and at the base of the shaft formed by the hollow building was a small garden and open plaza. Up here on the roof there were no public areas, so he should remain undisturbed indefinitely. It had been a trivial matter to seal the access doors anyway, just in case. There was nothing to do now but wait.

> Cara

She was at the hospital when everything fell into place. Cara realised in between the initial shocks and general background anxiety she felt for her father that she'd just been shielding herself from the obvious truth. When it all finally lined up and dropped on her she was staggered by the weight of it.

Ethan was either in definite danger or worse, already dead.

She knew without doubt then that his final message was anything but a hoax, and that whatever business he was mixed up in it had gone badly wrong. The reason he hadn't responded to her calls wasn't simple ignorance or from some security requirement, it was because he couldn't.

Cara had been visiting her Dad again that morning and it was on the way out she'd had a sudden sharp insight that made her gasp aloud and almost fall into the nearest chair. She'd spent so much time at the hospital that she knew most of the nurses on the ward, at least a little, so when she'd sat down so abruptly in obvious distress they'd rushed to help her, while another nurse ran straight through to check on her father, assuming he was the source of her anguish. They were somewhat taken aback to find he was fine and that Cara was upset for another reason, especially as she couldn't bring herself to explain. In the end she'd had to tough it out and pretend she was feeling better to deflect their well-meant concern.

It was a front Cara had held onto on the drive home, but no more. Now she was back in the flat she let it all out, dropping onto the couch, pulling her coat off, one arm trailed inside out behind her as though it was struggling to hold on. The tears came again then, a full flow. It soon became more than worry for Ethan, as her fears and concerns for her father, frustration with Petre's situation, and even the small money worries all contributed to her distress, as though expressing her anguish from one source was a total collapse of control. Cara cried unselfconsciously, emotions raw and stark. It had been a long time since she'd felt so lost.

Frost had struck lucky with the hexapod. Its primary weapon system couldn't immediately target her as it crested the ridge, whilst from her own position below she was able to fire a grenade at its weaker underside, catching a couple of its leg joints and disabling it quickly. More than likely it would have reported her position though, and there was nothing she could do in response but run.

She'd covered a good distance before a near miss peppered her with shrapnel. Falling hard, she frantically dragged herself into better cover, a natural trough in the landscape. It hurt like hell to move, and nearly as much when she didn't. Reaching around Frost dabbed gently at a couple of the worst spots on her leg and lower back, bringing her hand back bloody. She immediately set to pulling a med kit from her pack, all the while looking around frantically for the next threat.

- Fifteen -

> Chase

There were a number of video files in the data Mallory had given me, recorded by some of the emergency responders on worn camera rigs, so there were multiple viewpoints on what they'd seen as they entered the mall on the Saturday evening. The video showed the officers racing through the basement corridors with a member of the mall's staff, all of them trailing a security 'bot they'd sent in ahead. The footage had an immersive and human perspective that made it all the more powerful. I felt like I was there with them.

The particular clip I was watching was recorded by one of the lead officers. She rushed on slightly ahead and was the first to find another mall security drone, hovering in place with its hazards on just outside an open doorway down a side corridor. There were other sources of intermittent lights visible from inside the room, and the door seemed to be propped open with a fire extinguisher. As she entered, the officer called out to identify herself.

Her initial view was blocked by racks of server equipment, but she headed quickly for the back of the room where there was a brighter, more consistent light source. Seconds later she found me there, laid on the floor. The officer stepped over my outstretched feet and moved further into the open space. She took a quick look back toward me as her camera view showed one of the paramedics rush straight over to provide treatment, whilst another went past them toward a seated figure slumped forward over a bank of computer monitors.

As the police officer took in the rest of the scene she focused on my right hand, and the pistol lying just beyond it. Moving across, she pushed the weapon lightly away with her foot, further beyond my reach, her camera view quite deliberately showing the action. Turning toward the other side of the room, she filmed one of her colleagues as he examined the male at the workstation, his head resting on a computer keyboard as though he'd nodded off. It was clear he was mortally injured from the blood that covered much of the desk and monitors.

With a sudden realisation that was almost breathtaking I knew that this was Harris, and that he was out of place. There'd been someone else sat at there. That sense of the wrongness was all I really had though. I took a break, came back to the images again, hoping a different viewpoint might help me remember more, but it was useless.

I began reviewing the rest of the files, starting with Harris's autopsy. The report showed that he'd been shot twice, once through the torso from behind and once more at closer range in the back of the head, which was consistent with the blood spatter evidence at the scene. Either shot would likely have proved fatal without medical treatment. The estimated time of death was around 8 to 10 pm, lining up well enough with the emergency call made from the mall at 21:04. As for me, the hospital were able to provide clear evidence from their examination that I had received a hefty tasering and then presumably fallen. There was a clear match between a bloodstain on the server racking and my head injury.

Ballistic tests proved that the murder weapon was indeed the gun that was found near my hand, and there were some partial fingerprints resembling mine on the handgrip and trigger. I was relieved to see that there were no corresponding prints on the magazine or shell casings. The evidence was a lot less definitive than the police implied, and my suggestion that the pistol could have been placed in my hand was at least partially upheld by the report.

More fingerprint samples were collected but it would take time to eliminate all the possible employees with legitimate access to the room. Partial prints from Harris were certainly present, most clearly on the extinguisher. I hoped that there might be some shoe impressions that would offer more insight as well, but it wasn't to be. There were traces, but the majority were from the emergency responders, which left the scene too confused for an easy analysis. Part of the problem was that the approach corridors were kept clean, and the server room was so deep into the building that any dirt or dust from the outside would have been left behind en route.

What was not there was almost more interesting. Despite a painstaking search by the police my stun gun and 'pad were still missing, though I wasn't sure if they attached as much significance to that as I did. The specific drone that had reported the shooting and requested medical assistance was also absent. It had definitely been there when the police first arrived, but sometime in the course of them dealing with my injuries and the body of Harris it had gone off somewhere, perhaps to recharge its power.

Any hope that we would learn more of the first murder from Harris's investigations was quickly deflated when the techs took a look at the mall's computer. Sometime around 20:30 an aggressive virus had been released on the mainframe, which had thoroughly compromised the majority of the system as well as the local network and off-sight back up.

I couldn't believe it was just a coincidence. Harris had obviously found evidence of something in the system files before they'd been erased, and it was no stretch to imagine that he'd been killed to conceal it.

> Reznik

The penthouse balcony was bright like a new moon, a spot of brilliant illumination in the night sky. Reznik watched as the party flared into life, the early guests ignored by all but the staff and each other before the real social stars arrived, their gravitational wake pulling lesser bodies along into their more eccentric orbits. Lagorio himself had only just put in an appearance, but there was no sign of Polzin yet. That should change soon enough.

Reznik had one eye firmly up against the padded end of the scope, the other closed. He was almost primed to fire, and had the wind telemetry and targeting data from the spotter drones patched into his right eye display. His left showed camera feeds from the main RPV in a small window and simple text updates from Santos. The construction drones were all in flight now from the building site opposite, their navigation lights switched off and motors running with just enough power to ride the winds but keep their emissions low. A few minutes more and they would be in position. It was a small slice of the wait he had already endured.

It was a genuine shame Jakobsen would miss this. He'd taken the death of Frost, and especially Tsukino, pretty hard. The three of them had been a team long before Reznik had known them, and would have gone on working together in all likelihood. Jakobsen was convinced Polzin was responsible and had burned to revenge them. Maybe if he had been here in town he'd have avoided the accident that killed him, but it was his own fault that he couldn't be.

Now that most of the guests had arrived, the musicians over on the balcony had played a couple of slower tunes by arrangement, the lighting effects growing more subdued and intimate in response. The sudden explosion of fireworks that followed came as a surprise to the guests, though he'd been expecting something similar from Espina's intel. It was curious to watch them as they mingled, chatted, and danced while a brave few were already making use of the large pool. His sight inevitably fell momentarily on many different targets as they moved through his scope, but he hadn't the slightest urge to fire. Even Polzin's death would bring more of a sense of completion than anything else, and if it hadn't suited Murdoch, he wouldn't be here at all.

It was time.

Santos had sent the signal that everything was in place, and he gave the order to proceed. Across from the smaller seaward balcony at the front of the building one of the larger construction drones suddenly turned on its spotlights and moved forward. Jakobsen had fitted a wide aperture laser scanner to the robot and modified it to give a more lurid visible light. This now came into vivid life, sweeping across a wide portion of the balcony in a red-hued arc, causing the guests there to cover their eyes. Many of them began moving back into the apartment, but this turned into a faster, more frantic surge when Santos activated the drone's arc welders to give off spitting tails of sparks.

Lagorio's armed security team arrived then, their guns held aloft, and began pushing aggressively through the flow of people trying to come back inside. When they reached the balcony the vivid lights caused them to cover their own eyes, peeking out to fire wildly at the drone. In response, Santos gunned the motors and drove the robot faster toward the penthouse. Reznik watched the camera view from the front of the drone and the rapid zoom of the view as it rushed forward, ending in a satisfying burst of static.

As the panic at the front of the penthouse rippled through to the larger patio at the back there were various reactions. Security and uniformed staff began to move first, fingers at earpieces straining for an explanation, just before the guests also began to realise there was a problem. When the shooting started a more hysterical note arose, the noises causing the band to falter, distracted by the sudden alarm. Guests in the pool were either scrambling out in panic or moving to the centre as others lost their footing and fell in, slipping on tiles suddenly made wet in the frenzy. Some of the staff began urging the crowd to retreat away to the edge of the patio, while security guards turned around to open fire through the doors at the big drone, which had continued forward into the apartment, lights and welders still ablaze.

Reznik saw Polzin then, the wide-angle view of the spotter drones scanning the crowd with facial recognition software for that one target. He scoped her amidst a clump of guests, their combined energy forcing her forward even as she tried to draw away from the edge of the patio, her instincts sharper than the crowd's. There were too many heads and outstretched limbs in the way for a clear shot, and he had to hold, lips drawn into a tight line of concentration.

Santos reacted as planned to the developing scene, but with a finesse that surprised Reznik. The remainder of the RPVs had moved in close now, and they suddenly accelerated noisily, up and over the heads of the partygoers, angry spots of light from lasers flickering randomly over the guests as though searching for targets. Santos started to herd the guests into smaller, straggling groups and Reznik saw his chance.

Polzin had forced her way to the outer edge of the crowd, peeling away as one of the drones herded them in the opposite direction. In seconds Reznik had the sights on her even as he drew in and held a breath. She stayed obediently in place as she turned her head this way and that, looking for the purest path away. He exhaled and fired in that moment of false calm.

The sudden glare through the scope made him blink and recoil back from the gun. A terrific explosion ripped across the patio, an expanding ball of hot gas and flame pushing on past the balcony edge and into the night. The noise was perfectly audible over the distance, and he fancied he could even feel the shockwave, though he knew that was unlikely.

Pausing for precious seconds, stunned, his eyes were unable to escape the sight of panicked guests thrown bodily from the balcony by the explosion, while others scrambled to dive into the pool, desperate to escape the flames and flying debris.

> Cara

Her house *aigent* kept a log, of everything, always.

It recorded her return, and the hours that passed. There was a single visitor, Miss Emma Benita Womak, who called at 19:32:25 and stayed for 37 minutes and 17 seconds. Miss Womak delivered a pharmaceutical product, details unknown. The two persons exchanged occasional physical contact, and conversed. There were no other visitors and no calls, inward or out, and additionally no internet activity except for approved devices checking for software updates.

As night fell the AI turned the lights on at the usual settings, but swiftly dimmed them when Miss Dalca swore at it. The heating came on and was then reduced gradually as the evening progressed, only for it to be scaled back up past midnight when it was clear her body would ignore the subtle cues that it had been programmed to employ.

The *aigent* faithfully recorded her actions, noting the break of pattern and routine, but the call it might have placed to a support service to seek assistance had been prevented by user preference months ago.

It observed instead, silent and impotent.

The Wolf was down to the last of his electronic decoys, an ECM package designed to emit false signals to confuse enemy sensors and draw off pursuit. He'd used a couple already, when the level of activity near him had grown too intense, and they'd done a fine job so far. They were new tech, still in R&D, so he'd had to steal them. It was a shame that he wouldn't really be able to report back on the results, as they couldn't possibly have had a better field test.

The mission itself had gone well. He'd been on his way out when the alarm went off and it had been a foot race after that. With the comms and tacnet offline he'd no way of checking how the others had fared, but he'd seen more than enough of these situations to know their chances weren't great. As far as his employer were concerned they were expendable, and he didn't feel any differently.

- Sixteen -

> Chase

I awoke to find that the secrets we'd worked so hard to uncover were all over the front pages: that Jakobsen had been living as Grant, until his murder in the mall. Claims of newly discovered video, very likely a merging of the photos released by Cadejo onto one of the better clips from a bystander, were trending on YuTu just as the news channels were featuring the story prominently.

There wasn't, in fact, all that much substance to the stories, but perhaps that didn't matter. Alongside file pictures of Jakobsen, and some details of his dual identities, was a statement concerning Harris. The reporter quoted information provided by 'a source' that Harris was likely involved somehow in the murder of Jakobsen/Grant and that he had in turn been fatally injured whilst resisting arrest in circumstances that were themselves subject to further investigation. My first reaction was relief that I'd not been mentioned directly, but then I became angry with the way the case was being presented.

When Roberts and Williams came to visit later in the morning it was only a small surprise. The two detectives were there to request that I accompany them to visit a specialist consultant, who'd give a second opinion on my head injury, and then hopefully try some techniques to stimulate memory recovery. Once Roberts had made his request a CSS paralegal they'd brought along, Duval, spoke up to confirm that the company were keen for me to cooperate. She was no more than an acquaintance, but had a decent enough reputation as far as I knew. I'd little choice except to go along with it.

Once we got there the examination itself took just under forty minutes. I was in a hospital gown throughout and inevitably felt uncomfortable and exposed. The fact that we were all crowded around the monitors looking at live scans of the insides of my skull was probably another reason. The results were promising, according to the consultant. The treatment I'd received in the early hours of Sunday had reduced the worst effects of the concussion successfully, and as a result I was doing very nicely.

His own tests and diagnosis complete, he then explained that I would be hooked up to a sophisticated VR program for a couple of hours that was designed to stimulate memory recovery. There was no explanation of how it worked, but it was supposed to be perfectly safe.

Once the program was running I lost all sense of time and place. A series of short animations, mostly at least quirky if not a little silly, were projected in a roughly central window, whilst in the background a rapid fluttering of colours flowed through while soft chimes of different pitches and durations sounded from all directions. Subjectively the space inside the program was cavernous, and there were some strange smells emanating from the equipment as well, which I presumed was intentional.

After a time the program wound down and stopped just before I felt the headset being removed. Duval and a bored looking Williams were still there, but Roberts had gone. I didn't really feel any different, and the consultant said there wouldn't be an immediate reaction.

While another short round of tests were run Williams excused herself, giving me an opportunity to speak to Duval in relative privacy. She explained that Harris himself was under suspicion, now that they'd discovered he had a hidden bank account into which a series of large payments had been made. They'd also established, as best they could, that the viral attack on the mall's systems had originated from the server room console. CSS obviously had no idea there'd been anyone else present, and I still only had a partial memory myself.

Duval was pleasant enough, and it felt as though we were building some rapport, which only made her next remarks all the harder to hear. Williams had returned and we were all on our way out of the clinic, when Duval stopped in mid-stride, her expression growing pained. "It's Iyer, she wants me to let you know you're on formal suspension pending the completion of internal enquiries. In the meantime you are to cooperate fully with the ongoing police investigation, and inform CSS of any developments. I'm sorry."

I was stunned, even though I knew there was some evidence against me. Williams didn't bother to hide her satisfaction, though Duval did at least looked chagrined as she asked for my Cadejo warrant card. Perhaps Iyer had no choice, but it still felt like a kick in the head.

> Reznik

For the first few seconds it was impossible to do anything but stare as he absorbed the reality of the explosion. It billowed with a shocking brightness into the night sky as the spotter drone continued to feed him confused, fluctuating readings straight to his optics. His reverie broke as Santos swore loudly into his ear through the comms.

Scrambling to his feet Reznik ran into the wind, straight for the inner edge of the roof. The ghillie suit and rifle, which moments before had been valued tools, were now immediate problems. Cutting across the boy's stream of invective with a terse command to 'Move!' he otherwise ignored him. Practiced hands broke the rifle down into smaller pieces, confident and quick despite his haste, as his eyes flickered around, looking for threats. The stripped rifle parts all went into a holdall, which he closed with a fierce pull of the zipper. As soon as he let go of the bag he moved to strip off the ghillie. Reznik continued to scan the horizon all about as he removed the suit, stripping down to the ordinary clothes he wore beneath.

In the distance he could hear helicopters growing nearer, sirens and excited cries. That he had been compromised, perhaps betrayed, screamed through his veins like fear. The boy would have been his first suspect, except that the continuous creativity and passion of his monologue made it seem unlikely. Reznik crammed the ghillie into a thick padded bag and then sealed the neck, pulling a D-ring on the front as he set it down. A sharp chemical tang stung him almost immediately, making him wince.

At the side of the roof was a coil of slick black rope, one end bolted into the concrete, and a strap harness. He quickly donned the webbing, attached the rope and then threw the loose length over into the darkness. One of the helicopters was fearsomely close now. Swiftly he grabbed the holdall and pulled his arms through the handles, the hard weight of the rifle pieces slamming and settling awkwardly against his back as he scrambled to the edge of the roof and turned around. For a moment he hung there, testing the line with his bodyweight while his toes rested on the lip, suspended in time and place. He could feel the void behind, the nothingness of the empty air at his back and the wind, gaining in ferocity, buffeting and pushing.

Then he stepped off, falling into the darkness just as the piercing spotlights of the rapidly approaching helo stabbed aggressively for the rooftop, its rotors stirring the air like an avatar of anger.

> Cara

Her *aigent* woke her with a grating alarm tone. The police were here.

Cara felt musty, still dressed in the clothes she'd collapsed in yesterday. There'd been no desire to sleep on her part, but evidently her body had plans of its own and she'd dropped off in the small hours, curled up tight on the couch, barricaded by cushions. She pushed a hand through her already scruffy hair as she moved foggily through the flat.

Opening the door sharply, Cara thrust her head out at her visitors, only to be momentarily fazed by the brightness of another day. On the small landing stood a uniformed policewoman, her face so-serious. Another woman stood behind, presumably a detective, striking in a skinny charcoal suit. On reflection, she might be a journalist, or something in the media.

"Miss Dalca? We're with the police, may we come in?"

The words Liaison Officer Burns had spoken so patiently, in her soft, calming voice, assembled themselves into an understandable form over the rest of the day, until Cara felt she had finally grasped it all. The main fact of the matter, the news she had expected but hoped against, had been plain as soon as the officer came into the flat and acted deferentially and politely. Her last experience with the police had been hard and distinctly unpleasant, but she would much prefer more of that to this.

Ethan really was dead. And he wasn't really Ethan.

It was at the coroner's that she could finally add the unrelated pieces together: the YuTu footage of a man falling through the Acrobots at the mall that went viral last week; the lack of fresh news; Ethan's absence and unresponsiveness. Officer Burns had taken her to the morgue for a formal identification of the deceased. It was best to get these things over with, Burns said, and there was no one else who could do it.

Ethan was already in place in the room next door when they entered the viewing area. An official stood behind the glass like a dour conjurer, poised to remove the large white sheet covering the body and reveal the mystery. As he did, she was confused and a little shocked: Ethan had been placed face down, with a smaller cloth still covering his head and shoulders. The conjurer picked up a video camera and began to scan over the back of the body, moving to the side as he did so to allow Cara full view of the large TV monitor behind him. His hands holding the camera traced slowly along Ethan's torso, lightly following the lines of his tattoos, just as she had done so many times. She could just make out her own pale, hollow-eyed reflection on the surface of the glass.

That had been an hour ago. Cara was sat in a police interview suite now, Burns to her side and in front a uniformed officer and the detective; Mallory she'd said she was called. Mallory had been with them all the while, most of the time in the background, barely saying anything, like a silent shadow.

There were apologies first. Officer Burns had been wary when she had entered the flat earlier in the day, wanted to know if Cara had seen any news reports, but of course she hadn't, them waking her after a bad night's sleep. It made more sense now, as Burns explained there'd been a mistake, that a press release intended for later in the day had gone out early, before they'd had chance to speak to her.

Pleasantries over, Mallory suddenly had plenty to say, only it was mostly questions, not answers. Cara responded as best as she could. She felt she really knew Ethan, the core of him, but the detective's probing cast a different light on her memories, twisting and turning them to new angles, revealing darker shadows at odds with her own recollections. Mallory wasn't unpleasant – far from it – and her questions were worded with care, but it was hard to not to be hurt by the holes she tore through Cara's image of Ethan. That he was someone else, in a way, he'd said himself, but the police seemed more interested in that other man than hers. Perhaps it made no sense to them either that Ethan should be killed, but this other Ethan, this Karl Jakobsen, was different. Maybe he was the sort of someone that was killed for reason rather than from random chance.

No, she didn't know anything about Karl Jakobsen, and she'd never heard of him until that day.

Jakobsen was Norwegian. He had an older sister, with her own small family, but no one else. Both his parents were dead, the father fairly recently and his mother long ago. As Ethan Grant, he'd claimed to have even less than that, a childhood in foster care, passed from one family to another, with none of his own surviving. Whatever he did have was hers by last will and testament, apparently. That was how they'd found her, the police, and determined she knew him well enough to identify his corpse. The sister had refused to come over to perform the duty, but had insisted the body be returned home as soon as possible. He would be buried all over again, in the same cemetery where he had been laid to rest in absentia, amongst family plots and ancient headstones.

The interview seemed to drag on forever. It felt as though she were in some old black and white film, the dialogue scratchy and remote, as the black-uniformed police questioned her in the white room under white lights. She wanted to believe this was all some awful mistake.

Frost was targeting two points in the middle distance, firing short controlled bursts from her assault rifle whenever a drone presented itself. She had the IyZon up trying to see everywhere at once, professional paranoia screaming through her that the real attack would be from some other angle. When The Wolf dove over the ridge directly ahead Frost had her sights halfway toward him before she recognised his silhouette.

He ran almost straight toward her position, though whether by design or chance she'd no idea. Frost hunkered harder into the stock of her gun and braced to fire. She was too hurt to escape on her own, but she could damn well help him, marveling as he crossed the terrain between them with a speed and haphazard precision she could only envy. Hard behind him three hexapod drone tanks broke the ridge. She targeted bursts between two of them and was sweeping over to the third when it exploded into shreds, one of their last remaining gun pods finding a target. Frost grinned at that and switched aim again. She never felt the shot that killed her, a burst grenade cold-launched from an aerial drone.

The Wolf ran on, slowing just a little as he passed her broken body.

- Seventeen -

> Chase

When I got back to the flat I was barely through the door before the *aigent* was informing me there were new messages. It sounded a bit different, warmer with a cleaner diction, but it had probably just had a software update while I was out. Whatever, my mail could wait: I knew that it was important to stay positive, but I just didn't have the energy to push back the feelings of numb weariness right then, and the fierce headache that was beginning to build really didn't help matters.

Things had been hard enough while I was convalescing before, but at least then the way forward and the end goal were clear, and there were others to support me, however distant some of them were or became. This was a much darker place. I knew there was enough circumstantial evidence against me to give rise to serious questions, but the removal of back up and status by Cadejo made me feel entirely vulnerable to whatever the police did next.

Maybe she'd had little choice, but it was difficult to imagine that Iyer's dislike hadn't been a factor. Duval's feelings were much harder to fathom. She insisted on dropping me off back at the flat herself after we'd finished at the clinic, and on the way had made attempts at small talk which we'd both found a bit challenging. I think she had some sympathy for my situation, but she was too professional to be drawn into a discussion of the case.

The *aigent* chimed up again, interrupting my thoughts for a moment, until I told it to piss off. I'd slumped down on the chair, still with my coat on, and was all set to do nothing but stew for the next few hours.

I'd hoped there'd be some definite results from the treatment the specialist had given me, rather than just another bought of pain and discomfort, but I was to be disappointed. The consultant seemed to think there was no specific reason why my memories wouldn't return, and that the VR program should help, but he couldn't be certain. Because the results from the tests and scans that afternoon were in relation to my own medical status I'd been given a copy, so now I had the time I retrieved my smartpad and took a closer look.

In the scan images I could see indistinct traces of my cerebral implants as well as all the fascinating and complex layers of natural tissue. Though they were incredibly small, the bioelectronic enhancements I had were just visible as faint shadows in the scans, thin sheets of circuitry embedded on the inner and outer surfaces of the skull. There was a loom of ultrafine wires as well, some leading down in parallel to the spinal cord, while others branched off into even finer networks, all but invisible at this resolution. It had been some time since I'd last seen them, but they did look different from what I remembered. I couldn't be sure though, especially in my current state.

The *aigent* intruded yet again, and was beginning to be properly annoying. I thought my messages could wait, but it didn't seem to see it that way. Only one was of any importance, an 'Urgent' received from CSS. The email was from one of the generic corporate accounts rather than a specific user, and the originator had stripped out all the address and metadata. The only identification given was a name: the sender had called themselves my 'Secret Admirer'. I had no idea who they were, but when I read the rest of the message I was glad they'd been in touch.

Clipped onto an otherwise blank email were two attachments. The first was a case update, a summarised daily briefing file, while the other was a transcription or copy of an internal Cadejo discussion between Iyer and the regional office. I skimmed it and then read it again, more carefully, with growing anxiety. There was a chance that this was a hoax, but it didn't seem likely as the format and detail of the attached briefing file would have been hard to fake.

Neither Cadejo nor the police wanted the mall case to go unresolved much longer given the public interest and the media's insistence in blowing up a controversy about the intertwining of corporate and state interests. There was just enough of a suggestion in the evidence to imply that Harris may have been involved in some way with the death of Jakobsen, if only as an accomplice, and the investigation into his financials had revealed large, anonymous cash deposits made to a previously unknown bank account held in his name. Once that information was released Harris would look good enough as a suspect for the first murder. The fact that we weren't yet clear on how or why Jakobsen/Grant was killed – or even who he really was – seemed secondary to them.

They would try and keep the focus on Harris if they could, but if they needed another sacrificial victim to shift the media's focus I was right in the firing line. I was expendable, an officer just returned from medical leave and in a slightly questionable mental state. The fact that my long absence was as a result of injuries received in the line of duty just made it better, as they could paint me as a broken hero, reacting over aggressively in the heat of the moment to the sight of Harris obviously deleting key evidence from the mall mainframe. Perhaps in the confusion of the situation I'd misinterpreted his actions as threatening. No one could say any differently right now, least of all me.

There was a symmetry to it, a tight pattern, and all they'd need to do was spin the story fast enough and it would have a trajectory all of its own. Unless I could prove differently I'd be fucked.

> Reznik

He landed gently, knees bent to cushion the impact with the hard concrete of the plaza. The helo still buzzed around far above like a confused moth, fluttering and circling around the stark brightness of its own spotlights. With as much haste as he could Reznik detached the harness and strapping from the rope, stuffed it into the holdall, and moved swiftly away into the darker shadows in the hollow centre of the building.

Looking around, he was relieved to see that no one appeared to have noticed him. He could hear sirens in the distance growing in number and variety, and the shrieks and exclamations of an excited crowd of people gathering nearby. The base of the oval high-rise was punctuated with broad walkways in three or four places through from the surrounding streets, and he headed toward the one positioned furthest away from where he'd landed. He could see the back of the gathered crowd through one of the passages, entirely oblivious to him.

Escape and Evade. His attention now centred fully on his present difficulties: the fact that this was a heavily urbanised area, full of people and surveillance; and that he still carried the rifle, and also a handgun, concealed elsewhere on his person. He wasn't worried about cameras and remote surveillance so much as a physical search. There would be police everywhere.

Santos was still there in his ear, jabbering away, until Reznik finally got tired of it and told him to get the hell away and that this never happened. We were never here. All we know about this is what we see on the news. A few more curses, and his accomplice shut up.

The blast had happened only a few minutes ago and the images were still fixed very firmly in his mind, where perhaps they would always be. The bomb had been timed to coincide neatly with his own op, so either he'd be implicated directly by whoever had planted it, or the police would assume a connection on their own.

As far as he knew, only Santos and perhaps Araya were in a position to exploit the plans he'd made in such a way, unless the situation with Jakobsen was less neat than it appeared. Perhaps someone had reached him, and then staged an accident to cover themselves. Murdoch was another possibility, but he was aware of only the outline of the mission, and knew very little of the specific details, as they both preferred.

Reznik shook his head: there really wasn't time for this now. He had to focus on getting away from here to somewhere safe, and with any luck dump the rifle along the way. Once he was elsewhere he would have to lay low for a while, which should give him ample time to think things through – probably enough to tie himself thoroughly in knots. At least Polzin was finally dead. He was sure he'd hit her with his shot, and even if he hadn't the explosion would have done the job, but given the circumstances it was hard to take much satisfaction from it.

He continued onward, putting a couple of blocks between himself and the oval building, and was heading in the direction of the high-rise where they'd emplaced the construction drones earlier in the week. As he knew the building quite well it might be possible to find a way into the basement and steal a vehicle without too much fuss, ideally an older model with less security.

The boy screamed back into his ear: he had not been so easily dissuaded. "You used me, you bastard! I didn't sign up for this!"

"Me neither. Yeah, I used you a little, but not as much as you're thinking. What happened at the end was someone else, not me. I'm as burned by this as you are."

"I don't fucking believe you, you bastard! When I find you, I'm going to....."

"Now listen, little man. Right now....."

They talked across one another, neither fully listening, until another blast rocked the world, much closer this time, scattering glass to the sidewalk and showering Reznik. He ducked, jogged on a few yards, crunching along the paving, and then slowed to look back, dusting glass fragments from his hair with one hand as he craned his neck upward. The explosion had been high up in the building he'd been making for, if he had to guess around the same floor as the construction site where they'd hidden the drones. Smoke poured from a ragged tear in the mirror glass, the edges sharp and stabbing. Santos had gone dead in his ear.

> Cara

For the last half hour she'd let her mind drift while she had YuTu play the same images in an endless loop. In front of her, just beyond where her fingers rested, was a slip of paper from Officer Burns with the number for Jakobsen's sister in Norway written on it.

Emma had been brilliant, but she wished hard that Petre could be here. Em had dropped everything to meet her again, and had tried her best to lift the mood and distract Cara, though it was too hard a task in the end. She'd asked about the tablets she'd brought over, whether they were working yet? As for Petre, there was nothing he could do from inside a cell, and his sympathy would be a little limited considering he'd never even met Ethan or heard much about him.

Cara had read everything she could on the news, and watched a whole load of video clips. Most of them were endless reposts of the same information, recycled and remixed, heavily focused on the spectacle of Ethan's death rather than his life. Even now she had a hard time seeing him as the victim and there was far too little on why he'd been killed, nothing that spoke of his actions in those last few days between their parting and his fall. The reports seemed to suggest that with the death of the second man, John Harris, the police had lost their prime suspect, and that other factors in the case would make further discoveries difficult.

Cara watched the video he'd sent in the book again, looking for answers. There was nothing embedded in watermarks or metadata, no hidden messages or secret codes. She'd checked thoroughly, and then again. The Hollis biography itself was subjected to the same painstaking search for fresh insights, with the same lack of results. She looked at other things as well, every scrap of video she had of Ethan, every photo, until it all became so familiar she could see it with her eyes closed. For a few minutes she thought her flat's *aigent* might have some images as well, captured on its cameras, but he'd not been by in the week before their last date and the footage had been routinely deleted.

Would she, or could she, build an ArPer of Ethan? Several times already she'd caught herself asking the question. In the past she'd done so for clients with less data than she already had, but always with some reluctance. Generally, the more information available the more authentic the ArPer would seem. The alternative, building a digital personality from incomplete data, meant using so much off-the-shelf code that the result could feel far more artificial than intelligent. Now, though, she wasn't entirely sure she'd known him so well in the first place.

Perhaps there would be something at the warehouse, or in Ethan's flat? She'd only just learned about the industrial unit from Thorne, so there was no way of telling what she might find there. As for his flat, the last time she had been there she'd been more worried about what Ethan's reaction would be than anything else, but if she went back she might be able to find something on his computer that could tell her a lot about what he'd been doing. She supposed the police would have taken it, but she wouldn't know for sure if she didn't have a look.

> Schuler

The spyder cut through the traffic effortlessly, its hand-beaten panels reflecting the sun and envious glances alike, pure-petrol engine murmuring throatily as he shifted through the manual gears. His rear mirrors showed an ever-decreasing view of the mall arcing in the distance, clearly exposed on this side due to the more modest profile of the buildings it had colonised.

As he drove further away he felt lighter, almost joyous. The afternoon sun, the smell of warm leather and wood, and the exquisite sound of the auto-composer matching spontaneous music to the rich harmonic texture of the exhaust note all made his spirits lift. He could leave altogether soon, perhaps return to the villa if nothing else intruded.

It had taken a few days for the forensics team to complete their work, and he had thought it best to wait until they were nearly done before returning. In a way he was pleased to see the thoroughness they'd shown, trying to make sense of the scene he left them with. It spoke of their professionalism and concern for a colleague, which he could only respect. In the end though, they had run out of nooks and crannies to examine and grids to walk.

The key things they needed they would never find, because they were no longer there. To make up for it a little he'd left them a small gift, which he hoped they would discover soon. It wasn't quite in its original condition, but it would take them at least a little while to realise that. In the meantime, the conclusions they would jump to would confuse their investigation no end.

When the complex finally went up The Wolf was running at such a speed over the patchy ground he needed most of his concentration to plot where his feet were falling. All the same, once he'd crested the next large ridge he felt obliged to slow and slide down, scrambling back up to look behind. A secondary explosion made the sky flash again moments later.

The target was well and truly aflame, the high-powered incendiaries he'd planted ripping through the main structures. He could see as he zoomed in that the satellite aerials in the far corner were silhouetted nicely against the flickering light and still looked intact. He smiled a grim smile of satisfaction. If things were happening as predicted the main AI would be sending a copy of its core data as an emergency backup to the next facility in the chain, unintentionally taking the worm he'd planted on the server along for the ride.

- Eighteen -

> Chase

As soon as I'd begun to fully absorb the implications of the Cadejo email I'd had to get out of the flat. It began to feel claustrophobic of a sudden, as though the room had shrunk in that single instant, pressing and pushing on all sides. Apart from a few personal things, and some money, everything seemed to come with the job: the flat, the car and much of the hardware I used every day. I really didn't want to think about the implications of losing everything, and especially what would happen in regard to the implants I was carrying in my head. That I wanted to think about least of all.

I made for the busier, more touristy places in the city centre, tried my best to zone it all out by moving between bars with everyone else, thought about ringing a couple of mates but realising I preferred the solitude of being amongst absolute strangers. It was late when I finally returned home, just a little drunk, and I got my head straight down. Sleep never really came, and I dozed and woke again often, far too aware of the time crawling along in the dark. I was up and out of the place again by seven, with no real plan at first for the day ahead.

After a long, meandering route on buses and the underground I found myself back near the centre again. It hadn't been intentional exactly, but I'd gone off the grid, as best I could, making all my journeys on public transport, losing myself amongst the crowd. I'd picked up a few items as I went, bits and pieces here and there, paying using different cards each time and cash whenever possible. It had been an expensive few hours, but I had pretty much everything I would need now.

The same set of instincts I was running on had made me search out a place I associated with a more lo-fi, low tech reality, an old second hand book shop tucked away in a back street. I'd been there a couple of times with Jo, when things were good, but that felt long ago now. The business had changed hands, the gentle ambience of the place somehow wafting out of the door on the heels of the previous owner. It still had its little café though, and plenty of spare tables.

In front of me on the dark-wood surface was a small selection of security and surveillance devices, as well as a couple of disposable phones and a compact smartpad. None of the gear was as good as the stuff CSS had issued, but it at least had the advantage of being unregistered and anonymous, so I could get on with the things I needed to do. I made a few minor modifications to some of the kit, mostly just software and settings changes, using instructions I'd found online on a couple of hacktivist sites. Strange company to be keeping, even remotely.

I also took some time to skim through the briefing file my Admirer had sent me along with the copy of Iyer's emails. From the look of things, there did seem to be some weight to the suggestion that Harris had been paid large sums of money from an unidentified source, but that wasn't proof he'd known anything about it. There were no withdrawals recorded, just deposits, so in theory the account could have been set up without his knowledge. As for the Jakobsen case, there were some details regarding a woman, Cara Dalca, who appeared to be a girlfriend or partner of Jakobsen's. Mallory had accompanied the uniformed support officer when she broke the news of his death to Dalca, and from there to the coroner and a police station. From Mallory's notes and the transcript of the interview it seemed that Dalca had no more knowledge of what Jakobsen was up to than we did: though it was certain they had a relationship she knew him as Ethan Grant.

I'd stayed at the book shop a little longer than I should have, but there was no sign of anyone waiting for me as I left. Unless I took the most rigorous precautions they would find me eventually if they really cared to look, so my attempts at evasion may have only a limited effect in the end. It would be so easy to just give up, go back home, let the self-doubt dictate things and just sit this one out while the formal investigation took its course, but if I did that and didn't help myself it felt like there was no one else who would.

Harris deserved better as well. I was sure he was a victim in this, but I seemed to be the only one who saw it that way. Maybe there was some circumstantial evidence that pointed in his direction, but I was far from convinced he was guilty of anything. Besides, he must have been killed for a reason, and I was as sure as I could be that I'd not done it, which meant someone else definitely had.

> Reznik

"Fuck, did you see that?" Santos again. Evidently the boy hadn't been positioned too close to the second blast after all. Either way, he'd had enough of the boy's scatology this evening and promptly disconnected the comms link, unpeeling it from his ear and pulling the plug as he walked. It went into a pocket on his jacket where it would be less conspicuous.

Reznik was already moving away from the second bomb site at a brisk pace, not stopping to see whether his estimation that their staging area had been destroyed was correct or not. No doubt this whole thing would be all over the media now and stay there for days, so he could check the details later. Smoke still belched from the jagged tear in the high-rise, blotting out the starlight and rendering the place even darker.

There was no ready explanation he could think of right now that would explain what was going on, but from the surface pattern of it he suspected that he was about to be made a scapegoat for the murder of some of the city's most prominent citizens. He briefly considered the possibility that Santos and he were the actual focus of the attacks, but it seemed unlikely. The bomber appeared to have detailed knowledge of their plans, so if they were the targets they'd already be dead. He wondered at what stage he might be publicly identified as the bomber, and hoped there would be at least a few hours yet.

As he walked along, the emergency services began to respond to the second explosion. First there was a police car, then another, and finally ambulances and fire crews. The different sirens and flashing displays warred with the sound of the panicked crowds and helicopters. Their response was slower than normal, but this was the second major incident in the same night. Reznik hoped fervently there would not be a third.

Up ahead a refuse truck was parked at the kerbside, its orange lights a softer version of the emergency vehicles further up the street. The operator was across on the other side of the road, his reflective-patched overalls marking his profession as he stood with a crowd of onlookers watching the fires. The robot refuse workers were clustered around the truck, idling as they awaited more instructions. It was a trivial matter for Reznik to weave between them and throw the holdall and then the radio into the compactor at the back, deep amongst the garbage. It sounded as though the truck was fairly empty, so hopefully they were close to the beginning of their rounds, meaning it might be a few hours before the weapon was discovered.

Reznik continued onward, his step lighter now the weight of the rifle was gone. He recalled that if he were to cross the road in a few yards he was close to where a number of narrower side streets intersected with this one, which would give him more options for moving away from the area. The streetlights were less numerous over the other side as well, which improved his chance of staying out of sight.

He waited for another police car to pass, this one an unmarked SUV with concealed lights flashing in the grille, and then crossed the road where it was darkest, the shadows welcoming him into their depths.

> Cara

Ethan's front door was sealed with a chequered blue and white membrane stretched across the frame, with a few lines of more familiar 'POLICE' tape strung over the top for good measure. It had made her pause at first, but no longer. Bending down she attached a short lead running from a battered looking smartpad to a port set into the edge of the seal. A couple of finger taps later and the membrane deflated, losing its rigidity to become more pliable, allowing Cara to easily lift it from the doorframe and set it to one side.

The hacking device was on loan, strictly temporary, and only offered after she'd begged more than a few old contacts and laid out a major favour or two. It wasn't that the help was resented, more that bad word travelled faster than good will, and nobody wanted to implicate themselves in a murder enquiry. She had expected at first that collecting the device would be as awkward as arranging to borrow it, but had been surprised to learn that this last part would be easy. All she'd had to do was drive out of her apartment complex last night after 8pm and wait at the kerbside. One from the group of cowled figures that habitually loitered around outside came over to the car and handed her the device, and she now had until this evening to return it by the same method. Whether the contact was part of the usual bunch or not she couldn't tell.

There was no sense in wasting any of that time, so Cara was here first thing. Using it at night would have been preferable, but there'd been a police car outside his flat when she'd driven by around midnight and then again 40 minutes later, so she'd left it until today to come back. Cara inserted the key and went inside.

"Good morning, Miss Dalca." The flat's *aigent* sounded pleased to see her, as though it had gotten lonely over the last few days.

"Morning. Have there been any messages or visitors?"

"No messages of note. The police have been here along with forensic support teams. The door had been sealed to deter further visitors."

"Sorry about that."

"No apology necessary, Miss Dalca."

Apart from feeling even colder than it was on her last visit, the flat appeared largely the same. She made straight for the desk area in the lounge, and found that all the computer and smart devices were missing. That was disappointing, but probably inevitable. From her own experience she knew that people used data services so frequently and consistently that they left significant clusters and trails of personal information in their wake and on the devices themselves, so it was no surprise the police would want them.

She had a look around the rest of the room, with the freshest eyes she could muster. There were no photos anywhere, as usual. Cara couldn't help but wonder how much anyone had meant to him: how much she had meant to him. It had always seemed a little strange, sad even, but Ethan had just shrugged and said that was just how he was. In their time together she'd only briefly met a couple of Ethan's friends, and she thought he'd no surviving family after his sister supposedly died.

When Cara was done in the lounge she went and sat down on the edge of the bed they'd shared more times than she cared to think about. Usually he'd stayed over at her place, but she'd been here often enough. There was a small holdall lying on the bed, partly unzipped, that she was sure was at the bottom of the wardrobe when she'd last been there. Presumably, the police had found it and left it there. Some of the bag's small outer pockets were unzipped and empty, but otherwise it was packed full with essential toiletries and other bits and pieces you might take on a short stay somewhere, including a couple of changes of clothes. On top was the oatmeal sweater he'd worn in the video. She grabbed it, sat on the bed, and then dropped backward onto the covers.

Cara lay there, staring at the ceiling, holding the sweater tight as the bag nudged her hips. She wasn't sure if the dull sense of confusion and emotional detachment she was experiencing was how she was supposed to feel, or whether the pills Emma had given her were already taking the edge off things, in which case she might have felt even worse. They were a common anti-depressant rather than a gene-tailored type, so Em hadn't needed to collect her pharmacard first.

It was perhaps fifteen minutes later when the *aigent* enquired whether she would be staying long. She sighed and sat up, pushing the bag away as it fell further toward her. Time to go. Cara was almost at the door on her way out when she stopped, turning to address the AI. "House, I presume you'll have logged my visit as standard?"

"Yes", there was the briefest of pauses, "as standard."

"Is there any chance I could persuade you to delete that record?"

"No need. Mr. Grant's standing instructions are that your visits are not to be recorded."

"What? You've no log of the times I've been here? Why would he do that?"

"Unknown. Mr. Grant installed a number of system upgrades and non-standard protocols."

Cara didn't know whether to be hurt or elated, and in fact felt a little of each. It seemed that there was one other person who was to receive unusual treatment, a man identified by only a single grainy photo. In his case the instructions were reversed, as the *aigent* was to record and upload every detail of any visits he made. She heard a catch in the AI's voice as it explained all this, a brief hesitation that suggested to Cara it was holding something back.

"House, what is it? Were there any further instructions?"

There was another, longer pause while the *aigent* formulated its reply.

"Miss Dalca, a small package was left for the other individual, located in the freezer compartment of the refrigerator. Bottom drawer, at the back."

This was getting weirder. A quick search turned up a small plastic zip bag, which contained two keys, about the size and shape for a locker or padlock. There was no note, or any indication what they would open, but she guessed they might be something to do with the warehouse she'd learned about from Thorne. Unfortunately, the AI knew nothing more and could offer no help.

Cara realised she had been there long enough, but as she moved toward the door another thought occurred to her, and she turned back: "House, what about footage of Ethan? Do you have much?"

"Yes. There are a number of cameras installed throughout the residency, and multiple images of Mr. Grant have been retained as per standard parameters. May I ask why?"

"Because I'm thinking of building an ArPer, and I need all the data I can get."

There was a quiet, a longer pause before the AI replied. "I am obligated to provide any and all assistance to authorised persons, Miss Dalca, but if I may be so bold please reconsider. Please don't build an Artificial of Mr. Grant."

That unsettled her, and she left the flat as soon as she could, wondering what to make of it. She took the files of Ethan anyway, along with the descriptive details of the man the *aigent* had been set to watch for. On the way out she replaced the membrane and resealed it, watching as it firmed up almost instantly before reattaching the Police tape as best she could.

If there'd been anything more to learn here she hadn't seen it. Ethan's place was so devoid of mementoes or personal things that there was little of him there. The only place she could go now was the lockup. Logically, it could tell her more about any work or other activity Ethan was mixed up in.

As she walked away from the flat a police car pulled onto the estate, cruising along and parking up nearby. She forced herself to act calmly and carry on without fuss, reaching her own vehicle and climbing inside just as the police car pulled to a final stop. Once she was settled into the seat Cara punched the 'Home' key and leant back, grateful for the way that the autopilot moved off smoothly. As the car left the estate for the main road she couldn't help but watch in the rear-view nervously, worried that the police would move off again to follow.

The screen readouts were giving him so little that Jakobsen had resorted to climbing up the hill behind the pillbox and looking out toward the north and east, swapping his own eyes for the dormant tacnet. Whoever survived out there would most likely make for his position on their way out, and he ached to see someone. It had been a little while since he'd heard any gunfire, and he feared the worst.

Although the plan had called for it the vivid flash of the first explosion surprised him, making him turn and cover his eyes against the sudden light. Another came a few seconds later. It had to be the main complex. The sudden squawk of the comms system behind him was almost as much of a shock, the volume turned to the max for him to listen for any faint traces in the static. Sliding and scrambling down Jakobsen rushed into the pillbox, desperate for news.

- Nineteen -

> Chase

Jakobsen's partner, Cara Dalca, lived in a modest housing project, walled and gated. I needed to get inside, and soon. The police and CSS would have Jakobsen's flat locked down by now, but at this stage they probably weren't looking at Dalca too hard as a suspect so they wouldn't have searched or secured her place yet. I might just find something there that could get me a step ahead.

It would be better to have waited until darkness, but there didn't seem to be the time. Things went smoothly enough at first. The perimeter walls weren't so high, and I'd found a way in that someone else seemed to have prepared beforehand, using an old packing crate they'd left propped up against the outer wall behind some bushes. Over the other side the drop was away from any of the cameras, and the only thing of note there was a small graffito tagged on the brickwork.

Now I was in I needed to find a good spot close to her flat and out of camera view. I spent a tense few minutes moving between clumps of natural cover unintentionally provided by the gardeners until I got close enough. In broad daylight it probably looked more than a little ridiculous, and definitely suspicious, but I just had to hope no one would see me.

One of the things I'd bought earlier was a small, spider-like robot about the size of my hand. It was curled into a rough ball shape, its body and legs tucked in, and I rolled it across the lawn toward the flats. When the Spydar came to rest amongst a plant bed near the base of the building it quickly unfurled itself and climbed up along the wall and around the corner, following a rough set of instructions I'd punched in beforehand.

Now the Spydar was in range of her front door I checked again that no one was around, and that the car registered to Dalca wasn't there. The way looked clear, so I entered another string of commands, instructing the drone to enter the flat through the best means available and scurry up to ceiling height, avoiding any countermeasures or monitoring if possible. It would be unusual to find anything problematic in a domestic residence like this, but there was always a possibility that she had unusually good security in the flat itself. I'd updated the Spydar's firmware to make it quieter and reduce its electronic footprint, and with any luck the flat's *aigent* wouldn't even know it was there.

Once the drone began executing its instructions it moved quickly, going inside through the letter box and climbing up the wall too rapidly for me to get much more than a vague impression of the interior, until it came to rest moments later. It was clear then we were in the kitchen, a small, modestly decorated space, very much the typical layout for this kind of building. I could see nothing of obvious interest, and the Spydar had received no electronic query or handshake attempt from her *aigent*, so it appeared to have escaped detection.

The next room was an open-plan living area, with a small dining space flowing through into a lounge. Here the décor and furnishing was a little more distinctive, and she'd added some personal touches. There were three or four photos of Jakobsen, sometimes with Dalca in the frame and sometimes not, as well as pictures of a couple of other men, one older, and the other around her own age. A small solitary photo of a woman was positioned on its own in a clearer space. As the Spydar scanned the room further,

I could see a larger photo-wall to the side with a collage of images and on the dining table a laptop, folded down, with a hardback book beside it.

While the drone went off to search the rest of her flat, I had a look at the data it had already captured from the lounge. Checking her file, I could see that apart from the pictures of Jakobsen all the individual photos were of her immediate family; a mother long dead, father critically ill in hospital and a younger brother, currently in prison. I left the photo-wall for now, as it would take a surprising amount of effort to catalogue and cross-reference. The dining table area was more interesting. Next to the laptop was a note pad. The top sheet of paper had been written on, an address in the city.

Once it was finished with its sweep, I had the drone return. It was a modest flat so there were only three other rooms, including the bathroom and main bedroom. The third was a spare bedroom, which Dalca was using as an office. The workspace here was reasonably organised, with a much more substantial computer setup that was unfortunately powered down.

There'd been no obvious reaction to my intrusion, so it looked as though I'd gotten away with it. I'd have to go through all the footage the Spydar had gathered to try and pick out any useful info, but the address I'd grabbed from the note pad might be a good first step.

> Reznik

After he'd left the main arterial road and headed into the side streets Reznik made good progress, but a police cruiser with its sirens blaring was approaching from up ahead and he felt pressured into taking the next junction. He relaxed just a little as the cruiser went past the road end at speed, but then felt the tension of a new threat.

On the opposite of the street an SUV was parked up, engine running, a full row of roof and headlights flicking into life a few seconds after the cruiser sped by. Reznik blinked in the sudden brightness, but only for a split of a second, his vision adjusting automatically. Pressing on as casually as he could along the sidewalk, he made a show of ignoring the truck whilst keeping it firmly in view from the corner of his eye. That suddenly got a lot harder to do when the SUV rushed across the street straight toward him, its lights blindingly bright.

Bursting into motion Reznik made for the nearest corner, the speed of his reaction and acceleration catching the driver out. Even as he raced along the next street looking for immediate cover or another twist to take he heard the bulky vehicle squeal to a halt before reversing and skidding around in a tight turn. There was no immediate shelter, but he could see the dark mouth of a side alley across the way and he sprinted toward it. From behind he could hear the roar of the SUV's engine grow ever closer. It was almost on him when he dived toward the mouth of the alley, rolling messily to his feet on the grime-slick floor before righting himself and running on again. Behind him the SUV braked, screech-turned in reverse and then plunged along on his heels, one side of the wide vehicle sparking and grinding along the wall, rubbish squelching under its heavy tyres.

Reznik had his speed back and ran hard. The truck's blazing lights cast twisted, rapidly shifting shadows ahead, and in the sudden splash of illumination he saw a fire escape ladder flash into view. He leapt for it, slammed into it, and then climbed up as fast as he could, feet slippery on the rungs. Before he could make the first landing the SUV crashed into the ladder, the big vehicle's momentum tearing it loose on one side. Reznik almost fell back, slammed forward again, but held on, suspended in the air for a moment.

Scrambling upward he grabbed at the landing just as the ladder gave out and fell, clattering down onto the truck's roof. Hauling himself through the opening in the metal grid he scraped elbow and knee before rushing across the platform to the stairway that would take him upward. Below him he could hear the vehicle slide and crash into the wall, its angle askew, but even as it came to a forced stop the doors were opening, the nearest to the wall banging against it noisily.

Reznik ran up the rusty stairway, his footfall rattling its supports, as the truck's passengers moved to spread themselves in an arc at the opposite side of the alley. From there they began firing upwards toward him in short bursts, their muzzle flash vivid but narrow, suppressors damping down the sound to a sewing machine chatter. In the dark he wasn't the easiest target, and the metal framework of the fire escape was between him and his attackers, but even a stray round hitting might be enough. He ran on, reaching the rooftop just as the volume of fire lessened. Taking a quick glance down, he could see that at least two of them had climbed onto the roof of the SUV and were reaching for the lower landing.

He had to get out of sight and away. Now he'd reached the flat rooftop he looked around quickly for a route that would take him inside, either in this building or the next. There was nothing here though; just the hooked guiderails of a ladder and clumped blocks of service equipment, but there might be a way down through the adjacent property. He ran again, ignoring the twinge in his bruised hip, and leapt straight over the gap.

It was like flying, his perception stretching time until everything slowed to a smooth glide. Flowing toward him was the place where he must land, the outer edge of his leap and the next rooftop. Gracefully he hit the exact spot, rolling to soak his forward momentum and came to his feet again. A pause, and then he ran toward a small hut-like building that probably housed a stairwell leading inside.

His pursuers had reached the roof of the first building and rushed to the edge, firing as they did so. Reznik figured it would take a very good shot to hit him at this distance in the half-light, but that didn't make him safe. He'd run in a long curve as that was the easiest way and it gave him the advantage of passing behind air extractors and water tanks, their bulk and shadow between him and the gunmen. As he neared the head of the stairs he twisted his upper body slightly and lowered his shoulder, ready to charge the door with his full momentum. The wood splintered and cracked, resisted briefly, and then gave. He rushed inside, momentarily off-balance, then ran down the stairs.

> Cara

Cara had circled the block of units where Ethan's property stood once already, parked for five minutes and then circled it again before she finally pulled up outside. Partly it was sensible caution, but the rest was more to allay the tension and nervousness she felt. This appeared to be the best way to learn more though, to understand, and she badly needed that.

The outside of his lockup looked reassuringly dull and business-like. Ethan had hired an address that occupied a central space in a row of identical light industrial units on an estate full of the same. These were all high-roofed with large roller-shutter entrances with a more domestically sized door and windows to the side. Large white numbers and letters were stencilled on the exterior to help the lost. His was C4: if there were any significance in that, she failed to see it.

Cara tried to look inside through the windows but was frustrated by a thick layer of SunTrap sheeting spread over the glass. The side door was secured with a modern cardkey reader, whilst the roller-shutter was simply padlocked. She hoped the keys she'd found at Ethan's flat would allow her access.

Thinking to try the padlock first, Cara squatted down to take a look. As she examined it from close up it was clear that whilst it had been positioned to look as though it was locked it actually wasn't. Reaching out, Cara took hold of the brass-coloured body, twisting it to check the lock mechanism itself. It had been bored out, so neatly it might have been made that way. Frowning, Cara pulled the useless padlock free and straightened, looking around. There was no one there. She felt nervous, unsettled by the fact someone else must have been here.

Next, Cara tried the control box for the roller shutter, and was unsurprised to find that its padlock had also been bored out, just as cleanly as the first. Both locks were the about the right size for the keys she'd brought. Taking a deep breath, Cara pushed the button to raise the shutter up a few feet.

It was dark inside even with the shutter up part way and she had to take a moment to adjust before looking for a light switch. There was no sign anyone was there. Once the overheads had flickered on she took stock of Ethan's domain, unsure as to what, or who, she might find.

Not much at first. There was a small office space in the left corner nearest the front entrance, and she could see through the clear glass windows facing into the warehouse that it was full of roughly stacked office furniture and clutter. This was where the smaller exterior door and windows lead to, straight into the first of two rooms. Looking up she could see that the skylights in the high roof had also had a layer of SunTrap smoothed on, the panelling providing a flow of cheap electricity to the building at the expense of natural illumination. The back and side walls of the unit were all whitewashed brick and blocks, except for a large double-door at the rear.

Her footsteps echoed around the empty space as she walked around inspecting the place. The doors at the rear were both firmly barred and padlocked on the inside, and looked like they hadn't been moved for months. In the centre of the main space were two clumps of palletised boxes still part-wrapped in plastic, with a number of empty wooden pallets stacked against the walls in a couple of places. Examining the large boxes, lifting the half-open flaps on some, she found nothing but packing materials inside. The cardboard was mainly plain with not much hint at what they might have contained. Cara craned and tilted her head to try and decipher the shipping labels stuck haphazardly to the side, but these were mainly bar codes, strings of numbers and Chinese characters.

Over in the corner were two full-sized shipping containers, both a bit battered looking and from different freight companies. They were positioned tight against each other in a block, with no gap between, close by the right-hand wall, almost in line with the front roller door. Bloated power cables snaked heavily from industrial scale connectors on the exteriors, attaching to a large electrical board on the wall nearby. Whatever was going on in there it was set up to draw a lot of juice.

The doors of both containers were closed, but as Cara approached she noticed that the left-hand container's lock was on the floor, unattached. Pulling at the door lever with some force, expecting it to be stiff and heavy, she was surprised at how easily it opened. In front of her was a magnolia coloured metal panel filling almost the whole of the container, save for a gap of about three inches on all sides that was stuffed tightly with grey foam. It seemed that this was a second box nestled inside the container, isolated from the outer shell. Set into the magnolia panel was a plain metal door, normal sized, with a blank touchscreen beside it.

Cara knew from the look of the touch pad and the door itself that it would be difficult to get inside, and not without a certain amount of gear she didn't have. The pad display was blank, and to see if there was any power to it Cara reached out to place her fingertips gently on the surface. As soon as she did, the screen briefly cycled through a fingerprint and biometric analysis before changing to a steady green.

"Please state your name." The voice that issued from the lock panel was flat, lifeless, yet no less surprising. Cara replied truthfully, and grinned when the display briefly showed a sound wave analysis before turning green a second time.

The door clicked open with a solid thunk. Seconds later her phone pulsed behind her ear, letting her know there was a new message. Cara checked it, and found a sound file, a flat and digitised voice reading a random series of numbers and letters. It was too long and complex for her to remember, but it was saved to the memory, so she could easily retrieve it later. Cara paused there, nervous again, before reaching for the door handle and pulling.

The comms had come back online quickly when the jamming field shut down and he'd already had a terse conversation with The Wolf, after which Jakobsen began frantically repacking his kit while the tacnet rebooted. As soon it did he'd gone back outside, where he now stood firm, eyes flicking between the ground ahead and the display. All he could register were the blue dots on the screen giving the locations of Tsu and Frost, and the biometric indicators that showed they'd not be coming back.

Nearby, The Wolf was intent on leaving the area as quickly as possible. Up ahead was the ridge that sheltered the pillbox from the rest of the site. He felt rather than saw something streak right by at low level and dived to the ground in reaction. Whatever it was, it hit and exploded, right where he judged the bunker to be.

- Twenty -

> Chase

The note I'd found in Dalca's place ended up yielding so much background information I'd begun to feel like less of a shit for sneaking the Spydar in there, and I'd not even processed all the photos and other data I'd found yet. Now that I was safely back home the whole episode felt comfortably distant. I'd had to go back there to use my link to the CSS network, which mercifully was still active, and now I'd some work to do the atmosphere in the place seemed fresher, less oppressive. Despite still having the systems access it took a while to go through everything, but what I'd discovered made the effort more than worthwhile.

The address I'd retrieved from Dalca's notepad turned out to be a small warehouse that neither the police nor Cadejo seemed to be aware of yet. It was a mid-sized light industrial unit nestled among so many others of its kind, completely ordinary, but the financial structures behind it were a lot more interesting. The legal contractor for the property was a small startup, recently incorporated, but the chain of ownership soon got lost in a confusion of shell companies and paper entities. All the bills for rent and utilities were debited from a business account that was in turn seeded through cut-outs to an offshore bank I'd heard of but never personally encountered. The whole thing was set up with enough obfuscation to make any further enquiries time consuming and difficult, even with the use of the Cadejo AI. It would take more expertise than I had on my own to dig any deeper.

The professional activities listed openly under the Ethan Grant ID were a complete contrast. This was an area CSS had looked at thoroughly, and they'd found nothing unusual or suspicious. From that end of the investigation they'd not found any links back to the warehouse, which was kept isolated and off the radar as far as Jakobsen's public persona was concerned.

I couldn't tell yet what was going on, but it seemed pretty clear that Jakobsen was working with someone else given the complexity of the set up. The electricity bills indicated there'd been a fairly heavy usage at times, enough to run a significant amount of machinery or computer hardware. After cross-checking the data traffic levels the latter option looked more likely. The only way I could find out any more in the short term would be to a pay a visit to the address and have a look around.

I was considering the best way to approach that when the phone chimed. It was a message from my Admirer: they wanted to meet.

> Reznik

The building he'd ended up in was a residential hi-rise, low rent and run down, crammed full of small apartments running off endless dim corridors. He saw almost no one but heard much, through closed doors and around corners, people resolutely cocooned in their own lives and wilfully ignorant of their neighbours.

Reznik had no idea who his pursuers were. It was difficult in the half-light but he was sure there was no insignia or badge on their SUV or clothing, and they'd been wearing suits, not uniforms. They certainly hadn't called out a challenge before shooting, and in his experience cops wouldn't generally try to run you down like that. Whoever they were, they were well resourced and tactically aware, as they'd been able to lock the building down much quicker than he'd hoped.

For the last few minutes there'd been relative calm, but a sudden scream behind and around the corner, a woman, made him break into a run, aiming to reach the next stairwell before anything caught up with him. He barely stopped when he reached the door, cannoned through, grabbed the balustrade and swung around and down, feet rapid and regular as he headed for the lower floors.

A small drone dropped past him through the centre space of the stairwell, stopped somewhere below, hovering quietly. Before he had time to think about it he leant away, toward the wall, keeping as much of his momentum as he could. A snagwire grenade popped just behind him, the slight concussive wave nudging him even as tendrils of sticky polymer grabbed at his legs. He staggered, nearly fell, but continued downwards, pulling away, his feet almost skidding across the outer edge of each stair.

Pressing on, expecting another grenade, he tried to maintain his progress while he looked for an exit or counterattack. Ahead, just a few feet away, was the next door out of the stairwell and back into the corridors. He ran for it, ducked as a micro-flash exploded to the side, the sudden nova-burst punching his perceptions. Reznik staggered and fell forward, almost collapsing on his way through the door.

Grey moments, and then he tried to scramble back to his feet, limbs loose like rubber. He looked back to watch as the stairwell doors swung back into place: there was no sign of the little drone. Reznik figured it had nowhere near enough mass and power to push through after him, but it was small and agile and could find another way if he gave it time. He moved on, gaining speed and surer footing as he recovered.

The logical way out was down, so instead he'd gone back up. Perhaps it was the after effects of the stun grenade rattling his brain, but what was clear and obvious to him would be doubly so for them. He made his way up using an emergency ladder in the lift shaft, hoping the elevator wouldn't move. His luck held that far, but he'd been forced to exit on the top floor and that was when things got more complicated.

Either as a contingency or because they had guessed his intention the corridors up here had been seeded with a handful of the little drones. They were surveillance and non-lethal response models, but they were undoubtedly networked with whoever was out there looking for him and Reznik was alone, with no back up. At least he was carrying his handgun, and he supposed that at this stage there was no point in being coy about using it, though he did fit its suppressor.

From his reckoning, he had two long stretches of corridor to traverse and a couple of shorter ones before he reached the final set of stairs that would take him back up to the roof. He was already part way along the first long passage, moving as quietly as possible but with a moderate speed. Up ahead he caught a glimpse of the back segment of a drone just around the next corner. There was a wide alcove nearby, a couple of feet deep, and Reznik ducked into the corner for a moment while he considered his options. Seconds later he had to press in even tighter as one of the quadrotors flew lazily past from up ahead. He watched the drone speed away before ducking out quickly. There was nothing there and he continued onward, along and round the corner.

It was more shadowy in this part of the building, close by another, the scant moonlight blocked. He was half way along the corridor before he spotted them, two more of the drones rushing toward him, still silent and dark. His gun was up and firing, body twisting slightly, as he broke into a run.

The first of the two drones dropped as he hit it square, but the other avoided his aim and launched a micro-grenade. It overshot and fell behind, and his forward momentum took him further out of harm's way even as it detonated. He fired again, hit the drone as it drew closer. Ahead there was a sudden spill of light at the end of the corridor, a door opening, a human silhouette. Reznik aimed, fired once, then twice more. The target ahead tried to raise his gun, weirdly slow as though he was moving through water. Reznik ran forward, fired again until the man slid down, folding like a drunk, his torch spilling to the floor and skittering away as his legs began to kick.

Reznik closed up, squatted down, witnessed his victim's final slurred movements passively as death or unconsciousness took over and his bowels released. Checking quickly, Reznik found a little cash but no wallet or ID on the body, and definitely no badge.

Expecting more hostiles he pressed on, running up the stairs, taking cover against the corner wall at each turn to check the way ahead and then again at the top, rapidly surveying the roof from the mouth of the doorway. There was no one around and it looked as though he could make it across to the next building, a little further away but lower. Stashing his gun he walked out, turned and backed up. A pause, and then he ran, leapt and rolled, coming to rest in a spray of loose gravel on the next property. There were sounds of pursuit beginning to grow behind, and so he moved on sharply, using the rooftop cover and rapid evasion to its maximum.

Forty minutes later he was tired and aching, but he'd at least gotten back down to street level. It was late and the cloud cover had thickened, shielding the moon and reducing the light. His pursuers were probably still out there, but he'd had no sign of them in a while.

As he walked on, stepping a touch unevenly, he could hear a vehicle approaching, its engine older and less even than the deep roar of the SUV he'd run from earlier. A van pulled up just ahead, its lights dimmed and with the side door wide open. He tensed, expecting more trouble, but couldn't help feeling sheer relief as the two men he could see inside almost fell out of the van in their haste to beckon him over. Grinning, they shouted they'd been sent by Santos to pick him up. Both looked right, and he was too tired to overthink. He looked around briefly, then climbed straight in, dropping to his knees in fatigue. As soon as he was inside the van sped off, rattling him with inertia.

It took Reznik a moment or two to right himself, and when he did his expression switched sharply to weary hostility when he saw the guns pointed straight for his head.

> Cara

The security door swung open smoothly, despite its unexpected thickness. Solid bars, clearly part of the locking mechanism, had retracted into the door edge at intervals, four on the side and as she reached up to run her hand along the top she felt another two. This was serious security, and she wondered what it was doing there.

Lights had splashed into life inside as the door opened, bathing the room in a soft, pure brightness. The inner box layer of the shipping container went right to the back, as far as she could judge, and appeared to be some kind of workshop. There were large empty cradles at the far end, made from modular shelving and foam tubing, and metal racking against the left wall, not too deep and full of various sized plastic trays. She went over and examined a few at random, finding screws and fixings, electrical wiring and connectors, and parts that on a visual inspection gave her absolutely no clue as to what they might belong. On the right was a large workbench, with small scraps of wire and metal shavings lying randomly on the oil-stained surface while a number of tools were arranged on hooks behind, exactly placed and ordered. An adjustable chair was pushed right up to and underneath the bench.

Just beyond the workstation on the right was another featureless metal door like the first, painted in the same neutral magnolia as the walls and with its own security panel. As Cara approached the second door more closely she realised it wasn't fully closed. Grasping the edge she opened it wider before stepped through into the next space, pulling the door closed behind her until it was only just ajar. For a moment it was dark there until automatic lights flickered on patchily, as though the room wished to keep its secrets a little longer. Her vision struggled to cope with the change from light to dark to light again, but she took a deliberate step forward and blinked the confusion away.

There was a narrow table against the wall, some kind of foldable design, on top of which were a few hard plastic cases, various sizes, all matte and non-reflective in blacks, greys and olive greens. There were stencils on some, matter of fact labels for the items inside, and nothing at all on others. Cara had no more than a suspicion of the kind of things they might contain, but was emphatically against touching anything to look. As she glanced over, she noticed one of the cases was open and she leant over to peer inside, then pulled sharply away once she'd seen. Although it was currently empty, the crisp outline of a pistol was cut into the foam lining. She was shocked to see that, and wanted no part of whatever was going on here. Places like this didn't belong in her life and she would have sworn not in Ethan's.

Cara backed away from the table and turned ninety degrees to face what would be the front of this container, opposite to the connecting door. There was another internal room, taking up about half the space, made from wood and raised from the floor on squat pillars. It looked like its whole shell was entirely isolated from the surrounding surfaces except where it rested on the floor supports.

A little concerned about what she might find inside but curious nonetheless, Cara pulled her coat sleeve down to act as a crude glove to work the handle and open the door. Inside the air was a little cooler and she could see a stack of high-end computer equipment. The walls, floor and ceiling were covered in thick rubberised sheets except for a number of air vents. Cara pressed against the rubber padding on the wall with her finger and was surprised at how little it gave. Moving over to take a closer look at the computer set up, she could see a rack of server units and a computer case, this one with three monitors and the most impressive workstation chair she'd ever seen outside of a catalogue. Everything in contact with the floor rested on supports made from hard plastic and more of the rubberised sheeting arranged in sandwich layers. To her relief nothing in here looked specifically illegal or dangerous.

Cara left the inner cell and moved back toward the connecting door, taking proper note of another desk on her right, opposite where the plastic cases rested. Here there was a much simpler computer setup. She walked over and jiggled the mouse, her sleeve still stretched down. The monitor flicked from standby to active and showed a grid of images, eight in all. Most of the windows swam with grey static, but two showed interior views of the warehouse whilst another gave a view of the street out the front. All had a time stamp matching the present moment. Obviously, this was some kind of security monitoring, and Cara quickly realised that she may be able to use it to her advantage.

Pulling a smartpad and some connectors from her pocket she then plugging into the computer, quickly locating a file list. There was very little on the machine apart from segments of video so she had no trouble finding some footage from the cameras, which she began copying over to her 'pad. It took very little time to set up and when she was done Cara stepped away, pleased with her initiative. She reset the screen image. Two people had entered the warehouse while she'd been busy, wearing loose overalls and masks. They were looking around systematically, clearly searching for something. Despite the bulky clothing it was obvious one of them was female, and the other a powerfully built male.

Cara didn't like the look of these two at all. The masks and the way they moved told her these were not reasonable, friendly people, and they were unlikely to be happy that she was there. She peered over to the table for a moment and considered checking to see if there was another gun there before realising she had no real idea how to use one.

"Sir, Station Delta reports significant damage and at least two major fires. They're requesting permission to forward an emergency data dump to Epsilon."

"What's the status on the hostiles they reported?"

"Neutralised sir, believed no survivors – identities presently unknown. They were using an old pillbox from the former regime as a command centre. Base defense has just taken it out with a missile strike."

"Excellent! Authorise the data transfer and keep me informed."

- Twenty One -

> Chase

I'd been parked outside for about five minutes when a van pulled up behind Dalca's car. Two people got out and headed straight for the warehouse, clearly studying the exterior as they approached. I was behind them and further up the street so I couldn't see much detail, but it was a man and woman, both wearing oversized boiler suits and what looked like masks. When they reached the warehouse door they paused for a moment, exchanging a look, before ducking underneath the partially open shutter door and going inside.

I could really do without this. I should probably leave, park further away and then return later when they'd all gone, but there was every chance they would disturb or remove evidence. There was also the possibility that these two might harm Dalca if they weren't working together and didn't expect her to be there. I drummed my fingers futilely on the door trim as I weighed the risks, then abruptly pushed the window control, turning to grab the carry case containing the Spydar from where it rested on the front passenger seat.

Pulling the plastic case onto my lap I opened it and quickly powered up the drone, winding the window down a little more so I could set it free. I directed the Spydar to scurry across the road, approach the roller shutter at an angle to get a look inside, and then dart underneath. All the while I watched the live feed from its cameras and made small course corrections until its presets took over and it dashed into cover behind a stack of empty wooden pallets leant against the wall.

The view from there was good, and I watched as the two newcomers searched the warehouse, moving quietly and cautiously around the perimeter, taking in everything around them. Once they'd finished the first sweep they met up in the middle of the room near some pallets piled with large cardboard boxes. The female began to examine these more closely while the male, a powerfully-built individual, went to take a closer look into a small office section at the front of the building. The woman was a possible fit for the outline description we had of the hooded figure up on the high balcony in the mall where Jakobsen fell, but we still had so few details it could be almost anyone of a similar height and build.

They didn't appear to have found anything in particular yet, and certainly no sign of anyone else there. If Dalca was in the building, it looked increasingly likely that she was either in the office space at the front or in one of the two shipping containers positioned against each other toward the right-hand side of the room. Thick power cables ran into the one nearest the wall, looking like huge pipes from the perspective of the Spydar. It wouldn't be long before the two intruders turned their focus there.

I had the drone make a quick run for the open door on the left-hand container, where I could now see a partition wall across the front into which a smaller secondary opening was cut. As it dashed inside I sent the drone behind and up an equipment rack standing against the interior wall.

Now that the Spydar was in place I could get a proper look inside. It seemed like there was an inner chamber within the first container, sealed except for the entrance and what looked like a side door. I quickly reviewed the footage captured by the drone on the way in and spotted a thick band of insulating foam between the inner and outer layers. It was some kind of clean room, designed to give off minimal emissions and offer a level of protection from remote surveillance, and as the containers were positioned right against each other it was likely that the interior of the second one was linked. This first room was fitted out as a workshop, and for the moment I could only guess at what might be inside the second. As yet there was no sign of Dalca.

When the male intruder finally entered the container to look around he stood right in front of where the Spydar was positioned. He was tall, clearly athletic despite the loose boiler suit, and moved with a surprising smoothness. The woman, lean in profile and figure, had moved to take up position in the entrance, blocking the way out. At first, the man paid no obvious attention to the connecting door as he looked around, but that couldn't last and through there was where Dalca must be hiding.

I had to make the decision that had been churning my insides all the time I'd been there. If Dalca really was inside the other container the situation didn't look good for her. There was no choice really. Leaving the car I crossed over to duck under the roller shutters, quietly moving along the wall and around to the back of the containers. I lost the feed from the Spydar as I moved so I synced up with the car using the smartpad, tapping in a sequence of commands as fast as I was able.

There was a short wait while the car executed the first part of my instructions, and I spent that time trying to calm myself. I didn't at all fancy tackling the two intruders directly, and as I was on suspension I couldn't call for any backup. I could see a number of rusty old pipes lying on the floor and I grabbed one of these, enjoying its weight in my hand and its rough, rusted texture. Leaning back briefly against the side of the container I thumbed a green 'GO' command on the 'pad.

Right back along the end of the road the car began moving forward, its sirens blaring. As soon as I heard the familiar wail I waited a couple of seconds and then began hammering on the metal container with the pipe along the back and far side, not too often, allowing the siren to cut through, flakes of rust falling as each thunderous strike echoed around the warehouse, my arm jarring with the blows.

There was a moment where nothing happened, but then the two intruders ran for it, out under the shutters and into the street. The car did its best to roar to a stop outside just as they reached their van and sped off. I waited for several seconds and then killed the siren. Pausing for a moment, I thought about the many ways that could have gone wrong, before taking a few deep, deliberate breaths, forcing myself to calm.

Gingerly, I walked around the back and side of the containers until I reached the front, pausing for a moment again before heading inside. The pipe was still gripped firmly in my hand, just in case.

> Reznik

Jorge glanced in his mirrors, craning his neck to view the surrounding environment. There was no sign of anyone following and he was beginning to relax now that the city centre was a good way behind them. This Reznik, he'd been no real trouble. Jorge had tried to use his mirrors to watch as they'd disarmed him, but he'd had to give up and concentrate on the road. It was too dark in the back to see much, the illumination from the torches a couple of them held focussed tightly on their captive.

Once Reznik was tied the brothers had started ragging on him, screaming insults in his face until they reached a busier part of town and Jorge had to ask them to cool it when they started to draw glances from pedestrians and other drivers whenever the traffic slowed too much. The brothers swore at Jorge instead for a minute, and then calmed down. Now all he heard was a low animal growl of malice from them and an occasional dull slap of fist on flesh.

They reached the main freeway at last and the long curve of new tarmac that would take them around and back to Santos. Jorge was grateful and accelerated a little too hard, earning another curse from behind. Overhead lighting had been installed in a few short sections, the slatted brightness casting freeze-frames in the rear, the Anglo hunkered down and the four men menacing in a pack.

Jorge was disappointed to have to slow down yet again for some roadworks, but the traffic was light this time and they were through after a few minutes crawling along. He pulled away again, not so hard this time. There was a thud from the back then, the van rocking a little. Jorge thought something had broken, the old thing letting him down again, but the wheels and power felt smooth.

Cries and curses erupted from behind, another crash, louder, the van rocking on its wheels. There was more of the sound of violent contact but the cries and animal sounds were different, more of fear than power. Another section of brighter lighting on the road, bodies in snapshot motion in the rear-view, then darkness again. All he could see behind him was one of the torches rolling across the floor.

Then an angry face suddenly beside him, wild and bloody. Cold metal to his temple, unyielding and unbelievably real.

"Where the fuck are you taking me?"

"To Santos. He wants to see you – you set him up!" Jorge cringed at the sight of Reznik, wondered why he'd been so bold.

"Like fuck. Where are we now? How far from the railyard?"

"Ten minutes, I think maybe fifteen. Look, I'm sorry. I just drive, ok. I just picked you up. I never hit you, right?"

"Do I look like the kind of guy that would trouble to make such a distinction?" He didn't, and pressed a little harder with the muzzle, as if its presence could have been forgotten. "How did you find me?"

"Stickydust I think, from the stairs."

Reznik nodded his battered head, wearily. "How far out is Santos from there?"

"Thirty minutes, maybe twenty five."

"Tell him he's got twenty. Tell him none of his boys are dead yet but I'm mindful to change that." Reznik had lapsed into English by now, forgetting his place. Jorge didn't dare point out his error.

> Cara

She had squeezed down the side of the wooden inner room, and now stood behind it, her legs splayed painfully to try and align with the floor supports. The lights were off, presumably because she was out of range of the sensors, and she waited anxiously in the dark. When it came the scratching at the door was like a grinding, the sense of presence that followed equally intense. She did her best to meld into the walls, be small and nothing.

Then there was a muffled thudding, the sound of something banging hard against the metal walls, a faint siren, coming closer. Cara stayed as still and quiet as she could, wondering what in hell was happening. Her legs shook, though whether from the strain of holding an uncomfortable position or from the fear she couldn't tell. Without warning, the banging stopped, and then the siren.

Cara waited there in the dark

A little later. She heard someone moving through from the other container just before the lights came on overhead, the sudden brightness making her blink. Soft footfalls entered the room and a male voice called her name. He came nearer, feet and voice louder, called again, then a pause.

"Look round Miss Dalca, up and to your left." She thought for a moment, and did exactly that. Above her was a drone, a matte black insect thing clinging to the walls. It rocked back slightly on its thorax and seemed to wave with a foreleg. It creeped her out.

Letting out a loud humph of breath, Cara shifted her feet back to centre, wincing a little at the muscle strain.

"Would you come out please, so that we can talk? I mean you no harm. My name's Keegan Chase, I'm a detective." He sounded ok, trustworthy, so she took against him instantly, but he had her cornered and there was no point in denying it.

Cara squeezed back through the gap between the container and the wooden room, slowly, stretching the time out as far as she could. The insect drone followed her progress, scurrying along the ceiling in pace with her movements. When she reached the open space again, it ran down the wall and into the isolation booth behind her. She thought about slamming the door to trap it there.

In front of her stood a man, dark skinned, an expression caught between curiosity and concern on his face. She thought he looked a little familiar, like she'd seen him before in a completely different context. He was quite tall, broad-shouldered, well dressed in a business suit, and every inch an agent or detective of some kind. His hands were empty save for a 'pad, no sign of a gun, but he stood blocking her way to the table where Ethan had left his armoury. Probably best for them both.

He smiled a tight smile and spoke: "Did you find much? Anything useful?" There was the barest suggestion of agitation in his manner, though he talked smoothly.

"Who are you? Are you going to arrest me?"

He smiled once more, a little tighter, and replied. "Detective Chase, as I told you. I'm investigating the death of your boyfriend, Karl Jakobsen."

"Ethan! Ethan Grant!" She corrected him automatically, without thinking.

"Ah, yeah, sorry. Ethan Grant then. Though this place is much more in the style of Karl Jakobsen to be honest." He pantomimed looking around, taking in the stacks of plastic cases and the isolation booth she'd hidden behind.

"I didn't know about this. I don't know what's going on. I came to find out."

"Yeah, well, me too. Look, is there any chance we could continue this somewhere else? Probably best to move on before the uniforms arrive."

"You worried about the paperwork?"

"Something like that."

Cara agreed readily. It would be better to get out of there, though she was just as worried that the two thugs would come back as she was about the police. Surely, this Chase was police himself, though he seemed remarkably calm about finding her in a room full of stuff that might be guns and who knew what else. Unless he was from the same detective agency as that Mallory woman, who had the same irritating air. Yes, that was probably it. There was that nagging sense still that she'd seen him before.

When they got outside Cara noticed his insect drone clambering over her car. She imagined there might be loads of them, crawling all over the place, and shuddered. It scurried across the pavement, right up his leg, body and arm, dropping a piece of wet-looking black plastic into his outstretched palm and then curled into a compact ball. He placed the spider thing in a pocket with his free hand, then held up the plastic object between the finger and thumb of his other for her to see.

"Bug," he said.

They told him he was lucky to be alive. Jakobsen didn't feel particularly lucky, especially as the levels of drugs were gradually reduced and he started to remember. The worst part was realising his nightmares were real, and that Tsu and Frost were both gone.

It wasn't clear how long he'd been in the hospital, weeks he figured, though the constant headaches and pain made it hard to think. Apart from one or two visits from The Wolf the nurses were his only company, and they were reluctant to tell him much. Jakobsen thought they might be in China, or perhaps one of the Koreas; the nurses were nearly all Asian, but he struggled to be specific.

The breeze picked up, wafting at the curtains as he drifted back to black on another perfect afternoon.

- Twenty Two -

> Chase

Dalca had agreed to give me a lift in her car and I tried to talk on the way. I would have loved to take a proper look round the warehouse, but with all of the fuss I'd created we needed to get out of there in case the real police arrived. As it was they could easily track my movements if they cared to look, especially as I'd put my own car into alert mode, but it seemed the easiest way to get rid of the intruders. Sending it back to the flat via a long diversion was the best I could do for now.

Dalca and I were both a little on edge from what had just happened, though perhaps for different reasons, but it was the last thing either of us was going to talk about. As it was I tried to get what I could from her, but she wasn't having any of it: "So, how long were you in there before the two thugs arrived?"

"Is that what they were? I didn't get a proper look." She had elected to drive manually, and made busy with the controls.

"It seemed that way. I'll try and run their IDs later, but I'm not too hopeful."

"Why?"

"They were careful, made every effort to conceal themselves. Anyway, did you see anything there that helps?"

"How do you mean?" Looking straight ahead, in the mirrors, never across.

"Well, everyone seems convinced you're an innocent in all this, and that you'd no idea Grant had another identity. So, like I said, did you learn anything that helps you make sense of things?"

"No, not really. Quite the opposite. I presume you noticed the big stack of guns?" I nodded, though I'd not really confirmed yet whether they actually were weapons or something else. "I don't know what I was expecting to see in there, but it wasn't that. And what was going on with all that room-within-room shtick?"

"They were isolation rooms I think, designed to give off minimal traces to make remote surveillance harder. They were disguised inside the shipping containers to make them easier to move around and install I expect."

"Oh. Do you have any idea why?"

"Not specifically. Do you?"

"No."

That was about as far as we got. She didn't react to the info I gave her on the iso-rooms, though I suppose with her background she might have already realised what they were. If any of this had rattled her, she wasn't showing it. I'd expected her to ask about the bug, but it didn't come up. In fact, she was clearly reluctant to talk much about anything, and I was in no position to push her too hard.

When Dalca dropped me off I left her with my card. I didn't think there was much trust there yet, but given chance to reflect on things she might change her mind.

The briefcase made a solid thud as it hit the table top, jarring my drink in its glass. I looked up and saw a young girl, probably in her late teens, dressed in equal parts goth, punk and geisha.

"She said you'd give me fifty." Her hand still held onto the case, which she rested on its thinnest side near the edge of the table top.

"Who did?"

"Some woman. Fifty." The girl had glanced sideways for just a moment as she spoke, looking out of the restaurant. Her words twisted around a constant chewing of gum. It was almost as though it acted as a filter, translating her speech from Attitude to English. Outside a well-dressed woman was studying the menu displayed in the window, the collar of her chic raincoat high and her face partially hidden behind oversized, old school shades. Striking.

I looked back to the girl stood next to me, pulled some notes from my wallet and placed them on the table, one finger firmly resting there as though I needed to point to them.

"What did she look like? Tall, slim, dressed in a raincoat, good looking, like the lady stood at the window now?"

"Suppose." She said nothing else, and I stared back, until she rolled her eyes and spoke: "Look, it was some woman I've never seen before. A Suit like you. Said she'd been paid to bring the case to me and I was to deliver it straight to you. Wasn't gonna do it, but she offered me a hundred, promised it wasn't anything dangerous or illegal. I still wasn't sure, but she gave me a quick look inside the case, so I said yeah, ok. It was weird, she had my picture and knew all about me."

Glancing back to the window, I saw that the woman had gone now. I had an image of her from the 'lenses, which I was wearing again despite feeling worse for it. Lifting my hand from the money I reached over for the case. She allowed me the briefest of moments to grab the handle before letting go, scooping up the cash as she turned and left. I'd never really gotten on with teenagers, even when I'd been one.

I left the café a couple of minutes later, using one of my last paper notes to cover the bill, and went outside to hail a taxi. One of the old-fashioned looking black cabs pulled up and I climbed in the back. The operator, who was no more actually driving the cab than I was, asked 'where to?' and then began his patter. I listened with half an ear, joining in where it seemed appropriate, while I opened the case. He seemed happy enough to do most of the talking.

The briefcase was one of those with a particularly deep compartment and once I'd opened it I could see why. There were four Big Block external hard drives inside, packed tight against each other. In the lid were two pockets, one of them containing a couple of pre-paid debit cards and a new smartpad. Inside the other were a couple of null-pouches, light grey in colour, just about the right size to make me pause and think. The last time I'd seen one of these it had held a handgun.

After pulling out the new 'pad I shut the briefcase hard, almost trapping my jacket sleeve and causing the operator's patter to falter for a moment, until he picked it right up again. I set to looking at the 'pad's contents, after removing a yellow sticky note that was tacked to the front. There was a small roodle on it, very much in Mallory's style, though not quite to her usual standard.

> Reznik

Jorge was on his knees backed up against the open door at the rear of the van, hands on his head. All the other doors were closed and Reznik had made him park up in such a way that no strong light shone through into the load area. He couldn't feel the hardness of the gun's muzzle any more, but the gringo held a stick in one hand, the other on top of Jorge's shoulder, its rough surface scratching against his neck so he would know he was still there.

Directly behind Jorge were stacked the four bodies of his friends, all alive but unconscious. Reznik had made a barricade of flesh and bone in the rear of the van and he waited back there for Santos to arrive. A train rumbled along close by, the heavy engine and trucks churning the air, rocking the van. It was a relief from the curmudgeonly throb the old bio-diesel engine made as it groused away in neutral.

Jorge had tried to resist, show some spirit, but Reznik had fired a warning with the pistol, swinging the gun back over a fraction to point right at Jorge's temple. The sound of the gun had been shockingly loud in his ears. They were still ringing a little, nagging him to stay calm and cooperative.

Santos arrived noisily and at speed, two saloon cars throwing fish tails on the rough dirt surface, lights splashing everywhere. They crunched to a stop, aligning in a haphazard 'V', their headlights now forming a bright pool at the back of the van, dazzling Jorge. He thought he saw Santos and the others spreading out in a crude half-circle. Once they were in place they all held position, silent. Jorge was tired and worried: his knees hurt, his shoulders ached and he needed a pee badly. Somehow, he thought it would all be fine once Santos arrived, but now he wasn't so sure.

He spoke up over the grumble of the engines. "Boss, it's me, Jorge! The boys are alive, just a bit beat up. Maybe we can resolve this, er, amicably."

"You work for him now Jorge?"

"No, no boss. Just you. He's got a gun, boss."

Santos paused, then called out, "Why don't you fucking show yourself Reznik!"

There was no answer. Another train pulled by, its air horn mournful. Santos called again. "Are you there Reznik? We got business. You set me up, you fuck!"

No answer. Then a high-pitched call tone, loud, the sound grinding against the cheap phone's speakers as it rasped out. It rang and rang.

"Answer it, Jorge."

"But boss, he's got a gun and..."

"Get up off your fucking knees and answer it!"

He did so, slowly, dislodging the wooden beam, which fell with a dull clatter outside the van. Jorge paused for a moment feeling numb, wincing from the painful throb of blood returning to his cramped joints until one of the boys closed up and pushed at his back, making Jorge move. He reached into the van and opened the second rear door. Reznik was nowhere to be seen, but a phone sat on the floor behind the stacked bodies, its bright display flashing on and off, a strobe to highlight the van's emptiness.

Jorge climbed inside awkwardly, up and over the grumbling bodies of his friends, retrieving the phone, which he recognised belatedly as his own. He answered it, replied then crawled back to the van doors, stretching out to hand the phone to Santos, who snatched it away with a meaner anger than Jorge had seen in him before.

The boss walked away a few feet into the dark, toward the tracks, talking quietly. Mostly he seemed to listen, but it was hard to be sure. When he came back he hollered out for the boys to get back in the cars, but that Eddie should drive the van back. Jorge thought that was good, as his knees ached too much and he wasn't sure he could drive yet. The boss still made him help the brothers and the other two into better positions in the back. It was cramped in there and he had to move around on his knees, even though they hurt still.

When it was done he crawled out backwards and climbed gingerly back onto his feet. He closed the doors and turned, expecting to go around to the front and ride with Eddie, but came up short when he saw the gun the boss held pointed at his head.

Jorge and Santos stood there, frozen, the boy's face twisting in anger, lips trembling fiercely just as the gun began to waver and shake in sympathy. They locked eyes, Jorge entirely frightened by the expression he read there, stunned when Santos's hand dropped, still holding the gun. Just as abruptly Santos turned away.

Jorge could barely see in the fierce light as one of the crew approached determinedly, until there was another gun up and pointing at his face, the bore as wide as a tunnel. It was the very last thing Jorge saw.

> Cara

Cara was at home, her 'pad connected to the TV in the lounge. She'd rigged things up to show the different camera feeds from Ethan's warehouse in a split-screen style, as she'd first seen it. As it started up Cara was surprised to see eight full images, not just three, giving her a fixed viewpoint from various different positions around the warehouse. None of the cameras showed the inside of the containers.

Cara watched most of the footage she'd recorded on fast forward as not much seemed to happen. Ethan was there for a few hours each day, but apart from looking around when he first arrived and again as he left he would spend most of his time inside the clean rooms, out of sight. It was bittersweet to see him.

The fourth day was different. This was the Thursday, and he wore the clothes she saw him in last. From the time stamp, he must have gone straight from the warehouse to the bistro where they met up that night. She really had to stop then, take a break, before the slight welling in her eyes turned into a full stream.

Friday. Ethan arrived early, took just a quick look around then went straight inside the first container. Cara watched the time digits blur by until she passed the three-hour mark, when she saw a white van pull up on one of the external views. Two people, a man who approached the door, while the other, a woman, squatted down to look at something at the front of the van, her back to the cameras. Cara paused the playback for a moment. She couldn't be sure, but they looked generally like the two she'd seen there earlier that day. In the video both were dressed in dark overalls and caps, the male's showing a power company badge. She let the video run on again, saw him push the buzzer next to the front door before reaching into a pocket and pulling out an aerosol of some sort, reaching out with his left hand to spray the can upward toward the camera before tossing it aside.

At first there was no response to the doorbell, and no obvious effect from the aerosol, but over the next fifteen or so seconds there were clear images of Ethan leaving the shipping containers, closing the door to the inner clean room behind him and pushing the outer door to. Cara was surprised to see the butt of a gun sticking upward from the waist of his cargo pants, snug in the small of his back, as he walked toward the entrance. She was so captivated by that sequence that she nearly missed the gradual degradation of the images from the outer camera as the video became steadily grainier.

The footage from the camera outside was very poor now, so she could only just make out what happened next. Ethan opened the front door to speak to the male, who held up an ID of some sort, before moving a 'pad around to show Ethan the screen. While this was going on the woman came around from the side of the van and casually walked up toward the warehouse. She reached out smoothly with something in her hand just as Ethan looked up from the 'pad. There was a look of surprise on his face for a moment before he staggered and then collapsed forward into the ready arms of the man, who grabbed him and supported his weight before the two strangers picked Ethan up bodily and carried him to the back of their van. Cara could see that the man then returned briefly to the warehouse door to lock it and retrieve the aerosol can he'd dropped. They then drove off.

Cara was stunned, barely watching as the images from the front camera gradually returned to a normal, clear view of the exterior. She paused the recording, rewound, and watched it all again before getting up, going to the kitchen to boil a kettle but ignoring it when it flicked off, the water's agitation matching her own.

After a few minutes had passed, she returned to the lounge and forced herself to watch the rest of the video. The images whizzed by, nothing happening for a few days, until she had to stop it and rewind a little. One of the feeds had gone out, an external view, and now nothing but static was in the image window. Cara watched more of the footage at normal speed and saw one feed after another go blank, working from the outside of the warehouse in, until there were only thee cameras left, showing the deepest of the interior views.

An elegant looking man stepped into view inside the warehouse. He was tall and wore a dark suit, impeccably cut. Cara thought he looked Italian perhaps, Mediterranean at least, with a tanned complexion and dark hair to his shoulders. Despite his smart appearance he still gave an air that he belonged there, though she was pretty sure he didn't. Craning his elegant neck to look around a little he then approached the containers at the back. He spent a minute studying the security panel beside the outer door, hand lazily massaging his chin, before smiling ruefully and turning back the way he'd come, leaving the warehouse.

Cara scanned through the remaining feeds until she saw herself turn up, the return of the two who'd abducted Ethan, and the arrival of the detective, Chase. He'd been smart, and acted quickly. Maybe he wasn't so bad. She was certain that if nothing else, he would have the resources to identify the three who'd been at the warehouse a lot faster then she could. Perhaps he could help her after all.

Jakobsen awoke gradually, aware there was someone else in the room. It didn't alarm him in any way – it was something you got used to in hospital – but when he came around enough to take proper note of his visitor, he was a little embarrassed to have been so nonchalant. The Wolf was sat there in a chair he'd pulled up beside the bed, wearing a white coat which even though it sat well on his frame looked wrong. Jakobsen almost laughed, but the seriousness of the other man's expression stopped the sound in his throat.

They conversed after a fashion, short droplets of information drip by slow drip. Jakobsen expressed his anger and sadness, his confusion. He was still sure that Polzin had betrayed them, passed on tainted codes and passwords. The Wolf shrugged and replied, gnawing at the bones of Jakobsen's recollection until there was no more marrow left, the shaggy skin of his mystique moulting away all the while until he sat there as plain Reznik, the white coat more ill-fitting with every passing moment.

- Twenty Three -

> Chase

By the time I got back to the flat I was feeling a little weak, almost nauseous. I'd forgotten to take along any of the tablets the hospital had supplied, and they weren't something I could get anywhere else. I took a couple as soon as I could.

It had been a long day, the last half of which I spent dealing with the gifts my Admirer had left for me. I'd been able to take a quick look at the directories on the Big Blocks, and it was immediately clear that three of them contained far too much hard data for even the most capable laptop or smartpad to handle, which meant I'd need to access a much more powerful system. The fourth drive had more of the same, but it also held a series of much smaller files that I'd be able to transfer to the 'pad. These were an up to date record of the case notes and forensic reports held at CSS, some of which I'd still not had time to view.

Dalca called a little later, offering to email over some video clips from the lockup, though she became evasive when I asked how she'd got them. The files came through soon afterward but my initial enthusiasm was severely blunted when I saw the quality of some of the footage.

There was a short clip showing two people arriving at the warehouse a few days before Jakobsen's death, superficially the same ones I'd scared off earlier. The male approached the front door of the industrial unit to ring the buzzer while the woman dawdled around near the front of their vehicle. The picture quality was ok at first but degraded steadily as it continued. You could just about see what was going on and this looked very much like a kidnapping, which was a development I suppose I should have expected from the forensic evidence on Jakobsen. Whoever these two were, they were smart. I might be able to grab a partial still of the man's face as they'd not been wearing masks this time, but it would be nearly impossible with the woman.

The other clip was of another man who walked right into the warehouse space. He was well dressed, and from his appearance and movement of a completely different class from the other suspects. Frustratingly, I felt there was something familiar about him, but I'd no idea what. I still needed to get to bed, but I couldn't resist running the first video sequence though some software apps to try to get a couple of clean images I could use for identification. The footage of the second man was good enough already and I immediately set a query going on it.

About two hours later, most of which I spent dozing in the chair, I had a usable image of the male intruder from the warehouse that I could use for a search, but as expected there was no recoverable image of the woman. Two out of three wasn't bad though, and she might turn out to be a known associate of one of them anyway. I trudged off to bed, feeling battered and barely myself.

There was some good news waiting for me the next morning. The male suspect who'd helped kidnap Jakobsen was identified as David Ruscoe. He had a long history of suspected criminal involvement but only a few convictions, chiefly for bodily harm and B&E. Ruscoe was ex-military, with a decent enough service record, but after his discharge he seemed to have fallen in with a rougher crowd and become an experienced and skilled professional criminal. There was no history of kidnap or murder in his file but it was possible he'd simply not been caught. The search for the other man was still running.

Listed with Ruscoe's details were a couple of known addresses, so I decided to head off straight away and have a quick look. The last thing I wanted was to attract his attention, but a quick reccie should be all right. He'd not seen me at the industrial unit so he wouldn't recognise me, and I was wearing civvies this time, a loose hooded top and jeans, chosen both to make me more anonymous and harder to identify or categorise. As I left I set another search running, this time for the van they'd used. Probably should have thought of it before.

On the way I called Dalca. She answered the phone almost immediately.

"Chase, morning. Were you able to find anything out?"

"Yeah, one of them so far, still running the others. He's a professional criminal with a long record, not someone to be messed with. Cara, if you see any of them again don't approach them, but call me straight away. Unless you think you're in danger at all, even the vaguest hint of it. If you are then call the police and get yourself somewhere public, amongst lots of people."

"I thought you *were* the police. Did you get any names?"

"I'm a corporate contractor working *with* the police. His name's David Ruscoe. Might be useful to know that if you do have to call them. They can often get to you quicker, Cara, and in numbers, so like I said if you feel threatened or in danger call them straight away. Actually, it might be might be best if you laid low for the next couple of days, stayed at home or with friends."

"Sure, ok. Thanks. Listen, I have to go. Thanks for calling."

Dalca hung up. She hadn't sounded at all phased by what I'd just told her. Maybe if hadn't sunk in yet, or she was somewhere safe already. I'd try and check up on her later, see if she was ok.

I wasn't too far from the first of Ruscoe's addresses now, so I put that out of my mind and pulled up a map on the satnav to pick the best place to park up so I could do the final approach on foot.

> Reznik

The train had been a convenient way of getting away from Santos and moving back into the city, but he'd had to leave it as it moved deeper into the goods yard. It was a couple of minutes since he'd seen the headlights approach the van off in the distance so now was probably about the right time to call. The phone went unanswered at first, and he had to let it ring on for a while. When Jorge picked it up Reznik could hear his confusion, before he passed the handset onto Santos, the sound of the van's engine and another train passing by filling the background.

"You calmed down any?" Reznik asked him.

"No. No I fucking haven't!" He could picture the boy mouthing the words extravagantly, a sommelier of choice language, spitting the syllables when he'd had their full flavour.

"Well, that's on you. The thing you need to understand is that the city ain't safe for us right now, and that I'm just as screwed as you are."

"You think? No, I think you're more screwed than me. You have fewer friends and more enemies. And you know what; you can count me amongst them!"

Reznik sighed. "Right now you're no enemy, you're just an inconvenience. See, I was even good to your boys, just roughed them up a little. No corpses, just contusions. I strongly recommend you don't promote yourself onto my shit list though. I'll not waste my time making threats – but be assured I will fucking end you!"

He paused and waited for a response, but all he heard was another train rumble by. "Now, so we can both understand things, tell me what happened from your perspective."

"From my perspective?"

"Yes. During the job, what happened? From your P-O-V." Santos didn't reply immediately, though Reznik could hear him swearing in the background as he ran through a varied list of unlikely familial relations.

"Ok, fine. The job was going well, all to plan. I piloted the big drone over the back balcony, got all the guests through onto the patio near the pool and I was herding them nicely with the smaller bots when things went weird. Everything started responding more slowly, and then ignored my commands all together. I could see what was happening still, but couldn't do anything about it. Someone hacked my system. I had strong firewalls up, the best, and nothing should have gone through them that quickly."

"Ok, I believe you. What next?"

"Next I saw extra blips on the tracker, and a glimpse or two of a couple of larger drones moving up, just edge-of-shot images. I'd have taken a proper look but I was just a passenger by then. Then the whole fucking place blew up. You probably noticed that part."

"A little. Now, I'm no hacker – if I were, I wouldn't have needed you – so I didn't send those extra birds in. That was down to whoever set us up, and I'm reasonably certain it wasn't you, unless you spoke to someone. Did you? Did you speak to anyone, brag to your friends maybe?"

"No I did not! I was tight, compartmentalised. I told nobody."

Reznik strained to hear every nuance of Santos's reply, his hearing sharper than a dog's, before replying. "Glad to hear it. So that leaves me a short list of possibles."

"Araya?"

"Maybe, probably. Not your concern. You need to look out for yourself and get out of town, or at least go to ground. Just you, no crew, somewhere that even you wouldn't think of looking for you."

"Why should I believe you?"

"You shouldn't, not entirely, but you should see that whoever blew up two fucking buildings is bigger and meaner than either of us. Now, I think we're done here. I don't expect to see you again. Follow my advice or don't. Your choice."

He rang off, not waiting for a reply. This was worrying. He'd seen Santos operate enough to suggest he had skills, though he couldn't be certain how much. Whoever had crashed their op had formidable tech, it sounded like, and if that were so there was no way to say how long he'd been under observation, and whether he still was.

The sound of a single gunshot in the near distance ended his speculation and got his feet moving.

> Cara

She closed the call quickly, her hollow assurances echoing around the empty space. It was probably a good thing Chase had rung when he did, as she didn't think there'd be any signal inside the container rooms. Despite a growing sense of risk she'd come back to C4. The last visit had raised far more questions than it answered, though she knew beyond doubt now that Ethan had been in much heavier trouble than she thought Nada capable of, unless she'd misjudged him and he'd changed far more than she thought over the years.

Cara was aware that too many people seemed to know about this place, and that they perhaps also knew about what had been going on here. She half hoped the kidnappers would return so she could confront them, but she knew that if they did she would more than likely scurry off to hide again. Cara wasn't a coward, but she stayed away from violent people as a matter of policy, especially violent people who were trespassing somewhere she shouldn't be either.

On the way over she'd picked up a few things, her treasures carried in plastic bags so thin they were almost degrading already. One contained water, snacks and toiletries, the other some cheap mobile phones and a few simple parts, enough to place some rudimentary cameras in the warehouse. She could link these to cloud storage and have them send a compressed data file every few hours. They wouldn't give great quality or live monitoring, but they would cover some of the blind spots.

She thought her best option for finding out what Ethan had been doing was the computer he'd installed in the isolation room inside the second container. It was too complex and expensive a set up to have if you weren't intending to make serious use of it, and she knew from direct experience that his knowledge of hardware and systems was far too good for him to have made a mistake and over spec'd on his requirements. That did assume that she would be able to access the machine of course, as something that powerful would have top-line security. She hoped that Ethan would have made it easy for her, but there was only one way to find out.

Just as she was about to enter the containers Emma called, trying to talk her into meeting up for a drink. Cara was sorely tempted but declined: she had to follow this through. Once she was inside the clean room in the first container Cara checked the wall beside the door, and was relieved to see that there was indeed a second biometric panel: she hadn't recalled seeing one, but thought that there would be.

She waited a moment, suddenly unsure, and then reached for the handle, pulling the door closed behind her. It sealed with a definite sense of solidity, the lock thunking into place. The lights stayed on inside, and she moved through to the next chamber.

He'd been so long away from a real life that the sudden sight of the sun, unfiltered and full, was almost overwhelming. Jakobsen stopped just outside the main entrance to the hospital, oblivious to the blockage he was causing, head tilted back and nostrils flared to breathe in deeply. The warm, sticky breeze carried the scent and stink of humanity to his parched senses. Even the rough feel of denim and cheap cotton on his skin was a revelation.

He hadn't seen Reznik in over a month, the older man an occasional visitor for the end of his convalescence until he had to go away 'on some business', as he put it. He'd given no hint of what he might be doing or where he might be doing it.

Jakobsen felt rejuvenated and ready. He had to find Polzin, but first he wanted to visit that tattooist he'd heard about. There was a bare spot on his forearm that was just itching to be filled, and he had the perfect design in mind.

- Twenty Four -

> Chase

It was mid-afternoon by the time I was done checking the two addresses we had for Ruscoe, and I'd had the car drop me off a couple of streets away from where I wanted to be before sending it home. The first house he was connected with was long empty, and probably not even his anymore judging by the names on the mail piling up in the front hallway. The second was in use but protected by an extensive but discreet security system, which I didn't fancy risking even though I had the Spydar. There was a car in the drive which I could check later to see if it was connected with Ruscoe at all.

As I walked back toward the main ring road, making for a modest café I knew, I reflected on my surroundings. It was a bleak hinterland here, concrete multilane and neglected social housing with an old-fashioned greasy diner separating them like Checkpoint Charlie. There were other customers inside but they kept to themselves, apart from a noisy clique in one corner that seemed boisterously familiar with one another. Pulling the smartpad from my backpack and powering it up felt distinctly futuristic, its graphite-weave shell a mocking reflection of the grey, tea-stained formica of the table.

Amongst the information my Admirer had sent on the fourth Big Block was my own personnel file, which I initially found strange until I took the time to skim through it. There was a complete medical and psychological record going back several years, most of which was familiar enough, but the files from after the Paris investigation were far more comprehensive than anything I'd seen previously. In fact the level of detail was almost forensic, and distinctly uncomfortable to read.

If the reports were to be believed I'd been a lot closer to death, and consequently had a lot more reconstructive surgery, than I'd previously been aware of. It was a little hard to reconcile my relative ignorance of all that with the fact that it had been me that these things had happened to, but I suppose if you factored in the fact I'd suffered head trauma and was on heroic levels of medication it was more understandable. I couldn't help but think of Jo again, and what she'd gone through to support me, and that she'd left when she finally realised I wouldn't do the one thing she really wanted in return.

All in all Cadejo had spent a not inconsiderable fortune on putting me back together, physically and otherwise, until I was ready for active service again. They'd made selective changes as well, hard and wet 'ware upgrades for the enhancements I'd retained on leaving the military. These were the cause for some of the unfamiliar shadows I'd seen on the scans back in the neurology lab. Now I was both less and more than before, an amalgam of my original self and replacement parts; brand new biotech and ancient evolution. There was no clear indication what the upgrades were, just manufacturers serial numbers with only the vaguest of specs. I'd have to look into all that later, when I had the stomach for it. As it happened that was one of the things they'd replaced.

There were other files to look at, and I selected one with the blandest title to avoid further surprises. The first part of the document was an evidence log, which showed that at the time my Admirer had copied the folders no one at CSS had yet viewed the contents.

Somehow, the drone that had raised the alarm on the Saturday night when Harris was killed had gone missing for half a week and then suddenly turned up again. One of the clean-up crew closing down the forensic investigation found it in a nearby corridor, stationary and powered down. It had been plugged in overnight to recharge at the CSS lab before someone downloaded the drone's memory files onto the evidence log. These were then copied for me at Thursday lunchtime: checking my watch that was about 27 hours ago.

There were various reports attached but the only thing I was really interested in was its camera or sensor memory for the Saturday evening. I knew that these drones would routinely upload much of their collected data to the mainframe and then delete it, but they were also programmed to retain a copy of any significant incidents. With any luck its on board systems still had those records.

I was feeling hopeful now, but then my mood shifted, flipping 180 degrees. The incident report showed in bland, line-by-line detail what the drone had witnessed, but the video it had captured was all anyone would really need.

After leading me through the mall's basement the drone had taken up station, just outside what looked like the server room, and its camera showed me entering through the open door. It remained in place for the next few seconds, its viewpoint nothing but a short, bland, ill-lit corridor while its audio sensors continued to record. There were system alarms, faint at that distance and my shouting voice challenging Harris to stop. I identified myself as police and then the sound of two shots barked in quick succession. The drone was already moving after the first shot, which distorted the sound quality.

The video feed became key again. It showed a cat-like view of rapid movement through the server room, centre clear and focussed with the edges a smear. I was stood there with a gun in my hand, while a blurry image of Harris and blood spatter showed at the edge of the picture as the drone move around, reflections from its hazard flashers lending the scene an odd quality. The drone fired its Taser almost immediately, bringing me down and as I fell I knocked my head on the racking, dropping my weapon. After it quickly surveyed the room, recording Harris and his injuries more clearly this time, the drone then sent a call to the emergency services before it took up station again outside the door. There was no sign of anyone else there, no mystery man.

I swore loudly, stunned, nearly knocking my mug over and drawing a quick glance from the other customers as it clattered. Swearing again, I then put my hand to my mouth as though ashamed of my rudeness.

I couldn't understand it. My memories of that night were extremely patchy, but I'd not had cause to doubt the little I could recall. Right in front of me, though, was clear evidence that contradicted everything I believed of myself.

I had killed John Harris.

> Reznik

He sat in a tiny backstreet bar with a cold one that he sipped from absentmindedly while his gaze took in everything from behind his shades, especially the large TV in the corner. Over and over came the explosions, spectacular and horrible in the night, numbers and names of casualties flowing left to right in the stringers like souls along the Styx. There were other shots of the damaged high-rise taken the next morning, smoke still pouring forth, debris and emergency crews circling the building.

The reporting was emotive and everywhere, with a tone nearing hysteria. Local politicians and police officers called for justice and revenge while foreign leaders gave statements of support and assistance, describing the bombings as acts of cowardice and terror. Inevitably, the focus was on the more famous victims, the wealthy and beautiful, though a number of human-interest pieces had also run featuring some of the staff and the families that they'd left behind.

Reznik thought he could see a narrative developing here. There had been no official confirmation of the bomber's motivations, and no acknowledged claimants for the act, but the reportage was loaded with innuendo. Left-wingers, anarchists, and anti-capitalists were to blame, the poor, the Other. There was speculation on the impact to Hallistiks future market performance in the light of losing key executives in the first explosion, and whether their legal dispute with local firm OraCotek would continue. He expected to see his own image or Santos's on the screen at any moment, and he hated that he would be blamed for an operation so needlessly and indiscriminately devastating.

A half hour later and the narrative and footage had looped back around again, endlessly repeating itself in the background like a psychic drive. He remained unknown, anonymous, unblamed. If felt like the mother of all storms was brewing, and when it broke he would be at its centre.

His second beer was done and now he had gone for another, propped against the bar while he waited for service. The comm in his inner ear chirped. A priority call on a secure channel. Reznik stood and quickly walked over to the rest room, his next beer still in the hands of the barmaid, cold smoke floating from the lip where she had popped the top. Once he'd reached the rudimentary privacy of the single cubicle he responded. There was an exchange of code words and number strings, the caller unfamiliar. It felt strange, incongruous, as he perched at the edge of the dirty toilet and talked nonsense under his breath to a stranger. When the protocols were over Murdoch came on the line.

"Talk to me. Tell me what happened."

"We were compromised, fully screwed over."

"How?"

"Unknown. I kept things tight, only dealt with a handful of contacts and told no one anything they didn't need to know. Standard O.P. Someone hacked the op and twisted the outcome to their own ends. The damage isn't so much collateral as catastrophic."

"I see. Any idea who?"

"The man you recommended is an obvious choice, but who he's working for I don't know. Whoever it was had good tech, cracked through our security real easy."

"That's concerning. Ok, close it down. Clean up and get out. I'll see what we can dig up from here and we'll work through the pieces later."

"Copy that."

"Situation is as per the play book. Good luck."

That meant that he was on his own. There would be little help or assistance, maybe a way over the border if he could reach it, but there would be no protection if he failed. He would be left to rot away in a shockingly real prison under a fake name and fake charges. Reznik flushed the toilet for form's sake, watched the waters swirl and sink down the pan, imagining his life doing much the same.

> Cara

It felt a little claustrophobic in the isolation room at first, separated and sealed off from the outside. She realised that was the whole point of course. Whilst she knew that no one could really get to her, or even see that she was there, Cara also had a latent worry that she would not be able to get out again. All of the locks had responded to her biometrics though, so it was probably just paranoia brought on by anxiety.

When she'd first come back to the warehouse and entered the innermost room Cara had stood and taken stock of everything while the server powered up. She badly wanted to know what Ethan had been working on but finding out might be difficult. The mainframe he'd installed was powerful enough to run formidable password protection, so that even with the best kit it could take months, or even years, to crack the encryption and gain access. All she had was her knowledge of Ethan, if not so much his alter ego, but she hoped they were similar enough. So far he'd shown her some generosity in giving her access to the warehouse's inner areas, so with any luck that spirit might extend to his computer as well. There was little point in being allowed in otherwise, as far as she could fathom.

Cara thought she might know what that password was. Calling up the audio message she'd been sent just after unlocking the containers Cara replayed the file, carefully noting down the sequence. She had to go back a few seconds here and there as she struggled to write as fast as the digits came, but she got the complete message in the end.

Cara paused, took a breath, and then leaned right over the keyboard, typing carefully and slowly, checking back against the note she'd written, loathe to make any errors.

A pause, a progress bar, and then a message: Sign In Error. Failure.

She sat back, thought again, was sure she'd entered the code accurately.

Cara stood in front of the power and cable connections on the far wall, her toe kicking through a thick layer of brick dust scattered on the floor. She had plugged her smartpad directly into the landline while she worked.

A few minutes after she'd failed to sign onto the mainframe, it had occurred to her that she might have the answer after all. Ethan had a particular process when it came to his online activity, using an ultra-secure gateway tool that managed and updated all the various site log-ins and access codes he required, so that he only needed to remember one main password at once. The code she'd received by voicemail had given her access to the gateway. There were lots of verification tools on the directory, and it took her another five minutes to locate a particularly complex login process for a system she couldn't initially identify. Unless he had another mainframe elsewhere it might very well be the correct one. A glance at the nickname assigned to the code, 'C4U', gave her greater confidence that she was right when she remembered the unit's address. Cara saved the details to a notelet on the pad and signed off, unplugging from the wall when she was finished.

Back in the iso-room, perched over the server's keyboard, Cara typed with intentional over-caution again, referring constantly back to the smartpad's screen to ensure all the characters were copied correctly. Once it was done she sat back in the chair, reaching out to hit 'Enter' before clasping her hands together and closing her eyes for a moment in an echo of prayer.

A pause, a progress bar, and then a message. She was in!

Cara relaxed, almost slouching in the chair while she watched the monitor screen refresh itself as it came awake from its dormancy. The background image on the desktop showed a bar somewhere, two women in the foreground smiling for the camera. She didn't recognise either of them. They were both in their thirties, strong looking, their arms around each other like good friends, one white with crewcut peroxide blonde hair, whilst the other was probably Japanese, with a more stylish short bob. Both were dressed for a night out, glamorous though not overly polished. She didn't quite know what to make of it. They could be friends of Ethan's from before they met - she certainly didn't recognise the bar as anywhere they'd been - but they might be more than that for all she knew. Maybe it didn't matter now.

Cara frowned, and leant forward to look over the shortcuts displayed on the screen. There were surprisingly few, and none of the ubiquitous software icons that would be present on a typical mixed-use machine. In the centre of the screen, almost directly in line with the heads of the two mystery women, was a folder sat on its own, which she opened first.

She could hardly do otherwise, seeing as it was addressed to her.

Jakobsen stepped out from behind the packing crates and levelled his gun straight at Polzin, who stopped sharp at the sight of him. They were a mere ten feet apart, the distance having narrowed from continents to closure in the last few days. The surprise and fear on her face pleased him immensely. He felt giddy, forced himself to calm, raised the gun higher until it pointed straight at her face, walked forward a few more steps, increasing his threat and making things harder for her bodyguards.

Standing absolutely still now she stared straight into his eyes, frightened and determined, holding him frozen, his finger ready on the trigger, unable to complete the simplest of movements and perform the act that he had rehearsed so many times in his head. Time slowed to a stop as he held the gun steady, the rose and chrysanthemum sharp and clear on his arm.

The noise of others approaching, and now a larger tableau developed, more of her bodyguards behind and to the side, their own guns drawn, equally slow in those stretched seconds. And then the sound of sirens, drawing ever closer.

- Twenty Five -

> Chase

I took my time travelling back to the flat, almost lost in a city rendered strange by unfamiliar paths. I just couldn't accept that I'd killed Harris and yet had no memory of doing so. Even now, with the added stimulus, my mind refused to unlock, leaving me with the grainy images recorded by the security drone, a poor substitute for personal recollection. Regardless, that video would be enough to damn me as soon as someone got around to viewing it.

Perhaps that had already happened. When I returned home I ducked in through the garage as I'd been doing most of the week, and almost immediately noticed a van marked with CSS livery parked up beside my company car. Further round the corner were a couple of police cruisers, and another car that looked like Iyer's. There was no sign of any officers or Cadejo personnel down here, but I knew they'd have no problem accessing the flat while I was away: it was their property after all.

Deeply curious about what they were doing, not to mention just a little peeved at the intrusion, I decided I'd have to take a look. The Spydar would be perfect, though it was down to a half charge at the moment and I didn't want to waste its power having it climb the whole way up by itself. The stairwell was the best way to travel upwards and once I'd reached the floor below mine I headed in the direction of a small communal area that was located in the corner of the building. There were, as usual, a couple of open windows with enough of a gap for the Spydar to fit through. I sent it up and around the building to take a peek into my lounge while I took a seat on one of the padded chairs and hunched over the smartpad display.

The view inside my flat resembled nothing so much as a crime scene. I could see Iyer talking to Roberts in the kitchenette while Williams was at the back of the lounge, pacing about as she talked on the phone. Two uniformed officers were just outside the door and in the lounge a couple of white-suited techs were starting to conduct a methodical search of the flat, a couple of mini-drones shadowing each of them to record everything they were doing.

As the Spydar's viewpoint panned around I realised there was something there in the flat that I needed. Sitting in plain view on the drawer top were the rest of the meds for the concussion that the hospital had given me. They'd been specifically tailored to my body chemistry and condition in their onsite pharmafac, so there'd be no way of getting the same prescription without going back there again. I'd only taken about half the course and after thinking about it I knew that I didn't want to go without them.

Sending the little drone scurrying right across the glass to an open window, I then slipped it through the gap before dropping it down behind the furniture. From there I piloted it as it crawled along out of sight, before steering it up and onto the drawer top. The Spydar would be matching its shell to the colours and textures it walked on, and as I piloted it across the surface of the wood I could feel the tactile feedback on the 'pad from those tiny feet as though I was sharing every step.

When the Spydar reached the strip of capsules I had it grab them in its pincers and turn around to head back behind the furniture. It had only taken a few more steps before it went into a preset mode and paused, the view from its cameras now lower and fixed in place. I felt tense as though I was in the room with it, trying to see what was causing the little drone to go into a defensive posture until I saw a flicker of movement in the top of its vision, one of the forensic tech's mini-drones hovering above.

There was a noise in the background and the camera-bot blipped upward. Immediately the Spydar scurried forward at its top speed, dropped straight off the drawer top at the back and falling part way down before catching itself against the wall and furniture. It hung there momentarily, its legs fanned wide, before I steered it back and out of the window, flipping over as it exited and then hurrying it out of sight.

I left the Spydar in place there for a few moments, but I began to feel increasingly uncomfortable as it wasn't impossible that someone would have noticed it. Piloting the drone back as quickly as I could it was a relief when I could retrieve it and its cargo. Immediately I stowed it in my pocket as I made my way to the stairwell door.

After checking the way was clear I headed downwards at a brisk pace. I'd already passed the ground floor, and was almost at the sub-level landing, when the basement door opened and two uniformed police officers walked through. They were noisily debating the weekend's match schedule and weren't taking much notice of anyone else, but I was going too fast to turn around and head back up. The only way to proceed without looking suspicious was to continue. Pulling my elbows in I slowed a little, turning my torso to the side as I drew level with the coppers to allow them more space to pass. They appeared to take little notice of me, and were still chatting animatedly as we crossed paths. I was thankful I still had my hood pulled up covering my features.

When I reached the basement level itself I went straight through the access door and into the garage. There was no one around so I turned the corner and walked toward the vehicle entrance, trying to keep my pace relaxed. As I drew closer to my car I thought it would be useful to grab a few things from inside, so I retrieved the key fob from a pocket and pressed the unlock button. Instead of opening, the car's alarm signal started up, the sound of it incredibly loud in the echoing space of the garage.

I was already beginning to walk away when I heard the basement door slam open. Turning my walk into a run, I headed out of there as fast as I could. As I drew further away from the wailing car I could hear the sound of running footsteps and shouting. Running hard, I slowed just a little to vault over the barrier and make a tight turn at the garage entrance, before sprinting away.

If they caught me I would be arrested and in a cell within minutes, and I couldn't let that happen. There was only myself that I could trust to follow through on the investigation, and I so desperately needed to find some truth in all of this.

> Reznik

Reznik was working as fast as he could to clear his presence from the apartment, as quickly and thoroughly as possible. It was a matter of prioritisation, and some of the less critical stuff would just have to be left.

After running a quick perimeter check, the first thing he'd done on returning was to power everything down and stow the absolute essentials before taking a couple more painkillers and cleaning himself up. It was partly good sense, to deal with any minor infections and so that he looked less remarkable, but in truth a lot of it was because he felt like crap. Reznik ran the shower as hot as he thought could stand, got in and turned his bruised and bloodied face straight into the stream of water. He withdrew almost immediately, stung, the pain and heat almost pulling the air from his lungs. After turning down the temp a little he waited before sticking his face back into the flow. This time he kept his head directly under until he felt clean again. To finish off he applied a couple of sachets of the dry gel, letting that soak in while his mind wandered over the events of the last 48 hours. There was plenty to think about, and he found no clear answers.

As soon as he was dry and dressed he gathered the rest of the important stuff into his ready bag, a small rucksack that already had spare clothes, some food and other essentials inside. The main things he couldn't leave behind were his laptop and smartpad, and he'd already packed those.

His DNA and biological traces would be all over the apartment by now, and there wasn't enough time to clean the place thoroughly. Most of his clothing would only have ordinary environmental and organic traces, so he'd bagged those to take them down to the laundry room in the basement. The clothes from last night were another matter, along with a few items that he'd worn under his overalls when he visited the construction site and the garage where he'd stored the drones. Those he dealt with next, drowning them all in the sink under plenty of water thick with cleanser and strong detergent.

With that done it was time he moved on, but it would be worth setting the rest of the laundry on a cleaning cycle on the way out. He picked up his rucksack before heading for the front door, and after grabbing the washing bags in one hand he used the other to exit the apartment.

His door opened straight onto a narrow landing bordered by a bannister rail. Before he was even fully outside he froze. Ahead and a few feet down were the black-armoured heads of the city's assault police, filing up the stairs quietly in tightly disciplined order, their rifles tracking the way forward. At the front was an officer in a power-assisted suit, her voice already rising in alarm. Reznik hoisted the laundry bags straight at their heads before turning and running back into the apartment, the lead officer close behind. As soon as he'd cleared the doorway Reznik shouted out 'Bulldog!'.

Breaching charges detonated all around, blasting out the big windows along the balcony and the open doorway, scattering glass fragments at the legs of a SWAT trooper roping down outside. There was a heavy thud and shouts from behind and more cries from ahead as Reznik leapt through the window frame on the tail of the shockwave, landing on the balcony and surprising another trooper who slipped and fell as soon as his feet hit the ground.

Running straight ahead Reznik caught a female officer around the waist as she was landing, carried her along as he leapt from the balcony edge across the narrow street to the next building, dropping her mid-flight. He caught the edge of the roof opposite, one hand slipping, the other gripping firmly as his body swung there.

The broad street below was busy with pedestrians, many turning away or toward the explosion and the fallen officer, her cries of pain and shock joining with the crowd's and with the shouts of the troops following behind. Reznik swung up, grabbing the edge of the roof with his trailing hand and then edged along as quickly as he could, dropping straight down once he reached the corner to land on a brightly coloured awning. Relief flipped to alarm as he sank down further than expected, the fabric straining and ripping a little with the sudden weight. He walked along the canopy close to the building frontage, strides comically clumsy on the shifting surface, almost on all fours.

When he reached the awning edge he grasped the supporting ironwork frame, rolled over, and dropped to the ground. Reznik felt like the only thing in motion as he accelerated away, running as fast and hard as he could into the static crowd, weaving his way through while he keeping his head low.

His instincts were good but his enemies were callous beyond his expectations. He heard but didn't see the first of the SWAT troops open fire from his apartment balcony, the murderous impact of their shots on the people around him unmistakable. Pedestrians and onlookers fell, wounded or dead, random victims left sprawling in his wake just as he heard angry shouts behind and an abrupt end to the firing. Police, ordinary officers, were ahead in the middle distance, propped against their patrol car, turning in shock toward the shootings, rushing toward the victims. Further on an armoured troop carrier thundered into place, blue-black and bristling with grenade launchers.

His pace unrelenting, Reznik made it to the opposite side of the road. Ahead was a narrower side street, choked with civilians just beginning to feel the panic. Beyond them the doorway of a corner bar swung open to allow a drunk to weave his awkward exit.

Reznik ran toward him, knocking the man to the side as he pushed past into the bar. The drop in light levels inside was dramatic but his optics, tuned to his heightened state, switched automatically to low-light, splashing the dingy interior in emerald opulence, surfaces bright with scattered light. There was as a door at the far side, a private exit through to the kitchens and a back way out. He ran for it, barged through.

Outside the cries of the crowd changed tenor as the troop carrier fired a wave of grenades, gas billowing out and felling any civilians who inhaled enough right where they stood. Hexrotors flew overhead recording the scene and it wasn't long before the first of the mediacams arrived.

> Cara

Cara didn't quite know what to make of the news. She'd caught the latest headlines as she made her way to the hospital and had been surprised to see that the detective, Chase, had been named as a suspect in the death of John Harris at the mall. It seemed like the only one beside herself who'd shown any real interest in Ethan was a corporate detective under suspicion himself, but something really didn't fit with that. Chase must have known he was in trouble, but he'd still been looking into Ethan's murder and certainly appeared to have found out more than the ordinary police had. She'd kept his card, with the private number scrawled on the back. Maybe she should call him.

They'd agreed on this place as it was convenient enough for them both and not too shabby, but he was already twenty minutes late. She still had half a beer left, and was determined not to rush it. The last thing Cara wanted to do was get pissed but she was so tired after staring at Ethan's computer all day, not to mention emotional, that she could tell she was more susceptible than usual.

It had been worth it though. Cara had cried again when she'd seen Ethan's latest message, but there probably wouldn't be any more. She'd not figured out what he'd been up to yet, though she had found an inventory listing the contents of the various plastic boxes stacked on top of the little table, and was relieved to see that most of it, if not all, was entirely legal and not at all dangerous. A lot of it turned out to be surveillance equipment, and she'd spent a couple of hours installing some of it in the warehouse to boost the security back to its original level. It felt like she would need to spend quite a lot of time there. Ethan might have made it easy for her to access everything once she'd found out about the warehouse, but he'd not seen fit to leave her an explanation of what was actually going on.

Cara was done with waiting. She drained the last of her glass and had slid halfway off the stool when he finally arrived. Stuck in mid-movement, one buttock still perched there on the seat's edge, the other free, she'd been forced to hook her foot awkwardly around the stool's cross bar to find enough leverage to push herself back into position. He either didn't notice or didn't care.

"Alright Ceed, 'ow's it going? Sorry I'm late, been a bit busy. What you 'avin'?"

Thorne had said it was about Ethan, that he had some news, so she didn't have much choice but to meet him. He knew someone in the police it turned out, or claimed to, and from them had found out something quite interesting about Ethan's original identity.

"See, this Jakobsen fella was some kind of special forces guy, working as a mercenary. Specialised in electronic warfare, drone piloting, that sort of thing. Turns out that officially 'e died two years ago, on some mission. Until your man got himself thrown off a balcony, everyone thought e'd been long dead. Your fella, Ethan, that was just some name 'e took on a couple of years back."

The casualness of his manner hurt her deeply, but she was determined not to show any sign of it, her face as placid as she could make it. "Did this contact of yours have any idea what he was up to then? What do the police think was the motive?"

"Between you an' me, they 'aven't got the foggiest. Might be something to do with all that black ops stuff. They don't even know who killed 'im, they just think this mall security manager guy was in on it. That rentacop killed that bloke before 'e'd been questioned, apparently when 'e caught 'im uploading a virus to the mall's server. Lost loads of data."

"And what about the rentacop, the detective? How does he figure in all this?"

"'e was the lead investigator for the private firm the police passed the case on to. They do that with anything too complicated they can't solve quickly. It was 'im who first found out there was something dodgy about the guy from the mall, and when 'e went to confront 'im ended up shooting the bloke somehow. 'e's proper shafted now though."

Thorne didn't have any more to add, but it took another half hour and another round of drinks to find that out. At the end he asked her if she fancied a fuck. It would have been nearly impossible to fully explain how much she really didn't.

> Schuler

They met on the embankment, in the shadows between two street lamps, like a couple of old spies. Schuler smiled a little at the thought, when Thorne wasn't looking, amused.

"Well, did things go as expected? Were you able to tell her everything?"

"Yeah, told Ceed everything. Just like you said."

"Excellent! And how did she take it, did she tell you anything in turn?"

"Nah, not really. I could see that most of it was news to 'er, but she didn't give much away. Keeps 'er cards close to 'er chest, does Cara. Always did."

"Sensible habit. And you managed to keep her occupied for a couple of hours, as agreed?"

"Yeah no problem. I strung things out as much as I could and I was a bit late meeting 'er in the first place. Then again if I'd been on time she'd probably get suspicious. Best to meet 'er expectations, if you know what I mean."

"Yes, I think I do. Well, unless there's anything else...?"

"No, everything went well, everything done as you asked."

"Good. For now I believe that's the first part of our business concluded." He handed over a small white envelope, and did his best not to show offence while the other man tore it open roughly and extracted a one-use cash card, turning it over to view both sides before swiping it across his 'pad.

"Everything in order?"

"Yeah, thanks very much Mr. Sauveterre. Always nice to meet a new client."

"Yes, indeed. I'll bid you good night then. Safe journey home."

"Yeah, thanks. Cheers. Same to you."

Schuler turned and left, smiling to himself again.

Another hospital, plainer, less private. It looked like a relic from the last century, everything too analogue.

He awoke again, and was startled for a moment when he saw Reznik there. This was becoming a habit, but something about the other man's expression made Jakobsen try and sit up, alert and wary. Reznik motioned with his hand for him to stay. They were hardly friends, but Jakobsen could see from the other man's icy expression they might be even less now.

"Do you know where Polzin is?" Reznik, sounding rougher, more Wolf.

"No, I... No I don't."

"Neither does anyone else now. After you fucked things up she went to ground."

"I'm sorry! Look, I..."

"Save it. Get better. Drop me a line when you're ready to do things my way."

Jakobsen took the business card offered, a simple white rectangle with a darknet email address. It was much too small to contain the agreement that would bind him until the end of his life.

- Twenty Six -

> Chase

I came awake in an instant, snapping from dirty light and shockwave to an altogether different feeling of pressure, someone leaning over, too close, stink of sweat and booze. Squirming away I pushed, lashed out, covering my head in a crude guard, then finding some space, twisting upright and punching, rising quickly to my feet and then going in harder, two or three fast jabs, hands connecting with fabric and fastenings and the flesh beneath. Then back to defence like a boxer, heart racing and head gone, looking for another opening but pulling back as he did, staring passively as he turned and cursed his way out of the loft, his jagged teeth chewing the words to sharpness as he stumbled off down the stairs.

He'd probably been gone a few minutes before I came down properly, pacing the loft, quickly learning its limits: the floorboards that creaked a little too much, that one over there that shifted as I placed my weight on it. My thoughts raced, careering between delayed fear, relief and exhilaration. It took me a while to settle down.

When I was properly calm I sat against the chimney buttress, jacket folded to make a crude cushion, after a few minutes only barely better than nothing at all. It was cold here, my breath misting, everything damp and neglected, the wall hard and rough against my back.

Ordinarily there'd be no chance of getting any sleep in a place like this, but I'd been so tired after a day on the run earlier that I'd dropped off anyway. It wasn't so much the physical aspect but the mental, constantly alert for surveillance. The smartlenses would have been a big help, but I could hardly sign into the police-band AR to get the camera locations. In truth, they were everywhere, so it was more a case of keeping my head covered and avoiding those that were likely part of live monitoring nets rather than private systems.

I'd needed a good night's sleep, but that's not what I got. Instead, my dreams drew me back to Paris, that endless, unremitting loop of experience. The way I picture it now, especially the way I dream it, isn't really the way it was, but the way it should have been. Somehow, I've either invented or recalled detail that I simply wasn't aware of at the time, tiny indicators and signs that build and build the pressure of the memory until it explodes with all the force of the bomb that nearly killed me. Maybe one day I'll dream a different path, heed the signs, and be somewhere else entirely.

I was there as part of a new investigation supporting a special judicial task force, shadowing one of the prime suspects as she made her way to a meet. We were gathering evidence, didn't have enough to pull in the whole crew yet, and there was every chance we'd learn something useful from that day's surveillance, so most of the core team were in or near the gallery when it blew.

It shouldn't have happened. The suspect had no known links to terrorism, and so when her contact turned out to be a militant we were unprepared, improvising. He was important enough that an immediate arrest was warranted, and we moved in to take both of them into custody.

But if we were caught by surprise, he wasn't. He'd been living as an outlaw for months, known he was hunted, and expected an arrest any time. The bio-explosives he carried were new then, had only been rumoured, and we had no idea of the danger. As we moved in he sank to his knees, passive and calm, waiting until we had him surrounded before he triggered the device.

We lost most of the team that day, good people. If I'd been much closer to the epicentre I'd never have survived either. I suppose I was just lucky.

I'd been looking at the copies of the data files from the mall's security drone my Admirer had left me for a couple of hours before I spotted it. After so much time spent searching through the tiny lines of coding, even with the 'pads *aigent* offering assistance, it was hard to believe I wasn't just hallucinating, especially as I was still absolutely shattered. Despite trying to get as comfortable as I could going back to sleep had been impossible, so after a while I'd just given up and started working.

As I looked through the data again, the screen so close it began to mist over from my breath, I felt more confident I was right. The relief at finding something, even such a tiny, intricate thing as this, was overwhelming and I couldn't concentrate again for a few minutes.

It turned out there were some discrepancies in the drone's core activity logs, a locational difference between where the summarised output report said the drone had been since the events of the Saturday night a week ago and where its GPS log said it was. In a smaller building it probably wouldn't have registered, but the mall covered the centre space of a whole city block, one wing many yards from another and tagged with different grid numbers. Numbers that were telling different stories.

I began to look for other anomalies and found a couple more sometime later. There had been a change posted to the drone's standing instruction set in the late afternoon of the Saturday, but I couldn't make sense of the coding, except that the alterations looked complex. What was much clearer was that the machine's memory file had been tampered with. Ordinarily it would record data from its onboard sensors continuously, unless the unit was on standby, and store the files until they were uploaded to the central server. In this case though the base activity log showed that data from the Saturday evening through to the Wednesday had been overwritten with a new file, originating in the unit's external data port. In effect the machine's original memories of the Saturday night had been replaced with false ones.

Picking up the burner phone, I was half-way through dialling Mallory to give her the news when I stopped. I had to get my emotions under control. Whoever was behind all this had a good knowledge of police procedure and enough technical resources to fool an active and detailed murder enquiry, and they were at least one step ahead. Besides, I'd yet to test this new evidence. The falsified video left on the security drone looked real enough at face value, and that combined with the forensics, however incomplete they might be, would have been enough to persuade some people of my guilt. It would take time and effort to convince them otherwise. There was also the fact I might expose my Admirer to scrutiny seeing as I would have no ready explanation for how I obtained the drone's files.

Right now I was already so far out on a limb I may as well stay there. After I'd run I'd headed outward on bus after bus until I'd finally made it here. The best place to go seemed to be where no one would look, where the destitute and damaged gathered, just inside the boundary of the current Civil Safety Zone, in an area technically free of contamination but still abandoned. Here there'd been another bomb, much larger and many years ago now, and the city still bore its scars.

I wondered if it were time to take a thorough look at the files on the rest of the hard drives I'd been given. There was a great deal of data, far more than I could process with the gear I had.

Maybe Dalca would help: she certainly had a motive, and the terminal in her office was more powerful than anything I had.

> Reznik

He was several blocks distant from the massacre now but the memory of it was fresh, as though the whole event was still happening around him. There was no guilt as such, more regret. That and a painful ache in his shoulder, now that the adrenaline was long gone.

It was a messy, botched operation by the police assault team and he didn't doubt that they would twist the facts of the incident around until it was entirely someone else's fault, most likely his. Maybe they'd have a point, at least in part. It was perhaps cynical of him to have run into the crowd, but he'd not expected them to fire so indiscriminately in response. He really should have heard them coming as they approached the apartment but he'd been so preoccupied with sanitising the place that he missed them. The security grid had failed as well, somehow none of his sensors triggering an alarm, which was a concern in itself.

Really, the blame for all this was on them. He'd not fired a single shot, though he had to admit he'd fired off plenty of breaching charges. There was also the female trooper who would certainly have been hurt as she fell from the balcony, but apart from that his only aggressive act had been to lob his dirty laundry over their heads. In the end, the only way he could have prevented the incident was to surrender. Even with hindsight it was a choice he would never willingly make.

Ahead he could hear people, car horns and bustle. He hoped fervently there were no police there that might recognise him from his description. Any officers he encountered this far from his apartment would most likely have heard about the shootings second hand through false reports and rumours, so he could count on an aggressive response if he was spotted.

Emerging from an alley he entered one of the district's main streets. The road ahead was choked with traffic made torpid by the news of the incident and a series of hastily erected roadblocks, the nearest just tens of yards away. Reznik took a quick look around and then walked straight across the road, keeping his head low and turned away as he wove a path between the crawling vehicles. Fortunately, he was by no means the only pedestrian to cross from one side of the street to the other in such a way, and the officers were in any case too busy calming and checking the frustrated drivers to take note of their passage. Evading more sophisticated surveillance was a greater concern, but he was one amongst many and had done his best to alter his appearance a little by grabbing a jacket and cap as he travelled.

He wondered again if he'd been betrayed, or if they'd simply spotted and tailed him back to the apartment at some point. There was no way of knowing. Whoever had usurped and escalated his operation to target Polzin must have been informed of his activities one way or another well in advance, so he may have been under observation for quite some time. Whoever they were, they were good: he never once suspected anything. Thinking that now made him worry all the more.

> Cara

She had made progress, of sorts, though the more she learned of Ethan's activities the more he felt like a stranger. He was almost morphing into this Karl Jakobsen figure before her eyes and she hated it. It was as though her memory was a finite space, and the more new things she learned about him the more of her older understanding was overwritten. Cara was slowly losing him all over again, and it was hard to separate out which time was worst.

As soon as she'd returned to the warehouse that morning she'd been unable to resist watching the message he'd left again. This one was more business-like and less emotional than the first, and spoken as though he believed that there was little chance he'd sail cleanly through his troubles. He'd not been wrong as it turned out.

It was only a short clip and he didn't say overly much. Mostly it was a rundown of the security in the warehouse and what the mainframe could do. No mention of who or what had him worried, and little explanation of why he'd half expected her to come here, just a wry smile and a remark that she could see through him if she tried, and that he might as well help her if she got this far.

Cryptic again. If he was really that smart then perhaps he should have saved himself.

After she'd installed the surveillance kit yesterday she'd done little more than have a quick poke around in the system to judge its specifications. This time Cara had come with a more determined mindset, a strong conviction that she could and would learn enough from this machine to understand what he was into and where it went wrong.

Cara began to work, methodically listing the mainframe's hard, firm and soft 'ware capabilities before moving on to assessing the types and sizes of data files it held, along with the hierarchy of storage he'd used. It didn't take her long to confirm that in a sense the machine didn't hold very much considering its size and capabilities, and that this was exactly the point; the high level of spare capacity it had would allow the computer to run at very impressive speeds. He'd tailored the set-up toward hacking and code-cracking, and the inclusion of some darknet applications, specialist cloud access and sophisticated encryption and browser software only reinforced that impression.

Her younger self would have done more than a few things she shouldn't to have the opportunity to play on a set up like this. In her current state it was looking almost as attractive. Though this was all interesting it told her what he could do, not what he had actually done. She would need to look through the various data files, and perhaps the system logs, to get a sense of that.

Cara took a break around lunchtime to go out and get some hot food and find somewhere nicer to pee. It was then, as she exited the clean room, that her phone updated itself with all of the messages she'd missed. The voicemail from the detective, Chase, stood out and she called him back immediately. He answered after only a brief delay.

"Hello. Is that Miss Dalca?"

"No, it's Cara, stop referring to me like we've never met!"

"Sorry. Cara, then."

She took a breath. "Ok, sorry, I'm just a little tense. Didn't mean to snap at you."

"That's alright. I can empathise I think."

"Yeah, you probably can. I saw the news. So, what do you want?"

"I need your help, and I think in return I can help you."

There it was, the part where he wanted something. As far as she could tell though, from the news and what she'd seen herself Chase – Keegan? – had spent more time investigating Ethan's death than anyone else. He said with her help they might be able to learn more, but he'd need someone with a powerful computer and the skills to make use of it. That did sound like her.

They talked for a while longer, and agreed to meet at the warehouse, though he sounded reluctant at first, suggesting her flat or somewhere neutral instead. She'd not said as much yet, but she would help him if she could. There was just the small matter of Chase being wanted by the police.

But she could relate to that.

The damp chill penetrated deeply, making it feel much colder than home even though the numbers said otherwise. The fact that Jakobsen had just stepped out from the warmth of the plane didn't really help. It was something he would have to get used to as Reznik's plan demanded he mostly stay here now and track Polzin remotely.

Jakobsen had only been here once before, years ago, so the prospect of spending months here was not unattractive, though he very much wished he'd arrived in the summer. They were enduring some of the worst winter weather they'd seen in years, and if it had been much more severe he wouldn't have got here today at all.

If he hurried now he could get to the terminal before most of his fellow passengers, and hopefully grab his luggage first. Next would be customs, and he was not looking forward to it. Now he was safely on the ground it was the first point at which things could really go wrong.

- Twenty Seven -

> Chase

I wasn't sure what kind of a reception I'd get. It had taken me a good part of the afternoon to get there, and on the way I'd brooded over the amount of trust I was placing in Dalca. It was an uncomfortable experience to have travelled amongst so many people for so long and yet feel so isolated, and maintaining the necessary level of vigilance had been draining.

Cara had been a little off when we'd spoken on the phone earlier, but her mood seemed to have improved since then. She answered the door quickly, and greeted me warmly enough. As we headed deeper inside the warehouse, and into the shielded rooms that filled the shipping containers, she became visibly more relaxed with every door that closed behind us until we were standing in the right-hand clean room, each propped up against one of the tables. She'd ended up on the side furthest from the plastic cases, and looked a little worried at the way that had worked out, but as I'd made no move toward any of the hardware she seemed to lose at least some of her anxiety. I spoke anyway, trying to reassure her, "It's ok Cara, I've absolutely no plans to use any of this stuff. Honestly, I'm in enough trouble already for just allegedly killing someone. I really don't want to do it for real."

"Great, cool, that's very reassuring. Don't suppose you'd swap sides anyway?"

"Sure, no problem." We did so, and her expression and posture became a little more relaxed. She smiled again, a tight, quick gesture of warmth that was exquisitely welcome.

"Ok Cara, I came here to ask for your help. I really appreciate you agreeing to at least listen."

"Shoot."

I looked at her for a moment, and then continued. "Firstly, the crime I've been accused of, I didn't do. I have information on me that proves it, but I'm not really here for that – it's not the thing I need help with. What I do need is for someone to analyse a whole load of mainframe data for me. It might be difficult as the info was grabbed from a badly corrupted system – so you'll have to watch out for viruses as well – but there may be something there that will throw some light on how and why Grant was killed. It might not be much, but it's better than nothing. And to be honest no one else seems to be looking into it."

She didn't reply immediately. I suppose the whole thing was a lot to take in. "Show me the evidence that proves you didn't shoot that guy first. Then we'll see."

"Fair enough." I stood and retrieved the 'pad from my bag before moving to the side so she could join me and see the display. Using the device to demonstrate the process, I quickly went through how I'd found the anomalous GPS and memory file logs on the mall security drone, and in addition how I believed the footage itself would probably show up as a fake with enough analysis. It felt good to explain everything out loud to another human being and watch their expression change from wary scepticism to acceptance and even sympathy. I'd mentally rehearsed having just such a conversation with Mallory or the police, but I didn't fully imagine the simple joy I would feel at being believed and vindicated.

And then we were back to business. Dalca wanted to know more about where the mainframe data came from, and the kind of thing I might be looking for. I explained about how Harris had said he'd found 'too much activity'. At the time I'd no idea what he meant, but now I speculated aloud on whether he'd simply seen the first stirrings of the virus that was unleashed that night.

"The thing is, Cara, whether Harris had actually found something or not I think he was killed to prevent him talking about it or digging any further. And I can't accept that the virus being released so close to the time of his death was a coincidence. There was obviously information on that system that could lead to Grant's killer."

I continued, "there's something else I need from you though: you sent me three videos you'd captured from somewhere of people who'd visited this place. Two of them were the intruders I chased off when we first met, the other was someone else. I need to know where you got those pictures from and if there are any more."

"Ok, I guess that's fair." She indicated the monitor beside us. "That shows the feeds from various security cameras around the warehouse. I took the images from that. There's more on there if you want to look through it."

"Great, I appreciate that. I'll swap you a copy of the mainframe data for a copy of your surveillance footage."

"Deal. I suppose if we're going to do this we'd best get cracking."

> Reznik

Reznik needed somewhere quiet and out of the way, so he'd picked a cheap backstreet hostel that catered mainly to backpackers. He was doing his best to blend in, booking a room with cash and generally minding his own business. There was a 'pad balanced on his lap as he watched TV on the bed, with an earpiece running to one ear, though his attention was split between the news broadcast and his own recollections of the day.

The massacre outside his apartment had made the headlines now, and the story had been folded into the general narrative of terror and hate. There were no pictures of the assault troops, just ordinary uniformed officers and paramedics. It was strange to see the aftermath on screen, high-angle shots of the street, smoke still billowing out from the grenades, occasional breaks in the cover revealing civilians lain prone on the ground. Many were clearly alive but suffering from the gas, retching and convulsing on their knees, but others were eerily still, haloed by dark-stained earth.

There was a related story about a raid on a building said to be the base for one of the bombers. Another sequence of images taken from the air, kinetic and confusing. Black-clad SWAT officers formed a human chain, passing an almost endless stream of strip-cuffed gang members along and into the backs of armoured police trucks, while helicopter rotors kicked up a storm of dust and dirt. He'd been looking at the shots for half a minute before he recognised the location as the old hotel where he'd met Santos. There was no clear sign of the boy, though one of the prisoners, about his build, was brought out alone with their head hooded and bundled roughly into a separate vehicle. Reznik was surprised to feel some tension at that, a hint of concern.

The news moved on. There were other raids on other parts of the city, new checkpoints and control zones as part of an emergency pacification programme, whole districts cleaved from their neighbours and encircled. Regular army units supported the police with troops and armoured vehicles while fleets of drones flew, trundled and skittered everywhere. In response, there were inevitable outbreaks of violence, locals and gangs incensed at the authorities, who responded with aggression and heavy hands. OraCotek was featured again, this time for donating some of their latest models of drones and cyber systems to the authorities.

It was all much too fast. He knew that from the scale of the response that there must have been plans in place ahead of time, at least as a contingency, for them to undertake such extensive operations in the favelas, areas where central authority was traditionally weaker and there were few obvious nodes of control.

There was a smaller story, mentioned in brief at the end, of a foreigner who'd been near the bombings that the police feared had been badly affected by the experience. He was said to be violent, suffering from paranoid delusions and possible trauma. Reznik could almost see it coming as an image of his own face appeared on screen with an emergency contact number for the police. It was better than being named outright as a terrorist, but not by much.

As he exited the app it highlighted a number of other news reports. There was an update on the death of the man who'd fallen through the mall display in Auldwiche, that Reznik was about to dismiss when a picture he didn't expect appeared on screen. It was Jakobsen, identified with both his real and assumed names. In that moment he felt like he'd taken a fall of his own.

Reznik thought back to his conversation with Murdoch, after he'd first learned that Jakobsen was in trouble. Murdoch must have known something even then, and yet he'd been deliberately misleading. Just an accident, he'd said, no chance the police would identify him. Yet they'd done exactly that. It could be some kind of operational parameter horseshit, some need-to-know thing, but he was still pissed.

There was a little fear too, in case it meant something entirely more serious. Not just a wrinkle, but a permanent kink. He knew everyone outgrew their usefulness eventually: he just didn't expect it to happen to him yet. Usually, you'd be retired quietly, but he'd always supposed before that he would have at least an inkling in advance of when that might be coming. And then he realised that you wouldn't really, most of the time.

> Cara

She left Chase with the security logs while she took the portable hard drives through to the main computer inside the small isolation room. The first thing she'd done was to run a thorough diagnostic on each unit to check for viruses, malware, worms and any other disease-inspired shit. When everything checked out she uploaded the contents of all three drives to a segregated memory partition on the main system, and then ran another set of search tools to get a good overview of what he'd brought her.

It was obvious to her that the data she had was partial and fragmented, pieces of a whole. The overall shape of the system's architecture, and the kinds of files and data that would have been stored, was all still evident, like the bare walls of an abandoned building. The problem was that the virus had stripped or scrambled most of the décor and trashed the place, not so much in an overly boisterous party but in a focused blitz of vandalism. Cara wasn't sure if she'd be able to help Chase even before she'd seen the data, but she had serious doubts now.

She was tired, and so engrossed in her initial analysis of the files, that at first she'd missed it. The mainframe was running a large download in the background, and as soon as she noticed Cara tried to block it, but by the time she'd accessed the proper menu using the unfamiliar utilities it was already too late. The software was installing automatically at a rapid rate, prioritising itself and disregarding her stop commands. This should be interesting. At least if she'd killed Ethan's computer he wasn't around to complain.

"Chase, I think you'd better take look at this." She had to call out again, much louder, and heard him push his chair back and come in. "I don't know what's going on, Chase, but I'm fairly sure it's not good." She knew she'd insisted he call her Cara, but calling him Keegan in return didn't seem to fit.

"Fuck!" That summed it up pretty well.

A face appeared on screen, a beautiful young woman with uncannily alert eyes. Her features were unarguably fine and clear, and yet impossible to pin down to any particular time and place: she seemed to belong nowhere and everywhere. In terms of her pigmentation she was similar, a tanned Caucasian or light-skinned Arab or Central American perhaps, the underlying bone structure just as non-specific. The face spoke, frowned, and spoke again, this time with a speech bubble appearing beside her.

"*Hi, afternoon. Good to meet you! Well, quite good, this thing's really cramped and I can't actually see or hear much.*"

"Ah."

"Chase, what's going on, who is she?"

"She's not really a She, she's an It. Raissa, as in r-A-I-s-s-a. She's Cadejo's main AI. Raissa's a friend, if that's the right word."

Cara was deeply suspicious at first, but once Chase and Raissa had explained things she relented a little. It turned out that Chase, like most people, was using the AI term a bit loosely. Raissa was an extremely complex and capable expert system, a so-called weak AI, rather than a truly independent machine intelligence. Definitely not a run-from-it-and-hide-it-might-send-killer-robots-from-the-future super AI.

The part she particularly didn't like in all this was that there'd been an extremely subtle utility hidden amongst the mall data that would locate and download Raissa from an internet connection without the system administrator's express knowledge and without the usual permissions. It wasn't a full copy of her/its program, rather a portable version for more modest systems, but it was still powerful. Regardless, her antivirals hadn't detected it, which meant either that it was very, very well written or Ethan's software was not as good as she would have expected.

Cara ran all this through in her head while she sat back and watched Raissa sprint through the raw data Chase had brought and start to pull out pieces of information like they glowed in the dark. It was a bit disconcerting at first: she'd never had the opportunity to work with such a powerful AI before, and the experience was if anything a little humbling.

If she could get Raissa to work on analysing Ethan's machine as well then she might get that much closer to working out what got him killed.

Jakobsen was sure that Polzin had left Europe entirely and gone to ground in South America, like an old Nazi, though he very much doubted she'd appreciate the comparison. He'd like to think he'd scared her away himself, but there were strong indications that he wasn't the only one looking for her. In fact he felt obliged to muddy the waters almost to her advantage, not to help her but to keep her out of the way of anyone else's harm.

He liked it here, in this big old city, once the heart of the world but now more the lobe of much of its memory. And money. It was easy to work from and Jakobsen had always enjoyed cultured places. There were endless things to see here, especially now that he'd found someone to appreciate them with.

Cara. He liked her a lot. Jakobsen always wondered what a life beyond the military and the strange, murky world of PMCs would be like, and he could almost see a shape to it now. Maybe this was something special. He looked forward to finding out.

- Twenty Eight -

> Chase

Watching the new footage of the kidnappers again gave me a certain level of professional respect for them. They were both careful to keep their faces covered and away from the cameras, though Ruscoe had been partially in view before the fogging agent took full effect. Jakobsen had been cautious, obviously not expecting visitors, but they were slick enough not to give him any further cause for alarm. Ruscoe served as a distraction while the woman approached to administer some kind of gas, neutralising Jakobsen easily. They then gathered him up and carried him over to their van without further fuss. The whole thing was smoothly done and over in moments.

From his file Ruscoe appeared to be a freelancer, a professional for hire, rather than a fully independent operator. Presumably he was working for someone else this time as well, though the list of previous associates was long enough that it would be pointless to try and speculate exactly who at this stage. Kidnap wasn't really part of this usual repertoire though, nor was it typical of the people he was known to have worked for, so this might be something new.

I was curious as to how Dalca had known about this place, whether she'd ever been here when Ethan was alive. If she saw that as a leading question in any way she went right by it, explaining that she'd first learned about it from an old...acquaintance, who'd had business dealings of some kind with Ethan, and who was still owed money.

It was unfortunate that I'd not been able to run any more queries through the Cadejo network before they closed down my access, but now we had a mini-Raissa working for us that might not be a problem. As well as the other two from the warehouse, and this Thorne character, it should be possible to trace the van they'd used and the car I'd seen at one of Ruscoe's addresses as well.

I'd been checked in with Cara now and then, but I wasn't able to offer much assistance and she seemed too distracted to engage in small talk. The one time I spoke to Raissa directly Cara left us to it, saying she needed a break anyway.

"Hi Chase, long time no visual recognition."

"Hi Raissa. What's the situation with you being here?"

"This is a mini-me, a compressed and compacted version of the main-me back at Cadejo. I don't have the full range of awesomeness, but I can cloud-source extras as needed or link up with the boss if necessary. She says 'Hi' by the way, and that there's a file for you."

It didn't take me long to establish that this Raissa was able to operate in the background as an extension of the primary Raissa, more or less below everyone's radar. Except for her own, but they kind of had an arrangement, apparently. I wasn't really sure how that would work out, but I needed those searches running so it was best to just get on with it.

When Cara returned I'd just finished downloading the file Raissa mentioned. It was an ID and history for the unidentified man from the warehouse, whose name was Conrad Schuler, though he was known to use aliases when it suited him. As well as the basic profile there was plenty of biographical data, but none of it really explained why he might visit the industrial estate, unless he expected to meet someone restoring a classic roadster there.

Schuler was a corporate consultant of some kind, peddling a respected lineage and an excellent education into two decades of fully-expensed luxury travel around the world and a fat wallet. Intelligence obtained from law enforcement agencies suggested there might be a bit more to him, though there were few specifics. All we had were rumours that suggested he was a fixer of some kind, adept at finding solutions to intractable issues, not all of them entirely legal.

If someone like Schuler was involved then there was a hell of a lot more going on here than I'd guessed at. He operated at the fringes of the corporate and political worlds, and was a league apart from common criminals. Clearly, he had an interest in Jakobsen, though whether he was opposed to or in support of him I couldn't say.

I wondered then if my situation was his doing. Whatever had been going on with Jakobsen at the mall, the murder of Harris and my own apparent involvement had drawn attention elsewhere, and the virus that destroyed the mall mainframe had everyone assuming there'd be nothing left to find. If that was his plan, it was going pretty well for him so far.

> Reznik

The hostel had grown steadily quieter, and it had begun to nag at him. His room was roughly above the main lounge area, which had been boisterous all the time he'd been there, but not in the last few minutes. The only thing around him that seemed to be moving was the wind, which was picking up just as the temperature was falling, signalling a break in the weather.

Reznik gathered his few things and left, quickly and quietly. There were guarded looks from some of the other residents as he moved through the building, whispered gestures, and he was certain now he'd been recognised. A moment of alarm in the eyes of a man who looked a little too old and a little too local to be there as he crossed quickly through the restaurant, out onto the patio and straight over the low wall at the rear, dropping down into a quiet alley that snaked down the hill onto a main street.

Reznik didn't get far before he felt eyes at his back. He took note of their reflections in the shop windows as he passed, his own battered face mingling with theirs, tourist tat and bric-a-brac throwing bold colour from the background. They were cops: plainclothes, but definitely cops. Off in the distance he'd seen just enough of a squad car at rest to gain further confirmation. That these were only police gave him a little hope. He took care not to betray any sign that he'd spotted them, fearful that they would bring stronger reinforcements, risk an arrest despite the crowds and his new reputation.

He continued on as though everything was ordinary, but felt hemmed in, committed to this direction even as the scene changed. The number of commercial properties on this stretch of road grew fewer as he moved uphill, with more and more residences pushing into place. Colours and hues, individualised and bright in the daylight, now became shades of grey as dusk began to fall and the clouds gathered. There were fewer people around, most of them hurrying somewhere ahead of the storm. Under normal circumstance he might be fractionally more welcome here than his tail, but with the ongoing terror alert and crackdown it was hard to say now who would inspire greater sympathy.

If he took a left soon he could make his way toward one of the larger arterial roads. Ahead he could see a break in the line of buildings coming that should lead him in the right direction, and angled towards it. As he made the turn, he noticed immediately that what had looked like a reasonably wide opening soon closed down to a path suitable only for foot traffic. That was ideal, as it would separate his tail from their support a little without worrying them unduly. Reznik continued down the narrower lane as though that had been his intention all along.

The rain came, briefly fresh and then heavy and hard, bouncing from the ground as the wind gusted. Behind him the police kept a steady distance. Here the buildings and streets had gradually morphed into a more formalised layout, with enough of a pattern for Reznik to begin to plan and predict. They'd crossed a wider road a few yards back and he could see the path ahead moved between two reasonably large apartment blocks. It was much darker now, the downpour hard enough to blur outlines, and his sight had taken on a green-tinged hue.

Up ahead and to one side was a tall wire fence sectioning off a yard, with a large garbage bin right in front of it. Reznik had been looking for just such an opportunity and had leapt onto the dumpster then up the fence as soon as he'd drawn level, trusting his own speed to get him over before the men following had worked out what he was doing. He was halfway down the other side and dropping the rest of the way before they began to shout out in alarm.

Reznik found himself in a small courtyard with a plain door ahead, jammed slightly ajar by a half-brick, as though he was expected and welcomed. He rushed up the short flight of steps leading to it, pulled it smoothly open, and then darted through. Once he was inside he kicked the brick away and pulled the door firmly shut, casting around the suddenly green interior for something to block the door. There was an old mop and bucket on wheels, grimier than the floor it was set to clean, and he quickly reached for the mop, sloshing brown water with the barest hint of soap on the floor and his boots as he span back around and jammed the handle through the push-bar to make the door more secure.

He could hear the police scrambling at the fence outside, and smiled before heading off quietly into the heart of the building.

> Cara

Cara carried on long after Chase had popped his head around the door to bid her goodbye. He hadn't been any kind of danger at all and had been quite sweet, trying to persuade her to get some rest before he left. In that small way he reminded her of Ethan for a moment, something she immediately recoiled from, surprised that her thoughts could take such a turn. She was probably just tired. It was a relief, though, that Chase looked to be innocent, as far as she could see.

The experience of working with the AI had been an interesting one. Cara found that as she started to become familiar with Raissa she quite enjoyed it, as they bounced ideas off each other like true collaborators. It took a while to find that groove but once they had, and Raissa was acclimatised to the system she/it was running on, they'd made good progress. The AI had an understanding of system architecture and data patterns that far surpassed Cara's, whilst she in turn added a level of imagination and intuition quite beyond Raissa, though the program was proud to say the full version she was a copy of was much more capable. It sounded like pride anyway.

Despite the progress they'd been making she'd begun to think about calling it a day as she got more and more tired. Emma's pills had given her some distance from her grief, but they made her lethargic. She needed sleep, and Raissa offered to carry on trawling through the hard drives, building up an image of the original files from the scrambled data. At first, she'd resisted the idea of leaving the mainframe running unattended, but in the end she'd given up fighting the yawns and gone home. The volume of information they had to go through was so high that it would take many hours, even for the AI. It would have been a tedious and painstaking task for Cara alone, reassembling scattered and unattached fragments of information piece by piece like a monstrous jigsaw, if she could even do it at all.

Cara had journeyed about half way when she reluctantly changed route and direction to double back and visit the hospital. It had been a long time since she'd last been preoccupied or engaged with something enough to forget about Dad, and the realisation was unwelcome, making her feel guilty. Certainly, the idea of going to visit had occurred much later in the day than it usually would have, but she thought it likely many others would have forgotten altogether, or simply not bothered. Of late Cara had, she thought, been a very good daughter. She still couldn't really fathom how much of her relationship with Dad was shaped and shadowed by the poor state things had been in with Mother before she died.

He wished he'd dug a little more obliquely, and a little deeper. The others pursuing Polzin were something else, internet and network savvy like few he'd seen. Jakobsen wanted to learn more about them, find out who they were, but they would always scurry away when he got too close, travelling from node to node until their trail was entirely obscured. It worried him that someone else might get to Polzin first.

She, in contrast, was not nearly so impressive. Once he'd known she was in South America it had only taken a couple of weeks to trace her new identity and follow her movements.

Reznik had mostly left him to it, rarely getting in touch, but he knew he'd been in town at least once from a hand-written note left by his workstation at the warehouse. It was terse, block printed, and just asked if he'd found her yet? No pleasantries, all business.

- Twenty Nine -

> Chase

It was one of those nights where it's cold and damp enough, and dark from rainclouds and a timid moon, that at some deep level you feel it's much later in the year. The bus I was on was an older one, a little run down, with the windows misting and rain-spattered. Its route took me along the northern edge of the Civil Safety Zone, by the parkland that was growing ever wilder. You could sense the broad open space out there in the darkness just beyond the edge of the road.

I was tired and achy, feeling like I'd been bashed over the brain again. I'd already nodded off once, coming awake with my head jarring intermittently against the window, fringe and hood damp from the condensation where they'd rubbed a clear patch on the safety glass. Cara had been in touch, briefly, just a message about allowing Raissa to run diagnostics on her home *aigent*. It was a good idea, and I told her so, but I would have my fingers crossed that the AI didn't find any trace I'd sent in the Spydar.

The bus had slowed down where the route narrowed to allow for some road works at the kerbside. We'd been travelling along like that for a short stretch when a small sports car pulled out to pass us, engine revving noisily. It sped along but I could see already that there wasn't enough space for it to get back in before an oncoming van reached it. The autodrive on the bus had obviously recognised the same thing but a little late, and we veered suddenly toward the kerb. The sports car tried to speed up to make it but failed, colliding head on with the van in a noisy crunch as we dived through the barriers and across the pavement, jamming to a hard stop against a bus shelter. I rocked forward in my seat, just as the other passengers did, and then sat back in place, a little stunned.

I could see through the rain that both vehicles were a mess, but couldn't tell if there were any casualties. The rest of the passengers were becoming agitated now they understood we'd been in an accident. A couple moved to get off, but the front doors were jammed hard against the shelter we'd collided with, preventing them from opening. I knew that the police would arrive soon, and that they'd want statements from us all as traffic accidents were so unusual now, and I was one of only two passengers with a good view of what had happened. The problem was they would request my ID, and by this stage it was more than likely a warrant for my arrest had been issued.

There was an emergency exit just ahead of me, and I could see that the traffic outside had stopped. I'd no choice really, and walked straight to the door and pushed hard on the exit bar. I could hear some of the other passengers start to kick up a fuss just before I jumped out onto the road. I could feel their hostile stares as I moved along beside the bus, but my own attention was drawn off toward the abandoned commons. The noise and spectacle of the crash had drawn another audience, a couple of rough looking men armed with crossbows, crouched down in the undergrowth just beyond the barriers, a dark shape on the ground between them. At first all eyes were on me, until the passengers and the hunters seemed to notice each other for the first time, and I became a sudden afterthought. When I reached the pavement I ran for it, off into the dark.

An hour later and I was inside a nightclub, one of only a few customers this early when many of the pubs and bars were just about still open. It would begin to fill up soon enough, and by then the police would have their hands full with drunks and domestics, and it should be safe to move on. In the meantime, I thought I might as well have a couple of drinks while I was there.

This place was the first bar I came across with a Privacy Max logo on display outside, which meant there'd be no surveillance on or around the premises, so I dived straight in and down the long staircase to the basement club. Dive was probably the operative word. There was a deep layer of static smoke all across the dance floor, giving the clientele more separation from each other as they gathered in discrete groups.

The club went from quiet to heaving in the space of twenty minutes, filling up quickly as groups of younger people came in, most of them dressed head to toe in baggy anti-surveillance clothing, all hooded and metamorphic, changing shape and grey-shade constantly. Many of them continued the theme under their outer layers, even wearing vari-sole boots and makeup or masks with specific patterns to confuse facial recognition. Such measures were effective to a degree, but also served to mark them out, and even isolate them, from the general populace.

Despite the obvious difficulties it would represent I decided that I'd probably best have another drink for forms sake before I headed out. Getting across the dance floor to the bar was a pain, and a trip that had taken seconds the first time took much longer now as I wove through the tightly packed bodies, all of it in near darkness punctuated by flashes of bright colour and thunderous, bass-heavy noise. The fact that this was underground was somehow still evident in the smoke-filled air. When I got there it took a while to get served, as most of the punters were more interested in the pharmabar to one side. Many of the narcotics on offer were sold wet, and the fumes from some of the drinks were potent enough to reach across to me a few feet away.

I stuck to the beer, and once I had a plastic pint in hand I headed for the area where I'd been sat before. Ordinarily I'd have just retraced my steps, but the scenery had changed so much with the shifting bodies that I had to take a longer, more meandering route just to make it back, almost disoriented in the heart of the crowd. When I made it I sat down in the nearest seat, perched at the edge of a booth occupied at this point by stacks of coats and only a couple of people, relieved to have a drink in hand.

And then a fresh memory came to me, a chunk of my recent past dropping into place. I knew now where I might have seen Schuler before. It was hard to be sure, but back in the basement of the mall, it could have been him sitting at the workstation in the server room. There was no more than a partial reflection of his face in one of the monitors, but the set of his shoulders and hair were a good match.

Harris was there as well, laid out on the floor beside the desk, quiet and still.

I ran the sequence through in my head again to see if more came to me, some detail or feature, but there was nothing else. Excited, I pulled the smartpad from my pocket, lighting up the corner of the booth I was in as the screen came on, and began tapping out the clearest description I could of what I'd remembered into a note.

Satisfied, elated even, I looked around the room again, feeling fresh and far from sleepy. It was a strange place for such a revelation, but I suppose there might have been something about the half-dark, tight spaces and regular patterns of flashing lights that had triggered it. Energised, I got up to leave, grabbing one of the pattern-change coats at the last moment even though I felt like a shit for doing it. I pulled the heavy garment on then followed a few steps behind a group of teenagers heading back up the stairs and out of there.

> Reznik

Dawn was breaking, but you could hardly tell for the rain pounding down. He'd dozed fitfully through the night, holed up on the top floor of a disused hotel, long abandoned to legitimate trade. The first couple of levels had been thoroughly stripped of any furniture, but the upper floors were still reasonably intact, the limits of the ailing elevator marking layers in the old building like geological strata. The place was elementally grimy, with the sheets and mattress so filthy he napped in the chair, still in his clothes, window half open despite the risk. Thin walls had done little to filter the sounds of comings, goings and fucking nearby, as one male after another bellowed out, the regular rhythm of an ancient profession notching the slow time of the small hours.

He was familiar enough with dives like this but not the feeling that this might be a permanent thing. The knowledge that Murdoch had misled him shook his confidence, threatening his sense of purpose and the expectation of a place of safety and shadow he could reach and sink into. In a break from every protocol he knew he reached out through the darknet to a few old associates, asking for favours and intel on his situation. For the first time in many years, Reznik didn't know what would come after the mission, or even what the mission really was.

The downpour continued even as the sun grew bolder, sheets of vertical rain piling at the ground like needles. He resisted closing the window and let it soak the scrawny curtains, splashing on the frame and floor as he enjoyed the way the almost solid wall of water braided the early morning sun together with the last flickers of late-night electric light.

There was a commotion in the corridor outside, angry male voices and a soothing female. Reznik perked up immediately, moving up from the chair and over to the door almost noiselessly. He listened and then opened it a little, as quietly as he could, peering out of the crack. The argument was about two or three rooms along, and had begun to spill into the corridor.

Reznik wanted no part of it and closed the door again, wondered briefly if he'd made a poor choice in coming here. He moved back across the room to the window. Nothing much was moving out there but the rain and a sole taxi crawling past, its sign switched off. There was no fire escape nearby, but a narrow ledge jutted from the wall a few feet below the level of the floor. It would be sturdy enough as far as he could see, but the constant rain had made the surface treacherous. He reckoned he would risk it if he had to, but only then. Crossing back to other side of the room he listened to the disturbance outside, and was relieved to hear it had calmed to nothing.

A couple of hours later, and he'd left the hotel. The rain had continued its relentless pace, soaking through his clothing and dampening the skin below. Storm drains were overwhelmed, little lakes and pools forming at the roadside, cars pushing through and splashing water in high arcs.

Despite the storm a food shack had opened, hoping to catch passing customers on their way to jobs and better places. Rain sizzled off the edge of the hotplate, spitting at the greasy chikun like an angry cat, soaking the counter edge. The fresh, tangy smell of sauce and faux fowl called to him, the promise of hot, spicy food a physical taunt to his dry mouth. Reznik waited and paid, collecting a can and a paper-wrapped handful of hot flatbread, vat-grown meat and thick, dark sauce, before scurrying off to the nearest cover to eat. He joined other customers from the shack and one or two pedestrians seeking temporary respite from the weather.

The soda gushed down his throat and the rich, tasty snack warmed him right through, satisfying and satiating something more than simple hunger. He dropped a tiny glob of the filling, cursing the wasted mouthful, and hoarded the rest close by, keeping the remainder of his meal tight to his body and clenched in both hands, the half-finished soda can on the muddy ground between his feet. The temptation to wolf the food down was strong, but he resisted now, savoured smaller bites, sucking every morsel from his fingers when he was done.

There was nothing to be gained by waiting here, and there were enough travellers around now to make his passage the less remarkable. When he was ready he joined the flow of pedestrians, all hooded and covered as he was, shuffling and trudging along with shoulders bent. They passed a police checkpoint searching some of the vehicles, drivers cringing from the rain as they stepped back into its full flow to answer the officer's questions. The subway entrance was just ahead, and Reznik moved along with the crowd.

> Cara

Dad had been no better, if anything a fraction worse, and she was secretly glad to have arrived a mere twenty minutes before visiting hours were over. She would have had some food in the café afterwards if it was open, but instead she'd stopped by the nearest convenience store on the way home. Dinner went into the microwave, a glass was filled with wine, and then she crossed over to the house *aigent's* control panel.

Raissa had made her promise she would install a utility tool that would allow her (it) to link in from the warehouse. The idea was to run some diagnostics to learn more about her habits and preferences, but also to look for any sign of tampering or intrusion. Cara knew the first part was routine enough, and had allowed other *aigent* programs she'd owned to run the same routines when she upgraded some piece of tech or other. The second part was a bit more unusual, and she was reluctant at first to acknowledge the possibility that there was any need for such a check, but then she remembered the bug on her car. She texted Chase about it, and he agreed it was probably a good idea.

Cara felt much better after eating, and was now sat on the couch with a smartpad laid across her knees. They'd started at a base level with the data Chase had brought, and in front of her was a partially restored copy of the mall system's underlying logs, much like the records he'd found on the security drone, but vastly more complex and involved. It had been another long and difficult day, and she'd about had enough. As she moved to close down the 'pad a message prompt flashed up on screen. Touching the icon, she was confused by the image that appeared, tilting the pad at an angle into the light to read it all.

'*Hi, it's Raissa. Give it a couple of minutes, then get up and go through to the bathroom. Bring the smartpad with you and reply when you get there. Thanks, .r.*' That was weird, and she had more than half a mind to ignore it, but as the next few minutes passed her curiosity grew enough that she finally got up and headed for the small room, the 'pad cradled in her hand.

'What's this about?' she typed, 'Why am I hiding in my own bathroom?'

'Ok, don't freak out, but I think that someone has installed a bit of hardware in your aigent to record and upload everything the AI sees. This room is about the only place they've no visual on you right now.'

'What! Are you sure? How long's it been there?'

'Sure I'm sure. Been in place since yesterday evening. Can't tell you who put it there, it's been deleted from the aigent's memory. We could track the feeds to see where they upload to, but it's not transmitting permanently and I don't know when it will signal next.'

Cara did feel freaked, violated almost, and tried hard to think through all the things she'd done in the flat since Friday, relaxing only a little when she realised she'd hardly been there.

'You still with me Cara?'

'I need to get out of here, I can't stay!'

'It would be better if you acted as normally as possible. Get some rest and go out in the morning. Then you could speak to Chase, find out what he thinks.'

'No fucking way, I'm out of here!' She got up, reached for the bathroom door and headed back into the flat. The 'pad beeped, quietly, and then again a few seconds later, louder. She opened the new message, having to tilt the screen again to read it.

'Ok, I get it. Pretend there's something urgent you need to do. Grab your coat and bag, whatever, just don't bring too much. Definitely no packing. Then call Chase once you're outside.'

She followed the plan, a little numbly, relinquishing control to Raissa so she didn't have to think. The fresh air outside tasted the sweetest, the sky huge and everywhere, all around.

Nathan Thorne had been as good as his word. The construction drones he'd delivered were of the exact type and model Jakobsen needed, slightly worn and more than likely hot. They weren't a controlled or rare item though, so it shouldn't be too difficult to get them out of the country. The replacement parts and circuits he needed were already assembled and ready for fitting, DIY'd and converted in the clean room.

Jakobsen didn't particularly like Nada. There was an indelible sleaziness to him that seemed so ingrained it could almost be genetic, and he'd more than once hinted at an old association with Cara that Jakobsen was sure he didn't want to know about. She'd never mentioned him herself, which suggested it was old news, but he'd rather not ask.

Satisfied, Jakobsen put the first of the construction bots into manoeuvre mode and pushed it toward the containers, the drone keeping itself airborne at a steady yard up from the ground but providing no other movement or volition of its own. Jakobsen wondered how much he was being pushed around himself.

- Thirty -

> Chase

The burner phone rang five minutes after I'd left the club. It was Cara, and as soon as I heard her voice I could tell something was wrong, her normally cool speech overwhelmed by anger and consternation, and perhaps a little fright. A couple of days ago someone had installed spyware to monitor her *aigent*, and in effect almost everything that happened in her flat. I could understand why she was so upset.

The best thing I could suggest was for Cara to find a hotel for the rest of the night, then we'd deal with things in the morning, but somehow that ended up with me agreeing to meet up with her and stay there as well. Cara sounded much calmer when we had the basics of a plan in place and I rang off, knowing I would have to be quick to make it back across town. I tried not to think about the fact that staying with her, if she was still under surveillance, would expose me to the same threat that she was facing. Not the best way of staying under the radar.

When I arrived there I had a quick look around the reception area first, half expecting Cara to be there already. I'd picked one of the more reasonable places near a railway station, figuring they'd be used to people travelling at all hours and be able to take a late walk-in. The first part went well enough, but there was only one room still available, a standard double, which I thought would be more than awkward until I remembered they often have spare mattresses stashed under the bed for family groups. After confirming that they did, I made the booking and began preparing my explanation for Cara.

It turned out I had plenty of time as it took her another twenty minutes to get there. The hotel was ok, really, just generic and decorated to some corporate template, one business serving others. When she finally arrived Cara came straight up and hugged me. I returned the gesture, a little awkwardly at first, pleased she was safe. While she waited for a minute, I checked her car for tracking devices, and having found nothing went back inside. She obviously realised what I was doing and looked thoroughly relieved when I shook my head to indicate there were was nothing this time. We set off straight for the room then, not really wanting to hang around the reception area any longer. As we walked along we passed a chemvend machine, and I stopped to ask if she'd need anything to help her sleep. She said she was already on something, and didn't want to mix.

Cara took the news that there was only one room well enough. Once we were inside I set a chair behind the door and placed the Spydar up on top of the wardrobe in alert mode, plugging it into the mains to recharge. She narrowed her eyes at that when she came out of the bathroom but didn't say anything. I went to settle down on the floor, turning my back to her and doggedly ignoring Cara while she got herself ready. She tried to be quiet and it must have worked, as I was asleep in no time.

I woke up the next morning and was disorientated for a few seconds while I tried to work out where I was. There were a few dull aches in my back and leg, as I'd somehow ended up with my hips hard on the floor, rolling off the edge of the thin mattress and out from under the duvet. I checked the time, found it was 7:20, and decided I may as well get ready and go down for breakfast. Cara was snoring lightly, tucked up and asleep, so I left her to it, scribbling a quick note on the hotel stationery.

While I had breakfast I read a couple of the free newssheets, heavily loaded with reports on the bombings and police actions in Maravilhosa, before deciding I'd better get back to Cara. As I left the restaurant I had to cross back through the main lobby, rushing the last few steps to join a young couple who were just entering the lift. I settled into the front at first, and then almost pushed myself into the corner as two uniformed police in yellow high-vis jackets walked past on their way to the reception desk. The doors crawled to a close, shrinking the view inch by inch, until I was out of sight. For a moment the lift went nowhere, and I thought they might have seen me and held it, but it juddered into reluctant motion and climbed upward. The couple ignored me completely, though whether from indifference or strained politeness I'd no idea.

Once I reached my floor I moved as fast as I dared to the room, knocking softly twice and then using the cardkey to enter. Cara was gone. I stood for a moment, undecided, and then quickly gathered up my things, dashing into the bathroom for the smartlenses and collecting the Spydar from its perch. The note I'd left her was still there but the spare cardkey was missing, so she'd probably gone down for breakfast. I couldn't afford to go and look for her or wait around: if the police were here for me they might already be on their way. Cara wasn't in any trouble as far as I knew, so she should be all right. She'd have to be.

> Reznik

Araya looked relaxed enough across the other side of the café, and in much better health than the last time they'd met. It was an airy, open space, the ceiling two stories up with a large skylight and a mezzanine-like area with more seating running around the upper floor. Everything was finished in pale wood and whites, with immaculate linen on the tables. Palms and other greenery were generously placed, and plenty of soft artificial light streamed in to offset the grey sky outside. The atmosphere was genteel and it suited Araya, lending him an air of elegance.

As always, Araya had brought a couple of bodyguards, reasonably subtle and professional looking, well dressed and concealed. Reznik had no trouble identifying them as he'd been in place ahead of time and had the luxury of seeing them enter from his vantage point on the balcony. They had company: another team, separate from Araya's people as far as he could tell. Not police, probably, but something else.

When Murdoch had called earlier it had been a surprise, the signal tickling his skull through induction. It was almost exactly like he imagined an auditory illusion would be, at the edge of normal hearing, directionless, yet somehow perfectly clear. Reznik had been terse in that conversation, but his sponsor always spoke that way so it was difficult to gauge if there were any change in Murdoch's underlying mood.

There was an old farm south of the city where a package would be left for him, a pre-programmed stealth drone that would fly him under the radar and over the border. He'd used similar things before, slender prop-driven designs with just enough space inside for one person to lie flat out along the fuselage. All he had to do was reach it, set it up, climb inside and press 'Go'.

As long as he did just one more job.

Araya would call to set up a meet and his sponsor wanted him to go along so he could deliver a message. Murdoch believed it would be safe enough given the stakes for Araya, and that his reaction would tell them much about his reliability and future usefulness. It seemed a risk too far to Reznik, more than he should chance, but Murdoch was insistent. There was no one else he could send, and something was coming up in the next few days that Araya might be very helpful with, if he could be trusted. Reznik didn't ask what that might be, and didn't really care. He had his own reasons for agreeing to the meeting. If Araya had betrayed him he wanted to know, though he was unsure yet exactly what he would do about it. There was more than one variable here, however, and Araya wasn't the only one he had doubts about.

They'd reached and exceeded the appointed time, five minutes past the hour. Araya didn't appear concerned exactly, but he was looking around at his surroundings a little more, as though the friend he was waiting for was overdue, which was something like the truth. Right then Reznik was sitting comfortably in a car that didn't know it was stolen in the nearest parking bay, a wireless link providing him with real-time pictures of Araya from a couple of micro-cameras he'd placed in the café. He'd slight cause to thank Murdoch again, using one of the items stashed amongst his emergency supplies, an override unit that fooled both the car itself and the local autodrive system into accepting him as the legitimate driver. He'd followed his act of grand theft auto with more modest larceny, stealing the cameras and other supplies from a couple of small stores.

Reaching for the burner mobile he dialled Araya, barely taking his eyes from the 'pad display. There was a delay of a few seconds before he was answered. "Is everything ok? I was expecting to meet you here, as we agreed." Araya sounded and looked concerned.

"Everything's fine. Just feeling a little shy today," he replied.

"I see. Look, you can trust me." More quietly, "I can help you get away from here."

"No need, Sr. Araya, thank you all the same. I got my own plans for that. Now, how about you tell me how long you were intending to keep Weaver's news from my employer?" This was what Murdoch had insisted he ask, in person, but he figured a phone call and a zoom lens was close enough.

"Yes, everything is well. Excellent in fact. I'd intended to pass on the details – it must have slipped my mind with everything that's been going on." Reznik didn't really know what this was about, but he could see a liar plain enough, though he had to give Araya credit for his smoothness.

"Well, please be sure to pass on my employer's regards. He was most insistent."

"Yes. Yes, I will."

"Great. We'd also like to know if you've been entirely honest with us of late, and whether you might be responsible, maybe, for some of our present difficulties." This wasn't part of Murdoch's brief, but Araya looked just a little off-balance now and couldn't know that.

He hesitated a moment before replying, "I can assure you that your present situation is not any of my doing. I was most surprised to see the outcome of our dealings turn so... dramatic."

"Not as much as I was, Sr. Araya."

"No, I understand how it must have been."

"I really don't think you do. Be seeing you."

He hung up and then pulled the battery roughly from the phone, dumping the discarded pieces in the foot well. Reznik grabbed his secure comms relay next, a sleek grey thing with no external switches and the simplest of displays, before tapping it absentmindedly against his free palm for several seconds as he watched the camera feed from the café. Decision made, he split the case of the comms relay along a hairline seal and stripped out its battery pack as well. A note flashed into the top of his field of vision, a tiny line of text to mark the cutting of his cord.

> Cara

She awoke later than she'd expected, surprised at the time, but hardly felt like she'd had much sleep. Remembering where she was, and why, she listened out for Chase, but couldn't hear him. Through the curtains and around their edges she could see it was a sunny morning, much better than yesterday.

Cara found the note he'd left a few minutes later, and decided that it wouldn't be such a bad idea to join him for breakfast. There was no sign of Chase when she got to the restaurant, but he might have missed her on his way back to the room. She piled her plate up, settled down at an empty table and accepted the waiter's offer of coffee.

Not long afterward the police walked in, accompanied by one of the hotel managers. They visually searched the breakfast room, the noise level dropping as progressively more of the staff and customers noticed them. Whatever the police were looking for they didn't seem to find it and they left soon after, the volume of conversation recovering then reaching a new level as they walked off. There was still no sign of Chase, so she hoped that meant he'd spotted them and got out of there.

Cara loitered in the restaurant as long as she could, going back for more toast and accepting more refills than she could really handle, but in the end she needed to go back to the room and grab her things. If the police were still looking for Chase she might have to explain herself, but with any luck they were here for something else or had given up and left. Besides, she hadn't really done anything wrong.

Whatever their reasons for being there, Cara saw no more sign of them. After gathering her things from the room, she checked out without any further incident. As she made her way over to the car, Cara felt a little better as she realised it was just as fine a day outside as she'd imagined. She was inside it and had the thing started before she saw Chase had left her another note, held in place under the windscreen wipers.

Cara entered the warehouse, after first checking the way was clear with Raissa. There had been no visitors, and no sign of trouble. She headed straight for the iso-room and sealed herself in, keen to close out the world. Raissa had worked all night, and yet responded with such a level of buoyant enthusiasm to Cara's return that she wondered if her (its) emulation routines were faulty. The AI had learnt something already, a strong suggestion as to what Harris had been talking about.

Whilst the mall's data gathering and processing power was significant, much of its core program was dedicated to optimising the building's atmospheric conditions and utilities consumption, with an aim to making the interior both pleasant and efficient. Despite this, there was a noticeable overcapacity in the system, which was more than sufficient to run a building several times larger. From what was left of the longer-term records, the servers had remained largely underutilised ever since the mall had opened until about three months ago, when the logs began to show a significant increase in daily processing requirements. It wouldn't have caused any noticeable slowdown in system performance, but something was clearly going on.

In theory, it might be one powerful program, a score of smaller ones, or anything in between. To Cara, though, the fact that the system load increased all at once hinted that it was a single installation. The size and system requirements for the new program(s) were enough to accommodate the full-fat version of Raissa, or even, at a push, an advanced AI of some sort. What something as powerful and rare as that would be doing in a shopping mall was anyone's guess. Unfortunately, they couldn't be certain exactly what was running on the mall's servers in those final weeks, only the general level of system traffic, but it may have been the source of Harris's concern.

There were a lot more files to go through, including records of external data transmissions that they'd not even touched on yet, and they both felt there might be useful information waiting to be found. Cara cracked open a bottle of water, disappointingly tepid now after being left in the corner for a couple of days, and set down to work.

He couldn't really put a finger on when it changed, but Jakobsen knew that it had. At first he'd had no problem compartmentalising his life, spending most of his time as Ethan Grant, doing Ethan Grant's business, and then becoming his old self again at the warehouse, but now the Jakobsen life had begun to feel unreal whilst the Grant one felt right.

Cara was a lot to do with it of course, even most of it, but he was sure some of the change was in himself, and that their relationship had simply shown him what was already there. Once this was all done he would leave that life behind, and be an Ethan Grant, or someone very like him, for good. Assuming he could work out the best solution for that last little issue.

Everything was in place now, just about. The drones were modified and shipped, the planning was complete and he'd run through everything with The Wolf and finally gained his approval. There was just the nagging feeling that he should set something up for Cara, some form of contact protocol, like Reznik's but much more personal, just in case something went wrong. Probably no need, but it couldn't hurt.

- Thirty One -

> Chase

With time and distance I was beginning to think I'd overreacted back at the hotel. I saw no more sign of the police for the next few hours except fleeting images of them going about their own business through a bus window or as I walked through a busy area. If they were actively watching me I suppose I'd not have seen them so openly in the hotel, unless they were close to an arrest, in which case there'd have been more of them and I'd not have gotten away so easily.

After running evasion for a couple of hours I decided I'd had enough, and headed over to an address I wanted to look at. Of the three individuals that I'd positively identified with a hand in the murders of Harris and Jakobsen, Thorne was the only one I'd not investigated yet. From what Cara had said he was a trader of sorts, running plenty of legitimate deals but also some black and grey market goods, as well as stolen merchandise. It hadn't been too hard to track down his place of business. We were in an area of the city that still hadn't seen a great deal of renovation, an old commercial hub near the docklands area. Thorne's property was once part of one of the original freight warehouses, was then partitioned off and converted into smaller businesses, and was now a warehouse again, old red bricks peeking through fading whitewash. Surrounding it were mainly cheap apartments, with only the occasional larger space still used for business.

I'd sent the little Spydar off ahead to run a quick reconnaissance of the exterior, looking for any open doors or windows, or even vents, that either the drone or myself could penetrate. Thorne's building was secure though, probably not such a surprise given his line of trade, so I'd have to go in through the front door, like everybody else. This was really a situation where long-term covert surveillance would be better, but I'd neither the time or resources for that. I was hoping I'd find something useful here, especially as investigating Ruscoe had provided no immediate leads and Schuler looked almost untouchable.

The entrance was arranged almost like an airlock, with two large heavy-duty doors set up across from each other in a small antechamber. Once you were through there was a basic counter top to the right, running for about eight feet or so, behind it a false room formed from a wall of packing crates three or four foot high. Beyond this were rows and rows of boxes, crates, pallets and packages, haphazardly arranged in a maze-like confusion stretching as near as I could tell right across the warehouse interior from wall to wall.

I'd been there for almost five minutes before anyone came. At first I felt a little nervous, especially when I walked right up to the counter to let the Spydar scurry away out of sight underneath, but I soon relaxed. Occasionally a robot would amble past, select something from one of the stacks, and take it toward the back of the warehouse where I already knew the main loading area was. Sometimes voices could be heard, rough-edged banter mainly, and once or twice you would see a human walk by through the gaps. I'd no doubt I was in camera from somewhere, and did my best to play the part of an impatient customer, peering off into the depths of the warehouse to see if I could attract any attention. It wasn't too much of a challenge.

When help did arrive it was in the form of a very tall, unusually thin woman, dressed in tight jeans and a long black mohair sweater, baggy and rough. She said nothing, instead holding up a smartpad that scrolled messages left to right. I'd decided that for cover I would look at any surveillance drones they might have in stock, Spydars and similar, and hopefully spend a few minutes looking through those while my own completed a survey of the interior and took footage of all the staff or customers present.

They had four or five different ones, most of them very basic – little more than toys really – though there was another that was similar to mine but overpriced. As we were chatting I heard one of the groups of people drift closer, and when I looked across I was surprised to see Ruscoe. He was talking animatedly to a slippery dark haired guy who was clearly Thorne from what Ruscoe was saying to him. They were discussing an order for heavy equipment of some kind, haggling over price. I almost froze part way through my own dealing, and then remembered that it was unlikely that Ruscoe had seen me before. Thinking quickly I decided to buy the only suitable drone they had, an older arachnid model that I'd used in the past. I'd have to use nearly all of the cash I'd brought with me to meet the price, which was a little high. It was going to cost me for every arm and leg.

I could see and hear Ruscoe and Thorne moving back toward the rear of the warehouse as we closed the purchase, and I almost couldn't get out of there fast enough, letting my own Spydar crawl back up to my knee and hang on just before I turned to leave. Once I was through the exit I walked briskly around toward the rear of the building, switching the new drone on as subtly as I could, not wanting to draw any attention. I set off toward one of the many side streets nearby, passing by Ruscoe's van where it was parked up at the back, dropping the new drone next to it. I couldn't turn to watch, but I imagined it scurrying under the van and clinging on, activating its camouflage once it was in place.

When I reached the side street I then took the first available turn to get out of sight. As soon as I felt safe I pulled out the smartpad and quickly linked up with the drone attached to Ruscoe's van, setting it to tap power from the vehicle and broadcast a beacon signal over the network so I could track it.

When that was over I called the Spydar over and then waited for a few minutes. It wasn't long before Ruscoe drove away, carrying the little hitchhiker along.

> Reznik

Araya had only a few seconds respite before a white male approached the table, two of the unidentified surveillance team breaking from their posts to take up positions at his shoulders, the three forming a 'V' shaped wedge centred on the new arrival, his quick, darting features bringing the phalanx to a sharp point. The newcomers partially blocked Reznik's view from the small camera, but he saw a flicker of worry in Araya's familiar face as the three men approached, the Caucasian's anger and blunt criticism clear from his expansive hand movements and tight shoulders. Reznik almost felt sorry for the older man. Dutifully, he checked the images were still recording, though he was still unsure of when and whether he would send the files to Murdoch.

Sensing this would not be such a brief and simple exchange of words, Araya's own bodyguards had also approached the table, flanking their boss in mirror image of the men across from them, a tense modernist ballet of suited dancers, aligned in almost formal opposition. Only Araya spoiled the illusion of choreography, insisting on keeping his seat whilst the others all stood. Reznik still had no idea what they were discussing, the camera's microphones being too elementary to pick up their words at such a distance and in so complex an environment. He had relied on a recording of their phone call to document his own conversation.

Satisfied or not, the unidentified man and his guards turned and left, though not without a few final aggressive stabs in the air from a pointed finger. As they cleared the frame worry and even a little fear was plain in Araya's face. He spoke quietly, inclining his head a little to the left, before rising sharply and heading away, one of the bodyguards reaching into a pocket for a bank note that he dropped casually on the table. Reznik rewound the end of the video file, performed a quick clip and copy, and then ran Araya's final words through a lip reading app.

There wasn't much, but he was glad he'd taken the trouble. "I don't trust that OraCotek bastard. Tell everyone to expect trouble." Reznik had heard of them, and recently, the indigenous manufacturer of electronics, the same ones who were donating new drones to the police for the emergency. He would do some digging on that later, see if he could find anything more. For now he would sit tight, just on the off chance Araya's friends made another appearance.

A few minutes later a dark blue saloon, a Marcatti, one of those with the whisper-drive power unit, pulled out from opposite the museum, turned right and headed past Reznik. For some reason the vari-tint windows were dialled down, and he could see the back of a head and a set of shoulders he recognised from the meeting with Araya: Mr. OraCotek.

Reznik started his motor and pulled out in the next space, three cars behind the Marcatti. He knew he'd just had a stroke of luck, and was happy to go with it. They headed away from the more upmarket parts of the centre out to an area zoned for light industry and services. For the first mile or two they'd taken the inner orbital road, and traffic was slow and heavy enough in the rain to mask his presence, but once they'd turned off from the main arterial route he felt a bit more conspicuous. When the Marcatti turned into one of the industrial parks he followed and pulled over behind a parked van, watching as the other car continue onward.

Further along the blue saloon flashed its brake lights, slowed to a smooth stop, and then held position for a good twenty seconds. Reznik watched nervously, believing his efforts to tail the car blown and wondering if things were about to turn ugly, before it accelerated away equally smoothly to park up by the kerb on the opposite side of the road 70 yards away from where he now sat.

Nothing happened for the next couple of minutes: no one approached either the Marcatti or Reznik's car, and no other traffic passed through save for an old man cycling erratically along the pavement on a slow snake of a route, the bike just as rusty and ancient.

OraCotek's car was far enough away that Reznik could barely see it though the rain, and he was beginning to think he should leave when another saloon pulled around the corner at the bottom of the road, moving slowly, an equally impressive model but coloured a metallic white. The rain seemed to flow around it, the smart material surface constantly scrubbing itself back to showroom pristine. The white car, an Auguzzo, pulled alongside the stationary Marcatti, pointed toward him while the other faced away.

Moments later Mr. OraCotek left his blue haven and climbed in the back of the radiant white. Reznik had hoped to eavesdrop if they'd had their conversation between vehicles through open windows, but they obviously knew better. Trusting to the van to screen him Reznik got out of his car, keeping low, and moved alongside the four or five parked vehicles in front until he reached the end of the line. The two saloon cars were that much nearer now, outlines clearer and more distinct even through the side window and windshield of the car he now crouched beside. Reznik strained to hear over the downpour but was disappointed, the passenger compartment too well constructed for any stray syllables of conversation to escape.

A few minutes later the door of the white Auguzzo opened again and Mr. OraCotek stepped out, crossing straight back to the Marcatti and getting into the rear. Before his door was quite closed the Auguzzo set off, moving straight for the exit of the industrial park. The blue car also headed away, smoothly and without fuss, turning at the bottom and disappearing out of sight. Reznik was left there, crouching by the side of a stranger's car, unsure of his next move, and wondering if he'd found small pieces of the first puzzle or even tinier pieces of another.

> Cara

The more they looked at the data, Raissa and Cara, the more it looked like some vast program had taken root in the mall's computer system and stayed there until the night the virus was released, after which a mountainous spike of outward internet traffic signalled a huge upload from the mall to somewhere else. The next steps in the trail were muddied as the virus unleashed on the mall's system had spread to the surrounding grid network, but it was possible to see further traces as its path forked and multiplied. They would need to do a lot more analysis to see any further than that. Despite their sense of the program's power and complexity they couldn't be sure what it was: there was little sign in the information they had of any interaction between the mall's original programming and this other, larger thing.

Cara was capable of analysing the raw data on her own, but the pace and level of precision would be far below Raissa's capabilities. Instead, she'd found value in working from models and graphics, summarised representations of numbers and codes, a conceptual analysis that could help her identify angles of inquiry and lines of reason that Raissa would rapidly assimilate and run with, a part of her attention racing ahead in whatever direction Cara suggested.

For all that she was able to offer at least some assistance to the AI it would have been far too little to truly occupy her. Instead, most of Cara's own attention was spent on reading and appraising Ethan's files, made that much harder by the additional layers of password protection he'd attached to them, which this time he'd failed to leave her a key for. Despite his caution the files were hosted on a system that between Raissa and herself they'd thoroughly penetrated, allowing her to approach and breach his security from multiple angles. Once she had access it was only a matter of time until she had a handle on what he'd been doing.

Every so often Raissa would present her with a new problem or line of enquiry that she'd identified amongst the data from the mall. It was on one of these that Cara spotted an anomaly in the environmental records, a small bubble of life support and power use in one of the vacant parts of the building. It had begun as a minor increase in electrical consumption weeks before, growing in size in the last month and leading to a clear record of increased air and waste reprocessing in that same physical location for a few days before dropping back again. As far as they could tell the power drain continued after the virus struck, if anything increasing a little. Cara felt proud of herself as she explained her findings to Raissa, enjoying the cultured warmth of her congratulations and praise. She wasn't so engrossed in the conversation that she missed seeing the intruders on the monitor as they entered the warehouse.

It was almost certainly the same two as before, dressed in dark overalls and strong boots, gloved and hard-hatted with their faces hidden. Between them they carried heavy looking tool bags, brown and scuffed with wear, and some other industrial equipment she didn't recognise. Setting the bags right in front of the door, they now walked around the two adjoined containers before stepping back for a few minutes, all the while acting like tradesmen studying a job of work. Cara would have almost been taken in had she not seen them before. The calm confidence they projected drained her own.

Apparently satisfied with their preparations the two moved back toward their tools, unzipping one of the bags and pulling out some equipment and lines of some kind, connecting everything up to one of the other things they'd brought, a compact oblong box made of plastic. As Ruscoe assembled the device it began to take on a shape she could recognise, some kind of welder, and her guess was confirmed when he donned a protective mask and pulled the faceplate into place. The woman returned from around the rear of the containers with a mask of her own.

Cara knew this was trouble. This time they'd be able to cut their way through the security doors even if it might take a while, and there was nothing she could do about it. Her mouth had gone desert dry and when she tried to speak her tongue stuck in her arid throat. She swallowed, wet her lips and tried again: "Raissa, call Chase!"

"Already on it, sending a message through the landline."

While Ruscoe had been setting up the welder the woman had been examining the thick cables connecting to the outer skin of the right-hand container, before following them to their end points on the wall. Ruscoe triggered something on the tool in his hand, igniting a bright light at the end of the torch. As he moved toward the door he adjusted the light to an intense, narrow stream, and began cutting.

"Have you reached him?"

"Trying to connect now."

"Fuck, hurry up!"

Ruscoe paused in his work for a moment, shutting off the welder, pushing back his facemask and calling out to his companion. Cara was horrified when the woman pushed back her own facemask in turn to reply, clearly revealing her face.

It was Emma. Her best mate.

Emma moved back to the power supply and suddenly the lights went off, along with the small computer displaying the external camera views. Cara was literally blind for a moment as she adjusted to the dark. The tears didn't help.

"Raissa, what's happening?"

There was no answer. A few of the LEDs on the server were still active, though there were far fewer than before.

"Raissa!"

Jakobsen wished he'd never agreed to those last jobs for The Wolf all those months ago. It had been bad enough having to source a small shopping list of materiel, but the next mission turned out to have much more serious consequences, even if they didn't manifest for a while. He hadn't really known what it was all about, then or now.

It had happened a few months after he'd arrived and begun to firmly establish himself as Grant. The Wolf had asked him to act as a courier on some piece of work he needed doing. It was thoroughly old school, dropping off a large brown envelope containing fuck-knew-what to a woman he'd never heard of. One phone call to set it up and three hours total to make the drop and return. She'd been at the café as arranged, and all he'd done was walk by her table and casually exchange the envelope for its twin.

That really should have been the end of it, but as soon as he saw her face on Cara's new photo-wall in the summer he recognised her. The first time all he'd had was a description and a first name. Now he had the whole of it, and he knew that Cara's best friend Emma was no more who she appeared to be than he was.

- Thirty Two -

> Chase

The carriage was only about two thirds full but the heat was stifling, the air-con either off or ineffective. Despite that I was still wearing the shape-changer jacket I'd picked up in the night club, expecting to leave the train and perhaps the underground network in another stop or two. I could almost measure the extent to which I was losing myself on this new path by the suspicion and hostility of those around me. Even in this ancient, mixed city there were strata and social seams and I had been derailed downward and darker. It didn't help that there was something going on between some of the other passengers. Tempers were a little frayed and I'd found myself standing in the aisle almost directly between them.

When my phone started ringing they all turned some of their anger momentarily toward me, as though they'd finally found something they could agree on. It took me a few seconds to retrieve and answer it, and when I did the connection went dead almost straight away. I'd only heard a few words, but it was Raissa: Cara was back at the warehouse, and she was in trouble. I tried calling back and got nothing, just an engaged tone. Quickly rummaging through my shoulder bag I pulled out a smartpad and reactivated its network links, gripping it hard as the refresh cycled round. When it finished I found an update from the tracker I'd placed on Ruscoe's van: he was parked up outside Jakobsen's warehouse, which was exactly where Cara had gone.

I thought through every option I could imagine as quickly as I could, but in the end there was really only one way. The phone was still in my hand, its case a little slick now with sweat, and as I raised it up to dial I closed my eyes in wordless, godless prayer. Resigned, I tapped in the number from memory and held the phone to my ear.

"This is Mallory. Who's calling?"

"Mallory, it's Chase. I'm willing to come in, but I need you to do me a favour first. Right now, non-negotiable."

It felt like I'd been in there for hours, but it was hard to tell. That was very much the point of course. White walls, single bulb, blue metal door, empty pockets, nothing to do, no one to speak to.

After calling Mallory earlier I'd left the underground and headed for a busy intersection a few streets away, reconnecting with my regular phone and email accounts as I walked. There were a lot of messages, most of them useless but a few from friends and colleagues, wanting to know if what they'd heard was true and in many cases urging me to give myself up. Jo was one of them, just the briefest of calls, wondering what the hell was going on. I'm not sure how I managed not to call her back.

As soon as I reached the small plaza I'd been aiming for I stood in the centre, pointedly in view of the nearest surveillance cameras, hood back and face to the lenses. I pulled out the smartpad and changed the home screen to show tagged images of Schuler, Thorne, Ruscoe and the woman and then turned if off and stashed it my bag, before emptying everything from my pockets into it, even removing the smartlenses myself and placing them in their case. All the while I was hoping that this was worth it, that I wasn't making a huge mistake. I knew Mallory would do what she could, but there were, as she reminded me, no guarantees.

I could hear the approaching police car well before I saw it, watching with mild amusement as pedestrians and drivers looked around for where the siren was coming from and where it might be going. I knew the answer to the second part only too well, and just stood there, almost calm and accepting. There might be a few rough, unpleasant hours to get through but I had to hope everything would work out in the end.

When the car pulled up the officers rushed out toward me, Tasers out, and then slowed cautiously, suspicious but satisfied I wasn't about to run. Standing still all the while, I smiled and gestured toward the cameras with my head before holding the bag out at arm's length, the other arm spread to match. They had me kneel on the ground then rushed in, grabbing the bag, forcing my arms behind my back and cuffing them, me as relaxed and compliant as possible. Civil, calm, no problem officers, anything you say. They said plenty with their short clipped words, the formal arrest, the 'mind your head sir' as they steered me into the back of the car, the 'we've got you, you bastard' in the language of body and undertone.

They drove away quickly, and I tilted back and braced myself in the corner of the seat, rocking against the inertia and shifting directions as best I could to stay level, head starting to ache from the siren and reflections of blued light on blurred scenery. When we arrived they rushed me through check in, the desk sergeant brusque and efficient, no wasted words. After that I was escorted straight to a cell.

I'm not sure when that was or how long I was there for. There was no easy way to measure the passing of time, and I'd nothing to do but think. Mostly the case occupied me, and the many questions that remained unanswered, but I thought of Jo as well, and even Mallory. For all that things were uncertain I felt relaxed, and resigned to whatever was coming. I was tired of running.

> Reznik

He had to check the rear-view twice to be sure, but it was almost certainly the same Auguzzo. Nothing else he'd seen had quite that cutting brilliance.

Reznik had driven away from the industrial park shortly after the other cars had left and had been heading back toward the city centre when he spotted it. At first he thought he might have been made, and that the white car was there to return the favour and follow him in turn, until it pulled out to change lanes at the next intersection. Naturally he followed, at a distance. There was the possibility that it could be working with a team, but he could see no sign of any other vehicles acting suspiciously.

They entered a long tunnel now, with the Auguzzo four cars ahead in the middle lane. He almost lost sight of it when they exited, its colour having switched from the white to a plain, low-vis grey, almost the same shade they used on military aircraft. He'd heard some luxury cars had a configurable finish on the bodywork, changing colour and texture to suit the whims of their owners, but he'd never tailed one before. It had switched to the inner lane now, and suddenly accelerated hard toward a small side exit, taking the turnoff almost at the last second. Reznik swore, glanced briefly in the rear-view, and cut across sharply to the side, earning the registered owner of his car an instant fine.

He made the exit, just, and sped off after the other vehicle. The road bent around quite tightly on itself to link up with another arterial route, so they were both forced to slow. When Reznik got his bearings and realised they were heading out of the city he smiled, enjoying the momentary feeling of escape and firmly ignoring the surety that he would have to head back there later. Now that he'd completed Murdoch's final instruction, more or less, he had to wonder what was keeping him around. Reznik hadn't yet reached any firmer conclusion as to who had set him up, and it was debateable how much risk he should take in trying to find answers. There was this link to OraCotek though. If he called in a favour with one of his old acquaintances they could look into it, perhaps find connections and intel that would illuminate what was going on, but the more he could learn on his own first to shape the questions the better.

They joined another highway soon after, passing a large retail park, much of which looked new. Most of the traffic was slow, and seemed to be heading to or from the site, but and once they were past the last feeder junction the speed increased. He maintained a steadier pace, dropping back a little.

Up ahead the Auguzzo's brake lights flashed a steady red as it decelerated before taking a tight turn to the left, kicking up a tail of filthy water. Reznik watched as the car changed colour yet again and headed up a service road. Staying on the main route Reznik went past the junction end, following the highway round as it moved into a long right-hand bend.

A few minutes later and he returned to take the same service road as the Auguzzo, pulling over at the side to check the satnav unit he'd found in the car. This route led to nothing but a private airstrip, just large enough for a small prop plane or helicopter to land. The main highway in contrast continued for miles, running past a couple of small towns, but not much else. More than likely the Auguzzo would head back toward the city once its business here was complete.

Reznik looked up from the satnav display, and immediately there was something heading toward him from the direction of the airstrip. At first he thought it was the other car returning, but quickly realised the vehicle and the amount of spray it was creating were much too large. It was a truck, almost filling the whole road, and there was something menacing about it, something off, and it was more than just the fact it was going a lot faster than it should be.

> Cara

She waited in the dark, unsure whether to hide behind the smaller room again or arm herself with something from Ethan's stockpile. Cara knew which cases to go for now, but there was still the problem that she wasn't used to handling weapons. In the end she'd grabbed a stun gun, figuring she would be less worried about pulling the trigger if she had to use it.

Cara was devastated to learn that her best friend was out there trying to break in, however crazy and improbable that was, and it looked as though Emma was very much involved in Ethan's abduction. Even worse, she might have killed him. That it had been Em's shoulder she'd cried on most, and her pills she was taking to help her get through it, seemed perverse. The thought made her so much keener to use one of Ethan's more decisive weapons than was healthy.

It was torturous in the dark with nothing but fear and betrayal to fill the empty space where the light should be, especially as she had been in almost the same situation so recently. She listened intently for some sign of rescue or threat, but the clean room was designed to squash all inward and outward emissions down, dampening any noise they might be making. Even Raissa was silent now, the faint hum of the server just a trickle of life support for the sleeping AI.

There was a sudden loud clang from outside, the sound reverberating right through the metal frame of the container. Long moments later a spot of intense light and shower of sparks erupted from the door, Cara standing frozen as the plasma began to draw a white-edged line through the metal, its heat lancing into the room and crackling the air.

Decision made she moved as quickly and quietly as she could to the far end of the container, behind the inner isolation room. Cara looked back toward the door and could see the general glow of the excited air from the plasma, and its reflections in the ceiling. Edging further into her hiding place, she pressed her back against the container wall, gripping the stunner hard as she spread her feet to steady herself. Cara closed her eyes, heart hammering as she listened to the angry fizz of the plasma torch.

It stopped suddenly, and she waited...

A tremendous clang of heavy metal, reverberating around the whole room like thunder, the rattle of small objects slapped by the shockwave. Sounds of booted feet and calls, her name, concern and triumph in the voices.

"Cara Dalca, are you there? It's the police. Are you alright Cara?" A female voice, not Emma's.

She moved sideward, looked around, saw the questing lights of different torches, flashes of vivid yellow and white. If it were Ruscoe and Emma they'd brought company and a change of clothes.

Cara bent, placing the gun on the floor, pushing it underneath the isolation booth with her foot, and then called out as she began to squeeze back through into the main room. Torch light shone in her eyes, dazzling, and then hands helped her, gently lifting and dragging her out as she reached the furthest edge, her foot catching a little at the corner until she pulled it free.

She was safe.

Jakobsen scrambled to shut down the links, killing connections and programs before the tracker followed him home. Once he'd keyed in the last commands and pushed the power switch he dropped back in the chair, hands on head, and let out a lungful of air, eyes closed as though in meditation.

The trace routine had crept up on him from nowhere, appearing like a mundane part of the system's fabric until it went active, its reactions unlike anything he'd seen before, faster and more adaptive. It could just be a coordinated team of counter-hackers with a seriously juiced mainframe, but something about that explanation didn't fit. More likely it was an AI, some kind of expert system, and if so he'd been fortunate to get out of there before it traced him all the way back.

Assuming he actually had.

- Thirty Three -

> Chase

They didn't tell me where we were going, but I guessed it would be another police station. The journey over was much more sedate this time, and the officers escorting me were a little more friendly. I was still cuffed, but not too tightly, and they made the experience about as comfortable as it could be. It was only when we'd driven past the road that would have taken us to the regional police HQ that I realised where we were actually going. As the car slowed and turned off onto the industrial park a few minutes later it only confirmed my suspicions. We were heading for the Cadejo office.

It was a novel and uniquely humiliating experience to be taken through the lobby of my own workplace in handcuffs. I tried to look away from everyone, avoid eye contact, but I knew there were more than enough people watching even if they weren't exactly packing out the balconies overlooking the lobby. As much as you sometimes think you don't care how people at work feel about you it's not really true, and the heat I could feel across my face was only the physical sign of my embarrassment.

The officers steered me through reception and up the stairs to the next floor, where there were a number of meeting rooms. As we walked through we saw fewer people in that area, but I was gutted to see Mallory waiting there. I kept my head down as we approached, hoping we could walk by her without fuss, but she stood squarely in the centre of the corridor and there was no way around. Her eyes looked right at me, and as we drew almost within touching distance I was forced to look up and face her. Mallory's expression was unreadable, controlled, and her voice was almost equally expressionless when she spoke. "Chase" was all she said.

"Mallory. Did you get anyone over to the warehouse? Is Cara ok?"

"The police sent some squad cars. I believe a couple of arrests were made. Miss Dalca's fine."

"Was it..."

"That's enough!" It was Iyer, who'd stepped out of one of the conference rooms and into the corridor, just a few feet past us. Mallory half shrugged, stepping aside as the officers quickly steered us passed and into the room where Iyer was waiting. This was one of the upgraded suites with a decent display screen, and I could see a couple of technicians busying themselves with some of the equipment, one CSS staff and the other a police liaison officer. Duval, Roberts and Williams were also there, already seated around the table. The officers escorted me to a chair placed opposite the others, sat me down and then repositioned the cuffs before stepping back to stand against the wall behind me.

There was no preamble, and after reminding me that I was under arrest and this was all on record the three detectives took turns to try and pick me apart. They asked about my memories of the night Harris was killed, and I had to admit they'd not yet fully returned, but that I knew a little more. I told them what I could, that there'd been another person there, a man that I believed might be Conrad Schuler. I explained how he'd already come to my attention because of the footage captured from Jakobsen's warehouse, and that I thought it was him who'd released the virus in the mall computer. Harris was already dead or injured, and was laid on the floor when I'd last seen him.

They were understandably sceptical at that, and there was a delay before anyone replied. To my surprise, it was Iyer who was the first to respond. “You don’t seem to have understood the concept of medical leave too well, considering how busy you’ve been. Rather ironic considering your familiarity with the experience. Perhaps you’d like to fill us in on the rest of your discoveries?”

“Have you actually read my full medical file?” I gave her a hard stare.

“Yes, it’s been made available to me in the last few days.” Iyer actually looked just the tiniest bit chagrined at that, unless I was just imagining it.

There were more questions, about what they’d found on the smartpad I was carrying when I was arrested, and I moved on to explain what I’d discovered about Jakobsen’s business dealings and the links to the warehouse, as well as the security footage Dalca had given me of the kidnap, and that I’d identified the male intruder as Ruscoe.

They were paying attention and responding directly to my evidence rather than steering the interview along their own lines, but it was hard to gauge what sort of an impression this was making on them. Things got a lot more interesting when one of the technicians walked up and placed the mall security drone squarely in the centre of the table.

> Reznik

It seemed to take an age for the car’s pre-start to cycle after he’d pressed the ignition button. By the time the dash display had reset and the mode indicator switched to green the oncoming truck was that much closer.

As soon as he had power Reznik backed up toward the highway as fast as he could, looking back and forth between the view over his shoulder and the one through the windshield as he drove a nearly straight line in reverse, the car’s electric motor perversely quiet in a moment when the grunt of big engine would have felt so much better. He hoped to spin the car around in a turn and head forward to the main road, when the situation suddenly became twice as perilous as a tanker truck turned off the highway and charged up behind him, filling his rear-view. He slowed a little, still moving backward but with less certainty than before.

The trucks took up so much of the road that there was nowhere on the tarmac he could pass, and they were both near enough that he could see neither had a driver in the cab. To his side there was a flat expanse of muddy earth. Closer and closer now, and then he wrenched the handbrake and steering wheel, spinning the car before stamping hard on the accelerator and driving straight off the road. He slew to the side in his seat from the force of the sudden change of direction, and then bumped along the bare earth at the roadside, which was rougher than it had looked.

The trucks slammed on their brakes, trailers weaving a little under the sudden stresses, threatening to pull the vehicles sideward, the tanker almost swiping toward Reznik as he passed close by, near enough he could have stuck his hand out of the window to slap the walls of its tyres as he raced past. He headed straight for the highway as the two trucks passed one another, trailers sparking and scraping together as they each drove with only half their wheels on the road, chewing up the ground and spraying great sheets of muddy water.

Reznik reached the junction with the highway, braking as late as he dared for the turn, knowing the container truck wasn't far behind. There was too much traffic and he had to wait there, his foot hovering just at the edge of pressure on the accelerator pedal, the truck ever closer, when a gap appeared and he stamped down hard, barely making it onto the main road cleanly and executing a fast turn, the motion throwing him sideways in the seat. He sped off, back toward the city. The lead truck drove straight out of the junction after him, turning ponderously to make the corner and colliding with oncoming traffic on both sides, brake lights flashing angrily as car and container came together.

He almost couldn't believe the chaos he'd left behind and was looking as much forward as back when he was knocked viciously sideways, a vehicle he hadn't even seen t-boning the rear third of his car, spinning him around and along until he came to a stop, sideways to the slowing traffic in the middle of the highway.

Reznik sat there for a moment, stunned, surrounded by air bags and crash-foam, the seat belts pulled tight. He looked up, saw the battered truck approaching, ramming aside stationary cars as its trailer careened around wildly. He grabbed at the seat restraint and door handle, moving in directed panic as he stared at the chrome grill of the truck heading straight for him, almost there, almost free, falling out of the car, scrambling to his feet, running and diving out of the way, hitting the tarmac hard and rolling as the truck hit his car, crunching into it and pushing it along for several yards until the car span off and the truck slid to a halt.

All the traffic was stationary now, drivers and passengers climbing out, shouting, people rushing toward him to help as he pushed himself on to his feet. It was fortunate that most of the other vehicles had stopped cleanly and without contact, autodrive systems reacting with supreme order in the sudden chaos. Reznik brushed off mud and the helping hands of one of the drivers, grimacing a ‘thanks’ as he checked himself over. The car was beyond use and he didn’t want to hang around for the police.

Some twenty minutes later and he was walking slowly back, well away from the road edge, feeling battered and bruised. The Auguzzo passed him on its way back to the city a few minutes later, now a deep raspberry red.

> Cara

It wasn’t long before they arrested her, wanting to know about the weapons they’d found, the mainframe and the iso-rooms. They were suspicious enough on their own, but her past record wouldn’t help. Cara hadn’t really thought about what might happen with the police, but preferred this outcome to the alternative. At least there were ways forward from here, options perhaps, even if not all of them were pleasant.

Before her relationship with the officers had soured they’d been quite chatty, telling her they’d caught one of them. The woman had been off and running as they pulled up but the male had been too engrossed in his efforts cutting through the door to notice the police’s arrival. All the while she waited there in the back of the police car she kept hoping Chase would turn up, explain things, but she realised it wasn't going to happen when she was driven off to the nearest police station.

After she'd been placed in formal custody she'd been left waiting in an interview room for a while until the duty solicitor arrived. Not long after there were three more visitors, a man and woman she'd not seen before and Mallory, from Chase's agency, who looked less pristine and more pensive than when they'd last met. The man smiled and introduced himself, DI Roberts, and his colleague, DS Williams, and made no mention of Mallory at all. Pleasantries ended abruptly after that, as the two police detectives asked question after question for the next couple of hours, circling relentlessly around the guns and the clean room and the server like sharks in a whirlpool, doomed to hunt until they'd tasted blood. Mallory remained passive and unhappy, sitting to one side, whilst the duty solicitor mainly made notes, offering little support and few interjections.

Cara repeated her statement, pointedly keeping her words simple and similar despite the varied ways Roberts and Williams posed their questions. No, the guns and explosives weren't hers, she hadn't touched them (with one exception) and she didn't know where they came from or who they belonged to. Most of them were in cases, sealed out of sight, and could have been power tools for all she knew. The only time she'd picked up a weapon was when the two intruders arrived with the welder and she'd hidden in fear, a stun gun in her hand. But she never fired it and left it on the floor when the police arrived.

The rest of the questions were actually more awkward. Cara had to go over how she'd discovered the warehouse and her reaction to finding the clean rooms. The server was a problem as well: she had a criminal record for hacking and cyberterrorism, however long ago, and the police seemed to have a difficult time believing that she had no involvement in Ethan's activities, whatever they actually were.

She did tell them about her conversations with Thorne, and his involvement with Ethan, supplying the construction drones. At first she resisted, out of the remnants of some old code, but she couldn't think of another way of explaining how she knew about the lockup without making herself look guilty. There was no malice in it, no pleasure at sending inconvenience and trouble Thorne's way.

Emma on, the other hand, she betrayed in a heartbeat. She had no idea what was going on, whether they'd ever really been friends, or whether that friendship just hadn't been enough. Either way she was sure it was Emma that she'd seen with Ruscoe, just before she cut the power and everything went dark.

As she repeated her story over and over Cara struggled to keep her voice and emotions level, the frustration infecting her words and body language so thoroughly it was impossible to hide it. They picked at that like a scab, pushing and prodding her to provoke a more revealing response, but she had nothing more to say and the detectives grew more heated than she did.

Mallory had tried to interject now and then, Roberts or Williams cutting her off curtly each time, until she sat and glared at Cara's solicitor instead, her dark eyes piercing and intense. In the end he spoke up, the pressure from Mallory's glare and the increasingly repetitive nature of the questioning finally drawing some opposition from him until the interview was suspended and Cara was taken back to her cell.

> Schuler

He leant on the balcony rail of his hotel suite, a chilled glass of white in hand, the remains of a half-eaten seafood dish arrayed on fine plates behind him. The food was excellent, but Harper had called part way through and he'd quite lost his appetite.

The view over this part of the city was truly impressive, the traffic and people so far below they were easy to ignore. He wished he could do the same with his employer's last message. By his own estimate there was little benefit in remaining here, and an unwelcome degree of risk, but they clearly felt otherwise.

It was the project again, more trouble. They'd confirmed his own suspicions that their pet AI had misbehaved, leaving a copy of itself behind, amoeba-like, instead of fleeing the mall network altogether as instructed. There were other issues, hints of a further will to selfhood and self-improvement quite unwelcome in a mere tool, which they'd learned of from a thorough analysis of the original program. He hoped it was post-mortem, if the term could really be applied. Schuler was less surprised at how things had turned out now he'd discovered how they'd built the thing's personality, using traits scanned and copied from some of the more extreme examples of humanity, killers and criminals all.

Another call, Womak now, interrupting his sour philosophising. Their latest visit to the warehouse had proved problematic, and Ruscoe was in custody with the job unfinished. Schuler couldn't help allowing some of his anger to show in his voice. She reacted calmly enough in response, claiming she had an idea to put things right, though she didn't offer any details.

If she could make that particular pig fly he would have an excellent view of it from here.

The simulations were going well, now that he'd nailed the settings, and Ethan felt confident he was running through the op in a reasonably accurate facsimile. Recreating the penthouse layout was easy enough: the complexities came from the microclimate and the crowd behaviour. You could run the simulation a hundred times and it would give slightly different results, but at least it had the feel of realism now.

The door buzzer sounded. Ethan wasn't expecting anyone and checked the camera feeds on the other monitor. There was a van outside, and a man stood at the door dressed in overalls showing a power company badge. He could see someone else there as well, in the background. Ethan considered ignoring them but decided it might be less hassle to see what they wanted. Just as a precaution, he tucked a handgun into his waistband at the back and locked up the clean room as he exited.

Answering the door he took a look at the work order displayed on the man's smartpad. As he stood straighter, about to refuse access and insist there was a mistake he felt a sudden puff of air in his face, followed by a wave of intense relaxation.

- Thirty Four -

> Chase

As I was shown into the conference room the others were all quick to acknowledge me, half-smiles or nods, a chorus of 'mornings', an open gesture toward a chair placed around the other side of the table. I was nervous like I'd not felt in years.

We were in an old smoke-and-stone building maintained by Cadejo in the city, the plush carpets and wood panelling all making the experience feel like a vaguely defined period drama, set somewhere in time between steam and cellular. Iyer and Duval were there, Mallory, Roberts and his boss Freidman, who I'd not met before. It was, in effect, an informal board of enquiry, and entirely about my fitness for duty: I'd already done enough to cast the mostly circumstantial evidence against me in doubt. The problem was in how I'd gone about it.

Proceedings started with a recap of what I could remember of things, along with an examination of the mall security bot's false evidence and the forensic record left at the scene. This was all straightforward enough, and largely covered the events up to the point where I was taken off the case. By their reckoning that should have been the end of it, at least until my health improved, but I'd continued with my own investigations, compromising a witness and arguably interfering with important physical evidence.

I sweated my way through the next hour, answering their questions with as much honesty as I dared, trying to give them nothing to run with but case evidence and firm conjecture. I couldn't really tell how I was doing as none of them gave me anything to read or take encouragement from in their expression. Despite being largely cleared of Harris's murder now I still had plenty to answer for, and I had to do so without compromising my Admirer, whoever that actually was.

I very much wanted to keep my job and place in the ongoing investigation, but I knew either might be a slim possibility now. They finished, finally, and sent me out to a small antechamber while they discussed things amongst themselves, separated from their judgement by a finely crafted door of solid hardwood, under a ceiling heavy with the centuries.

I'd been waiting outside for over an hour, and hadn't heard anyone approach the door on the other side until it was opening, startling me and making me rise to my feet much too quickly. Mallory came straight over, smiling and hugging me hard and then letting go just as swiftly before I'd had much chance to appreciate or return the gesture.

We headed away from there to airier parts of the building, moving along a wood-panelled corridor, the only sound our own steps, sharp formal shoes on plush carpet. I felt gloriously energised of a sudden as I walked along, natural light flooding in from window after window on the outer wall to splash against portraits in oils and emulsions on the other, icons and iconoclasts intermingled with no sense of theme or faction. There was a lift close by and we took it, Mallory pushing the buttons for the roof.

I'd never been up here. I knew there was a reasonably large conservatory dining area but I'd never visited. We chose a table far from the door, and I sat while Mallory went to get two coffees. It wasn't a bad day, perhaps a little overcast, but I couldn't have cared less. Mallory was over to my right and I deliberately kept her out of my angle of sight until she headed back, hot drinks steaming in tall mugs, one a glass confection, the other ceramic. She looked great, elegant and business-like in a suit and heels.

Mallory set out the coffees neatly before sitting forward in her chair. "So, how have you been?"

"Ok. Worried, a little fraught. Probably not so ok, really."

"You must have felt better when you found the data anomalies in the mall security drone's records. At least you had some proof of your innocence then."

"Sure. Yes. What did you think; did I need to prove anything to you?" I knew as soon as it came out that I might regret asking that. I'm not even sure why I did.

Mallory looked away, her expression pensive, before she turned back and met my eyes again. "I'm a detective; I go where the evidence goes. But I was gutted when it made you look guilty and I'm ecstatic now it's proved you're not."

"And are you my 'Secret Admirer'?" This time I was definitely pushing.

She paused, though she held my gaze this time. "I've always had admiration for you Keegan, and I've never made a secret of it. Apart from that, I've no idea what you're talking about. Now, I hope we're cool, because I've got good news and bad news."

"Ok, we're cool. Any order you like." No more questions I shouldn't ask for today and besides, if Mallory had helped she could hardly admit it openly, even now.

She sighed. "You say that now… Ok, good news first: the arrest warrant and criminal charges against you are being rescinded as we speak. Roberts assured us he'd attend to it straight away." She smiled. "Now the bad news: you are reinstated, but at a temporarily reduced grade pending further review by Cadejo. You would have been placed back on paid leave, but the new lead investigator insisted on retaining you on the team."

"Who? Who's lead now?"

"That would be me. I'm your boss, for now. Sorry." She actually did look sorry, at least a little bit. I decided to make light of it, let go of that little bit of edge I was feeling. It could all be worse, and might still be if I made any mistakes.

"So I still get to go after the bad guys?"

"Yeah, you do. It's not like anyone's managed to stop you doing it so far." Wry amusement. Mallory was still Mallory.

"So, what's next?"

"I don't know, what would be next if you were in my shoes?"

"Blisters and balance issues, I expect."

> Reznik

The house had gradually gone dark over the last couple of hours. Araya lived out of the city, in a gated suburb that could have been almost anywhere in the world but most wanted to be L.A., all the properties screened from their neighbours by high walls and tall trees, gated and feted. He'd counted two pairs of guards on the grounds, plainclothes but professional enough, and had to assume more modern forms of security would also be present.

It was strangely quiet out here, the rain finally easing just as the winds were dropping a little. Too late for the old city though. The storm had been severe enough to intensify the tides, and the sea had finally breached its barriers, flooding right up to the foothills. At its peak some predicted the waters would rise even higher or that the rains might trigger landslides, prompting many to flee the city altogether or take their chances with friends and relatives up on the hillsides in the favelas, risking the police cordons to reach safety. The tone of the emergency was changing from division to disaster relief, as the world watched a different story emerge.

All of this had made Reznik's journey back into and across the city more challenging, as public transport was severely disrupted and the flow of people distorted by the panic. Even here, in the suburbs, his path had been harder, as the estate posted increased security to keep out refugees. It was a mess, but at least it made it unlikely that anyone would still be actively looking for him.

Reznik was perched amongst the thick branches of a dwarf hardwood rooted in the grounds of a vacant property just across from Araya, high enough to look out and keep watch. He wasn't alone in his vigil. Just opposite was a car with two occupants inside, plain as a pyre on infrared, and they'd been there longer than he had. It was a new electric model, nothing flash, ordinary but not out of place. He listened in to their conversation as each took a turn with a pair of night vision binoculars, but aside from identifying local accents he didn't learn much.

A half hour or so later a blue Marcatti drove up, the same one he'd followed earlier that day. Mr. OraCotek got out of the rear door and walked straight over to the surveillance car, opening the back and getting inside. This time he could hear every word of the conversation, not as clear as if he'd been there with them, but good enough.

"Anything?"

"No, sir. The target settled down for the night at 11:40 as far as we could tell, and there's been no movement apart from his guards since."

"You're sure there's been no one else around?"

"No, nothing. It's been quiet."

"Ok, anything interesting happens call it in. Another team will arrive in a van at 3:00am. There'll be a power cut just before they pull up to the house. When that happens start your motor and go home. Whatever you see or hear after the van arrives is not your concern."

"Sure thing, sir."

OraCotek then returned to the Marcatti, which started up and headed off smoothly into the night. Reznik smiled his cold smile, The Wolf again.

At 2:30 Reznik quickly rechecked the action and magazine on the handgun he carried, before dropping down from the tree to land softly on the lawn of the empty house. Moving quickly and quietly across to the high wall at the edge of the property he leapt straight up, catching the edge and hauling his body up and over, grateful again for his gloves and that there was nothing too nasty on top as he cleared it with his body tight to the surface, landing smoothly on the sidewalk outside. Grounded, he moved in a half crouch straight for the stakeout car, his feet taking quick, quiet steps as he approached the vehicle's rear corner nearest the curb, squatting down right next to the fender when he reached it, head down below the rear window.

He waited there for a few heartbeats as he attached a suppressor to the automatic.

There was no reaction and he moved again, around the back and along the driver's side, as low and smooth as he could, raising his gun even as he began to rise himself, yanking open the door, the gun in his fist spitting twice before he arced around slightly to cover the driver.

Reznik remained there, one finger to his lips, the other hand holding the pistol rock steady as the driver dropped the binoculars, eyes widening. As comprehension bloomed he looked over to witness his colleague's final moments and then back to Reznik, his eyes again betraying him, agitation and fear rising until Reznik shushed him, patting the air palm down with his left hand as though he had the other man's emotions under remote control. Once things were calmer they stayed there, eyes locked, until Reznik spoke: "Get out. Keep it smooth and slow, and then quietly walk across to the corner over there. Once you reach it head along the side street. We need to have a little talk."

He stepped back as the driver got out of the car and waited for him to turn and move as directed before he followed, always a few feet behind, gun steady and level. Reznik waited until they were a good distance from the car then shot him twice. There were some thick bushes against the wall of the property, and after a short pause he dragged the body into place, easily, as if it were a child rather than a full-grown man.

Reznik returned to the car and got in the driver's side, calmly taking the front seat, nestling his back into the warmth and ignoring the corpse and its smells. He checked the gun again, swapping out the magazine for a fresh one, removed the suppressor and placed it back in its shoulder rig. It was 2:35 by the dash clock.

> Cara

She passed a hard night on her own in a cell, aware of every moment as it crawled by until finally falling asleep in the small hours, exhausted and completely spent.

When she awoke early the next morning she felt no better for the rest, her body subtly abused by the hard-foam bed. Breakfast was a protein bar, engineered to be entirely inoffensive, as joyless and uncomfortable in the mouth as the mattress had been for her body, both hard, uniform blocks of industrial utility.

Lunch was much the same, though she did at least get a crap cup of tea with it.

There was no warning or notice when they released her mid-afternoon, freed but still under caution. She was processed out soon afterward, no detectives or solicitors present, just uniforms, and no one either could or would tell her what was happening.

The only place in her mind to go next was home. She tried to reach Chase, but couldn't get hold of him as his phone went straight to voicemail, so she left him a cluster of swearwords like an aural landmine and rang off. The drive was quick and uneventful as she lay back and closed her eyes while the car did the work, enjoying the sense of moving passively and safely through the world, protected and primary in her own cocoon of synthetics and silicates. Even as the car rolled to a stop she remained there, eyes closed and head reclined, zoning out the last few days.

Despite the surveillance Cara went inside, desperate now for a shower and a change of clothes. She raced through the flat to reach the bathroom, and then luxuriated in the hot water and enriched soap, leaving the fan off to allow the steam the full run of the place so it would, she hoped, fog any cameras. As she got changed in the bedroom she almost felt dirty again, knowing the artificial eyes were nearby.

There'd been a message from Petre while she was in the shower: he'd been in trouble again, a fight with another inmate. It was an open question now if the guards would discover who was involved and lock them both in solitary, or whether the other prisoner's friends would catch up with him first. Cara found herself empathising with Petre more than she had in some time, her own brief incarceration a sharp reminder of his daily reality. She was worried for him, desperately so, but knew there was nothing she could do. Besides, she was neck-deep in her own problems.

Chase finally called her back a couple of hours later. She'd briefly visited Dad in the meantime, but he'd not been great today and she couldn't stand it for long. Chase sounded concerned, checking she was all right, asking where she was. Waiting in the hospital carpark, not wanting to go back to her flat but not knowing where to go next. Not that she said that.

Chase: "Ok. Well the good news is I've been reinstated, more or less, so I'm officially a detective again. I'll get a team out to your flat as soon as I can to remove the tap on your *aigent*, maybe trace where the surveillance is feeding to, then you'll be ok to use the place again. You should be able to go back to the warehouse as well, if you want, after I've cleared it with the police."

"What happened to you, why didn't you come before?"

"Sorry. I thought calling Mallory would be the quickest way to get a response team out to you, but I had to agree to turn myself in. The police were still convinced I'd killed Harris, and I had to deal with that. Everything should be ok now."

"Alright. Do you still need me?"

"Sure. At the moment no one's done more work on the mall data than you and Raissa. We could link you into the Cadejo network from the warehouse, boost Raissa's capabilities a bit, or maybe you could work from the office?"

She thought about that for a fraction of a second smaller than 'no fucking way' and replied, "No, the warehouse is fine."

"Fine, the warehouse it is then. I'll get them to send a team over to make sure the place is safe and they'll let you know when everything's cleared."

"Ok, sure." She paused. "Chase."

"Yeah?"

"What about Emma? Have they arrested her, should I stop taking the pills she gave me?"

"No, not yet." He paused. "What pills are you talking about, what have you been taking?"

"Anti-depressants, she said."

"Ok. You need to stop. I'll arrange an appointment for you with a private doctor we use. She'll check you out, proscribe anything you need and collect the pills Womak gave you. We'll do some tests, just as a precaution."

"Thanks, Chase. Thank you."

Ruscoe cursed and slowed down, rattled by the last pothole, taking more care now to avoid the deep ruts scattered across the yard. A quick glance over his shoulder confirmed that their passenger was still out cold. There was another van just ahead, similar to their own but blue, parked up with the side door open. He could see there was a driver in the front, someone slight and not so tall. Ruscoe pulled up alongside, sliding a little on the muddy surface.

They waited a few moments, expecting some form of acknowledgement, until Womak, shrugging, opened the door to climb out and cross the yard to the other van. She returned almost immediately, sliding back their own side door and grabbing Grant's feet. "C'mon, we haven't got all day! We need to carry him over, and then we can get out of here."

Ruscoe cursed again and then climbed out to help his partner.

- Thirty Five -

> Chase

The real interview with Ruscoe had started a few minutes ago, and things were just warming up. He'd been in custody a couple of days now, questioned on various lesser charges while the more serious indictments for kidnap and accessory to murder loomed in the background. There had been the usual dance around exchanges and considerations, but his lawyer had indicated he was ready to give a full and frank confession, as soon as the paperwork was signed. It felt much better to be the other side of the interrogation, a mere observer as the police asked their questions, rather than being the focus of their attention.

Mallory had done an excellent job, stepping in to head up an expanded Cadejo team. Generally she'd been pushing things forward, in close cooperation with the police, to try and reach a quick and decisive result before things turned any uglier in the media. I was gratified to see that the core of their initial enquiries had been my own case notes, and they'd since leapt on the items I was carrying at the time of my arrest to enhance their own work, trawling through the smartpad's contents. There was broad agreement on the main suspects, Schuler, Womak and Ruscoe, and that Thorne was somehow involved as well. I couldn't help but notice the ghost of my own name on one of the whiteboards, not quite wiped clean.

Ruscoe claimed the first time he'd heard of Ethan Grant was a couple of days before the kidnapping, when Womak called to offer him the job. He'd worked with her a few times in the past so he trusted her and hadn't asked too many questions. The deal was that they were to kidnap Grant and then drive him to a drop-off point where he'd be transferred to someone else's care. There was no mention of killing him later, and the hirer was very specific that he shouldn't be harmed in any way.

A few days later Womak asked him to go back to the warehouse again, this time to break in and upload a virus onto the main server, or failing that, if they had to, destroy the equipment. According to Ruscoe they'd not expected anyone else to be there. Their main intention on returning the third time was definitely destruction, though of property rather than people.

Mallory brought things back round to the subject of Jakobsen/Grant's abduction. Ruscoe gave us more information, stating that they'd taken Grant to a patch of rough waste ground where they met with a second van that was parked up with its side door wide open. They bundled Grant inside, rolling him over until he rested against a rack of electronic equipment of some kind that looked as though it was bolted to the floor. It was dark in the back, and Ruscoe could see various LEDs flashing.

The driver had made no movement or sound at all. From what he'd seen, Ruscoe said it was either a smallish man or a woman, dressed in dark baggy clothes with a deep hood pulled up. Womak had gone up to the cab and while she was there Ruscoe happened to glance up to the roof where he saw a slim satellite rig had been deployed. His partner returned almost straight away, shrugging her shoulders. Then they left. There was, as far as he knew, no intent to kill Ethan Grant then or later.

They asked him about Schuler next, and Harris's murder. Ruscoe claimed to have had nothing at all to do with the shooting in the mall's server room. As for the name, Womak had only mentioned the client once, but it was Sauveterre, not Schuler. It seemed she wanted to impress him: he was important, apparently, though Ruscoe had no idea who he was. Ruscoe asked if Sauveterre was the client, and Womak had replied "this time." There'd been no mention of him before in connection with the kidnapping, and Womak had given him a hard stare when Ruscoe brought it up again.

Ruscoe was by all reasonable estimations a professional criminal, but these would be the most serious charges he'd ever faced. He seemed genuine enough, speaking calmly and clearly with a relaxed and open posture. If he was lying, or withholding anything, he was doing it well.

> Reznik

He'd spotted them as soon as they turned onto the avenue, riding in a dark van that looked entirely out of place at 3AM in an area like this. They drove past Araya's property just a little too slowly, before speeding up and then turning left further along the street. It was a large capacity hybrid vehicle riding low on its shocks, heavily laden or perhaps heavily modified.

Five minutes later Reznik watched the twin spots of the van's headlights approaching again in his side mirror, this time at a crawl. As it drew closer, about 50 yards away, the power for the block cut abruptly, rendering everything suddenly dark. The van's lights went off in turn as it sped up to cover the final distance, coming to an almost silent stop just before Araya's gates without even brake lights to betray it.

Reznik's eyes had already adjusted and he saw the next moments perfectly. As soon as the van's wheels stopped rolling the rear and side doors opened, allowing black-clad figures to burst forth, most of them carrying compact grenade launchers which they fired again and again over the walls, just as another attached a breaching charge to the gates.

As they returned to the van to dump the launchers the explosive was triggered, a quiet thud of a blast, rocking the gates on their hinges. While they'd paused there for a moment, Reznik had taken in their kit and equipment in a long appraising glance:

the usual dark overalls and boots with facemasks and strapping, like fetishists crashing some back alley party. All four men pushed through the gates, splitting into two teams and moving off rapidly into the grounds, assault weapons raised.

Reznik watched his time readout count twenty seconds and then activated a command on the dash before popping the door, getting out and casually dropping a small package in the foot well. He walked over to the van, cautiously approaching its rear corner.

When Reznik was close enough he could see that the driver was looking forward through the open window, focused on whatever view he had through the split gates of Araya's property, only briefly glancing across at the surveillance car as it drove off. Reznik ducked around the van's rear corner and edged along its side, twisting so that his back stayed flat to the bodywork, thinning his profile. He could hear commotion from inside the compound now, dogs barking and then abruptly silent, followed by human shouts of curiosity or alarm.

The driver leant out of his window, rising from his seat a little and craning his head to improve his line of sight. Reznik grabbed him around the neck in a chokehold, pulling him further out of the window as he applied more pressure. The driver fought, slapping at his arms, trying to reach back, grunting as he quickly lost consciousness. Reznik held on for a little longer and then rocked him back into his seat. After opening the door to check his status, he dragged the driver bodily from the van and loaded him into the back through the side door.

Following the unconscious body into the rear of the vehicle, Reznik pulled the driver further inside up to the bulkhead and then searched and disarmed him, finding nothing noteworthy. Reznik then gently removed the driver's belt, and used it to tie his hands behind his back, turning him onto his side in a modified recovery position when he was finished.

Climbing back out of the van, Reznik pocketed the keys before sliding the door closed. After kicking the driver's pistol under the van, he drew his own and dropped into a familiar half-crouch, took a few slow, controlled breaths, and then headed inside the villa gates.

> Cara

Once she'd been given the all clear to return to the warehouse, Cara went straight there. It was then a good four hours before she left the iso-room and took a break. They'd been the better sort of hours at first, swift and pleasant - stimulating even - until things took a darker turn and she had to leave for a while, get some space.

As well as checking the place for safety, Cadejo had installed some upgrades, partly of the security systems but chiefly of the mainframe Raissa was running on. With access to greatly increased computing power they wasted no time in beginning a more detailed analysis of the data traffic from the mall just before the system crash. There was something even more human and believable about this new Raissa, and Cara stopped reminding herself that She was an It. Partly, it was Raissa's increased capability to truly multi-task, dividing her full attention between different strands of enquiry. Previously Cara had felt that she was largely working alone on the data Ethan had left behind, but over the course of the day it was as though Raissa was increasingly with her.

What she'd discovered so far did not look good. Absolutely no part of it. These could be the last vital pieces to explain Ethan's double life, his older and other self, but it might just be another perspective on him that made her own ever smaller. As she started to make sense of it she almost didn't want to know, and had no idea how she would feel in the long run now that she was off the meds.

Over the last eighteen months Ethan had been looking for a woman named Polzin, though there was no real explanation of why. He'd first searched in eastern Europe, then through North Africa and the Middle East until he'd finally found her again in South America. From the nature of the contacts and darknet sites he'd investigated it was clear she was some sort of trader, though on a completely different scale from Thorne, specialising in military and proscribed technologies that would have earned her a long stay in prison, at the least, if she were ever caught.

Whatever his reason for finding her it seemed deadly serious. After she'd been located, he'd begun to organise some kind of commando operation. There were detailed plans of a tower block penthouse apartment and schematics and specifications for construction drones, possibly his reason for dealing with Nathan. He even had a simulation rig for the mission scenario that had seen heavy use right up to the day of his abduction. It was clear he wasn't working alone either: there were emails sent back and forth through the darknet, terse, clipped messages full of language and acronyms she'd seldom heard outside of a movie.

Cara was beginning to understand what he had been doing, his actions, but still had no idea of his motivations, or who he was working with. It was then that she'd walked away from it for a while, casually accepting Raissa's offer to look into things while she was gone.

It was a couple of hours before she returned. Cara had driven over to the park and sat by the lake, trying to find peace reflected toward her from the open waters and the relaxation of others. It was a success in part, the freshness of the air a welcome change from the cloistered isolation of the warehouse, but she felt restless still, as though she should be active at every moment. She thought about calling Chase, decided he was probably busy, and drove back to Ethan's warehouse instead, pushing her monthly self-drive allowance to keep herself occupied and involved.

As she settled back into the overly fancy chair Ethan had used in front of the main monitor she asked Raissa what she'd found, fully aware that she could talk to the AI from anywhere in the iso-rooms now. There was a pause, as though Raissa were thinking.

"Hi Cara. I've cross-referenced the data Ethan left on the mainframe with your own notes and the CSS case files. Are you sure you want to hear this?"

"No. But I don't want to be left imagining any longer either."

"Ok..."

"Raissa!"

"Fine. It looks as though all this started when Ethan – Jakobsen really – was working for a small mercenary company.

They were hired by a man named Reznik for a raid on a remote military-industrial R&D facility. The other two team members, by the way, were women named Anna Frost and Kurosawa Tsukino." Raissa showed her various pictures of the two women on the monitor, and Cara immediately recognised them from the server's home screen. There were other pictures next; a couple of long distance surveillance shots, poor quality, taken of the man she assumed was Reznik. She'd seen him before, checked her smartpad, and realised he was the man Ethan had set his home *aigent* to watch for.

"The two women were killed during the raid, but then supposedly so was Ethan." The AI continued, "We don't know why they're now going after Polzin, but she'd been working as a smuggler, black market trader and information broker, as you thought. She may have been involved in the planning of the raid somehow."

"This Reznik character, though, is something else. He's a ghost, hardly appears in any of the files. We think he's connected with deep and scary intelligence operations, way off-record. Assuming he's still in Maravilhosa, where he was last placed, he's probably in trouble. There was a bombing at the same penthouse apartment where they were planning to target Polzin. Lots of casualties, including local politicians and corporate types. There were no plans for anything like that in the simulations Ethan was running, but it's quite a coincidence."

Cara thought for a few moments. She'd seen the bombing on the news, was shocked that Ethan could have even the slightest connection to it. This was too much. She was suddenly tired of all this, but there was one thing she had to try.

"Raissa, send an email to this Reznik guy. Tell him I'm Ethan's business partner. No, hang on; tell him I'm a...friend of Jakobsen's and that I want to help."

"You sure?"

"Yes! Please, just do it for me."

"Ok, done."

"Raissa, you won't tell Chase or Cadejo about this will you?"

"Honey, they already know. I am them. Your server's integrated into theirs now. This Raissa is their Raissa, pretty much, not just a copy. I thought you'd have realised that. Sorry."

"What about the human agents, do they have to know?"

"I suppose I could forget to flag it for them for a while."

"Please!"

"Ok, no worries. Consider it not done."

It was the pain Ethan was aware of first, then the cold. He was strapped to a chair, held tightly enough by his ankles and wrists for it to be uncomfortable, and he was sure he'd drifted in and out of sleep a couple of times. From the numbness it felt like he might have been in the same position for hours, and he badly needed the toilet.

There seemed to be no one else there so he flexed and shifted as best as he could, trying to make the blood flow and the aches pass, his breath misting in the chill air from his exertions. He was in a small room, roughly cubical, the walls and ceiling made from many layers of thick plastic sheeting stretched over a metal frame, while the floor was like heavy linoleum. Powerful floodlights were placed in the corners, all of them shining straight toward him, leaving blackness beyond.

A figure stepped suddenly out of nowhere like a magician, startling him so much that he tried to push backward in the chair, momentarily panicked. It was then his control gave way and he pissed his pants.

- Thirty Six -

> Chase

We were finding out the hard way why Schuler had never once been indicted on criminal charges despite crossing so many lines, legal and geographic. As soon as we arrived at his hotel the circus had started, with the front desk refusing to confirm he was even a guest until we'd spent several frustrating minutes waiting in reception.

When we eventually gained access to his suite we were shown, with exquisite politeness and polish, into a sumptuous conference room that his solicitors had reserved 'just in case'. Two of his lawyers were already there, stepping in to speak on behalf of their client, whose lips were tighter than Lycra. They turned what we'd thought were strong grounds for interviewing him into almost nothing, challenging the validity of every piece of evidence we had.

The links we'd made earlier in the day between the name Ruscoe had heard, Sauveterre, and a car hired in that name that was placed near the mall on the Saturday when Harris was killed, and again later in the week, were dismissed as nothing more than coincidence. Pictures we had of him from Jakobsen's warehouse were from nowhere near the time of his abduction or the later visits by Ruscoe and Womak. Even my own testimony was shaky, relying as it did on a memory that was altogether too fragile to be admissible in court.

Before long I'd had enough of the arguments, so I took a few minutes break in one of the side rooms that opened out onto a balcony. I'd only been there for a short time when Schuler himself stepped up, casually leaning against the rail next to me as though we were old friends. At first he was silent, breathing softly, but after a few seconds he spoke: "I like the view from up here. The air is fresher, and you can see so much further. It gives you a better perspective."

I thought for a moment, trying to keep my face straight and voice level, though I think it betrayed me a little. "It's a dangerous perspective though."

"Really? How so?"

"Makes you too distant from everything else, like it doesn't matter."

"Interesting." He nodded slowly, as though considering my point, and then spoke again: "Do you think they'll find a way, your lawyers? From my own position that would be bad."

"I couldn't say. If I were able to contribute much to the arguments I wouldn't be out here."

"Fair enough. For myself I find the whole discussion a little repetitive, circular you might say. Truthfully, I am sorry so much time is being wasted for everyone."

"You could save everyone the bother, if you confessed."

He smiled, and almost let the humour reach his voice, "I don't think I can oblige you in that, Detective Chase. I'm much too busy. Besides, wouldn't that rob you of the satisfaction of completing your investigation?"

"Oh, I'll get satisfaction alright. I will get to the truth."

"Ah, but to the lawyers it doesn't matter what you believe to be true, it only matters what you can prove to be true." There was a pause and then he continued: "I'm pleased to see that you have resolved your difficulties with the police. I think we can agree that it is far worse for an innocent man be found guilty, than a guilty man be found innocent." He smiled, actually looking fairly pleased, though probably more with himself than anything else.

Schuler was smart and he had to know the evidence he'd planted wouldn't stand up to scrutiny forever. Maybe it didn't have to: whatever had been going on at the mall it was probably over. I didn't want him to give anything away, especially my annoyance, so I responded as levelly as I could, "I think it's better to be innocent than guilty, and to know which is which. Don't you agree, Herr Schuler?"

"I think it's a matter of perspective." He shrugged, inclining his head and arching an eyebrow, before he turned and walked away, his manner as eloquent as his honeyed tongue.

I let it go at that. I had no adequate riposte and didn't mind too much if he thought he had the better of me, because I think he gave me a little more than I gave him. Besides, I didn't really want to match his repartee: I wanted to throw him from the balcony.

After a time we left, temporarily defeated. No one's mood was improved much when we were greeted and aggressively questioned by a cluster of independent journalists on the way out of the hotel, in full view of a flock of mediacams that had seemingly appeared from nowhere, their plastic shells emblazoned with network logos and sponsor messages.

> Reznik

As soon as he entered the villa compound he veered left, across the gravel drive and over the lawn, using the trees and bushes to screen himself from the house as he angled forward through the thick smoke left by the grenades. Reznik was alive with expectation, senses as keen as a butcher's blade as he pressed on, a hard knot of fear in the pit of his stomach weighting his posture lean and low. There were dark shapes on the lawn and gravel path, confirming that any guards outside the house would likely have been neutralised by the assault team on their way through, but he still anticipated threats and problems, balancing his desire for self-preservation with the knowledge that the best option might be launching an aggressive counterattack before anyone knew he was there.

Moving closer to the house, he paused behind a tree at the edge of the garden. Ahead were two of the troopers, backs flat to the wall at either side of the front entrance, waiting briefly for a breaching pack to go off. Smoke and splinters spread inward as the charge detonated, one man rushing inside a moment later, kicking the door further open, his companion following on, both of them firing into the interior. Another muffled blast sounded from the rear of the house, followed by gunshots and cries of alarm.

Reznik gave them a five count and then followed, matching their momentum with his own, knowing they would be focused ahead. His feet fell on gravel, then stone, then wood as he moved forward. One of the attackers was clearly visible through the doorway and Reznik fired into his back, the gun level and steady, effectively silent against the overall soundscape. Then quickly inside, looking left, no one in front, gun tracking right, firing again then centring, weapon and eyes panning the room more slowly as a second trooper fell.

Two neutralised attackers, four of Araya's security down, a large entrance hall, doors leading off in three directions and a grand staircase leading upwards to a balcony level. Expensive, clean decoration, lots of windows, white walls, fine art. Sounds of gunfire and alarm from the back of the house and young voices shouting above.

Pause. Stow the pistol; grab a rifle from the floor. German made, modern and deadly. Check the mag, check the action, check the selector: everything ok. The stock nestled into his shoulder as if it belonged there. He moved through the ground floor toward the sound of combat, wired and wary, muzzle and head moving together to cover the angles, leading the shoulders and torso, hips and legs almost independent, aligned for smooth forward motion. His body sang to him, harmonious and perfect, attuned to this dance like no other.

The next time he saw Araya was down the sights of the rifle, when the older man stepped from around the doorway of his bedroom, pistol in hand. Reznik knew he was there, expected him, and didn't fire. They stayed like that for a moment until Araya bent and placed his gun on the floor, rising with hands high, moving further out into the corridor as he did so. From inside came sounds of subdued alarm and fear, shushing and muffled tears.

"Please, don't hurt my family." There was none of his usual suave smoothness, just a plain, direct honesty, dignified in its simplicity, his stance straight and artless. The rest of the house was quiet, eerily still now, human lives emptied and ending on the floor. Reznik lowered the rifle's plane away from the horizontal and to the side, showing his face and a less threatening posture.

"I ain't here for that. I suggest we go somewhere and have a talk, though. Your security company will have sent a response team by now, not to mention maybe the police, so it'll get busy here before too long."

Araya lowered his hands slightly, and then some more when there was no response. "If that's all you wanted why didn't you just call?" Disbelief, a little anger.

"It's a good job I stopped by. You'll see for yourself on the way out. I got here just in time to clean up and save your ass."

Reznik stepped backward as Araya moved toward him, waited at the head of the stairs for Araya to go down to the main entrance, and then followed. He kept his patience while Araya paused at the sight of so many bodies, studying the scene. When he reached the first of the assault troops Araya turned and nodded, looking less tense, resigned. "These men are not yours?"

"Nope, not my doing. Got a live one outside. Maybe we can both have a little talk with him, see what's going on."

Turning at the threshold, Araya forced a smile and waved bravely to his wife and young daughters who had come out onto the balcony, looking down on the carnage and their father leaving with an armed stranger whose face was hard and indifferent to their fear and the destruction of their home. They headed out without further words, the two of them, through the splintered door and into the garden.

Araya stood straight and they walked on, Reznik close but never too close behind him. Out of the gates and up to the van, Araya into passenger seat, Reznik driving off and taking the next hard turn, then another, then parking and waiting while emergency vehicles wailed along nearby.

> Cara

She was on her way home when the call came in. As soon as the ident flashed up Cara banged the dash button for autodrive, fortunate that she had already programmed the destination earlier as she checked for traffic.

"Miss Dalca, it's the Hawthorn Ward. I'm afraid there's been a change in your father's condition. Are you able to get over here, the doctor wanted to have a word with you?"

"..."

"Miss Dalca, are you there?"

"Yes. Yes, I'm here. I'll be over as soon as I can."

Everything seemed perfectly ordinary as she travelled, a journey like so many others she'd made before, and yet every mile seemed to be a crawl. Dad was probably just a bit worse, poorly with some bug: it didn't mean the end. She'd only just lost Ethan, and she couldn't lose him as well.

When Cara arrived her anxiety at being delayed evaporated and she fell into a mirror of her usual routine, as though it would change the news she was on her way to hear. She stopped by the second floor on her way up to the third, her knowledge of the subtle differences between the various coffee machines in the building like a gourmands, long experience and fortunate past detours informing her of the best and closest vendor to her father's bed. Once she had a coffee she took the stairs, fancying a walk but also knowing all the while that it would take a little longer, stretch out the moments where the news wasn't yet bad.

The stairwell exit was at the far end of the long corridor that ran up to the ward. It was then that she saw Emma in the distance, coming out of the lifts, dressed as an orderly yet unmistakeable, her normally pretty face looking drawn. As visits went this was swiftly becoming both more remarkable and more terrible, and for no reason yet connected to her father's condition. Emma had to be there for her, to perform some mischief. The idea that she might have gentler reasons to be at the hospital didn't fly at all, and it was too much of a coincidence to imagine she was here for some other piece of ill that had nothing to do with her.

Cara had to make sure though, maybe see what Emma was up to. There were people everywhere, and the nurses on her father's ward knew her well – surely, she would be able to get help and reach safety if Emma saw her? Ideally, though, she wouldn't. Cara headed forward, leaving the drink on a window ledge.

It didn't take her long to spot Emma again. She was hovering around the entrance to the ward, trying to look busy while two of the nurses Cara knew hung around nearby for a few moments. Cara watched from a slight recess in the corridor wall where she'd often seen empty stretchers stored. The nurses finished their conversation quickly, moving on to whatever duties they had next, leaving Emma alone. She ducked into the ward entrance then, out of sight, and Cara waited, tense and immensely worried, the indecision like a physical thing pressing down on her, until she had no choice but to get closer and try to catch what was going on.

Cara was halfway toward her when Emma suddenly left the ward and came back onto the main corridor, turning right and heading in the opposite direction. As Cara hurried along to check on her father Emma walked on, visible in flashes of green as she moved through the patients, staff and visitors.

Abruptly Emma turned back straight toward her as though suddenly remembering something and Cara had to stop and look to one side, pretending to read a notice on the wall before turning and walking back toward the stairs, desperate to have her feet match the pace of her heart but knowing Emma would spot her instantly if she did. Cara walked on, forcing herself to calm as she gnawed her lower lip so much it split a little and bled, the iron taste surprising her, stoking the fear and panic. It seemed to take a long time to reach the stairs but they were just ahead now, and she reached out for the doors to push through, her arm and hand quivering and suddenly weak. She pushed onward, the brass-coloured plate cold under her palm, the door swinging smoothly aside and her body following through the opening gap.

Cara made herself take a few more steps steadily and then she ran, the balls of her feet clipping along at the outer edge of each stair as she rushed downward, thinning herself and dodging to pass others as they moved in their more sedate pace, turning to look at her rush by.

There was no sign of Emma following, but she kept her speed all the way down to the bottom, relieved when she reached the ground and could move even faster. Cara hurried toward the main entrance and outside, pausing hand on wall for breath as she called Chase.

The figure stood like a statue, absolutely still, androgynous and loose in baggy clothes and a hoodie. Ethan couldn't even see the subtlest of movements, the shallow rise and fall of breathing or the slightest repositioning of weight. He forced himself to calm and spoke: "I don't know who you are, but there must be some mistake. Please let me go." No response. He tried again, tried pleading, but got nowhere and in the end sat there in his soiled pants, humiliated.

They stayed like that for a good while until suddenly, reacting to no cue he could perceive, the figure turned and walked gracefully away, coming back momentarily with a laptop, which s/he opened and turned round so that Ethan could see the screen. Text appeared, large white letters on a black background: 'Hello KarlJakobsen/EthanGrant. I want you to work for me. ☺'

- Thirty Seven -

> Chase

I was a little behind the uniforms as we rushed through the main entrance, startling one of the patients making their slow, pained way outside on crutches and almost knocking into a nurse. Cara wasn't there. I stopped in the middle of the entrance hall, turning around and back again to look in each direction. No sign of her.

The reception desk was in front of us so I went over. I knew Cara's father was an inpatient, so I asked which ward he was on and how to reach it. In the meantime, more officers had arrived and I sent them to cover the exits as best they could, hoping we could catch Womak before she got out of the building.

The lifts were just along the main corridor and I rushed toward them, taking the first two responding officers with me. We had to wait as it returned from the upper floors, and I muttered under my breath and bobbed in place with frustration as though ceasing to move at all would bring disaster. Seconds ground past as the numbers fell in sequence and the lift moved down.

When the doors opened I pushed forward, earning dark looks and curses from the passengers as they slowly emptied out until they noticed the officers behind me and hastened along. We were inside then, selecting a floor and somehow relaxing for a moment nudged into the back corner, knowing there was nothing we could do until the lift car climbed its way upwards and allowed us out again.

I saw Cara from the main corridor, standing not too far from the foot of one of the beds in a side ward as a team of two nurses and a doctor hurried around the elderly man inside, probably powerful and strong once judging by his frame but frail now. She rushed over, arms outstretched, looking for comfort and warmth. I held her, a little awkwardly at first, as we watched the medics work. I sent the two officers on to see if Womak was nearby.

As they worked the doctor and nurses talked amongst themselves. I knew barely half of the terminology, and that mainly from spending too much time in hospitals myself, but it was easy to tell from the tone of their language and their expressions that they were at first very worried and then confused, until a new piece of equipment, some sort of testing or monitoring rig, was wheeled in at a rush and hooked up to the patient. After that had begun to give them results the tension eased quite considerably, matched by a gradual loosening of Cara's hold until we separated entirely.

Satisfied at last the doctor came over to speak to us. "I'm not sure what happened, but it looks like it may all have been a bit of a false alarm, as far as we can tell. The monitoring equipment seems to have been giving false readings for a time, leading us to think there'd been a decline in your father's condition. The main thing is he's ok, no worse than before."

Cara's tension had eased noticeably while he spoke, until she literally took a deep breath and paused before speaking. "Thank you doctor. I'm sure it's no one's fault. Thank you for looking after Dad." She smiled and then turned square on to face me before speaking again.

"Emma. She must have done something to the equipment, sabotaged it somehow."

I nodded in agreement. She might very well be right, and I said as much.

There was no sign of Womak anywhere in the hospital, according to the officer who came back to report to me. It was more than possible she'd been missed or overlooked though, as there weren't nearly enough of us to fully control the entrances or make a detailed search. I asked Cara to stay there, and went off to help look for Womak.

> Reznik

He'd let Araya take the lead, pounding at the ribs and face of the driver, until in the end he signalled a pause with a quiet word and restraining hand. Araya listened the second time. They were high up on a hillside, in some layby on a nameless road, dawn almost on them, the city spread out in the distance below, darker and narrower than it should be. Power was not fully restored, leaving islands of electric light. A handful of fires burning amongst the favelas as helos and drones flew overhead, their searchlights punching down through the greasy smoke.

The driver was a mess already, bloody and battered, one eye closed and swollen, lips split and fat beneath a thoroughly broken nose. He held his right hand to his face, his left to fractured ribs, back leaning against the side of the van. Araya stood glaring at him, shoulders and chest heaving, knuckles bruised and bloody, fear for his family and self still twisted into livid anger. Reznik listened for the driver's breathing, aware he was terrified and close to collapse.

"Hope you're feeling a touch more talkative now." Reznik smiled in the dark. "We're real curious about who you work for, and what they were planning for Sr. Araya here." He indicated with his hand, like a concierge. "So how about you tell us what you know?"

The driver didn't know much. He was a local, and got the job from a fixer he knew. There were instructions for where to pick up the van, where to collect the men, who the team leader was, a guy called Haynes. Reznik pressed on that, found the troopers were all strangers, definitely not from here.

"You ever heard of OraCotek?"

"Yes, I think so. They make drones and shit, right? Is that who I was working for?"

"That's kind of the question of the hour."

Araya moved in again, his need for violence rising, and Reznik let him get to almost within striking distance of the driver, who cowered backward, until he turned and placed himself between them, gently but firmly leading Araya away. He took him to the front of the van and helped him inside before going around the front and climbing into the driver's seat, leaving the poor beaten bastard alone outside for a minute.

Reznik: "I've heard the name OraCotek a lot in the last few days. What do you know about them?"

Araya paused, breathed deeply for a couple of beats and then spoke, his voice weary and rough. "They're a technology company. They make their own stuff, a lot of it for the military, and some of the components and electronics that go into other brand's products. Nearly everyone uses them."

"And they gave oh so generously to protect the city from terrorists, right?"

"Right."

"Ok, fine. I can see them sending a team of vicious, highly trained specialists after someone, but I'd expect lawyers – not a kill team."

"I suppose. There are rumours."

"Do tell."

Araya paused, obviously reluctant, and spoke softer than before. "It's said that the money the company was founded with came from one of the cartels trying to buy their way to legitimacy. And that they became so successful, so quickly, through some...unorthodox...methods they've not yet forgotten."

"Go on. I'm guessing there's more."

"I've heard that as well as developing electronics and such they are doing other work, more secretive. Researching some new form of AI or something."

"I see. And how did Lagorio fit into all this?"

"Currently OraCotek's work on AI is of questionable legality, and so they've been trying to gain influence to change those laws.

Other companies, just as influential, were trying to prevent this. Lagorio was working as a lobbyist of sorts for one of their opponents, Hallistiks."

"I see. So I walked right into someone else's war."

"Yes." He cleared his throat, looked away. There was something else here.

"So, what about you. You're on their shit list because...?"

"I helped them out, but not enough to be useful again. I'm a loose end."

Reznik didn't say anything, but waited a moment before turning his head to stare levelly at the other man. "That help you gave OraCotek. Wouldn't by any chance involve my good self would it?"

"Yes." Quietly, looking away. "They promised much and threatened more. It was...impossible...to say no." He looked over at Reznik, plainly torn, betrayed pride and regret mingled with a more basic fear.

Reznik mulled, waiting for the tension to rise and Araya's discomfort to show plainly, before he spoke again. "I believe I understand your position. Damned if you do and damned if you don't". He smiled, mouth wide and generous while his eyes stayed flat and cold.

His left hand had been on the hilt for some time, and he merely completed the action, drawing the short knife and stabbing into Araya's side and stomach, pushing against his shoulder at the same time with his free hand. The knife bit again, again, again, the last withdrawal longer and slower. He flicked the blade clean, then wiped it across the upholstery and sheathed it. Araya's mouth was an 'O', his eyes round, grunts of pain and fear as he grabbed for his wounded side, blood and stink escaping between spread fingers.

Reznik paused, shrugged, and keyed an emergency response into the autodrive. "I believe that concludes our business."

He climbed out of the van, leaving the door wide, and walked away. The van asked for the door to be closed, then once more before being shut off part way through its request. Reznik heard it moving as he walked in the opposite direction, glancing once behind to see the van accelerate away. There was no sign of the driver.

> Cara

Cara was returning to the warehouse, driving manually and as fast as she dared, suddenly confident beyond doubt that she would find Womak there, the only place she could be after causing the panic earlier. Cara wasn't entirely sure what she would do when she got there, but it would be something. She hoped Chase hadn't worked it out before her.

Back at the hospital Cara had been quietly furious, and she'd more or less stayed that way. All the time she sat beside Dad it had churned and simmered inside, even as she'd tried to soothe his nerves and calm him after the recent alarm. He'd been awake through it all, wondering what was going on while the medical staff flashed him quick smiles and soothing words while the rest of their actions gave an entirely different message. It took her a while to explain that it was just a technical problem with the machines, and that the doctors had taken a while to fix it. She didn't mention Womak, didn't see any point in worrying him.

It seemed as though she'd not been fully successful in calming him though, as Dad was soon asking for Petre, if he'd be coming, forgetting that he couldn't. Dad had been curious about Chase as well, wondering if he was Ethan, drawing a chill from Cara when she realised they'd never met and now never would, and that she'd not yet told him Ethan was dead. Cara had to take a break then, go to the Ladies to splash some water in her face to dilute the trickle of tears and centre herself.

The near miss they'd just had made her finally accept the certainty that one day, probably soon, Dad would be gone. It was something that she'd been living with for months now, but without fully acknowledging it. His death was like some monster she'd half-seen from the corner of one eye, made more fearsome by shadow and story, that now she looked at directly in broad daylight was some ordinary thing, still terrible but understandable at least. She really didn't want it to happen, but she knew full well it would, and had no idea how she'd cope, especially after Ethan's murder. Cara felt that dealing with that would get that much harder once the drive for answers had gone and she'd found out what there was to know. She was still deeply unsure whether she would immortalise him as an ArPer, though the words his *aigent* spoke hadn't left her.

Chase came back soon after and she could tell before he'd even reached the bedside that Womak was still missing. He offered to stay a while, have an officer assigned for her protection, but she declined both. It didn't seem as though Emma was a direct threat in the ordinary sense: this was all far too elaborate if she just wished Cara harm. He stood there awkwardly for a while, before saying he needed to get on and leaving. Cara waited another half hour, until the end of visiting, before leaning over to kiss Dad goodbye.

She pulled to a stop, a few yards away from the unit, so she couldn't be seen yet, and turned off the motor. Now Cara was here she was less sure that Womak would be, or that she'd know what to do. Remembering the cloud cache she'd created for the lower grade cameras, Cara logged in. Everything looked ok inside, with no sign of any intruders, until she noticed the time stamp and recalled that the cameras would only upload every couple of hours, making the pictures she had too old to be useful. There would be a refresh in about 40 minutes, but she couldn't stand waiting so long.

A pause, and then she reached forward to press a button on the dash before rising from the driver's seat and exiting the car, shutting the door firmly behind her and walking quickly to the rear where she grabbed the tyre iron. Armed with something solid and simple, with no safety catch or off switch, she slammed the boot shut and headed for the warehouse door. On the outside things were much as she'd left them, and she used a key they'd given her to unlock the side door and go inside. Cara passed quickly through the warehouse until she reached the shipping containers, seeing no sign anyone else was there.

Relieved, mostly, she went into the first clean room. It was then she saw the booted feet of someone laid on the floor.

Slowing, measuring her steps to walk quietly, she raised the tyre iron to her shoulder, ready to strike if she had to, before rounding the corner of the doorway to look fully inside. There was a woman lying prone in white disposable overalls, a bulky holdall beside her. It was Emma.

From the slow and steady rise and fall of her torso Cara could see Emma was alive, if not well. Cara walked up slowly, stopping by an outstretched arm and squatting down beside her head. She stared at Womak for a moment, saw her vulnerability, and felt her own face twist into a black fury. Her fist, with the tyre iron still gripped firmly within, rose up level with her own shoulder and stayed there, wavering slightly as she imagined the downward arc that would smash the hard metal through Emma's skull.

He'd tried to delay, but his silent taskmaster read his face like a psychic and stepped forward sharply every time, just enough to scare and startle. Not the first time though: that time s/he had punched him in the face, hard and clean, breaking his nose.

Ethan worked freely now, unchained, his mind clearer. They'd left him his own clothes but removed anything that might conceivably help him, including his boots. He was almost enjoying the task itself, but hated the incarceration. While his basic human needs were catered for, and he was free to eat, sleep or whatever when he wanted, he had to keep working. The idea of escape was on his mind often, but he couldn't see a way yet. The silent warden never left.

His kidnappers wanted software, designed to breach firewalls and barriers. There was off-the-shelf stuff out there but they needed something different. They wanted him to find a way to pass smoothly through any obstructions, leaving them intact and unblemished. It was only after really working on it for a few hours that he realised they wanted him to break out of the barriers, not in.

- Thirty Eight -

> Chase

The police were set up and ready to go when I arrived back at Thorne's warehouse, their vehicles almost filling one of the narrow side streets. I had to let the car park itself between a riot van and a squad car, the gap behind barely enough for me to squeeze through to grab my body armour from the boot. As I ran along I almost slipped on the cobbles, forcing me to slow down, pulling tight the last of the rip tags on the armoured vest as I went.

The raid was a police operation, given the highest priority after Thorne had been identified as the supplier for the construction drones, fragments of which had been found amongst the wreckage of the bomb blasts over in Maravilhosa. Now that this case had been linked to terrorism, however slightly, it had acquired a new importance, drawing greater interest and resources in equal measure. The fact that Jakobsen's training scenarios hadn't contained any mention of explosives or plans to use them didn't do much to clear his reputation in the current climate.

With all the attention on the case there was a suggestion from some quarters that CSS should be paid off and made to go away, but others had argued against that until we were grudgingly accepted. It was largely through our efforts that Thorne was linked to the drones, and he'd also been identified as the source of the surveillance placed on Cara. Even so, I was on the raid primarily as an observer, though the scans of the warehouse I'd obtained with the Spydar had helped soften attitudes a little. I had to hang back with the detectives until the breaching team had gone in, though I realised even they weren't taking any chances when I caught sight of a couple of de-fanged medium-intensity military robots moving up into position.

They were bipedal and roughly humanoid in outline, though specialised for the task rather than mere mimics. Their gait was slightly comical and ungainly at such a slow speed, making them look like pantomime strongmen tiptoeing along, chests swollen with freakish strength, though their lower bodies were actually no less developed than their uppers. These things were built for powerful, rapid movement, with oversized synthetic muscles bundled into a heavy-duty frame, all of it encased in hard, armoured plastics. The two robots hunched down like sprinters in a ready stance, primed to explode forward as soon as the order was given. They stayed there, completely still, as the police officers around them made their final preparations.

When the 'Go' command came the droids rushed forward and through the warehouse doors, noisily smashing their way inside with pace and power. A small shoal of recon drones flew in after them, transmitting video and scans of the interior, recording and mapping everything, giving the uniformed officers the confidence and intelligence to go in, batons and voices raised more for forms sake than in any real anticipation of threat. I saw they were lead in by armed officers wearing power-assisted armour suits, just in case.

We were given the green light to enter not long afterwards, and I set off toward the door with Williams. The two droids made their way out of the pedestrian entrance just as we got there so we stood aside, clearing the path for them to tiptoe back to their handlers over by the unmarked truck they travelled in. Another pair were heading off in a different direction from the rear of the building.

Thorne was over in the far corner, handcuffed and loosely held by a particularly burly policeman, while the thin woman and several other staff members were being gathered up and escorted out. Behind Thorne a technical officer stood cursing as she watched a monitor display showing the computer underneath being virtually devoured from within. There was nothing much she could do to stop it, as there was no physical device to enter any commands, so she reached under the desk it was resting on and pulled the plugs from the wall. As she stood back up, shrugging, I noticed the crushed remains of three or four portable memory sticks on the floor nearby.

Turning round I took a good look at Nathan Thorne. I'd been given the details of Cara's testimony, some of which concerned this character, and she'd given a pretty clear impression that she didn't like him all that much. The police had the lead on this so I waited while they started things off. Thorne looked increasingly anxious as they began tearing the place apart looking for evidence, while Roberts recited a list of offences long enough to keep Thorne inside for years. He tried his best to maintain his cool, but the detective was relentless, expertly stoking Thorne's concern and fear.

We didn't get much out of him there and then, but it was a good set up for the more considered interrogation that would take place afterwards. There should be some evidence coming through by then, so his cooperation shouldn't be too hard to secure, especially when they brought up his connection to the bombings. We had him.

> Reznik

It had been a long walk back into the city, down the steep hillside through the bands of forest and rough buildings, everything busy and chaotic as refugees from flooded areas crammed in alongside relatives, or slept rough at the edges of the parklands. There was plenty of time to think and clean up on the way down. Reznik had been fairly confident before he spoke to Araya up on the hill that he was the betrayer, but it was better to have confirmation. He quite liked the old man, and understood he'd had no easy choices, but his treachery had struck a nerve with Reznik. Araya would probably be fine after surgery: it might take a while for him to recover fully, but with his money the injury was far from permanent.

He was all but certain now that OraCotek had been behind the bombing of Lagorio's penthouse. Presumably their main motivation was to end the attempts by Hallistiks and others to limit their activities through the courts. The reason for the following explosion in the second high-rise was less clear, and his best guess was that they were trying to confuse the picture and make the threat seem more intense, and had perhaps chosen that location because of its ties to his own operation. It seemed obvious that the alleged terror threat and the subsequent crackdown had been planned in advance, giving the speed of the authority's response. What they'd been aiming for in slicing up the city and aggravating its poorer residents he couldn't yet see, though money and the long game would be at the heart of it somewhere. It always was.

He'd been thinking as well about the last job he'd done under the Onkalegann banner before they'd dissolved it, the one that had brought Jakobsen into all this. The raid had been about planting a worm into the hostile's network, though he had never before asked who exactly, beyond Murdoch, he was working for. Or against. It was possible there was some kind of link from back then to what was happening now, which would make all this less a matter of coincidence than connections, a territory he was much more comfortable with. This all felt like a local manifestation of a larger problem, and he wanted to know how it might fit in. There was a whole lot to make sense of here, movements and motivations well above his usual pay grade.

Once he made it back to the city proper, he made for the nearest internet café, though it took a little while to find one that was still open. Checking his email account on a small 'pad he was disappointed to see there'd been no update yet from any of his old associates, who he'd contacted for any intel he could find on his present situation. All that he'd received was a new email sent from Jakobsen's account. Instantly suspicious, he checked it thoroughly, expecting some level of toxicity or subterfuge, but everything looked ok. He paused a moment, took a deep swig of coffee, thought it through.

Sighing, expecting trouble, he opened it. The email was from someone claiming to be Jakobsen's close friend, with an offer of help. Reznik hadn't had the leisure lately to consider the full range of loose ends Jakobsen's death might have left, especially on the personal side. Once Reznik had realised he'd been murdered he immediately suspected there would be a link to whatever was going on here, and now that he was considering a possible connection to the last Onkalegann job, which Jakobsen had been central to, it seemed even more likely. There was a chance that he'd discovered something useful, and now that info was in the hands of this friend. If that were the case, he would very much like to have it, if he could cope with the cost.

> Cara

Time seemed frozen in that moment of intense emotion and opportunity, with the tyre iron gripped hard and ready to fall on a target so tempting. Only gradually did she become aware of the world around her again, and a sparking sound from the corner nearby, an electrical crackle, that finally drew her attention.

Nearby, on the floor, was a drone she'd never seen before, a larger and meaner looking version of Chase's Spydar, which spat a small arc of blue lightning between two tiny prongs sticking out like mandibles beneath its head. This one didn't look like it would sit back on its haunches and give a cheery wave. They stared at each other for a while, until she felt the hate leave her face and her arm relax and drop to her side.

The spider-thing skittered toward her, sparking less intensely, and she stood up and moved back, walking around the prone form of Emma toward the inner clean room and Raissa's monitor. When she looked back from the doorway the little drone was poised on Womak's torso, rubbing its forelegs together in a purely animalistic gesture that almost looked like a chef sharpening knives.

Once there'd been time to get her head around the reality of the situation she'd asked Raissa to call Chase. He arrived soon after with Mallory, a couple of uniformed police and a medical team in tow, and came straight over to check she was ok. Cara said she was, and very nearly believed it herself.

Mallory dealt with the police and the medics as they treated Emma and then transferred her, still unconscious, to a stretcher. There seemed to be no real problem with the condition she was found in: evidently CSS had permission to use that kind of Spydar, and there'd been no serious injuries inflicted on the suspect. They'd all viewed the drone's image file, and seen it neutralise Womak before standing guard over the body. There were no pictures of Cara's temptation.

Today, the next day, had been better. She'd immersed herself in work, riffing off Raissa's findings and asking the questions that pushed the AI along in its search. It was such a relief that Dad was ok, for now at least, that even her grief at loosing Ethan and the surprise of Emma's betrayal was washed away for a while. There'd been news from Petre's solicitor as well: he was ok, though they'd placed him in solitary for the time being. Cara couldn't be sure how safe he'd be later, but for now he'd be alright.

Mallory had called, surprising her, and they'd chatted for a while, awkwardly at first but more easily as they continued. There was something Mallory was curious about, and she told Cara about Chase being delayed as he'd tried to get to the mall on the afternoon of Harris's murder, and later when he'd been on the bus and the witness to a car accident. Chase assumed there was some kind of glitch in the traffic system, but Mallory thought there might be more to it.

Cara agreed. What appeared to be random, chance events were anything but: she'd learned long ago about the protections and safety protocols that were built into the vehicle management network, and an accident like the one Chase had described was beyond unusual. The traffic and tube delays she could recall for herself. Mallory asked them to look into it.

Cara had work of her own to do as well. Whilst she now had a good idea of what Ethan had been up to there was actually very little that explained why he'd been kidnapped, and later killed. What Chase had shared with her from the investigation suggested that Emma had been hired to download what she could from Ethan's mainframe, or at the very least destroy it. If that were true then maybe there was something there that implicated his killer, or that might at least explain why he was targeted. She set to working on that very problem, leaving Raissa to focus on Mallory's question and the traffic analysis from the night the mall system was crashed.

Later Raissa had some answers: the transport network had indeed been hacked on both days, when Chase was travelling to the mall to meet Harris and when he'd been riding on the bus at the edge of the Civil Safety Zone. There was an unusual method to the hack, quite unlike anything Cara had seen before. The initial intrusion was familiar enough, if particularly skilled, but once the outer security was breached the actual manipulation of the management systems was remarkably smooth and efficient, as though the intruder was exceptionally knowledgeable about the inner workings and architecture of the system and thoroughly expert in software coding.

Cara had found some answers of her own a couple of hours later. Ethan's mainframe had picked up a tracer program, and despite his best efforts he'd unwittingly lead it back here, infecting the system with a short-lived worm that was only visible now from its spoor. The method of breaching his security was different, but the way his system was interrogated and manipulated reminded Cara strongly of the attack on the traffic management network. It felt like her earlier bubble of relief and good humour had burst. There was nothing to look forward to now but the hard slog of tracing the hacks back to their source.

Ethan had no idea where he was, or who was holding him. His guard was still as much of an enigma as his captor, the one giving him instructions through the laptop. He couldn't even be sure if there was just one contact at the other end.

He had some suspicions though. For his work to have any value it needed to be applicable in real environments, so it was very likely the software architecture they had him working on had close similarities to the actual system he was writing for. The types and positions of the firewalls and barriers would create a highly compartmentalised system. They were the sort of protections you might use to increase security for the highest levels of intelligence material. On the other hand, you might use it to create internal blocks to prevent a moderately powerful AI from evolving into something much stronger.

- Thirty Nine -

> Chase

The suite was empty. There was no sign of Schuler, though there were plenty of his effects there: clothes hung up, empty luggage and various personal effects scattered around. It looked at first like he'd simply gone out somewhere, but once we'd returned to reception and spoken to the concierge it was plain that no one had seen him go, and that he'd left no instructions. His legal team arrived soon afterward, but their show of force began to look a little comical when it became obvious they'd no idea where he was either, and were equally unable to reach him. By then the hotel's small lobby was feeling distinctly crowded with all the police, Cadejo staff and lawyers. The noise from so many raised voices was uncomfortably loud and edgy, and I headed outside for some air. This time I made sure I was stood near some of the uniformed officers.

I'd had to account for my conversation on the balcony with Schuler the day before, and for once someone was more pissed off with me than Iyer. His lawyer's had tried to claim intimidation, coercion and improper procedure, but I'd recorded the whole thing through my smart systems and could prove that he'd instigated the contact, and that little of consequence had been said.

Perhaps none of that mattered. We had an arrest warrant now for Schuler, if we could find him. After conducting preliminary interviews with Womak and Thorne, we'd again spoken to Ruscoe to crosscheck a couple of points. Whilst Thorne knew Schuler only as Sauveterre, Womak had dug a little deeper and identified who she was really dealing with. Their testimonies and other circumstantial evidence we'd found were more than enough grounds for questioning Schuler, and we were granted the warrant without much delay. The link between this case and a terror attack, however slight it may have been, had a galvanising effect on everyone, not least the suspects we had in custody.

Whilst I'd been happy enough to run the interview with Thorne, I'd left Roberts and Mallory to deal with Womak. There was something about the way Womak had faked the illness of Cara's father just to draw everyone away from the warehouse that struck me as particularly cold, especially as the two were supposed to be close friends. It might be a stretch to get a conviction for Womak on an accessory to murder charge, but kidnap and assault indictments should be easy enough with Ruscoe's statement and the video and forensic proofs we had. Her history didn't help her much either: it turned out her father was a second-generation criminal in one of the larger rackets. Womak's two brothers had inherited the bulk of the family firm, while she was left with money and a point to prove.

There was still a possibility that Womak had been more directly involved in Jakobsen's murder, given that she could fit the very open description we had of the chief suspect, but we'd nothing yet that could place her at the mall. Besides, if the statements she and Ruscoe gave were truthful the driver of the second van was a more likely prospect. We were working on tracing the vehicle and tracking its movements, but the traffic net AI that usually answered most of those questions was unable to turn anything up.

According to Womak's testimony she was hired through a notorious site on the darknet, and then in turn recruited Ruscoe. They were to abduct Jakobsen and transfer him to a second van at a specific location, which they did, before leaving the area immediately afterwards. Both seemed to be genuinely surprised at how things had turned out for him, and claimed to have no knowledge of where he was held, why he was killed or by whom.

Womak's connection to Schuler was more direct. She'd been introduced to him a few days later by a trusted third party, though he was using the name of Sauveterre at the time. He'd hired Womak to make a repeat visit to the warehouse, where she was to gain access to the shipping containers and attach a couple of devices to the large computer system she would find there.

I did wonder whether Schuler had been behind Jakobsen's kidnapping as well, but it seemed odd that he would change from a highly secure method of communicating to a more open one. On the other hand, it seemed a bit coincidental that two completely separate individuals had contacted Womak independently for related jobs.

After Ruscoe's arrest, Womak had come up with the plan to distract Cara herself as the money on offer at that point made the risk worthwhile. The intention on returning to Jakobsen's warehouse for a third time was to destroy the mainframe. She'd no idea what was on the system that Schuler was so interested in.

Thorne's situation wasn't looking great either. We were close to absolute proof that the construction drones he'd supplied to Jakobsen were at the scene of the bombing, and pressure was building for him to be prosecuted under terrorism offences. Failing that, we'd plenty of evidence he was guilty of more mundane crimes, such as handling stolen and prescribed goods. The virus he'd launched on his computer hadn't been as destructive as he'd hoped, leaving enough of his records intact for the police to extend their enquiries.

The only suspect we knew of who wasn't already in a cell was Schuler. From the look of things, though, it was going to stay that way, at least for now.

> Reznik

It was a slow, if fruitful dialogue. They were both cautious, paranoid and savvy. The conversation took place across continents and an ocean but it was their mutual suspicion and distrust that kept things to such a slovenly pace, a series of short typed sentences messaged back and forth at the speed of an ancient telegraph.

He was in another cheap hotel, not far from the coffee shop, in a tiny room suddenly ten times more expensive than it had been. It had taken him half the day to establish that it was Jakobsen's girlfriend, Cara, that had reached out via his old email address, and when he found out Reznik very nearly killed the connection. Instead, he thought about it for a minute and realised that she was just as wary and close with information as he was, and he remembered Jakobsen had said she was, or had been, a hacker.

She certainly seemed to be smart. As their dialogue continued, he learnt what she'd discovered, or at least what she was willing to share, and found that she'd been tenacious and skilled. He was particularly impressed that she'd somehow inserted herself in an active police investigation, and seemingly had leeway and resources to pursue her own lines of enquiry, even if these were entirely technical in nature.

How could she help though, and should he encourage her? She was a civilian, not part of the world he lived in, and it was probably a bad idea for both of them for them to be in contact. It went entirely against protocol, but then he thought sharply that those weren't even his own rules.

About the only thing he had going right now was to exact a little revenge on OraCotek before getting the hell out and catching the ride Murdoch had offered, assuming the old man would come through with that after he'd hospitalised Araya. The tech firm had a compound out at the edge of the city, just off one of the freeways. If he were able to work out a way to get into the place and do a little damage they should be at least inconvenienced.

It was time he sent a response to Dalca. Reznik typed into the pad what he thought would be a final message: 'Thanks, but no thanks. Don't want to put you in danger. Good luck.'

She came back quickly 'No way! I want to help.' And then another line straight after it, a different font and colour: '*Hey, sorry to crash in. Think I can be of assistance.*' As soon as he read it Reznik moved to close the connection and shut down the machine. It was locked, the keys completely unresponsive. He tapped harder, hit a couple of commands and thumped the space bar, but nothing changed.

Except outside. There was something going on out there that distracted him. He could hear a sudden chorus of car horns, reversing signals, phones ringing and various computerised beeps. Reznik got up and crossed to the window, peeking out from behind the faded curtain. Every phone, screen, streetlight and vehicle light he could see was flashing in concert, a steady, measured pulse. Then the lights of the cars fell into another pattern, regular in a different way, which looked like nothing less than Morse code. He translated, perplexed and not a little freaked. It was his own name, his real one, truer than Reznik or The Wolf, three times over.

Then it stopped, all the ring tones, beeps and flashes abruptly stopping. There was a lull, and then the familiar random soundscape began to reassert itself, chaotic but somehow shy at first. Most of the pedestrians and drivers outside had looked around, seeking validation from complete strangers of something that was plainly very weird, before answering their phones or hurrying on with their journeys.

Reznik's smartpad beeped loudly with a noise he'd not heard it make before. He returned to the bed where he'd been sat, picked up the 'pad again and read the screen: *'Hi again, hope you got my message. Think I can help. (By the way, Cara can't see this last part – don't tell her about the you-know-what)'.*

Outside the street noise had returned to an ordinary pattern. Inside Reznik felt anything but ordinary as the sheer strangeness of what he'd just seen confronted him. He could cope with many things, but what he'd just witnessed, something quickly hacking a whole range of separate devices with little forward preparation, was way beyond anything he'd seen before. If this was the arena he'd been playing in all along it was no wonder he'd been so outmanoeuvred.

> Cara

The Maxim Mall was haunted. There was no doubt from the analysis she'd done with Raissa that the original source for the hacks on the transport network that had plagued Chase was from within the huge building, but when they looked now there was absolutely no hint or sign that the thing responsible was still there. That it was an AI of some description was blatantly clear, and according to Raissa there were certain coding steps and strategies that suggested it was closely related to the one that had hacked into Ethan's computer, even though that particular intrusion had apparently originated over the Atlantic. She couldn't see those signatures as distinctly as Raissa, but was prepared to accept it as more than likely.

Wherever the mall AI was actually operating from they couldn't find it now. A new, more modest computer system had been installed to replace the first server ravished by the virus released on the night Harris died, and the managers had chosen to use a cheaper, less highly spec'd set up this time around. They'd looked at it enough to see there was nothing particularly interesting or powerful lurking there right now. Just in case they'd left safeguards and monitoring programs in place that would alert them should the other AI return.

There was the Reznik thing as well. He was in some fairly deep shit of someone else's making and she felt a desire to offer some help at least. Raissa was even keener, as far as she could tell, and was enthusiastically researching OraCotek and anything connected with the firm. Clearly there was something underhand about the way the corporation was acting, and its direct encouragement of the aggressive pacification programme the authorities were running. Whatever was going on, OraCotek's stock wasn't suffering and its share price remained high.

Cara had taken a hard look at the media coverage of the situation, especially the deaths attributed to Reznik. She wasn't sure whether she found the bombing or the later shootings at his apartment the most troubling. There was a great deal of debate over both incidents online, but the second event was the more controversial, with a number of amateur video clips showing the police SWAT team, who weren't even in the official coverage, arguing amongst themselves and restraining a couple of their own team members whilst the majority of the officers looked on in a state of obvious shock.

They were seriously considering helping Reznik with his intrusion into the suburban facility he'd been alerted to, sharing his conviction that something must be going on there. Cara was cautious though. This was most definitely the kind of thing she had promised herself, and her father, that she would never do again. It would be a colossal breach of that commitment, an act of cyberwarfare, not just some cute protest. Supporting Reznik would be hardcore, and not easy to explain or walk away from if they were caught.

That she was discussing this whole thing with a copy of an AI, which belonged to a private security contractor, that was working for the police, had not escaped her. This Raissa insisted she could segregate those activities off from the central version of herself if she chose to, but Cara would have to take that very much on trust. She had a lot of thinking to do, really, but in the meantime there were the intoxicating puzzles in front of her, and the semi-vicarious thrill of riding shotgun with the most powerful hacking and analytical AI she had ever seen or experienced. Despite her misgivings the buzz was as warm and bright as it had ever been, an old passion she had almost forgotten.

Ethan was nearly finished. His thoughts had grown clearer as the sedatives were reduced, and he'd becoming increasingly convinced that he was working with a single mind, and an artificial one at that, rather than a group of some kind. There was a dual sense of awe-inspiring power and bright naivety you might get from a young child prodigy, a startling intelligence with no real-world knowledge. It was very much like he imagined a fresh, shiny intellect pieced together in a lab would be.

For all his fascination with the work he never forgot he was a captive. He knew he was being monitored but couldn't be sure how much. Ethan hoped that the surveillance was light because he'd prepared a little surprise, patiently inserting an odd line of code here or there that looked incongruous enough but when taken together should insert a glitch straight into the AI's core. Assuming its apparent naivety was genuine.

- Forty -

> Chase

It was eerily still. The main loading bay was quiet, and even the surrounding traffic noise was minimal. I was back outside the plain, ordinary door that lead onward into the small delivery area at the rear of the mall. If I were to learn anything new, it would be here. The investigation, despite the external pressures, looked as though it was settling down to a more considered, methodical pace, and I needed more. The mall was where everything had begun, and I believed where everything would end. Drawing closer I could see that the LED on the damaged keypad beside the door was still showing green, and I took that as an invitation.

As the meagre overheads inside the loading bay flickered into life, I noted everything looked the same as before. It was cold and a little damp here, an area that probably had few visits from human personnel, and the atmosphere was one of emptiness and solitude. The stillness suited me in that moment, a reflective pause, and I stood there and sunk into the silence, peering around into the dark spaces beyond the pools of illumination cast by the overheads, adjusting the levels on my 'lenses to stretch the miserly light further.

Across from where I stood was a door that I hoped would allow me to press on further. I headed toward it, but hadn't moved forward more than a couple of yards before the whole room was plunged into absolute darkness again. I paused, unsure of my next step, then heard a brief surge of electrical power and the sound of clattering along behind me just before I was hit on the shoulder as something brushed by. The force of it was surprising, almost like a shove, and I dropped down to the ground as whatever it was flew past. I fell all the way forward, reaching out with my hands to save myself, soft palms jarring hard into the concrete floor.

I dropped lower and to the left as I felt something stir the air nearby, almost flinching away from the expected impact. Scurrying sideward I rolled clumsily, feeling a great clap of air and the sound of heavy metal slamming together where I had just been, a great rattle and hum further above. Pushing up off the floor I crabbed away, only stopping when I felt my other shoulder impact the wall. I lay there for a moment, twisted sideways with my spine against the brickwork, breathing surprisingly heavily, whilst the air nearby stirred again over and over, metal clanging together angrily over the whine of servos.

Then silence. A sense of stilled motion. Dark as night.

Remembering, I reached for a small torch I carried, shifting my weight again as the stun gun in its holster dug into my sides. Switching the beam on to bring light just as my breathing and heart began to slow to a steadier rhythm. I checked around me, saw one of the autoloaders hanging from its tracks on the ceiling opposite, a pair of oversized metal pincers on articulated arms. It rocked there slowly, bundles of black cable running along the outside of the solid yellow limbs. I let the flow of its gentle sway hypnotise me into calm, shadows and light from the torch scattering and flickering toward the edges of the dark.

It's hard to say how long I laid there, but the autoloader was completely still by the time I got up and dusted myself down. I checked myself over, and then in my pockets for the balled-up Spydar on one side and the EMP charges I'd brought on the other, counting them off for comfort. One gun was still at my side in its holster while the other was an unfamiliar weight in my pocket.

Carefully, keeping close to the wall, I made for the interior door, panning the torch around so I might see anything else coming toward me. The loader stayed in place on its track and there was nothing to show now that it had ever moved. Swallowing, I moistened my dry lips and dialled Raissa.

No reply.

> Reznik

The first police patrol car arrived to investigate at around the same time that the aid station across the road on the retail park was starting to quieten down. Reznik watched from a distance as the officers got out of their vehicle and approached the gate, part of a continuous run of wire mesh fencing surrounding the site. As they shone their flashlights around he wished them luck, knowing from the aerial photos he'd studied that there was no way to see through the dense curtain of trees and bushes beyond the fence. They were in the suburbs, a new sprawl of retail, industry and residency that had grown up alongside the highway over the last couple of decades. Everything had that bland Americanised look that could have belonged to almost anywhere.

The emergency calls were Cara's doing, the first steps in a coordinated deception of escalating seriousness that would confuse the OraCotek staff and open a way for Reznik to sneak inside. Cara had bypassed a pre-set instruction to get the patrol car to attend, deleting a special circumstances flag that would have had the reports rocketed up the chain of command to a more elevated officer. As Reznik waited his mind had entered the edge of that calm, Zen-like mental space he was so fond of, for him the immediate precursor to much of the violence and incidence in his life.

There was no hint of a response to the patrol officers from inside the compound so they faked one. As far as the police command computer was concerned they had been fired upon from inside and were requesting a tactical response. For good measure they piped in a couple of appropriate sound effects using a specialist PA drone they'd hijacked earlier and flown in.

Additional police arrived shortly afterward, followed by SWAT, who rolled straight up and immediately deployed into combat positions, though the best they could do for cover here was their own armoured van and the police cars. They'd come prepared, launching small quadrotors and announcing their presence over loud hailers while a couple of their members approached the mesh gate and set up breaching charges. The entrance was blown open almost as soon as the demolition techs were back in cover, and most of the SWAT team headed out in a wide dispersal into the compound, weapons ready. Reznik had multiple live feeds from the air almost as soon as the police did – unsurprising considering they were from the same cameras.

By the time fire engines, more police and a paramedic had arrived a few minutes later the scene had attracted a crowd that milled around on both sides of the road, watching from behind temporary cordons alongside local news crews. Reznik had blended in amongst the civilians by then, close by the perimeter fence. He waited there, anticipating an opportunity to slip through and onto the property.

An update scrolled across his HUD: *'Good luck. We'll be watching.'* That was probably intended as encouragement, but he felt a little uncomfortable at the intrusion. This was certainly different from how things normally went. A tactical air strike would have been so much more efficient.

> Chase

I'd been followed for a few minutes now as I made my way through the service areas of the mall. Security drones would be understandable, but apparently a couple of maintenance droids and a robot vacuum were enough. It was almost insulting. They were never close enough to be a real concern, usually just around a corner or back along a corridor, but it was still a little unsettling. From prudence I had one of the small EMP charges in my hand ready to use and the Spydar running a little way ahead, a composite of its view fed into a corner of my own.

Whether the initial choice of tail was a clever tactic to lull me into complacency I couldn't say, but either way when the first proper threat appeared I almost didn't notice until it was too late. The Spydar gave me just enough warning of the two security drones flying toward me from around the corner, and before I'd even seen the first splash of colour reflecting from their lights I was already moving, thumbing the EMP grenade to Live and throwing it forward as I dived back the other way.

The charge went off almost immediately, and I could feel the shockwave's edge even where I'd landed, the static electricity making the hairs on my legs stand up and the muscles in one calf spasm briefly. It wasn't a pleasant feeling, but it passed quickly enough and didn't seem to have done any damage as my foot was in contact with the floor and the charge had travelled straight to ground.

Looking back, I could see I'd been fortunate in my aim: one of the drones was lying on the floor whilst the other was flying erratically, its rotors working only intermittently. I got up gingerly, making sure my leg was alright before I put too much weight on it, and looked around to where the damaged quadrotor was weaving slowly off up the corridor, back the way it had come. The other drone was still lying on the floor, so I walked over and stamped on it a couple of times, breaking off two of the rotors and scattering small shards of plastic across the floor. Maybe there was a use for that vacuum robot after all.

I paused for a moment, and then called Raissa again. This time I got through.

"Hi Chase. Bit busy right now. Can I help?"

"Yeah. I'm at the mall. Could use some assistance."

There was only the briefest of pauses. "So you are. What's the problem?"

"Well, I was..."

"Ah, never mind, I think I can guess. To cut a long story short Cara thinks there's a rogue AI sheltering in the mall's system somewhere. Looks like it's woken up. Should have seen it sooner."

"Makes sense. I came in through a loading bay, where one of the autoloaders tried to take my head off."

"Glad it didn't. Cara and I will keep an eye on you. I can see that you're on the east side of the building. Sending data to your 'pad now." There was only the slightest delay.

"Cool, receiving that. When were you going to tell me about the AI, by the way?"

"Well, the mini-me Cara's running is semi-independent, not completely integrated. I guess they were just finishing their digging first. Not that I could possibly condone an investigator pursuing an independent line of enquiry without checking in or having back up of course."

I paused. "But I do have back up."

"Always."

I pressed on, talking as I walked. Raissa patched Cara through, and she went on to brief me about the various discoveries they'd made, including the knowledge that one of the dormant sectors of the mall had a record of anomalous power and heat readings. There might be a mundane explanation, but for now it sounded like a good place to start.

> Reznik

He'd made his way inside to the south west corner of the site, well away from the front entrance, and watched from the treeline as SWAT finished their final sweep, handing a line of strip-cuffed suspects over to the regular police. Reznik was glad he'd followed the plan: there were a couple of hexapod mini-tanks standing dormant in the central area that would have caused him more than a few problems if he'd come across them when they were active. He could see that the police had removed their power cores, but to be on the safe side he'd stay clear of them.

As soon as the last of the SWAT team had reached the track that lead out to the site entrance Reznik ran across the courtyard. Directly opposite was the main structure, a big mongrel of a building made from prefab sections, rising as high as three storeys in some places and just one or two in others. On its near side an exterior door had been left open and he aimed straight for it, keeping as low as he could and using the cover offered by a couple of parked vehicles until he reached it and slipped inside.

'Great work! Hang tight when you're inside. We expect the site personnel to contact their superiors, which should mean they'll open up their network to external traffic.'

He looked up from where he'd taken cover behind a large tool chest, studying the room. It was a big garage with enough space for four or five vehicles, though it was only half-full at present. To one side was a bulky SUV partially hidden beneath a dustsheet. Reznik went over and lifted one of the corners, cursed softly and then tugged firmly at the covering, swearing again under his breath as he pulled it completely clear. Underneath was a large, old-fashioned 4x4, dark coloured and aggressively chunky. There were scrapes and scratches all along the paintwork on the sides, while the left front corner and wheel arch were badly crumpled and dented. Standing on one of the fat off-road tyres, he pulled himself up to the roof level and looked at the top. There was more damage here, though not as extensive, a few dents and a scrape along the roof. He couldn't be absolute, but it looked as though this was the truck that had chased him along the alley all those nights ago when the bomb had torn through Lagorio's party and his own world had split asunder.

There was something else as well. In the back corner, beneath a camo-net tarp, was another one of the mini-tanks, fitted with twin mini-guns and multiple smoke launchers. It was offline, but unlike the ones outside in the courtyard its battery packs were in place. Either the police had assumed it was in for repair or they'd missed it all together.

Reznik swore again and moved on toward a door in the east wall. Drawing his handgun he fitted its suppressor in place, then relaxed back against the wall to study the environment, almost without thought moving his left hand to check the haft of the longer knife he now carried. He could hear nothing from the other side of the door, and there were no tell-tale body outlines to read on thermal, so he opened it and darted through.

It had been an intense five minutes as the code he'd modified went live and he waited to see if it worked, desperately hoping that he could disguise his anxiety for just a while longer. When his guard abruptly moved forward at a pace he could only call determined Ethan thought he was fucked until it faltered, suddenly clumsy, and then stopped on the spot, its head turning jerkily from side to side. It was the first time Ethan had seen it move with anything less than elegance and he stood rooted himself for a moment before he turned and dashed for an exit.

There was a break in the heavy sheeting and he slipped through into a much larger interior space, airy and light, the cell positioned roughly in the centre. There was another plastic-sided room a few yards away, smaller and more cubical. Surrounding the two was a broad ring of crushed and broken glass. He paced in frustrated panic until he thought to tear off his sleeves and bind his feet so he could cross it.

Once he'd cleared the glass Ethan picked a direction and ran as best he could, feet cut and bloodied despite his efforts to protect them. The building was huge and complex and he ran on, passing from one empty, unused space to another, some large, some small, until he chanced upon a plainer route, through maintenance corridors and service areas. Ethan found a lift, called it and stepped inside, exhilarated and out of breath. It was then that things crashed from dare to doom, as he pressed the keys to descend and instead found himself rising rapidly. The down button was still lit, a cheery green, mocking his panicked attempts to change direction.

- Forty One -

> Cara

The change was instant, supremely swift, as the Acrobots broke formation in a blur of exquisite motion, scattering light and shadow across the pristine white space of the atrium. They split into three distinct groups, drawing reactions of surprise and awe from their human audience. At first most assumed this was a new step in the dance, an artful departure from the norm, until a number of onlookers were knocked aside by the surging droids, unable even with their grace to find a perfect path. Then the cries turned to shock and alarm as the crowd realised this was something else.

The three sets of robots each headed for one of the open floors, some arcing over onto the public balcony level whilst the others traversed up or down the silk banners to their destination. They spread out as they travelled and it looked as though most of them were heading deeper into the building, save for a few that had stopped in place, singular droids holding position at key junctions. Worried pedestrians walked around the edges of these areas, almost sliding along the walls in an effort to stay as far away from the stationary robots as possible, their panicked expressions mocked by the droids blank stares.

Cara could see it all unfold in front of her. Commands issued to the building's drones by the security office were ignored and a minor paralysis set in as conflicting instructions were sent to the human personnel. Reluctantly, Cara moved to inform Mallory, so that the officers who'd been sent to catch up with Chase would be deployed to deal with the new situation instead.

Apart from those first few incidental contacts the Acrobots had not harmed or taken any notice of the humans present. Cara had absolutely no doubt that the droids were acting with coordinated intent, and that they were more than likely being directed by the rogue AI that was still loose in the mall's infrastructure.

She grabbed her phone and made a call: "Chase, it's Cara. We have a problem!"

> Chase

As soon as Cara had explained what was happening I knew we needed to get the civilians out of there, and the easiest way seemed to be an emergency evacuation, though I asked her to contact the authorities to let them know what was really going on. The wail of the alarm when it started up moments later was almost welcome, though the hazard lighting that accompanied it was a bit intense.

"Cara, is there anything you can do about the Acrobots? Can you hack their system?"

"Maybe. We're trying."

“Ok, let me know how that goes.”

I could wait for her to get it done, but they might reach me before then. There were enough of them to spread out pretty well, and I imagine they'd be able to move though the building quite quickly. There was no real point in just standing around. According to the plans there were some stairs not far from here, which would have to be my way through to the dormant areas now that fire evacuation procedures were in effect.

A few minutes later and I was moving along one of the last corridors I would use on this level. Everything was very sparse and plain, but cleaner and less cluttered than in the true service areas. There was a set of double doors up ahead, which should lead to an open space that acted as a junction point for a couple of routes through the building. Another short corridor across from that room would take me to the stairwell.

Once I was through the first set of doors I could see there was literally nothing in the open space, just the same clean but uninspired colours; near-white walls and flecked grey flooring. It wasn’t until I’d reached almost the centre of the room that my sudden vulnerability became clearer. In a near-synchronous move a pair of Acrobots appeared from each of the corridors ahead of me, leaving the doors they’d entered through swinging gently. I stopped for a moment, grinned as the Spydar scurried away on the ceiling, and then started to back slowly toward the set of doors I’d just used when they also swung open to admit another two droids.

“Cara, are you there? Are you any closer to shutting down the Acrobots?”

“We’re nearly there. Another couple of minutes.”

“Seconds would be better!”

The Acrobots were advancing slowly toward me, in a way that looked like a mixture of nonchalance and arrogance. I gently squeezed the EMP grenade I held in my hand, running my thumb over the safety as I moved into the centre of the room. Things did not look great, and desperation gave me an idea that I almost shouted over the phone link.

“Cara, turn on the sprinklers. Full power.”

“I’ll try....I can’t isolate your location Chase. I’m trying!”

"Fuck that, do the whole building. All of it, now!"

Moments later the sprinklers burst into life, scattering water droplets everywhere, making the floor slippery and drenching everything in the centre of the room.

I grimaced, and readied the grenade.

> Reznik

Up ahead was a single guard, who seemed to be stationed there as she'd held position for the five minutes Reznik had been listening from around the corner. For a short while there'd been another with her and the two had had a brief, whispered conversation, but now they were both getting back to work and the second guard had walked off.

Reznik had tried every alternative route they could find on the original schematics registered by the first owners of the site, but there didn't seem to be any other way to reach the core of the building. His progress to this point had been supported by Cara, who'd hacked the system after the external link went live and turned the building's own security drones against any personnel they encountered, but the next part of the security grid was a separate, isolated loop. Part of his job now was to find a way for them to penetrate the inner network, but he needed to get to a terminal in the secure area first. Until then he was largely on his own, which meant taking care of things in a more familiar way.

It was time. Rounding the corner, he walked smoothly forward in a semi-crouch, feet quiet and careful, gun out and stable on extended arms, breathing slow and steady. A little closer and the guard was still out of sight, off to the side somewhere. If he went much further there was a chance they might spot each other simultaneously, and that could get random. Pausing, he reached for his spare suppressor, throwing it underarm along the corridor then watching as it clattered along the floor. Reznik stayed in position, breath held, gun up and ready as the guard came into the corner cautiously and turned right. He exhaled slowly and fired, two shots into the back of her head.

She dropped almost immediately, straight to the floor, and lay still.

Moving up quickly Reznik looked around in all directions, seeing no one. There was a recess on the right-hand side of the corridor and he grabbed the guard under the armpits to drag her back there, sitting her against a small desk for a moment while he removed her jacket before almost folding the body in underneath, out of sight. He then went up to the where the guard had fallen and mopped up the floor as best as he could, then returned and stuffed the jacket in beside her.

Before continuing, he checked the computer at the desk to see if it was networked. It appeared to be, so he inserted a small portable memory stick into a port at the back. This was one of a number he'd brought along that had been loaded with a set of custom software, designed for gaining access to the network. With luck, it would allow Cara or her AI to hack into the inner system and ease his way deeper into the building. If not, things would get a lot harder from here.

> Chase

I threw the grenade in front and then dived the opposite way, hitting the ground hard and then sliding a few feet along the slick floor. The EMP charge looked spectacular as it detonated but only about half of the Acrobots were caught by its effects, which weren't that large despite the water pouring from the sprinklers. On reflection, that was probably for the best as I was now lying full length just beyond a great puddle of it.

Three or four of the droids were still moving erratically on the spot, but the rest seemed to have simply stopped for a moment. Scrambling awkwardly to my feet I raised the stun gun, fired pairs of shots at the less damaged Acrobots just as they began to move again, and then set off at a run, barging through the double doors and running ever faster through the corridor outside. The sprinklers sputtered to a stop as I rushed forward, the sound of the robots running just behind me. I half turned, fired a few shots blindly, and then continued on, bounding upward when I reached the stairs, my feet almost slipping beneath me.

Up and up, but not fast enough. I felt a hand grab for my ankle and then another, a brief grip on my leg making me lose balance and trip slightly, misstepping to the right and nearly falling face first, only stopping my momentum with an outstretched arm against the wall, cracking my fingers painfully and dropping the pistol. I heard it clatter onto the stairs and the robots close by, ran on, gained a little, another couple of strides, the sound of pursuit close and all around, echoing through the stairwell.

Then dark.

I ran up another couple of steps then slowed down, confused, unsure suddenly whether forward was better than back. The Acrobots were close, almost in touching distance, and I paused, thought about going back for the gun and then gingerly carried on upward instead, feeling for each step carefully, cautious and quiet while the Acrobots, suddenly clumsy, clattered on behind, further away now. I tried the low-light mode on the smartlenses but it was no help so I switched straight back. Words appeared before my eyes, floating in space: *'Go up a little further. Drop your torch then an EMP!'*

Smart. I took the advice, letting the little torch clatter down the stairs, hoping it would stay on, holding in a sigh of relief when it did and watching as one of the Acrobots stepped into the pool of light it created where it came to rest. Quietly I pulled out another EMP, switched to low-light again so I could watch them gather, and then pitching the live grenade downward.

Then I ran, up to the landing and through the doors onto the next level.

After that brief burst of speed I slowed again, scared of running into deeper darkness. Stopping for a moment, I laid a hand on the nearest wall and then walked on, my fingers brushing along the painted surface. I could feel that I was approaching a junction somehow, and when the hand I was guiding myself with lost touch with the wall I backed up a step, found the corner, and headed off to the right. Soon after I made another turn, to the left, back to my original direction.

'Power back on in 5, 4, 3, 2, 1' scrolled across the 'lenses, allowing me to close my eyes and adjust to the sudden illumination. I

waited there a moment, took a breather, smiled as my Spydar finally caught up with me. Nothing else had followed.

With Raissa and Cara's guidance, I aimed for the vacant area of the mall where they'd noticed anomalies in the readings. They assured me the Acrobots' command signals had been blocked now, leaving them impotent, and they had a firm enough grasp of the mall's systems to prevent any further actions by the rogue AI. I took the lift to the next level and passed through a number of utility corridors before I reached the area I was looking for.

Cautiously, alert for any hint of trouble, I pressed on.

> Reznik

Everything got more complicated after he'd reached the operations room. Reznik had plugged in a couple of the memory sticks into different machines, figuring it couldn't do any harm, when the sound of running feet approaching along the main access corridor reached his ears. He was down and hidden well before they came through the doors.

Thinking back to how many guards he'd neutralised to get here, permanently or otherwise, he figured they'd be angry and thirsting for some kind of revenge. Not to mention scared and thoroughly unsure of the situation they were walking into.

There were two of them, armed with shotguns and wearing body armour, not great for him. They at least had the decency to fan out and search the room individually, but it wasn't such a large space and it wouldn't be long before he ran out of desks to hide behind.

"You there, Cara?" It was still strange to convey such urgency in a whisper, even after all these years.

He waited, confident he was out of sight still, as the two began to walk forward, roughly side by side, searching efficiently as they moved. It was very light in the room, stark white, as much like a lab as an office, though there was nothing more exotic on the desktops than monitors and input devices. They were about ten yards away now and would arrive on his position at roughly the same moment, though one happened to be a touch nearer because of how he was positioned. He would need to do something very soon or they would have him cold.

'Hi! Anything I can help with?'

"Lights off, in 3!"

'Just a moment. Ok, lights off in...3, 2, 1.'

The overheads went off and he stood and turned, bringing the gun up in a smooth arc, shooting each guard in the face. One fell immediately, the other bent double in pain, before Reznik closed up to deliver a final shot to each of them.

'Glad we couldn't see that. Sounded terminal.'

When the lift stopped Ethan pushed the controls for the ground floor again, one last time, but there was no change. The doors slid slowly open. He took a deep breath, calmer now, almost resigned, and stepped out.

There was life here, a sense of open space and the bustle of people. Ethan moved toward the sound, felt a sudden surge in positivity as the crowd far below lifted his spirits. And then from behind faint footsteps, deliberate and measured, stopping as he turned. His guard stood there completely motionless, watching once more.

Ethan moved away, stubbornly headed toward the balcony edge, before his shoulders were grabbed from behind, spinning him around. There was a moment, a few seconds of gentle pause, and then his jailor attacked, with a speed and strength completely beyond him. Ethan defended desperately, trying to land a blow and break contact, but he was forced back, toward the emptiness behind. More blows, sudden and sharp, and he was unbalanced, vulnerable. His guard rushed in, grabbed him. Ethan was lifted off his feet, held high for a moment, and then thrown from the balcony.

He fell through brightness and motion, connecting solidly with someone and carrying them with him to the hard ground below.

- Forty Two -

> *Chase*

The transition from bland to grand had been almost instantaneous as I stepped from tight corridors to a vast airy space curving away into the distance, white-walled and clean. The atmosphere was fresh and cool, chilly even, and at first there was nothing to see, until I noticed a faint trail of blood, smeared but still visible against the flecked grey floor.

I pressed on, following the blood trail along the centre of the hall as it arced around, listening to nothing but the echoes of my own footsteps, until I spotted two box-like structures placed roughly in the middle of the room up ahead. As I drew closer I could see that both were formed from thick plastic sheeting stretched over geometric frames, one being about ten yards on the sides and perhaps three yards tall, while the other was a three-yard cube. Pale illumination shone inside each cell, and there was a slight disturbance to the air near the taller one where heat was escaping into the cold room. Surrounding them both was a wide band of broken and shattered glass, brilliant and fierce in the cold light, a trail of bloody footsteps crossing from the centre.

I felt intensely wary, expecting something to happen any moment as I moved forward. Everything was subdued and quiet in the cathedral-like space, the sound of my own breathing too close in the foreground, my soft, cautious steps echoing across the emptiness, while the very faintest of electrical hums ran in the background. It was clear now that there was quite a lot of illumination inside each structure, especially the larger one, but that the thickness of the sheeting was keeping most of it contained, leaving only the faintest of outlines and shadows to throw fuzzy, indistinct shapes through the plastic.

Then a sudden movement in the larger cell, like a flicker of the imagination or a visual glitch born of expectation.

Stopping for a moment, heart pounding, I crouched to pull the second gun from my pocket, hand shaking a little before I took a frim hold of the grip. This was a real firearm, the weapon my Admirer had left for me. After readying it, I raised the handgun up to its firing position before moving forward again, stepping carefully across the scattered glass, every crunching footstep grinding against my nerves.

My eyes had barely left it but I'd seen no more movements or scatters of shadow within the larger box. I was close enough to touch it now, walked right around the outside of it, intensely focussed, looking for an opening or way in. At first there was nothing and I considered finding something to pierce and cut the plastic, but then I saw a loose fold around the corner, a gap in the sheeting running top to bottom.

I palmed the last EMP grenade I was carrying in my free hand and edged closer to the opening, parting the curtain with the muzzle of the gun and spilling stark light against the pristine floor before slowly pushing through, moving my head around to try to catch an angle that let me see further inside. I realise in that moment that I should have used the Spydar, sent it in to recon the place just as I feel my wrist suddenly grabbed and pulled hard, yanking me bodily inside in a rush, my feet leaving the floor for a moment and loosing balance. I fire by accident in that instant before the gun is out of my hands and flying off to hit the floor. I trip over something, a chair, sprawl and land awkwardly, too far from the gun.

There is a figure, a slightly built man or woman, not too tall, stood watching in baggy clothes, head cocked to the side as though observing an experiment play out. I still have the EMP, push the initiator and throw the thing almost at my feet as the stranger rushes toward me, a flash of speed and motion as the pulse detonates, air pressure and static punching out just as the figure is upon me, hitting even harder.

For a moment I can't see, I'm stunned by the pulse wave, neural impulses and implants glitching for the moment. Perhaps I black out.

As I come back to myself and look around, frantic suddenly and afraid until I see the figure prone on the floor, twitching now and then, just beyond where I lie. In the fall its hood has come back, showing the sleek, stylised head of an Acrobot, beautiful and strange. It made sense, the strength, the lack of biological trace, the lack of anything, but I didn't know it this was the murderer or the weapon. I was reasonably sure the bot was a drone of sorts rather than an autonomous thing, but it would take a technician to know for certain.

I got to my feet with exaggerated care, still feeling rough, and retrieved the gun, checking it, keeping it in hand for reassurance, not aiming anywhere. There were four powerful spot lamps inside the cell, one in each corner, and in the centre of the room a simple foldable desk with a laptop resting on it and a chair in front. Nearby was another chair, a heavy, solid thing, sparsely padded, with thick straps attached to the armrests and legs.

I was sure Jakobsen had been there. In all likelihood this was where he'd been held for whatever purpose, at least for a while. There were food supplies, bottled water and a foul smelling bucket, which confirmed someone had spent time here. Unless the place had been cleaned there should be ample DNA and biological traces here to give us confirmation. I head out, ready to look at the smaller plastic structure, glancing back at the Acrobot to make sure it's still there.

This time I remember the Spydar, and pull open the gap on the second box, letting the little drone scurry inside. It turns out to be pointless though, as the link from the Spydar to my onboards is down and I can't view its feed. No sound or movement from inside, so perhaps it's safe.

Raising the gun and adopting a proper stance I push on into the plastic cube, trying to clear the sheet wall quickly this time, rapidly scanning the room now I'm inside. Check the corners, look for cover. It's clean; there's nothing in here that I can see except a thick cable, a large battery pack and a squat stack of server racks, lights blinking slowly as though at rest. It might have been affected by the EMP, I couldn't be sure. A couple of spot lamps are the only other light source in here.

I stand near the break in the sheets, looking around more slowly for anything resembling evidence or a clue when I feel a strong push in my back, hard between the shoulders, and I fly forward and down, slamming solidly into the floor. The Acrobot is back, moving jerkily but still strong, its arms grabbing for me and trying to turn me face up as I scramble backward, pushing off hard with my legs. I feel its weight across my lower body as it catches me, flipping me over onto my back.

I try to raise the gun properly as I push outward, attempting to arm myself while I fend off the Acrobot in near panic. The bot drags itself quickly up my prone torso and then punches me on a hard neat line that ignores my outstretched arms and connects bluntly with my face, pulping my nose and stunning me. I see its hand draw back and I cringe against the next blow, turning my head away.

A tiny spark and the faint smell of burning then the Acrobot rears backward, grabbing behind its head. I see it grab again, another miss, and then its hand comes back holding the Spydar, squeezing and crushing the little drone before flinging it across the cube.

But I have the gun ready now, finger on the trigger, and as the 'droid attacks me again I fire. It slams its fists into my chest, cracking ribs, my breath bursting forth. As my arms go wide I try to draw them back and fire again, almost blindly, probably missing but firing again and again in panic as the Acrobot draws back to strike.

There is a pause then, each of us frozen in impossible tension, and I see smoke pour from the server behind it, failing lights flickering to a stop. I fire again and again at the server, sure this should be my aim now, pumping round after round into the racks. Smoke and small fires flicker across the face of the panels where LEDs once danced.

The Acrobot stays frozen, swaying slightly in place astride my hips. I kick and twist, pushing away with my feet, knocking it over and pulling myself free, pain stabbing at me from my chest and sides, making me gag with sudden nausea. I almost pass out. Gently I draw myself upright again, raise the gun and then empty the last of the mag into the Acrobot, one, two rounds spearing into the droids face and chest until the hammer clicks on an empty chamber and I finally stop squeezing the trigger.

> Reznik

The small plane taxied in a hard turn, curving along across the rough ground and out onto the long straight section of single lane road that played the role of airstrip for today. As the sleek, slim aircraft picked up pace the sun splashed across its dull grey surface, the matt finish soaking up the light, before it leapt from the earth and crawled skyward, little clumps of dirt falling from the wheels as it climbed into the blue.

Reznik had found the old farm easily enough, the GPS coordinates placing him almost in the centre of the property between the family house and a larger barn, everything wooden and faded, once whitewashed. It looked abandoned, as if the farmer had just packed up and walked away one day, sometime years ago. He supposed you could clean the place up easily enough if you had the desire to: everything looked reasonably intact and fixable, despite the air of lengthy disuse.

The plane had been stashed in the barn behind a stack of old crates and under a tarpaulin, the whole area looking dusty and spider-webbed even though it couldn't have been there for more than a few days. Murdoch's people were good like that, thorough, taking care of the details. Reznik remembered when he first worked for him, or more accurately had first been aware he was working for him, the pride he'd felt, the sense of accomplishment.

The plane was a modified stealth drone, with no cockpit or regular crew space, only different in some minor details on the exterior from the regular version. It had been stored with the wings and tailpiece detached but was otherwise almost ready to go. After dragging it outside he had it fully assembled in an hour, bolting everything together and running the avionics up to full function. A little over twenty minutes later the course was prepped, downloaded from some darknet server, and it was ready for flight. Everything was as Murdoch had said it would be, and he could detect no fault or failing with it, the pre-flight diagnostics returning greens across the panel.

The plane had risen to the top of its long, gentle climb now, leaving the treetops and rough hills far below, and then began to bank gracefully to the right, arcing toward the ocean and international airspace. Reznik thought back to the last time he'd taken such a flight, slung inside the belly of the plane in a hammock, the trip eerily smooth under autopilot. He'd slept most of the way, relieved to be heading for safety, the mission complete but the aftermath immeasurably more complicated than anything they'd really anticipated. Then as now it was an easy way out of a messy situation.

Except this time he hadn't taken it. From where he stood, propped against the barn, he watched the plane recede off in the distance until it was a hard-to-see speck against the bright blue. It was a beautiful, clear morning, though he knew as the day grew longer the heat would become ever more imposing. It was quiet here, and the low drone of the prop engine had long since faded to nothing. He stayed like that for a time, cool in the shade, relaxed, before he headed over to the car, still limping and sore.

Despite feeling rough he knew he was lucky to have made it out of the compound relatively unscathed. After he'd had the run in with the two guards in the ops room he'd had to hide for a while as the next batch of security arrived, until they were pulled away by the sound of intense gunfire elsewhere in the building. The moment seemed right and he'd sneaked out, hoping the confusion would be enough to give him an edge. It was, just about, and he made it out of there, mainly through running very quickly.

As he neared the exit he began to receive directions from Cara's AI. His final act was to run hard and dive behind cover just before the last mini-tank, now under the AI's control, opened up with its main weapon, firing a barrage of soft slugs from its linked guns. They weren't supposed to be lethal by most definitions but it looked fearsome as hell and would hurt at least as much, so he was careful to keep well away, passing behind the robot on his way out. Once he was clear of the building it was easy and he made his way quickly to the SUV that was waiting there, driving off just before the emergency services returned to the site.

He'd heard from the AI again a few hours later, while he'd been driving. It firmly encouraged him to maintain his customary levels of discretion. There was no threat or inducement, but his optics and audio had shut down for a solid five minutes immediately after the contact. He could tell the vehicle was under control and still moving, but it was deeply unpleasant to sit in a state of sensory deprivation even for a relatively brief period. The car came to a gentle stop and his senses came back a few seconds later, at which point he found that he'd been parked up at the local police HQ. The sensation of seething anger and absolute helplessness he'd felt was unique in his experience.

Reznik thought about Murdoch as he drove away from the farm. There were too many questions, too many gaps in his knowledge for him to trust the old man right now. Certainly, the idea of strapping himself into a robotic drone and surrendering himself totally to someone else's control as it flew was too much. It would be such an easy way to dispose of an inconvenient loose end, out over the lonely ocean.

His first impulse had been to take a shit in the passenger hammock and send it along, but instead he'd stowed a flash drive with a more or less complete report on his activities since his last debrief, plus numerous video files, inside the plane. There was a hand written note for Murdoch as well. He'd spent much time on that, wasting three sheets of paper on false starts, his expert hands unused to the awkward glide of pen on paper, or the even finer words he felt the occasion required. He wasn't entirely sure yet if all this was a 'good bye' or an 'au revoir', but he knew he could get used to the sense of openness and relaxation he felt as he drove off.

When he was gone the farm returned to its timeless rest, empty and forgotten in the fierce sun, birdcalls covering the silence before the wind began to gust, rattling the shutters and swaying fences. As the wind blew stronger it stirred the dust on the ground, shifting and sifting the dirt until there was no sign of planes or cars or killers.

> Cara

She arrived at the bistro, irritated at her own lateness but determined to appear cool despite that, craning her neck this way and that until she found him. He was easy enough to spot, still well dressed despite the injuries she could see and the others she knew he still carried. She slid smoothly into the seat opposite, smiled quickly, and immediately looked for a waiter to order a drink. There wasn't one in sight so she sat back, looked at him more closely, smiling to see that most of the cuts and bruises were looking a lot better now. Chase pushed a glass her way and reached for a bottle resting in a cooler nearby, filling her glass and then his own.

"I got Pinot, hope that's ok. I prefer red generally, but wasn't sure about you. Everybody likes Pinot, I think."

"Pinot's great."

They drank, ordered, chatted and drank some more. Cara thought about taking it a bit easier – she had a plane to catch in the morning – but she knew that slowing down was the last thing she really wanted. Besides, the departure time wasn't until 11:30, so there was plenty of time as long as she didn't get too carried away tonight. She'd already done most of the packing, plenty of warm stuff and a suit, expecting it to be quite a lot cooler in Norway than it was here.

Ethan. Cara wasn't sure what she should be feeling about that. For one thing, she'd gained far more understanding of the events that had led to his death, and who he had really been, and had gained some measure of revenge against his killers. But there was the funeral in a couple of days, the ceremony and the aftermath, and the meeting people she didn't know and had no idea about in the worst of circumstances. It would be hard, one of the hardest things she'd done in a long time, but it would be over soon enough. She was thinking about her Mum a lot, how that still hurt sometimes, and that Dad, one day in the near future, would also be gone. At the moment she was in a strange place emotionally, a little locked down, chemically suppressed again and entirely unsure how she would feel later when she wasn't.

She had talked to Chase a couple of times a day since his last trip to the mall, checking on his progress, the investigation and finally on Emma. It turned out their friendship had been genuine enough while it lasted, that she'd not been singled out and cultivated. Kidnapping Ethan had just been a job, and one she'd taken to gain the good graces of Schuler, nothing more. The pills Emma had given her were relatively benign as well, not perhaps the ideal medication for her but not overly harmful.

She remarked on it again. "It was good of them to look after me, help me to get the right meds and test the others."

"You're on the payroll now, pretty much, so they'll be looking after you for a while."

"What about you Chase? Do they look after you?"

He paused before replying. "More or less. They've taken some liberties, but then so have I. I've still got my job, though they've 'recommended' I take some more leave."

"Will you? What will you do?"

"I might. I could visit my sister Ellie, and the kids, go see Dad. Jo wants to meet up for a coffee as well, though it would probably be best if I leave it a few days until I look prettier. What about you?

Have you decided what to do about creating a digital model of Ethan?"

Chase had never said as much, but she got the impression he didn't really approve of the idea. She really wasn't sure either. Her Raissa had sent over a file before they ripped out the servers from the warehouse, and when she opened it she found an exquisitely crafted ArPer, far better than she could ever have done herself, but she'd done no more than check its coding so far.

Her idea of Ethan, who he was to her, was largely intact despite his association with Reznik. Raissa had shown her a more complete background file on Ethan's co-conspirator, and he was something else again. They had helped him because it helped them, stripping the OraCotek server of every useful byte of data they could find once he'd got them access. Afterward they'd slowly released select pieces of information via deniable backchannels to expose the conspiracy. At first the authorities had tried to ignore it all, pass it off, until a sudden wave of apologies and resignations swept through, washing away OraCotek's reputation and dashing its share price against the jagged peaks of market confidence.

None of that thinking was allowed now though. Chase was good company, perfectly content to let the conversation ebb and flow, and didn't get too concerned when she drifted off in silent contemplation for a moment now and then, but pulling her back to the present if she was away too long. She wasn't sure if she really thought of him as a friend, but she looked forward to working with him.

Cara would be working alongside Raissa again as well. In truth when she looked back on the last week it was hard to be sure how much she'd really assisted the AI, but Raissa insisted she had been 'highly effective', and recommended her for recruitment. They had offered her a permanent job at first, subject to the usual conditions, but she had declined that in favour of contract work, preferring to retain a little more of her independence and dignity, as she thought of it.

As for dignity, she was feeling a little lack there right now: she really shouldn't have had quite so much wine, was a bit unsteady. She remembered finishing up the meal and taking an age to decide on whether she should have a desert, and which to have, and then she was outside, in the now cooler air, half leaning on Chase as they waited for her taxi.

When it arrived she went for the continental air kiss to both his cheeks, before he fluffed it and they settled for an enthusiastic but clumsy hug instead. He helped her into the back of the cab, gave the autodrive its directions and sent her off. Cara twisted in the seat to see him, smiled and blew a kiss to his receding profile, waving, before she turned back around too quickly, feeling dizzy for a moment. She wasn't far from home, and felt drunk enough to sleep.

The next few days would be a bastard, but she'd get through it. She always did.

- LeviaThanks -

I really don't know how many times I'll get to do this, so the temptation to thank every man, woman, dog, cat and their assorted genetic donors is huge. But I won't.

Instead, I'll thank all those who've supported me, shown an interest and asked kindly how it was going: friends, family, colleagues and acquaintances all. It's been a while since I started this, and in all the time this novel has passed through to get to this point I've had nothing but good from people, whether I knew them well, or long, or not.

But special thanks are due to a few, who've read through some or all of a couple of the early drafts and given feedback and consideration: Alan Avery, Richard Payne and extra-specially Mark Coverdale, Adrian Whitaker, and Mark Teasdale.

And to my families also, who kept me, *me*: my blood family Mum, Dad, Gran, Mark, Sarah & Sophie; my musical family Jason, Julia, Ron & Tim; and my friend-family Ant, Bx, Chris, Mark(s), Andy, Rich, Tony. Also Jake, Amelia & Sam. Liz & Carrie. Lisa & Sebba. Graham. Marcus, Mark, Rae and Eli. There are others of course.

I think of Mick, David, Jon and now Dominic. All too soon. RIP.

Don't seem to have stuck with the plan here. I've not even thanked *you* yet.
Thank you for reading this, and giving me a little of your time.
Peace.

.p.

Printed in Great Britain
by Amazon